P9-CSV-912

THE FOREVER PASSION

Lisa laid her head on Eric's shoulder. "Why can't things be easy for us like they are for other people?" she asked. "Why can't we just love each other?"

"Maybe we had to go through all this so we'd realize how much we really do love each other." He turned her face to his and kissed her passionately. "I need you, Lisa."

Lisa closed her eyes and let herself by guided by Eric. She had waited so long for this moment. She wrapped her arms around his neck. "Eric," she said softly, murmuring his name over and over.

He pressed his mouth against hers, devouring her with his desire. He ran his hands up and down her body, remembering what it was like to touch her, remembering the passion she aroused in him. He opened his eyes and looked in her face. "Look at me," he said. He ran his hand along her cheek. "You are all I want in this world. I love you."

He felt her hands running up and down his back and he rose to his knees, unbuckling his belt. He knelt above her for a moment, poised like a statue, unable to believe he could feel this way about any woman. He knew it was time. It had been much too long.

Her hands went around his neck and he lowered himself so that his mouth was above hers. He watched her face as her passion rose.

He had never seen anything so beautiful in his life.

She lifted her head and looked into his eyes. "I don't want to lose you again," she whispered.

"You won't lose me again," he whispered back.

DESPERADO
DREAM

KAREN A.
BALE

ZEBRA BOOKS
KENSINGTON PUBLISHING CORP.

FOR DON — I LOVE YOU

ZEBRA BOOKS

are published by

Kensington Publishing Corp.
475 Park Avenue South
New York, NY 10016

Copyright © 1990 by Karen A. Bale

First printing: May, 1990

Printed in the United States of America

Chapter 1

Lisa lay on her side in the tall grass, staring into her husband's incredible blue eyes. How was it possible for her to love this man so much? The depth of feeling she had for him almost frightened her. "Do you have to go, Eric?"

"I told your brother I'd help him out with this land title. Since I'm from one of the old Spanish families, it will be better if I speak for Tom to avoid any misunderstanding."

"But Tom would understand if you were just a few days late . . ." Lisa put her arm across Eric's chest and nuzzled her head against his chin. "I'll miss you. So will Raya."

"I'll miss you both, too, but I'll be back before you know it. A month goes by quickly."

"Not to me it doesn't. There have been too many months I spent without you."

Eric pulled Lisa on top of him and kissed her deeply. "I love you, Lisa. I'm not leaving you. This happens from time to time, you know that. When Raya is older, you can both travel with me."

"Oh, Eric," Lisa trailed light kisses across her husband's face. "We've been apart so much. I don't ever want us to be separated again. I don't think I could

5

stand it."

"I'll be back in four or five weeks. Maybe I can even talk Tom into visiting for a while."

"Oh, I'd love that. I'd love for him to spend some time with Raya."

"It's settled then. I'll bring Tom back with me. I won't let him say no."

Lisa raised herself on Eric's chest. "I love you more than anything in this world, except for Raya. If anything should ever happen, I just want you to know that."

Eric reached up and touched Lisa's mouth. "Nothing will ever happen, Lisa. Nothing could keep me away from you." He pulled her mouth to his and he covered it, consuming her with his desire. His hands ran up her back and slid underneath her blouse.

"It's the middle of the day, Eric."

"So what? No one can see us out here."

"But—"

"Don't argue with me." He kissed her passionately. "I'll be gone for over a month. I don't want to leave without making love to you."

"You're not leaving until tomorrow," Lisa pointed out.

"Still, we should make the most of every moment." His mouth traced a line from her throat to her breasts. "God, you are beautiful."

"And you are bad. I thought only prostitutes made love during the day."

"We made love during the day when we were in the Comanche camp. You didn't seem to mind it so much then."

Lisa squirmed in Eric's arms, but he held her tight, rolling over until he was on top of her. He looked into her very soul and she closed her eyes as his mouth sought hers. She wanted him desperately and held on

6

to him as if he might slip away from her and never return. Before she even realized it, she began to cry.

He looked at her, wiping the tears from her face. "Don't, Lisa. It's all right. I love you. You and Raya are everything to me."

Lisa opened her eyes and stared at her husband. His eyes told the truth, but she knew how easily the truth could be cheated by fate. "I worry . . ."

"Don't worry. Nothing will keep us apart."

"I don't ever want to lose you again, Eric. I don't think I could take it."

"Lisa, look at me." Eric waited until her eyes met his. "Life can play cruel tricks on us, Lisa, but know that I love you and Raya with all my heart and nothing will ever change that. You have to believe me."

Lisa nodded silently, reaching up to touch her husband's face. "Make love to me, Eric. I want to feel you with me."

Eric and Lisa made love until they were spent, and then slept in each other's arms in the tall grass.

They rode slowly home in silence and spent the evening with their daughter Raya and Eric's grandfather, Don Alfredo. After they had put Raya to bed, they took a walk in the courtyard.

"Why do I have the feeling I won't see you for a long time?" Lisa asked, her arm through Eric's. "I had the same feeling once before, remember?"

Eric remembered. It had been in the Comanche camp. Lisa was going to have his child and she had begged him not to go on the raid. He went anyway, arguing with her before he left. When he didn't return with the other men, Lisa thought that he'd been killed. By the time he finally got back to the camp, he found her consumed by grief of such magnitude that she had lost her will to live. "I remember, Lisa, but this is different. I'm not going on a raid, I'm just

7

going with your brother to talk to some people about their land."

"Four or five weeks seems like a lifetime. I'm just so afraid."

Eric held Lisa's shoulders. "I don't know what to say to you. I promised Tom . . ." His voice trailed off. He dropped his hands from Lisa's shoulders.

"You want to go away, don't you?" Lisa asked, sensing the impatience in his voice.

"I think I should. I feel . . . strangled, like I can't breathe."

Lisa turned away. "I'm sorry, I didn't realize that I made you feel that way."

"It's not you, Lisa, it's everything. Less than two years ago I was a Comanche, living without restrictions, doing what I pleased."

"And now you have a wife and child for whom you are responsible." Lisa walked to a stone bench and sat down. "Maybe it's best that you do go. Take all the time you need, Eric. I want you here only if you want to be here, not just because you feel responsible."

Eric sat down on the bench. "I love you and Raya."

"We both know that's not enough. I won't force you to stay married, Eric. I'd rather live on my own with Raya than make you miserable."

"Lisa . . ."

She stood up. "No, you're right, you've been through a lot, we both have. Maybe we hurried into this marriage. I should have stayed at Tom's rancho with Raya. I should never have let you bring me back here."

"You belong here."

"I'm not so sure anymore." She reached down and touched Eric's face. "I'll sleep with Raya tonight."

"That's not necessary, Lisa. I want you with me."

"No you don't." She turned away.

8

"All right," Eric said impatiently.

"All right what?"

"You can come with me. I want you to come with me."

"Are you sure? I don't want to force you."

"Yes, I'm sure. Time apart won't make either one of us feel any better."

"Really?"

"Yes."

Lisa threw her arms around Eric's neck. "I do love you."

"I know." He pulled her to him, kissing her hair.

Lisa buried her face in Eric's chest, hoping that this time away would make their marriage stronger. She wasn't sure she could stand it if anything tore them apart again.

Eric looked over at Tom and shook his head in exasperation. They stood on the veranda of Casa de Teresa, the large rancho north of Monterey that Tom was trying to save. "The old man won't change his mind. He thinks simply because the land was given to him, he doesn't have to show proof of ownership."

Tom took off his hat and slapped it against his thigh. "He won't let me help him now, but he'll be the first one to scream when people start squatting all over his land—him and a lot of others."

"They've been here for a long time, Tom. Change won't come easily to them. Just look at my mother. She'd die before she'd ever give up her land."

"That's just my point. At least your mother is smart enough to have something in writing, and so is your grandfather."

Eric shrugged his shoulders. "I can try again, but I don't think it'll do any good. He's convinced that no one will ever take his land away from him."

"Just talk to him in a year when the 'niners have gotten rich and are looking for good land on which to build homes. Isn't there anyone who can talk any sense into him?"

"The señora says they have a daughter in San Francisco. The rancho was named after her. Maybe we could talk to her if it means that much to you."

"I guess it does, Eric." Tom walked to the other end of the veranda. "I like these people, they've been good to me. They also represent a lifestyle that is quickly disappearing. In ten years this place won't be the same. There won't be ranchos anymore, just hundreds of smaller ranches."

"Who's to say that's so bad? Why should one man own hundreds of thousands of acres just because he was lucky enough to be born into the right family?"

"I know you speak from experience."

"I don't know if this system is right, Tom. I see the men who work on our rancho. They break their backs for us. Why shouldn't they have something more?"

"They do, thanks to Don Alfredo."

"But not everyone is as kind as my grandfather. Look at it here, Tom. California won't be a secret for long. People are already coming by wagon train and by ship, and someday there'll be a railroad all the way across this country. All of us are going to have to be prepared to accept the changes."

"You're in a philosophical mood today."

"I'm tired, I guess."

"Then go home. There's no reason for you and Lisa to stay with me. I can handle it from here. I'll just go to San Francisco and talk to the daughter and that's that."

"You promised Lisa you'd come with us. She'd shoot us both if you didn't come."

10

"I guess I could use a few days off."

"You need to learn how to relax. You take your job too seriously. After we talk to Señorita Torres, I think you should put up a sign in your office saying that you'll be away for a while and then I think you should come home with us and get to know your niece."

"I guess I can't say no, can I? I would like to see Raya. I bet she's beautiful."

Eric's blue eyes sparkled. "Yes, she is, and she sure is active."

"You'd better get ready, man, because if your daughter is anything like your wife was when she was young, she's going to be a real handful."

"That's what I'm afraid of." He smiled suddenly. "God, I can't wait until she can ride."

"Just hold your horses, she's not even a year old yet."

Eric laughed and looked past Tom. Lisa and Señora Torres were walking toward them. Eric took off his hat. "Señora." He kissed Lisa on the cheek.

Señora Torres handed Eric a piece of paper. "Here is the address of my daughter. She may not want to help, for she and her father have not spoken for some time. However, if anyone can convince him to change his mind, it will be Teresa."

"Gracias, señora, we will do what we can. We will be leaving in the morning, so please accept our thanks now to you and Señor Torres for being such gracious hosts."

"It was nothing. You have both been such gentlemen, and it has been a pleasure to talk to you, Señora."

"Gracias," Lisa said.

She looked at Tom. "I realize, señor Jordan, that this means a great deal to you. I can see that you are trying to do what is best for us. For that I thank you."

11

"Por nada, señora."

Señora Torres turned to leave but paused in mid-stride, looking intently at Lisa and the men. "Would you please tell my daughter that her mother loves her very much no matter what has happened," she finally said.

"Yes, of course," Eric replied. When the señora was out of earshot, he looked quizically at Tom. "What was that all about?"

"I don't have any idea. I guess the old man and his daughter don't get along. This should be interesting."

"He's a tough one. Maybe he forced her into something she didn't want to do. I know only too well what it's like to be forced to do something by a parent."

"Maybe she just doesn't get along with her father. It's possible," Lisa suggested.

"Well, whatever it is, I suppose we'll find out about it when we get to San Francisco." Tom took the piece of paper from Eric and read the address. He whistled. "Whatever she does, she must do it well. Only the richest people live here."

"It's not as if her parents are poor, Tom. Look at this place."

"I guess we'll find everything out when we get there. I don't know about you two, but I'm turning in." He kissed Lisa on the cheek.

"Good night, Tom."

"See you tomorrow," Eric said absently. He took Lisa's arm and guided her to the steps. They sat down. Eric looked up at the deep blue sky and the twinkling stars above. It was a beautiful night. He felt Lisa's body against his. God, but he loved her, and with a depth he hadn't planned on. It seemed to have grown even more intense after Raya's birth. But in spite of their love for each other, there was something that was slowly driving them apart. Even on this trip

12

he had felt it. They argued over silly things. Maybe he should've come alone. Maybe they needed to see that they could exist without each other and still love each other as deeply.

"What're you thinking about?"

Eric wrapped his arm around Lisa. "I was thinking about us."

"Good or bad?"

"Why do you ask that?"

"Because you were right. I should've let you take this trip alone."

"It's not you, Lisa."

"I know that. A lot has happened to us both in the past two years." She leaned her head on his chest. "We both deserve time alone. As soon as we reach San Francisco, I'll take a stage back home."

"You don't have to do that."

"I know I don't, but I think it'll do us both some good."

Eric turned Lisa's face to his. He kissed her gently. "I love you, green eyes. I always will."

Eric and Tom walked up the steep hill. Tom stopped and looked at the address on the piece of paper, then at the huge mansion in front of them.

"What did I tell you? She's rich." He shook his head. "It's a good thing you left Lisa back at the hotel. You wouldn't want her to see this."

"So her father gave her some money and she moved to San Francisco to be on her own. So what?"

"How many young single Spanish women do you know who are living on their own in San Francisco?"

"Maybe she isn't on her own. Maybe she's married."

"The name on the paper says 'Teresa Torres.' She's

13

not married, my friend."

"So what? Her father is a very strict, stubborn old man who follows tradition. Maybe she couldn't stand to live there any longer. I know what that's like."

"Nah, there's something strange about this. This isn't just money, this is rich. Look at the size of that house."

"Are we going to stand around here speculating all day or are we going to go inside and find out for ourselves?"

Tom put his hand out. "After you."

Eric opened the iron gate and walked into the front yard. A brick path led up to a wide stairway that was decorated on each level by clay pots filled with colorful flowers. Eric walked to the door and lifted the heavy brass knocker and let it fall against the door several times. After a few minutes it opened, and a small Chinese man with a long braid looked at them.

Tom stepped forward. "Hello, we are here to see Señorita Torres."

The man just stared at the two men as if he didn't understand what they were saying.

"Do you understand English?" Tom asked, growing impatient.

Eric stepped forward. "We were sent here by Señorita Torres's mother to inquire about her. She is worried about her daughter. Would it be possible for us to see her?"

The small man stared at them a moment longer, then turned and walked into the house, leaving the door wide open.

"Does that mean we're supposed to follow him?" Tom asked Eric.

Eric shrugged his shoulders and followed the servant inside. They walked down a long, white, pristine hallway until they reached a large foyer. Tables of

14

different heights were everywhere, each one holding a vase of flowers. A floral scent permeated the area.

"Shall we wait here?" Eric asked the man, but he had turned and was walking out of earshot of the men.

"He seems to really enjoy his job," Tom said sarcastically.

They waited for at least ten minutes, and Eric grew impatient. He jammed his hands into his pockets and paced the foyer. "I wonder if there even is a Teresa Torres," he grumbled. "If there is, I bet she's short, fat, and ugly."

"I can assure, señor, that I do exist. Now what I want to know is who are you two and what are you doing in my home?"

Eric turned at the sound of the woman's voice and flashed Tom a surprised look. Teresa Torres was short but she was definitely not fat or ugly. She had long blond hair and large brown eyes set in a small oval face. She was one of the lighter Spaniards he had heard his grandfather speak of, a Castilian. He had never seen one until now and he was stunned. The combination of her dark skin and eyes and her light hair was stunning. She was dressed in a floral silk dressing gown that didn't disguise her attributes. She stood with her hands on her hips, tapping her slippered foot impatiently. She didn't seem to be the least embarrassed that she was standing half-undressed in front of two complete strangers.

"Well? Can either one of you speak?"

"Señorita Torres?"

"My name is Teresa. What do you want?"

"We'd like to talk to you about your father," Tom said.

Her foot tapped even harder on the marble floor. Eric had finally lost his patience. "We've just come

15

from your parents' rancho. Tom has been trying to convince your father to retain legal title to his land."

"And of course he wouldn't agree, so my mother sent you here to try to convince me to talk to my father." She laughed derisively. "She hasn't changed at all."

Eric was angry. "I don't think I like you much, señorita. I don't know what went on between you and your parents, but I do know that they are good, kind people. They sure as hell don't deserve a daughter like you." Eric started to walk out, but Tom grabbed his arm.

"Eric, I think you owe Teresa an apology."

"That's all right, I'm capable of defending myself." Teresa strode over to Eric and looked up at him, a defiant look on her face. "You're right, you don't know what went on between me and my parents and I don't think it's any of your business. If you two are like any of the others who've tried to help my parents, you're probably asking them for some money or some land in compensation."

"You are something, lady. I bet you even search your servants before they leave your house."

"Get out!"

"I'll leave, but before I do, I think you should know a little bit about this man here. His name is Tom Jordan and he's probably the most honest person I've ever met. He's been working tirelessly and without profit to help a lot of the old landowners. He doesn't want to see them all lose everything they have once more and more people start coming out here. But I don't suppose that matters much to you." He looked around the foyer. "You seem to be doing just fine for yourself."

"That's enough, Eric. I'm sorry, Teresa. We've intruded long enough. We'll be going now."

"*You* don't have to go, but I would like it very much if your friend left, and right now."

Eric walked down the long hallway, followed by Teresa. He glared at her when he got to the door. "I was raised on a large rancho and I was very spoiled when I was a child. My mother wanted me to be something I couldn't be, and so I left. I hated her, and until right now, I blamed her for everything that went wrong in my life. But I look at you and see your bitterness and unhappiness and I realize how badly I must have made my mother feel. I suppose I should thank you for that."

Teresa grabbed Eric's arm. "How dare you judge me when you know nothing about me. You're wrong about one thing, however. I do love my parents, and I care about what happens to them. I'm just not sure I can ever forgive them." She turned and walked back down the hallway, leaving Eric to stare silently after her.

He walked outside and waited for Tom. It was clear that whatever had happened between Teresa and her parents, no amount of talking could fix it. He walked outside the gate and looked up and down the street. All of the houses were clean and neat and large. Tom was right; rich people lived here. He paced up and down the street until he saw Tom come down the stairs, a wide grin on his face.

"What are you so happy about?"

"I don't think she liked you very much."

Eric started walking down the hill toward town. "Well, I feel the same way about her. She's a little —"

"Hold your tongue and reserve judgment until you get to know her better."

"I'm not going to get to know her better. I hope that's the last time I ever see her."

"It won't be. She's invited us to dinner tonight, and

17

she was kind enough to include you, even after your rude behavior."

"You didn't accept?"

"How could I refuse? We have to think of her poor parents."

Eric shook his head. "Don't get interested in her, Tom. She'll only break your heart. I know about women like Teresa Torres. She likes to dangle men on a string."

"I'm not asking you to marry her, Eric, I'm just asking you to come to dinner with me tonight."

"I think you'll do just fine without me there. I'll only make her mad."

"Come on. I need you there. You know the history of this place better than anyone. Besides, you two do have the same background, as much as you both hate to admit it."

Eric stopped. "All right, I'll go, but don't expect me to like it."

"I'm only asking you to be civil."

"You're asking a lot."

"You have to admit that she's a beauty. I didn't know Spaniards had light-colored hair."

"There are many blond-haired, blue-eyed Spaniards. My grandfather has told me about them. They come from Castile, I think."

"Rich and beautiful, a perfect combination."

"Why don't *you* marry her? You seem interested."

"No, thanks. I like being single just fine." He looked at Eric, a sly smile on his face. "If I didn't know better, I'd swear she's gotten to you a bit."

Eric scowled at him. "I'm just tired of being around you. Are you always so happy?"

"Is that what's bothering you? No, I'm not always so happy. I just like what I do, and sometimes I even make some money at it. Best of all, I don't have to

18

answer to anyone."

"Just make sure you don't fall for that little hurricane back there, or you'll have plenty to answer to."

"Shut up. Let's go get something to drink. Have you ever been to some of the places on the waterfront?"

"I used to walk down there with my father when I was a boy, but we never went into any of the places."

"I forget that you were away a long time, but you must know that after the Gold Rush started, it attracted all sorts. A lot of men couldn't afford anything when they came into town but a cheap drink, so they went to the waterfront."

"It never was very safe."

"Still isn't. Everything you can imagine and more goes on there."

"Then why the hell do you want to go?"

"It's colorful."

"We're going to a place where we could have our money stolen and our throats slit just because you think it's colorful?"

"Don't tell me an old Comanche like you is afraid of some city people."

"City people scare me a lot more than any Indian I ever faced. At least with most Indians you know where you stand." Eric and Tom had walked to the top of another hill and looked down at the waterfront. "God, this place has grown. It's almost too bad they found gold."

"Weren't you the one who was lecturing me about the importance of accepting change?"

"It's easy to preach it when it doesn't affect you, but when you see it —"

"It's progress."

"No, it's not. It's rape. People come in and take the land and use it and abuse it, and someday they'll

19

wonder why it isn't around anymore."

"Come on. We're supposed to be relaxing. When was the last time you saw Chinatown?"

"Probably when I was about ten years old. My mother detested it, but my father took me there and I loved it."

"Well, let's go."

They headed down Sacramento Street until they reached Stockton, and walked for blocks until they reached the heart of Chinatown. People hurried everywhere—Chinese, Caucasians, Mexicans, Spanish, and Hawaiians. The Chinese scurried around, some carrying cages with birds, some with laundry baskets hung on poles, some pushing carts with drinks, and there was the occasional one who asked if they wanted to gamble or have a woman. Horses and carriages passed by in the busy, dusty street, while people walked by each other with only cursory glances. Eric smiled to himself as he thought of the first time his father had brought him here. It had been like a dream—every imaginable color and sound and sight. This brought it all back to him.

They finally wound their way down to the waterfront, where the scenery changed drastically. There was no color here, and no people bustled about. Men slept on the streets next to old buildings, and worn-out prostitutes tried to ply their trade during the day.

"Don't say it," Tom said before Eric could speak. "You have to admit it's unlike anything you've ever seen."

"It was a lot like this when I was a kid, Tom, and it's only gotten worse. Why did you want to come here?"

"I don't know. I guess I like to remind myself where I came from and where I am now."

"I thought you and Lisa grew up with a rich stepfather."

"Only after my father killed himself. That left us with a lot of scars. Mother remarried and had a better life, but we didn't. Even though we didn't have much when our dad was alive, we were happy."

"Lisa doesn't talk about your family much. She just talks about you."

"That's because we felt like we only had each other after Dad died. Anyway, I like to come to places like this sometimes. It's a good feeling knowing that I can get out anytime I want."

They walked along the waterfront taverns, watching the people mill about. Even in the afternoon, whorehouses and taverns were already crowded. Tom took Eric's arm and pointed to a building with swinging doors.

"This is the place."

On the outside it looked just like any other waterfront tavern, but on the inside, it was a marvel. The huge building had formerly been an old warehouse that had now been painted, decorated, and filled with the tools of the gambling trade. Bright lamps hung from the ceilings, sparkling crystals dangling from the center as if to call attention to the poker tables that were scattered about the room, and the huge table for shooting craps. An attractive woman stood at a roulette wheel, managing to show the upper thigh of one leg every time she turned the wheel. There was a stage in the back of the room, and a long, shiny, wood bar ran the length of one side of it. A piano player seemed lost in his lively tunes, as if he were alone in a parlor.

"What do you think?"

"This place is unbelievable. How the hell do they keep from getting robbed blind?"

"Look around. There are lots of men in suits just standing around. They're house police. They make

21

sure that nothing goes out of here illegally. If it does, it probably won't happen again."

Eric looked around the room. He spotted at least five men, all large and serious-looking, who stood around, just watching the people inside the tavern. "What do they do when they close up?"

"There are doors on the outside that they lock up, but I can guarantee you there's nothing in here of much value by the time they go home. In fact, money is always going out so they won't have a huge sum at any one time."

"How do you know so much about it?"

"I'm the owner's lawyer," Tom grinned.

"Who is he?"

"I don't see him. He usually makes an appearance in the evening. You can't miss him. He's a huge man, looks like a bear, but he has the manners of an Englishman."

"Is he honest?"

"As far as I can tell. But who knows what goes on when I'm not here."

Eric gazed in fascination at the already raucous crowd of men eager to spend their new-found wealth on women, gambling, and liquor. He walked to the bar with Tom, leaning against the polished wood, and looked at the huge mirror behind the bartender, his eyes traveling to the portrait above it. It was of a woman, a beautiful young woman, draped in a red silk sheet. Only her shoulders and arms were visible but the pose and attire gave the illusion of nudity. The woman's eyes looked so real they seemed to speak.

"Tom," Eric said, grabbing Tom's arm. "Look at that."

"Jesus," Tom said under his breath. "I don't believe it."

"Did you have any idea the owner knew her?"

"No. Who would've thought — Teresa Torres and Bryant Davies. Of course, they may not know each other. It just might be a coincidence."

"Right. He has a half-nude portrait of her and it's just a coincidence . . . How rich did you say he was?"

"Very. Enough to own a house on the hill." Tom stopped as soon as he said it.

"And Teresa lives on the hill. I'm sorry to break it to you, Tom, old boy, but I think your Señorita Torres is a kept woman."

"Get you gentlemen something?" The bartender stood in front of Eric and Tom.

"Who's the beautiful lady?" Tom asked nonchalantly, pointing to the portrait of Teresa.

"That's Miss Teresa. She's a friend of Mr. Davies. Say, haven't I seen you in here before?"

Tom reached his hand across the bar. "My name's Tom Jordan. I handle Mr. Davies's legal affairs."

The bartender shook Tom's hand. "I thought I'd seen you before. I never forget a face. So, what can I get you gentlemen?"

"I'll have a beer, and Mr. Jordan will probably have a whiskey."

"That's right."

"Coming right up."

Eric leaned close to Tom, a conspiratorial tone in his voice. "So, didn't I tell you she was a kept woman?"

The men nodded to the bartender when he handed them their drinks. "I just can't believe it. A girl like that, coming from the kind of family she does, it doesn't make sense."

"It makes about as much sense as me growing up here on a rancho and spending ten years with the Comanches."

"You don't like her, but I think you understand her,

23

don't you?"

"I can't pretend to understand why she's done what she's done. All I know is that my mother pushed me too hard in one direction and I went in the other. And I know for a fact that families like ours are harder on their daughters. Why do you think my mother is the way she is?"

"I can't imagine your grandfather ever forcing Mariz to do anything she didn't want to do."

"I don't know, I wasn't around then."

"You sound like you're beginning to forgive Mariz."

"Maybe someday, I don't know. It would be easier if she'd just be honest with me for a change."

"Have you taken Raya to meet her? I'll bet she'd adore her."

"No, but I've been thinking about it lately. I don't like the idea of her being alone."

"Well, well," Tom clanked his shot glass against Eric's mug, "here's to Eric Anderson growing up."

"I'm a hell of a lot more grown up than you. I have a wife and a child who depend on me. What do you have?"

"My freedom," Tom replied glibly. "Ever gambled much?"

"Just in the Comanche camp. We used to play a game with bones, bet on how they'd fall. I once won ten horses, a rifle, and a mirror."

"I've never fancied gambling myself. I work too hard for my money. Look at these men. They work for months at a time up on the Mother Lode doing back-breaking work. Then they come down here and blow it all on women, gambling, and drinking. Doesn't make much sense to me."

"I guess it does to them. Maybe they figure they work hard enough to spend it however they want . . .

24

You want another?" Eric pointed at Tom's drink.

"No, I'm ready to go. Let's go back to my room and clean up for dinner."

"Dinner's not for another three hours. You're taken with the señorita, aren't you?"

"You'd do well to keep your mouth shut!" Tom angrily slapped some money down on the bar for their drinks, then they walked toward the doors just as a man came flying through them, falling against Eric.

"Get outta my way, mister," the man yelled, regaining his balance and heading out the door again. At the sound of a scream, Eric and Tom bounded out the swinging doors.

A woman lay on the wooden-planked sidewalk, her purse and packages strewn all about her. The man who had bumped into Eric and another man were fighting, totally ignoring the woman on the sidewalk. Eric reached down and helped her up, while Tom picked up her things. Eric strode to the man who had bumped into him and grabbed him from behind in a chokehold.

"I think you need to apologize to the lady."

"Hey, mister, this is our fight. Stay out of it," the other man yelled.

Eric drew his gun and aimed it at the other man, while still containing the one in front of him. "Did you say something?"

"No, I—"

"Well, *I* said something. You both owe that lady over there an apology."

"Hell, that's no lady, that's just a whore."

Eric pulled his arm tighter around the man's neck. "I don't think I heard you clearly."

"All right, all right," the man gasped.

Eric cocked his pistol and aimed it at the other man's head. "How about you? You have anything to say to the lady?"

The man sidled over to the woman and stood in front of her. "Sorry, Lily, I didn't mean no harm. I just had too much to drink."

"Now you." Eric turned the man around, tightening his arm around the man's throat. "Make it sound real sincere."

"Sorry, Miss Lily. I hope you're not hurt or nothing."

The woman looked from Eric to the two drunken men. "It's all right, boys, but I think you better sober up. You know how Mr. Davies feels about rowdiness in his place."

Eric loosened his hold on the man. "Now, why don't you two be on your way." He replaced the pistol in his holster. "You all right, ma'am?"

"Fine, thank you. You didn't have to do that. I'm used to it. The men down here are always like that. Besides," she looked from Eric to Tom, "the kind of business I'm in, I guess I get what I deserve."

"You don't deserve to be knocked down on the street by anyone."

Lily shook Eric's hand. "Thank you, Mr. . . . ?"

"The name's Eric Anderson."

"Thank you, Eric. You're a real gentleman." She turned to Tom. "And thank you, too, Mr. Jordan." She flashed Tom a brilliant smile.

"I didn't do much, Lily."

"Well, if there's anything I can ever do for either of you boys . . ." She smiled beguilingly.

Eric smiled back. "Thanks just the same, Lily, but I'm a married man. But Tom here . . ."

"Oh, I know all about Mr. Jordan. Most all of the women around here do."

Tom shrugged his shoulders. "Well, it was nice seeing you, Lily."

26

"You, too, Mr. Jordan. Thanks again, Eric."

Eric tipped his hat and bumped Tom's shoulder. "I'd say Miss Lily has it real bad for you, Mr. Jordan."

"Shut up and let's get out of here."

"You have to admit that was colorful, Tom," Eric said sarcastically.

"I'm glad you're enjoying yourself. I just hope you have as much fun tonight at Señorita Torres's home."

A frown crossed Eric's face. He had just about forgotten about Teresa Torres. The thought of spending an evening with her seemed unbearable. He shook his head. Life had certainly been easier when he had lived with the Comanches.

Eric tugged at his shirt collar as he, Lisa, and Tom sat in the library of Teresa Torres's home waiting for her to appear. "She certainly doesn't believe in being on time, does she?" remembering their previous meeting.

"Women are always late, you know that."

"Eric, you've been complaining ever since we left the hotel," Lisa noted. "She can't be as bad as you say."

"She's not," Tom added.

"I don't know why you're so intent on defending her."

"And I don't know why you're so intent on making her out to be a criminal. So she lives in a mansion, so a man pays for it, so she left her parents, so what?"

"I just don't like her attitude. I haven't met a woman like her since—"

"Since my sister."

Eric smiled and looked over at Lisa. "At least your sister can compromise occasionally. I don't think this woman knows the meaning of the word."

27

"Good evening, gentlemen." Teresa entered the room quietly. She looked from Eric to Lisa. "Señora."

Eric and Tom stood up.

"Please, sit down. Finish your drinks." Teresa walked over to Lisa and extended her hand. "My name is Teresa. And you are?"

"Lisa Anderson."

"My wife," Eric responded brusquely.

"I'm very pleased to meet you, señora."

"Thank you."

Teresa walked to a side table and poured herself a glass of wine. She was dressed in a low-cut, off-the-shoulder, brown silk dress. Diamonds adorned her ears and throat and her hair was pulled into a chignon at the nape of her neck. She looked beautiful, and she knew it. "You look especially handsome tonight, Tom."

"Thank you. And you look lovely."

"Thank *you*." She smiled and looked at Eric, her tone changing. "I didn't think you'd come, Mr. Anderson."

"And why is that, Señorita Torres?" Eric instinctively knew how much it bothered her to be called "señorita."

Teresa glanced at Lisa. "I was afraid I had offended you today."

Eric regarded her for a moment. "No, you weren't afraid you offended me, you were *hoping* you had offended me."

"Did I succeed?"

"I don't offend easily, but you did surprise me."

"And why is that?" Teresa walked around the room, holding her wineglass very delicately.

"I'm just surprised that a woman of your background would live the way you do."

Teresa stopped. She turned around, her brown eyes

28

angry. "There is nothing the matter with the way I live."

"Then why is it your parents haven't been to see you? Why did your mother have to send a message through us to get to you?"

"Eric!" Lisa interrupted angrily.

Teresa walked over to Eric and stood in front of him. "I don't like you very much, Mr. Anderson," she said angrily, then held her glass up and threw her wine in his face.

Eric stood up, taking a handkerchief from the inside pocket of his jacket. He wiped his face. "The truth is hard to hear. Even harder if you can't face it." He walked over to Lisa." It's time to go."

Lisa stood up. "Eric, what is the matter with you?"

"Nothing a little fresh air won't cure."—He led Lisa to the double doors of the study. "Don't worry about us for dinner."

"What's this? Leaving already?" Bryant Davies strode into the room, a huge bear of a man with a big smile on his face. He walked to Teresa and kissed her on the cheek. "So, Tom, who is your friend . . . and who is this beautiful woman?"

Tom stood up, feeling uncomfortable. "Bryant, this is Eric Anderson and his wife Lisa, my sister."

Eric walked from the door to Bryant. He shook his hand. "Pleased to meet you."

Lisa smiled and extended her hand. "Mr. Davies."

"A pleasure Mrs. Anderson. Then, glancing at Eric, he asked, "What happened to your shirt?"

"Spilled my wine," Eric answered, glancing at Teresa.

"Well, how about another before dinner?"

"Thanks." Eric couldn't say no. Bryant Davies was a likable man. *What,* he wondered, *is he doing with a shrew like Teresa?*

"Well, you both come back in then. We don't care what your shirt looks like, do we, Teresa?"

Teresa smiled at Bryant, then looked at Eric, an unpleasant expression on her face. "Mr. and Mrs. Anderson might have other plans this evening, Bryant. I'd hate to keep them from something else."

"Nonsense." Bryant handed Eric a glass of wine. "You don't have any other plans, do you?"

Eric smiled at Teresa, knowing his presence would aggravate her. "No, we don't. We'd be glad to stay, wouldn't we, Lisa?"

Lisa glanced at Eric suspiciously. "Yes, we'd love to."

"Good, sit down. I heard there was some excitement today down at the tavern, that a couple of the regulars got drunk and knocked Lily down on the street. Some stranger came up and made them both apologize to her. Lily said he was a real gentleman and he handled both men without much trouble. I'd like to meet that man."

"You already have," Tom said proudly.

"You? Was it you, Tom?"

"No, it was Eric. He can't resist a lady in distress."

"You?" Teresa asked, genuinely surprised.

"All I did was help the lady."

"Not many men would offer to help a woman down on the waterfront, especially a prostitute. You're either real brave or real stupid."

"Like I said, the lady was in trouble and I don't like men who take advantage of women."

"How commendable," Teresa replied sarcastically.

"If you ever need a job, I can always use men like you at my place to keep the drunks in line."

"Thanks anyway, but I think I'll stick to ranching."

"You're in ranching?"

"I run my grandfather's ranch."

30

"So, how did you meet Tom?"

Eric looked at Lisa and smiled. "It's kind of a long story."

"If you say so. And how about you, Mrs. Anderson? Are you from around these parts?"

"No, I'm from Boston. My story's a long one, too."

Bryant stood up. "Well, it's not for me to pry. If you all don't mind, I'd like to talk to Tom about some business before dinner. We won't be long."

Tom rolled his eyes as he walked past Eric. "I'm sure you'll all be fine."

Lisa stood up. "Do you mind if I tag along?" Lisa looked from Eric to Tom and rose. "I'd love to look around the house."

"Your wife's a very trusting person."

"That's because she knows she has nothing to worry about." Eric stared across the room in silence, trying to think of a way he could speak to Teresa in a civilized manner. "Bryant seems like a good man."

"He is," Teresa said. "He saved my life. I owe him everything." She stood up and paced slowly back and forth in front of the fireplace. "I don't suppose you and I could call a truce, just for tonight. Bryant likes you, and I don't want to upset him in any way."

"Frankly, I'm not even sure why we're at war."

"I think you said it earlier today without realizing it. Perhaps it's because we're so much alike and sometimes one sees things in other people you don't like about yourself."

"I'm sorry about today. I had no right to say those things to you."

Teresa smiled for the first time. "I understand that you were defending my parents, and for that, I thank you. However, you do not know what happened, so it's wrong for you to judge me."

Eric nodded his head, putting his glass down on the

31

table and standing up. "You're right. I, of all people, shouldn't judge you."

"But a man like you. . . ." Teresa shrugged her shoulders.

"A man like me? You think I grew up on a rancho and spent my entire life getting everything I wanted. That might be true for a good portion of my life, but the last twelve years have been very different."

"I don't know what you mean."

"I left home when I was sixteen. My father died, and I blamed my mother for it. I hated her. I actually think I could've killed her. After I left home, I wandered around and wound up with a group of Indians who saved my life. I stayed with them for ten years."

"You lived with Indians for ten years? Wasn't it difficult?"

"Not really. I needed to be with simple people. These people were fierce warriors, but they were also loyal friends. They became my family."

"What made you leave?"

"Lisa. Some braves had taken her captive from a wagon train. By the time I came back from a raid, I found she had been beaten, abused, and humiliated. Trying to defend herself, she got in a fight with one of the women." He smiled as he recalled it. "She was like a mountain lion. She fought like a warrior, showed no fear. Even though she knew she could be killed, she didn't stop. I think I began to fall in love with her right then."

"She's a brave woman."

"Yes, she is."

"And what happened then?"

Eric looked at Teresa. He couldn't believe this was the same woman he had met earlier in the day. "I took her for my wife. We had a good life until she lost our child and almost her life. I decided for her own good

32

she had to leave. I sent her away."

"But you found her again."

"Yes, I found her again."

"You love her very much."

"It's that obvious?"

"Yes, your eyes, they sparkle as you speak of her, and the love is all over your face when you look at her." She nodded her head. "That is good. That is the way it should be."

"What about you, Teresa?"

"That is the first time you have not called me 'señorita'." She smiled. "I don't love Bryant."

"But he loves you."

"Yes, he loves me, and for that I am thankful. He knows I do not love him, but he is still willing to love me and take care of me. I am lucky."

"You don't say that like you believe it."

"I *am* lucky, Eric. I know I could be working down on the waterfront for dollars a night. I have never fooled myself. I am lucky to have a man like Bryant love me. I cannot ask for more. It would be selfish to do so."

Eric looked at this lovely woman who stood before him, and she suddenly seemed like a different, softer person. He wondered what had happened with her parents.

She appeared to read his thoughts. "You want to know what happened between me and my parents?"

"No. I don't expect you to tell me."

Teresa ignored him. "My father forced me to marry a man thirty years my senior when I was just fifteen years old. My father said it was a good marriage. He said I would be well provided for." She laughed derisively. "My husband beat me. He showed me no love. But when he found out I was carrying his child, he changed and started treating me like a princess. When

33

I lost the child, he blamed me. He said I did it on purpose. He beat me so badly I almost died. I decided to run away. I had nowhere to go. I knew I couldn't go back home, so I ran away to the city. I didn't know how to support myself. Then I met a man. He said he would buy me dinner. He did, and then he took me to his room. He told me he would give me money if I did whatever he told me to do." She looked at Eric. "I did things that I will always be ashamed of, Eric, but I made money. I did well until I became pregnant again. This time I wanted the baby. But when my little girl was born, I knew I couldn't keep her. I knew she deserved a better life, so I gave her away. After that, I started to drink. Nothing mattered to me but staying drunk. I let men use me, and I didn't even care. I suppose I thought it was my punishment. Eventually I wound up on the street, in the gutter, and that is where Bryant found me. He took me home and cared for me and loved me. He never judged me." She circled the room and looked at Eric. "What are you thinking?"

"I was just wondering how we could scream at each other this morning and be talking like friends tonight."

"I don't know, but I must say, I like this much better."

Teresa looked up as the others reentered the library. "Are you ready to eat now?" She directed her question to Bryant.

"Yes. I hope you and Eric found something to talk about."

She smiled at Eric. "Yes, Bryant, we found out we have a great deal in common."

"Good." Bryant extended one arm to Teresa and the other to Lisa. "Shall we, ladies?"

Tom walked over to Eric. "What happened between

34

you two? She actually smiled at you."

"Must be my undying charm . . . Actually, we decided to call a truce, for Bryant's sake."

"Well, she must care for him more than I thought because she sure hated you this morning."

Eric slapped Tom on the shoulder. "She cares for him and she's fascinated by me."

"That's dangerous talk for a married man, especially a man who's married to my sister."

"Don't worry, Tom. It's only because I remind her of herself."

"Now what the hell's that supposed to mean?"

"We're both black sheep, Tom. We came from similar backgrounds and we both got away from them."

"And you both hated your parents."

"Parent. With her it was her father; with me, it was my mother."

"Did she tell you what happened?"

"Yes."

"Well, since you two are such fast friends now, maybe you'd like to convince her to talk to her father."

"Tom, I'm starving, let's go eat. We'll worry about Teresa Torres later."

Lisa sat down on the edge of the bed, taking off her boots. "Teresa is very lovely."

"I hadn't noticed," Eric said distractedly, slipping off his jacket.

"You're a liar, Eric. You noticed her."

Eric looked at Lisa, shrugging his shoulders. "She's all right, I guess, but she's not my type."

"And what is your type?"

Eric moved forward, lifting a strand of hair from Lisa's neck. "Auburn hair, green eyes, fiery temper." He pulled her to her feet. He kissed her softly. "Sweet

35

lips."

Lisa shook her head and smiled. "You are a devil."

"You wouldn't have me any other way, would you?"

Lisa looked up into Eric's startling blue eyes. "No, I wouldn't."

Eric wrapped his arms around his wife. "I love you, Lisa. I don't know what I'd ever do without you."

"You won't ever have to find out." Lisa kissed him, then pulled away. "There was something between you and Teresa tonight. Everyone could see it."

"That's ridiculous."

"Is it? I saw the way you two looked at each other."

Eric sat down on the bed, one foot propped on the opposite knee so he could pull off his boots. "She's a beautiful woman who has a chip on her shoulder." He pulled his other boot off. "There's nothing between us, Lisa. Hell, I only met her for the first time today."

"I know that, Eric. I'm not accusing you of anything." She shrugged her shoulders. "I guess it's hard for me to see you with another woman. I saw the way she looked at you. I can't help but remember that Consuelo used to look at you the same way."

Eric stood up. He grabbed Lisa's shoulders. "I'm sorry about what happened with Consuelo but that was a long time ago. Teresa means nothing. You're the only woman for me." He kissed her and pulled her to him.

Lisa buried her face in Eric's chest, trying to rid herself of the nagging feeling that something bad was going to happen. She hoped and prayed that nothing would ever change the way they felt about each other.

Chapter 2

Bryant Davies was a very rich man. He had started out in Boston as a deckhand on a ship and had loved San Francisco the first time the ship laid anchor there. That had been ten years ago. He had seen the possibilities even then of taking advantage of the population boom that he knew was soon to come. He started out working the docks and, whenever possible, he gambled. He worked, gambled, and saved until he had enough to buy into a small tavern on the waterfront. He and his partner ran a small but honest table. It was during one of these games that his partner was shot and killed by an angry loser. Bryant took over as full owner. Soon, he began to expand. By the time of the Gold Rush, what he called a tavern had become a large and elaborate gambling and drinking hall.

Bryant had also made investments along the way. He owned property in Chinatown, a mansion on Nob Hill, where he and Teresa now lived, and he had vast amounts of gold in a vault in the bank just in case something ever happened.

He sat at his desk tapping his pencil and looking over the figures in his books. He had done well this year, and it seemed that nothing would ever slow it down. But he knew better. He knew that the Gold Rush would end someday and then there wouldn't be men like the 'niners so eager to throw their money away. That's why he was building a hotel in the better part of the city that would cater to wealthy clientele. He wanted to secure a future for him and Teresa.

Teresa. God, how he loved her. His life had been so empty before her. He was a smart man, and he knew that she didn't love him, but he also knew that she would never leave him. It wasn't the mansion or the clothes or the money—it was the security that he provided for her that assured him she would stay with him. He opened his drawer and took out a blue velvet box. He opened it and looked at the two-carat diamond ring. He planned to ask Teresa to marry him tonight. He wanted her to be with him forever. He wanted her to be the mother of his children. There was a knock on the door, and he snapped the box shut and put it away in the drawer.

"Sorry to bother you, Mr. Davies, but there's a man out here who's anxious to see you. He says it's important, that it's about Miss Teresa."

"Send him in," Bryant replied, frowning. This had happened before. Men had come here trying to blackmail him because they knew of Teresa's past. He had never paid a cent. Now he leaned back in his chair, his hands folded in front of him. The door slowly opened and a young man walked in. He was of medium build, dressed in a tattered suit and hat, and it was obvious that he hadn't had a shave in weeks. He was probably no more than twenty years old.

"Hello, Mr. Davies."

Bryant took his time. He didn't want this kid to think he was too anxious. "Do we have some business to discuss?"

"I think we do." The boy walked over to the desk,

38

pushing his hat back on his head. "I'll make it real simple for you. I want twenty-five thousand dollars one week from today."

"Oh, is that all? Why don't I just write you out a check?" Bryant replied sarcastically.

"I ain't foolin'. If I don't have the money in one week, you'll never see your sweet Teresa again."

Bryant felt a stabbing pain in his stomach, but he forced himself to be calm. "What about Teresa?"

"We have her someplace safe, someplace where you'll never find her. Now, if you care about her like I hear you do, then you'll have the money for me when I come back in one week."

Bryant stood up, walking to the other side of the desk. "How do I know you're telling the truth?"

"You're not a stupid man, Mr. Davies. Why would I come here like this if I didn't have your woman?"

Bryant reached out and grabbed the boy by the collar, pulling him toward him. "I could snap your neck right now. You know that, don't you?"

"I expect you could, but if you did that you'd never see your woman again. She'll be killed if I don't come back by nightfall."

Bryant tightened his hold. "You think you've outsmarted me? I could make you suffer in ways you've never even heard of, you little bastard, and then, believe me, you'd tell me what I want to know."

"Like I said, you're a smart man. I don't think you'll do anything to me. You don't want to risk hurting your woman." The boy tried to ease back from Bryant's hold. " 'Course, you could take a chance and hurt me and I might tell you. Then again, you might get carried away in your anger and hurt me real bad. Then where would you be?"

"You bastard!" Bryant pushed the boy as hard as he could across the room. He stumbled and fell, hitting his head against the wall. Bryant rushed after him, pulling him up from the floor and slamming him against the wall. "I don't think you know who you're dealing with, boy."

"Yes, sir, I believe I do. That's why the man I work for won't tell me where he's keeping your woman. You see, you can beat up on me all you want, but it won't do no good. He's waiting to see if I'm safe. If I'm not—"

"He'll kill her." Bryant let the kid go. "But why would he kill her? He'd lose his chance at getting twenty-five thousand dollars, wouldn't he?"

"Yes, sir, but he told me to tell you that there's more men like you in San Francisco. If you don't come through with the money, some other gentleman will."

Bryant walked over to his desk. "I can give the money to you now."

"No, sir. I have strict orders to wait one week."

"What's your name, boy?"

"Edward."

"Well, Edward, you're not being very smart. All you have to do is tell me where this man is keeping Teresa and I can give you the twenty-five thousand dollars. You could be a rich man."

"I could also be a dead man. No, sir, I can't do that. I'd never be safe if I took the money."

"You'll never be safe anyway, boy. I'll hunt you down and kill you myself if anything happens to her."

"Nothing will happen if you do as I say, sir. I'll be back in one week." The boy walked to the door and left the office.

Bryant grabbed his hat from the rack. He could use all the strongarm in the world, but it wouldn't do any good if he couldn't find Teresa. He had to find someone who could think like this man. He left the office and ordered his buggy. His driver steered the horse

40

through the throngs of people. When they reached the small house Tom was living in, Bryant jumped out and ran to the door, pounding on it until Tom appeared.

"I need to talk to you." Bryant brushed past Tom and into the house. He walked into the living room, took his hat off, and twisted it around in his hands. "I need your help."

"What is it, Bryant?"

"Did you tell me your brother-in-law was a tracker?"

"Not really."

"But I thought you said something about him being a good tracker.

"He is, but—"

"But what?" Bryant screamed. "I need his help."

Eric walked into the room. "Is everything all right?"

"I need your help, Eric. Can you track?"

Eric looked over at Tom. "Yes."

"How well?"

"Well enough."

"Dammit, man, I asked you a question!" Bryant's face was turning red.

"Take it easy, Bryant."

"I can't, Tom." He looked at Eric. "Look, I'm sorry for blowing up at you. Someone has kidnapped Teresa. They want twenty-five thousand dollars in a week or they'll kill her."

"Do you have any idea who it might be?"

"Hell, I've made so many enemies over the years, it could be anybody who's holding a grudge because I kicked him out of my tavern or who lost a lot of money gambling."

"I can track, Bryant. I lived with the Comanches for ten years. But tracking in the prairie is one thing, tracking in the city another."

41

"But you've got the instinct for it. That's what matters. Will you help me, Eric? I'll pay you anything you want. Name your price."

"I don't want your money, Bryant." Eric thought for a moment. Lisa wouldn't be happy about this. She was already concerned about him and Teresa.

"Look, Eric, I don't know what to say to you to convince you to help me. Teresa is my life. She is everything to me." His eyes teared up suddenly. "If she dies, I die."

"Bryant, I'd like to help, but I don't want to leave Lisa here by herself."

"Do you love your wife, Eric?"

"Very much."

"And if someone did something to try to harm her, would you do anything to get her back?"

Eric recalled the time they had ridden into the band of Apaches and one of them had tried to take Lisa with him. He had killed the man. Yes, he would do anything to get her back. "I don't want her staying alone."

"She can stay in the mansion with me until you get back. "I'll even take her home if you like. Please, Eric."

"All right, Bryant. I'll help you. But don't expect too much. If I don't have anything to go on, I can't find Teresa for you. You've got to think. You've got to remember everything about the man who came into your office and ask around, find out if anyone has seen him before. For now, let's go back to your home. We need to find out if anyone saw her leave."

"Bryant, is it possible that if you just waited the week, Teresa will be safely returned to you?"

"That won't happen, Tom. I know what these men are like. They get what they want, and they don't care about the people involved. We have to find her before

42

next Wednesday."

"All right, let's go to work. I'll give you a note for your man to give to my wife. Make sure he gets there, Bryant."

"He'll get there." He shook Eric's hand. "Thank you. I don't know how to repay you."

"You don't owe me anything. I just hope they left some loose ends behind."

Eric, Bryant, and Tom sat in Bryant's office, talking to all of the employees of the tavern. Eric and Bryant had already talked to all of Teresa's servants. All they knew was that she went out for a walk and never came back. They had already talked to most of the girls. All of them saw so many men in a week, it was hard to keep faces straight.

"They were smart," Eric said thoughtfully. "The kid looked so ordinary that nobody noticed him."

"There's got to be something. These men wouldn't just come out of nowhere. Chances are, one or all of them have been in my place before."

There was a knock on the door and Lily entered the room, smiling at Eric before walking to Bryant's desk. "Mr. Davies, sir. I been thinking about this young man you were describing."

"Do you remember something, Lily?"

"I'm not sure. I see lots of young men during the week."

"Anything would be a help, Lily," Eric said encouragingly.

"Was he sort of soft-spoken?"

Bryant thought a minute. "Yes, he was. In fact, it surprised me. Even when I grabbed him and threw him against the wall, he didn't raise his voice or get upset."

"And you said he was medium height? Did he have light-brown hair, kinda longish?"

"Yes, he did." Bryant stood up. "Lily, you've seen him?"

"If it's the same guy, I seen him. He comes in here once a month to be with a woman and drink a little. He has good manners and never gets drunk. He's one of the few I don't mind being with."

"What's his name, Lily?"

"It's a nice name, almost English-sounding. Edward, I think."

Bryant looked at Eric. "It's him. That's what he told me his name was."

Eric took Lily gently by the shoulders. "Lily, I need you to think real hard. Has he told you anything about himself? Does he work a claim? Does he have family? Anything."

"I know for sure he has a claim someplace because that's why he comes in here every month. He puts his gold in the bank."

"Do you know where that claim is?"

Lily shook her head. "I don't think he's ever said."

"What about friends? Has he spoken of any friends or family?"

"He's talked about a man he calls Big John. He says this man was real good to him when his parents died on the wagon train that brought them west. I get the feeling he looks on this man as his father."

Eric glanced at Bryant and Tom. "Does he ever give you extra money?"

"As a matter of fact, he's always bringin' me little gifts." She reached under the collar of her dress and pulled out a necklace. "This here's a small gold nugget he had made into a necklace for me. He said I'd been real nice to him and it was the least he could do."

"Have you talked about many things, Lily?"

44

"Yeah, we talked about his family and mine. He told me about Big John and he . . ." She stopped suddenly, biting the inside of her cheek. "Wait a minute. I think he did say something once about it being real far to the claim. He said he got real tired of riding back there."

"You have any ideas?" Eric asked Bryant.

"Hell, if its the Mother Lode, it runs all the way from Mariposa to Amador. That's about seventy miles. There're the northern mines and the southern mines and between them there's the American River with all of its forks, and the Calaveras, Stanislaus, Tuolumne, Merced, and a portion of the San Joaquin. There's no way we could hit all those camps in a week." Bryant sat down on the edge of the desk, looking dejected.

"I'm real sorry, Mr. Davies. I wish I could remember more."

"Nonsense, Lily. You've been a great help."

Eric took Lily's arm and walked her out of the office and up the stairs to her room. "Can I come in for a minute?"

"Yes," Lily said, somewhat uncertainly.

Eric closed the door and pulled up a chair, turning it around so he could lean his arms on the back. "I get the feeling you're not telling everything you know, Lily."

"But I am, Mr. Anderson. Why would I lie?"

"I don't know. Maybe you should tell me." Eric waited for a moment, watching Lily as she paced nervously around the room. "Did Edward promise you a lot of money? Is that it?"

Lily turned to the window, staring at the curtains. "I don't know what you're talking about."

"Look, Lily, I'm not here to get you in trouble. If Edward offered you money to give him information on Teresa, then you're in big trouble. Do you know what Mr. Davies would do if he found out?"

Lily turned around, her eyes frantic. "I didn't want to tell him. I just want out of this business so bad. I hate it. I hate myself. Edward said he could give me lots of money so I could go away somewhere and start a new life."

"And all he wanted was some information on Teresa, like when she was going out and where?"

Lily nodded. "He promised me she wouldn't be hurt."

"Did you believe him?"

"I don't know. I'm confused. Edward is a nice man. He's always been kind and gentle with me. I don't think he'd do anything to Miss Teresa. He justs wants some money so he can get out of here."

"But Edward isn't in charge, you know that, don't you? Do you actually think the person who has Teresa is going to let her go once he has the money?" Eric got up and walked to Lily, gently touching her cheek. "You're a good person. You wouldn't do anything to harm anyone, would you?"

"No," she replied softly.

"Then tell me what you know."

"Mr. Davies will fire me if he knows. Then where will I be?" she asked frantically.

"Mr. Davies will not fire you. He'll be grateful you told the truth."

"But how do I know that for sure?"

"I don't think you have much of a choice now, do you? I know you're lying."

Lily nodded, tears running down her cheeks. "The camp is called Bear Alley. They're keeping her in some kind of a cave or something."

"Is it far from here?"

"Edward says it takes him a day to get there from

here."

"What about men? How many men are with him?"

"I don't know. All he's ever talked about is that Big John."

Eric took the woman's hand. "You've done the right thing, Lily. Now, I want you to tell Mr. Davies what you just told me. I'll be right there with you."

Lily nodded silently, grasping Eric's hand as tightly as if she were a little girl holding onto her father. They walked back down to Bryant's office and Eric knocked on the door.

"What is it? Did you remember something else, Lily?" Bryant asked.

Lily looked at Eric uncertainly, then stepped forward. "I lied, Mr. Davies." She told him everything she had told Eric and stared at her hands, unable to look at Bryant. Bryant got up from the desk and walked to Lily, taking her hands in his.

"Thank you."

"You shouldn't be thankin' me, Mr. Davies, you should be sendin' me to jail."

Bryant smiled and squeezed Lily's hands. "I understand why you did it, Lily. I know you care for Teresa, but I also know how much you hate what you're doing. That's why, as of today, you're not one of the girls upstairs anymore."

"I understand, Mr. Davies."

"No, I don't think you do, Lily. I want you to be my personal secretary. I've been needing help around her for a long time."

"But I don't know anything about being a secretary. I don't have any education—"

"I'll teach you. I've watched you for a long time. You're smart and you're good with people. I should've done this a long time ago."

"But after what I did to Miss Teresa . . ."

47

"Teresa would be the first one to understand. She'll be pleased for you."

Lily covered her face with her hands and began to sob. "How can you be so nice after what I've done to you?"

Bryant took Lily in his arms. "We've all been desperate at one time in our lives, girl. But you have to promise me something if you come to work for me."

"Yes, sir."

"If you ever feel desperate again, you come to me. I'll help you. I'll treat you fairly as long as you're honest with me. You could've kept lying, Lily, but you didn't. I'll be forever grateful for that, no matter what happens. Now go on up to your room and get some rest. As soon as we bring Teresa back, you'll start your new job."

Lily threw her arms around Bryant and buried her head in his chest. "Thank you, Mr. Davies. You're a good man." She walked toward the door and looked at Eric with a grateful smile. "Thank you."

"How did you know she was lying?" Bryant asked Eric when Lily left the room.

"Just a feeling. She kept stumbling over her words and she didn't make eye contact with you."

"I don't know how to thank you, either, Eric."

"Don't thank me yet. Let's get Teresa first. I'd like to leave as soon as possible."

"I'll have supplies packed for us."

"You might get a rifle for each of us and extra shells. Also, try to find some old beat-up clothes for me and Tom. If we go riding into a mining camp looking like this, they'll shoot us on sight."

"They may do that anyway. Miners don't take too kindly to people trespassing on their claims."

"Well, we'll just have to find a way in."

"I'd better dig out my old clothes," Bryant said.

48

"You can't go, Bryant."

"You can't keep me from going."

"No, I can't, but you'd be foolish to come with us. Everyone in this area knows you. Christ, you're so big, you'd stand out in a crowd of a hundred. You can't go."

"I can't stand the thought of not being there to help."

"You don't have a choice, Bryant. Eric knows what he's doing," Tom added. "Besides, they've never seen us before."

"But you've been in here before, Tom."

"Only on business. I don't frequent the tavern."

Bryant thought for a moment then nodded. "All right. I'll get your supplies. But please, be careful. Bring Teresa back to me."

Lisa stared out the hotel window tapping her foot nervously. She could see the bay and the white, billowy clouds that hung in the sky. Below her in the street, life went on as it always did, with the usual hustle and bustle.

"Would you please say something, Lisa?"

Lisa spotted a couple walking hand-in-hand on the street below. They were talking and laughing, and nothing else around them seemed to permeate their little world.

"Lisa, did you hear me?"

Lisa turned around finally and looked at Eric. He was already dressed in buckskin pants, boots, a worn shirt and hat, and he wore his holster. "What do you want me to say? You've already made up your mind to go."

"Bryant needs my help."

"So does Teresa."

"That's right, so does Teresa. Have you forgotten already what it's like to be taken against your will?"

"How could you, of all people, say that to me?" Lisa said angrily. "I'll never forget what those Comanches did to me, and I don't need you to remind me!" She turned back to the window, her arms crossed in front of her body.

"Lisa, I'm sorry . . ."

"Just go, Eric. You can't let your friends down."

"Bryant wants you to stay with him at the mansion; I think it's a good idea."

"I can take care of myself."

"I don't want you staying in this hotel alone while I'm gone, I'll . . ."

Lisa looked at Eric, her eyes hard. "I said I can take care of myself."

"Don't do this, Lisa."

"Do what? Do you expect me to be glad that you're riding off to rescue another woman?"

"Lisa . . ." Eric touched her cheek.

"I'm all right, Eric. I'm not angry. You'd better go. Didn't you say Tom was waiting for you downstairs?"

Eric nodded. he pulled Lisa into his arms and kissed her gently. "I'll miss you. We'll talk when I get back."

Lisa smiled slightly as she watched Eric leave the room. "I'll miss you, too, my love." She went to the closet and pulled out her trunk to pack. She was going home.

Teresa struggled against the ropes that bound her hands and feet but they wouldn't budge. She hated being in this place. It was cold and dank, and it scared her to death. She was afraid the whole place would cave in at any moment. She had already been here for two days and she felt as if she were dying. She hadn't been taken too far into the cave, but it was far enough so that she couldn't see daylight. She had never felt so alone in her life. The only light came from a lamp that hung on the side of the wooden railing.

She laid her head back against the dirt wall and closed her eyes. Bryant would never find her here and she knew it. Her only chance was to try to get her hands free and somehow maneuver her way out of the shaft.

There was a noise, and she closed her eyes, feigning sleep. She knew it was the boy bringing her dinner and she didn't want him to think she was overanxious or afraid.

"Miss, are you awake?"

Slowly, Teresa opened her eyes. "What?"

"I've brought you your dinner."

"No, thank you. I don't want any more beans."

"I brought you rabbit stew this time and some biscuits. I even have a cup of coffee for you."

Teresa looked at the boy who stood in front of her. He was so sweet and innocent she couldn't believe he was involved in this kidnapping. She took the plate from him. "Thank you, Edward. You can set the coffee down right there."

"Well, I'll be back in a while to get your plate."

"Don't go. Please."

Edward stopped. "I'm not supposed to stay in here except to bring you your food and see to your needs."

"Well, this *is* a need. I need to talk to someone."

"Ma'am . . ."

"You have fine manners, Edward. Your parents taught you well."

"Thank you. They was good people."

"They're dead?"

Edward nodded. "They was killed by some Kiowas

51

who attacked our wagon train. They even took my ma's wedding ring."

"I'm sorry, Edward. How did you escape?"

"My pa made me crawl up under the carriage of the wagon and I held on to it for over an hour. My fingers and arms hurt so bad I thought I'd die, but it saved my life."

"What did you do after that?"

"A man came along and took me to California with him."

"You were lucky then, weren't you?"

"Yes, ma'am. If it weren't for—" Edward stopped himself. "I really should be going now."

"Please, Edward, stay just a little longer. It can't hurt for you to talk to me."

Edward looked around him. "I suppose not."

"Are you planning to kill me, Edward?"

"Me, ma'am?" He looked genuinely shocked. "I would never kill a lady like you, ma'am."

"But there's someone else who will, right?"

"I can't tell you nothing about this place."

"Why? It really doesn't matter if I'm going to die."

"Don't talk like that, ma'am. Your man will have the money ready and you'll be let go."

"You don't really believe that, do you, Edward?"

"It's true, ma'am. There's no reason to kill you."

"Except that I've seen your face. I can identify you."

"But I'll be gone away from here. No one will find me."

"You're a sweet boy, Edward. It's too bad you're mixed up in something like this. You're not a murderer."

"You're not going to be murdered, ma'am, I promise you that." Edward stood up. "I gotta go now. I'll be back for your plate later."

52

Teresa watched Edward as he left the shaft. She prayed she had gotten through to him. He was her only hope.

"Can I talk to you, John?"

"Come on in, Edward. What is it? Is the woman giving you trouble?"

"No, she's real nice. I just have a question to ask you."

"Go ahead, boy."

"Are you going to kill her even if you get the money?"

"Now why would I do that? That wouldn't serve any purpose, would it?"

"But what if she seen you, she could identify you?"

"Well, that'd be different. Then I'd have to kill her."

"But why? We're leaving here, aren't we? We don't need to kill nobody."

"What's the matter with you, boy? You're not letting that woman fill your head full of lies, are you?"

"No, I just don't want to kill nobody."

"And I gave you my word that we wouldn't kill her if we got the money."

"And if we don't get the money?"

"Then we don't have a choice, do we?"

Edward stared at Big John, the man he had admired for so long, the man who had saved his life and taught him about survival, had even taught him to read. "I don't want you to kill her."

"You don't want? When did you start giving orders around here?"

"There's no need to kill her. That Mr. Davies will have the money."

"I already told you, boy, if we get the money, then the woman will be fine. If we don't, she dies."

53

"But she's innocent, John. She's done nothing."

"She's a whore. What do you care?"

"She's a human being. She ain't harmed you or me none."

"My, you do have a soft spot for whores now that you've spent all that time with that one down on the waterfront. You best be warned, boy. Whores will steal your heart and your money."

"Lily ain't like that."

"Just like this woman isn't like that, right?" John got up from his cot and towered over Edward. "Let me tell you something, boy. Women like that are dirt, they're less than dirt. They don't serve any good purpose except to please a man. You can't trust 'em; they'll steal from you and they might even stab you in the back while you're not looking. You best get your loyalties straight, boy. It wasn't either of those two whores that saved your life when those Kiowas cut up your parents, it was me. If you can't remember that, then you best get out now."

"I don't wanna leave, John. You been like a pa to me, but I don't like hurtin' innocent people."

"Nobody'll get hurt if the money's there on time."

"We coulda had the money."

"And they would've followed you."

"He could still have me followed when I go back for the money."

"He won't take the chance after a week without his woman. He'll be too scared. And why are you questioning me all of a sudden, boy?"

"It just don't make no sense, that's all."

"It's not supposed to make sense to you, boy. You're just supposed to take orders and not ask questions."

Edward stared at the man in front of him, angry but not angry enough to confront him. He had seen

Big John break a man's neck like it was a twig between his fingers. He turned around and walked out of the shack.

"Don't you be gettin' no crazy ideas, boy, or you'll be sorry."

Edward ignored John's threat and walked back to the mine. It was clear what he had to do.

It took three days for Eric and Tom to reach the Mother Lode. They passed small towns like Whiskey Gulch, Hangman's Canyon, Murderer's Row, Hell's Thunder, and Poker Face. They weren't welcome in any of the places and were usually greeted by a loaded rifle or shotgun.

They had already decided on a story. They told people they were looking for their brother, that their mother was dying and it was her last wish to see her third son before she died. As a rule, most miners had been away from their families for at least a year and they were soft when it came to hearing stories about families.

They had just left Thirsty Man's Ridge and were heading to Bear Alley. Although Lily had told them Edward had taken Teresa to Bear Alley, they stopped at every camp along the way.

"It's a good thing those miners aren't too smart," Tom observed. "If any of them had taken a closer look, they'd have seen we don't look the least bit alike."

"Doesn't matter, as long as the story works."

Bear Alley was named for a bear that had walked down the middle of the camp one night. They reached it four days after leaving San Francisco. Eric had wanted to go in by day, but Tom was firm, insisting they go in at night.

"If we go in during the day, someone might get edgy. But at night, we'll have a chance to check around without being seen."

"It's not that easy, Tom. I've been on plenty of raids at night. It's hard to see where you're going. Hell, we don't even know where the cave is."

"So, we're going to go into the camp come daylight, ask for our brother, and wait for Edward and Big John to mosey on up to us? You're crazy."

"Of course we're not going to wait for them to come to us. We just want to make sure Big John's in this camp before we go in at night. Save us a lot of trouble." He thought a moment. "Let's say our brother's name is David. That's a good biblical name. Ought to get us a little sympathy."

"Then what? You think they'll all stop digging to commiserate with us?"

"No, but I think they might let us hang around for a while, especially since we've been traveling for weeks looking for him. Then we keep an eye out for Edward or John, and at nightfall we pretend to ride off but we sneak back into the camp. How does that sound to you?"

"All right, I guess. I still say it would be better if we got a look tonight."

"And what if we run into guards, or trip over a bucket or wheelbarrow? We have to see what the layout of the camp is like first."

"Don't tell me you did that when you were a Comanche?"

"No, but we knew that most camps were basically the same. This is different. These men are jumpy and likely to shoot at anything."

"All right, we'll do as you say, but if something happens to Teresa, it'll be your fault."

Eric shook his head. "That's what I like. A man

56

who's willing to shoulder the responsibility. Let's find a place to camp and get some sleep. Tomorrow may be the day we meet up with Big John."

"What wrong, Edward? You're quiet tonight."

"Nothing, ma'am." Edward sat down uninvited and handed Teresa her plate. She barely glanced at it before she put it on the ground. "You should eat, ma'am. You need to keep up your strength."

"Why should I bother if I'm going to be dead in a few days?"

"You're not going to be dead, ma'am."

"Edward, you're a sweet boy but you can't do anything about it."

"Ma'am . . ."

"It's all right, Edward. I don't blame you. I blame the man who forced you to do this."

"He's not all that bad. I'da been dead if he hadn't helped me all those years ago. He cares about me."

"If that's so, why does he have you involved in something like this?"

"He says the money can help us to do anything we want."

"*We?*"

"Yes, ma'am. He's gonna share it with me."

"Do you really believe that, Edward?"

"He wouldn't lie to me, ma'am."

"Listen to me, Edward. This man, whoever he is, can very easily kill both you and me after he gets the money. There will be no witnesses and no one to question him. He'll probably leave our bodies right here in the cave."

Edward looked around him, pulling his coat tighter around his shoulders. "He wouldn't do that."

"I'm not asking you to set me free, Edward. I re-

57

spect the loyalty you have for this man, but you're a smart boy. I want you to really think about what you're doing."

"Do you know what he'd do to me if I set you free?"

"As I said before, are you sure he's not going to do it anyway?"

Edward thought for a moment. "But where would I go if I didn't stay with him?"

"I'd take care of you. I could give you money and find you a place to live so this man could never find you."

"You'd do that? Why?"

"Because I want to live, Edward, and you're my only hope."

"How do I know you won't double cross me when I take you to Mr. Davies?"

"You met Mr. Davies, did he seem like the kind of man who would do something like that?"

Edward thought back. "He got awful mad at me. Threw me against a wall."

"That's only because he was worried about me. He's a good man, Edward. He has a lot of money now, but he worked very hard to get it. He could give you a good job and a chance at a real life."

"I dunno."

"We don't have much time to think about it. You'll be going in for the money soon."

Edward stood up. "I'm gonna have to think about it. No matter what happens, ma'am, I won't let him kill you."

Teresa watched in dismay as Edward walked out, leaving her alone again in the mine shaft. She was trying to keep her sanity, but the solitude and the semidarkness was getting to her. She just hoped Edward was as good a person as she thought.

Eric and Tom waited until afternoon, when they knew most of the miners would be taking a lunch break. They made sure that they looked especially dirty, then pulled into camp very slowly, as if they had been riding for weeks. One of the miners stood up, his rifle resting over his arm.

"Can I do somethin' for you gents?"

"Yeah, we're looking for someone," Eric said in as tired a voice as he could manage.

The miner stiffened visibly, his rifle coming higher up his arm. These men didn't want intruders, especially intruders who might be looking for one of their own. "And who might that be?"

"Our brother," Tom said, taking his hat off and wiping his forearm across his face. "His name's David Jordan."

"He done something wrong?"

"He hasn't done anything wrong. We're trying to find him for our ma."

"Why's that?"

"She's dying. Last we heard, he was up here in the Mother Lode, but we haven't seen hide nor hair of him in over a month. We don't know how much longer our ma's going to live."

"He's our youngest brother, her youngest son," Eric added. "She hasn't seen him in over two years, ever since he came up here from down South."

"What's he look like?" another miner asked curiously.

"Looks a lot like him." Eric pointed to Tom. "We'd be most obliged if you could tell us anything."

"You boys had anything to eat today?"

"Had some hardtack this morning."

"Well, git on down and get yourself some food. We'll ask around and see what we can find out."

59

Eric and Tom dismounted and led their horses to a hitching post. They followed the miner into the middle of the camp and grabbed some plates.

"It ain't fancy, but it's fillin'."

"We're thankful for anything you got," Tom said.

"We been out on the trail so long anything seems good," Eric explained.

Eric and Tom filled their plates and greedily ate the bread and beans the men gave them. They both knew what an extravagance this was for the miners. Food cost them a ridiculous amount. Merchants in the city charged exorbitant prices. They had seen a loaf of bread sell for fifty cents, a pound of coffee five dollars, Kentucky bourbon thirty dollars a quart. Supplies were no better. A good tent could run as much as one hundred fifty dollars and boots could cost a man one hundred dollars.

"So, tell me about this brother of yours."

"He looks a lot like my brother Tom here, only a little shorter. His hair was long the last time we saw him. He's a decent kind of person, but he could get riled if pushed."

"Well, that fits just about any man here."

"We don't have much time," Tom said wearily. "The doc said for us to be back by the end of the month or we might not even be able to be with ma before she dies."

"It'd break her heart if none of us was there," Eric said solemnly. He and Tom were pouring it on thick, but they had to make these men believe them. They had to be allowed to stay.

"I'm real sorry about your ma. Lost mine a few years ago. Even though I'm a growed man, I still miss her."

"She worked hard all her life. We have a small ranch down by Los Angeles, and when my pa died, Ma and

60

Eric and I just took over. We all kinda spoiled David because he was the youngest. He never really had to pull his weight."

"Ain't it the way?" The miner shook his head. "What made him come up North? Didn't like ranching?"

"Always thought it was too much work. When he heard about the Gold Rush up North, he knew that was for him. We tried to talk him out of it, but he wouldn't listen. We haven't heard from him since."

"Well, I understand all about that. I been here fifteen months now and ain't seen my family in all that time. Have a little money saved, but not much. I sometimes wonder what I came out here for."

"Much obliged for the food," Eric said, putting down his plate. "We'd be more than glad to pay you for it. We know how expensive it is to buy supplies up here."

"Nope, that won't be necessary." He looked at both men. "When was the last time you two had a good rest?"

"Since we started lookin' for our brother."

"Well, I'll talk to my friends and see if you can put up here for the night. I should warn you, though, stealin' another man's gold is a hangin' offense around here."

"We're not interested in your gold, mister. All we want is to find our brother and get back home."

The man stood up. "All right then. Why don't you two find yourself some shade and stretch out. My name's Blackie. Let me know if you need anythin'."

"Thanks again, Blackie."

Eric and Tom walked to a pine tree that stood by the edge of camp. They sat down against the trunk.

"What do you think?" Tom asked.

"I don't know. I couldn't see much of anything.

61

Most of the men are working the river. It doesn't even look like there's a cave around here."

"So, what do we do?"

"We take a little siesta, just like Blackie suggested, then we get up and walk around. We can ask some questions about mining, ask if there are any caves or mine shafts around."

"And if they aren't?"

"I don't know. We'll just have to hope that we see Edward or John."

Both men relaxed in the shade of the tree, but still kept their eyes open and alert. At one point later in the day, some men came up from the river. Eric spotted Big John immediately.

He elbowed Tom in the side. "Look."

"Well, if that isn't Big John I'll eat my boots. Where's the kid?"

"Look behind him."

John walked up from the river carrying some equipment. He didn't pay any attention to Eric and Tom but walked on to a rickety old shack on the edge of the camp. The other men went to their tents. Edward soon followed John to the shack. He was exactly as Lily and Bryant had described him. They waited for him to pass and watched him walk to the shack.

"I think he's the one to keep an eye on."

"Why? John is supposed to be the boss."

"But the kid will probably do anything the big guy tells him to do."

They watched as Edward dipped a ladle into a bucket and drank greedily. Then he disappeared into the shack.

"You're sure Lily said Teresa was being kept in a cave?" Tom asked.

"That's what she said." Eric stood up. "I think it's

time for me to have a talk with Blackie. Keep your eyes on those two." Eric walked down to the river, passing men as they worked their claims. He saw Blackie farther on down the river and walked up to him. "Mind if I watch, Blackie?"

"Go right ahead."

"Have you gotten much gold out of here?"

"I've done all right, but this river's just about panned out. Pretty soon, we're gonna have to go to hydraulicking."

"What's that?"

"You ain't seen it done? Well, it takes some money and it takes some know-how. You use a big hose and nozzle and you just start watering down the sides of the hills around the river. The dirt goes into troughs and sinks to the bottom while the gold particles float on top. I seen a place farther south where the river was panned out so they diverted the whole damned thing! Can you imagine? That way they could work the riverbeds."

"What about mines?"

"That's what we'll eventually have to do if we want to stay around here. But that'll take lots of money. It's back-breaking work, digging a mine shaft. I done it before digging for silver in Mexico."

"Are there any mine shafts around here, Blackie?"

Blackie gave Eric a strange look. "Why would ya ask somethin' like that?"

"Just wondering."

"No, it's more than that." Blackie put down his pan and took a rag from his back pocket. He stared at Eric a minute and wiped his face. "Why don't you come clean with me, boy. I knew right away that you and that other fella wasn't tellin' me the truth."

"Why'd you let us stay?"

"Curious . . . So, are you gonna tell me or not?"

63

"We're not looking for our brother, we're looking for a woman who was kidnapped."

Blackie shoved the rag back into his pocket. "Is it your woman?" he asked Eric.

"No, but she's a friend of mine and I don't want to see her get hurt."

"Why was she kidnapped?"

"Her man is very rich. She was kidnapped for a ransom of twenty-five thousand dollars."

"My, that is quite a sum. More than I'll ever see in a lifetime."

"Have you seen a woman around here, Blackie?"

"See lots of women from time to time. We have women that come to visit us. We get lonely out here, you know."

"You seem like a good man. This woman hasn't done anything to hurt anyone."

"No, I ain't seen no woman around here lately. When would she have come here?"

"Sometime in the last few days."

Blackie shook his head adamantly. "Ain't seen no woman. I surely woulda remembered if I had."

"Are you sure there's no mine around here?"

"I told you before there ain't."

"What about a cave or something?"

"Wait a minute, come to think of it, there *is* a place farther up the hill. Was a cave, but John decided to work on it after he found a gold vein in there. He put up some timbers and lanterns and he works on it some of the time. He and the kid." He looked at Eric. "Are you tellin' me Big John stole this woman?"

"I think so." Eric stared at Blackie. "Look, Blackie, I know you miners stick together. I'm not asking you to go against this man, but if you could only show me where the mine is . . ."

"You'd never get in. He or the kid always guards it.

None of us is even been allowed in."

"Let me worry about that."

Blackie turned around and pointed upriver. "It's up there. You can reach it if you walk straight up from Big John's shack, but I don't 'spect you'll be wantin' to do that."

"You're right."

"Well, you can walk along the river here for about a quarter of a mile and then climb up the bank. You'll have to be careful 'cause the dirt's eroding and it's real slick. Once you get to the top, you walk a few hundred yards more up the hill. You can see a dim light from the entrance to the shaft. But you have to be careful. Like I said, John or the kid are always guarding it."

"Thanks, Blackie." For the first time, Eric felt some hope. "And listen . . . if you're ever in Monterey and in need of food and a bed, look up the Rancho del Mar. That's where I live."

"I'd be obliged to do that, boy." He clapped Eric on the shoulder. "Good luck to you and your friend. You're gonna need it."

Chapter 3

"Miss Teresa," Edward whispered quietly, turning up the lantern.

Teresa raised her head from the wall and tried to focus her eyes in the dim light. "Edward?"

"Yes, ma'am." He reached behind her and cut the rope that was tied from her wrists to one of the poles of the shaft.

"What are you doing?"

"I'm gettin' you outta here." Edward cut the ropes that bound Teresa's wrists and handed her a canteen. "Carry this. We might need it later on. Listen to me real close now. We're gonna have to make our way down by the river, then we'll have to walk downriver a ways. I have some horses for us there. Once we reach them, we'll be safe. We just have to get out of here."

"Where's John?"

"He's asleep."

"Why did you change your mind, Edward?"

" 'Cause you're a nice lady and there's no reason for you to get hurt. And maybe I could start me a new life somewhere. I'm really not a bad person, you know."

"I know that, Edward, and I give you my word I'll help you when this is all over."

"I 'spect we should be going now. You ready?"

66

"Yes." Slowly and quite unsteadily, Teresa stood up, shaking her legs out and rubbing her wrists. "Go ahead, Edward. I'll follow you."

Edward led Teresa to the entrance of the mine shaft and stopped, looking around. "Big John's never out here but it still don't hurt to look." He walked out a few steps and looked down into the camp. A few embers burned dimly from the dying campfires in front of the various tents, but there was little movement. Edward knew John's habits by now. He was always asleep after dinner. He offered Teresa his hand. "Come on, ma'am."

It occurred to Teresa for a split second that Edward might be tricking her, that he might actually be taking her out of the shaft to lead her to her death. But the second she hit the open air and took a deep breath, she knew it would be better to die out in the open than in the dank, musty darkness of the shaft.

She glanced down at the camp as they walked along the narrow rim outside the cave. She wasn't aware before just how high it was. She saw the shack that Edward had spoken of, where Big John slept. She shivered and grasped Edward's hand tightly.

They walked through the darkness as Edward led the way above the camp. The river sounded closer all the time, and Teresa realized they were walking toward it.

"This is gonna be kinda rough, ma'am," Edward said. "We're gonna have to slide down this hill. Otherwise, we might fall and really hurt ourselves." He looked at Teresa. "You're not dressed for this, ma'am."

Teresa hiked up the back of her skirt and held on to it. "I may look like a lady, Edward, but I'm tougher than you think."

"All right, ma'am. Just hold my hand."

67

Edward started sliding down the steep embankment to the river, and Teresa held on and followed. They started out slowly but went quicker as they neared the bottom of the hill. Before they knew it, they were tumbling down the bank, finally landing on the rocks near the river. Edward stumbled to his feet.

"You all right, ma'am?" he asked Teresa.

"I think so." Teresa stood up, rubbing her behind. She had landed on a large rock and she was sure she'd never be able to sit down again. "Let's just get out of here."

Edward started running along the rocks by the river, stumbling occasionally but never losing his balance. Teresa held on to him as if he were her lifeline, which, in fact, he was. They ran and ran until they were both out of breath.

"I have to catch my breath, Edward," Teresa said, gasping for air.

Edward looked around him. "Just for a minute, ma'am. I don't trust Big John. He could be anywhere around here."

Teresa leaned against a tree, taking deep gulps of air. She closed her eyes. She couldn't believe how tired and weak she was from staying in the shaft. She opened her eyes and blinked. "Edward," she said softly, "I think I saw something over there in those trees."

Edward moved toward her, his back toward the tree, his pistol drawn. "Whereabouts?"

"Over there." She pointed to where she thought she had seen the movement. "But I'm not sure I see it anymore."

"That's because it's behind you, little lady." Big John reached from behind the tree and grabbed both Teresa and Edward. He threw the boy forward and then pulled him backward, slamming his head against the trunk of the tree. Edward fell to the ground, limp.

"Edward," Teresa screamed out. She tried to reach down but John came from behind the tree and grabbed her. "Damned shame," he said, giving Edward an extra kick. "He was always such an obedient boy. Lately, though, he started thinking differently from me."

"Lucky for him," Teresa murmured.

"I don't want no sassy talk from you, woman. I'd just as soon shoot you as look at you. I don't have any use for a whore anyways. I just want my money and then git out of here."

"What makes you think you'll get the money?"

"Oh, I'll get it all right. Edward said that man friend of yours was real scared. Said he was willin' to give him the money that day."

"If you take me back, I'll give you the money. I have that much, and more. I don't need it."

"You must think because I'm big, I'm stupid." He pulled Teresa by the back of her dress. "Come on. You're going back to the shaft."

"No, please, not back in there."

"What's the matter? Don't you like our accommodations? Aren't they to your satisfaction?"

"Please, tie me up anywhere you want, but don't put me back in there."

"Sorry, lady, until I see my money, I'll tie you up anyplace I please." He pulled Teresa along beside him, but Edward's voice stopped him.

"Leave her alone, John," he warned, rubbing his sore head, "I can shoot you, even at night, and you know it. My eyes are good enough."

"You wouldn't do it."

"John, please. I don't want to hurt you."

"That's a laugh, boy. *You,* hurt *me?*"

"I don't want to do it, but I will."

69

"Sure you will." John took Teresa's arm and continued on in the dark. "You wouldn't risk hurting the woman."

"I, on the other hand, don't have to worry about hurting the woman since I'm right in front of you."

John raised his gun and looked around him in the darkness at the unfamiliar voice. "Who's that?"

"I've come to get the woman and I've got people with me. We don't mind killing all of you if we have to."

"You wouldn't hurt the woman."

"My orders are to kill the man who kidnapped her, even if she dies in the process."

"I don't believe you."

"Try me."

John continued to look around him in the darkness, but he couldn't see a thing. He fired his gun twice. "Where the hell are you? Show yourself."

"I'm over here."

John shot two more times. "You there?"

"Don't worry, you didn't get me. You'd better take careful aim next time, you only have two bullets left."

John fired again and again into the darkness, then grabbed Teresa and pulled her in front of him. "Don't come near me. I got a knife on her. If you try to hurt me, I'll kill her. I swear I will." He looked around him and back up toward the trees.

"How long do you think you can do that?"

John looked around him. Where had Edward gone to? He wanted to take the boy's gun from him so he could have it for himself. He shouted into the thicket. "Edward, you out there?"

"Who you talking to, ghosts?"

"Show yourself. Come out and fight like a man."

"Let the woman go and I'll fight like a man. She hasn't done anything."

John looked around him. "She's my ticket outta here. If I let her go, you could shoot me dead right now."

"That's true, but we'd prefer to have her alive. If you kill her, you're dead anyway. At least if you let her go, you'll have a fighting chance."

John leaned up against the tree. "I still got the woman and ain't no one gonna take her away from me."

" 'Cept me, John," Edward said, moving quickly from behind and hitting John on the head with his gun. John stumbled forward, loosening his hold on Teresa. "Jesus Christ, why'd you do that for, boy?"

Teresa was pulled to safety into the thicket with Tom and Edward. Eric walked into the clearing. "What's the matter, Big John? Does your head sting?"

John squinted into the darkness ahead. "Who are you?"

"I told you before, someone sent here to get the woman. Well, now that I have her, what do I do with you?"

John stood up straight, pulling his knife out from the leather sheath on his leg. "Come here and fight me. What's the matter? You afraid?"

"I was just going to ask the same thing of you, John. Is that why you kept that poor woman tied up alone in that mine shaft? Were you afraid she might hurt you?"

"Where are you? I swear if I catch you, I'll skin you alive."

"I'm right here." Eric stood in front of John like a shadow in the night. "Come on, John. Come get me."

John didn't wait. He ran toward Eric, swinging his knife from right to left. "Come on out. I'm ready for you."

Eric moved around in the darkness like a cat. "Over

71

here, John."

"Stay still."

"That's not the way the game is played, John."

"Damn you." John came at Eric again and again but he was gone, out of sight, unable to be seen in the darkness. He seemed to blend into the rocks and trees around him. "All right. What do you want?"

"I want you to leave Mr. Bryant Davies alone."

"Why should I do that?"

Eric moved so quickly John didn't see him. He had his arm around John's throat, his knife held to it. "Because if you don't leave him alone, I'll make you regret that you ever made trouble for him."

"He doesn't need all that money."

"He earned all of his money. He can do whatever he pleases with it."

"He spends it all on that whore of his."

Eric grabbed John's right ear and put the blade behind it. "I'd be careful what I say about Miss Teresa if I were you. I think you owe her an apology."

"You want me to apologize to a whore?"

Eric pressed the knife blade into John's ear, cutting the flesh. "Are you sure you don't want to change your mind?"

"I'm sorry, ma'am," John wailed loudly. "I didn't mean you no harm."

"Now, back to the original topic of conversation. If you ever give Mr. Bryant Davies cause for concern, you'll be sorry I didn't kill you tonight. Do you understand?"

"Yeah, I understand."

"Good," Eric said quietly, removing his hand from around John's throat and holding it to his back. "Back up here to the tree."

"What're you gonna do?" Big John asked in fright, but Eric was gone into the darkness, leaving Tom and

72

Edward to tie John to the trunk of the tree and gag him.

Eric took Teresa's hand and guided her through the thicket to their horses. He helped her mount and then climbed up after her. He rode for about two miles until he came to a spot by some rocks along the river. He dismounted and helped Teresa down. He tied the horses and led her between the rocks to a small clearing that already had a fire going. "This'll be our camp for tonight."

"Will we be safe here?" Teresa asked.

"Don't worry. Everything will be all right. Are you hungry?"

"Starving," she answered.

Eric spooned from the pot that sat on the rocks by the fire. "It's not San Francisco's finest, but it should fill you up. Here's some biscuits, and some coffee, too."

"You wouldn't happen to have anything stronger, would you?"

Eric walked to his saddlebags and took out a small bottle. He walked back to Teresa and handed it to her. "I brought it just in case."

Teresa took a small drink from the whiskey bottle and pursed her lips together as the liquid burned her throat. She took two more sips, put the cork back in, and handed the bottle back to Eric, who sat on a rock by the fire, pouring himself a cup of coffee. "Are you all right?" he asked.

"Yes, thanks to all of you."

"Did John hurt you in any way?"

"I never saw him until tonight. Edward did everything for me."

"That's strange."

"I guess he didn't want to be seen. How's Bryant?"

"He's worried sick about you. If you're going to ask

73

why he's not here, I talked him out of it. He wasn't thinking too clearly. Besides, Edward had seen him. Bryant is easily recognizable."

"It was brave of you and Tom to come after me. You didn't have to, you know. But I suppose Bryant offered you both a large sum of money."

"Wrong. We did it as a favor to Bryant, because we like him."

Relaxed from the whiskey, Teresa took the cup of coffee Eric offered her. "He wasn't going to let me go. Once Edward came back with the money, he was going to kill me and be off with it."

"He was going to kill Edward, too, I'm sure of it. What reason would he have to keep him alive? He sure as hell wasn't going to split the money with him."

"Poor Edward. He cared for that mindless oaf and didn't get much for his trouble."

"Oh, I think he got quite a lot. He figured out for himself that he could trust you and that you could help him. I think old Edward did just fine for himself . . . We'll leave before sunup, so you might want to get some rest. You don't look like you've slept too well."

Teresa put her hands up to her face. "I must look a fright."

"Actually, you look quite beautiful." Eric flinched as soon as the words were out. "Sorry, I—"

"It's all right. I appreciate being told I look beautiful after I've been in a mine shaft for days."

"Do you want some more to eat? There's plenty."

"No, thank you. When will Tom and Edward be back?"

"In a while. They're waiting around a bit just to make sure no one follows us."

"You're a strange man. I can't quite figure you out."

74

"I already told you about myself."

"But I sense there is more to you than what you tell me. For instance, if a man is as much in love with his wife as you obviously are, what are you doing here, rescuing another woman?"

"I already told you why. I'm doing it for Bryant."

"Is that the only reason?" Teresa's dark, exotic eyes met Eric's. "I think you're as intrigued by me as I am by you."

"Maybe."

"So, what do we do about it?"

Eric threw the rest of his coffee into the fire, where it sizzled and steamed. He set his tin cup on a rock. "I may be intrigued by you, Teresa, but I'm still married."

"If you say so," Teresa replied softly, unplaiting the shiny braid that hung down her back and letting her hair fall in long golden waves around her shoulders. "I wish I could have a bath."

Eric looked at Teresa across the fire and was reminded of the many times Lisa had sat by their tepee, talking about wanting a bath, and how he would walk with her down to the river. How many times had he watched her bathe and then come out of the water like some beautiful sprite? But this woman was not his wife.

"What's the matter? Are you thinking about Lisa?" Teresa's voice cut through Eric's thoughts. "Do you miss her?"

"Why do you keep asking about her?"

Teresa got up and circled the campfire, sitting down on the rock next to Eric. "I think your wife must be a special woman to keep a man like you." She reached up and touched his face. She could feel the muscle in his jaw tense as she moved her fingers. "I know you want me, just as I want you. I can feel it." She turned his face to hers and she kissed him deeply, moving her mouth sensually against his.

Eric returned the kiss and pulled away, a smile spreading across his face. "I bet you were good."

"I was the best. That's why I'm where I am today."

"And what about Bryant? Doesn't it matter that he loves you more than anything in the world?"

"Of course it matters. He's been good to me. I'd never do anything to hurt him."

"And you don't think this would hurt him?"

"He'd never have to know. Come on, Eric, I've seen Lisa. She's a beautiful woman and if she's as passionate as she is beautiful, then I'll bet you my house on the hill, that she hasn't been faithful to you."

Eric stood up. "Not every woman thinks the same way you do, Teresa. I don't know how Bryant puts up with you. If I were him, I'd have kicked you out a long time ago."

Teresa stood up and walked seductively over to Eric. "No, you wouldn't have kicked me out. You couldn't have gotten enough of me." She put her arms around his neck and pressed her mouth to his.

Eric felt her soft, full lips against his, and there was the old familiar gnawing in his groin. He put his hands on her arms to try to loosen them, but she locked them tighter around his neck and pressed her body against his. As good as she felt, he couldn't have her and he knew it. It was different when he wasn't married but now that Lisa was his wife, it wasn't right.

"We're not interrupting anything, are we?" Tom asked. He walked to the campfire, followed by Edward.

Eric tore Teresa's arms from around his neck and pushed her away from him. "You're back" was all he could manage to say.

"Yes, you were expecting us. Remember?"

"Hello, Tom," Teresa said playfully, tossing her hair over her shoulders.

"You all right, Miss Teresa?" Edward walked over to Teresa.

Teresa took Edward's hands. "Thanks to you, I'm fine, Edward. How about you?"

Edward couldn't resist a grin. "You shoulda seen Big John all tied up to the trunk of that big ole pine. I 'spect he's gonna have hisself a fit by the time somebody finds him."

"Would you mind walking me down to the river, Edward? I'd like to clean up a bit."

"Yes, ma'am."

"Take my rifle, Edward," Eric said. "If there's any trouble, fire three shots into the air."

"Yessir."

Eric looked at Tom and walked back over to the fire, pouring two cups of coffee. He handed one to Tom. "Everything go all right back there?"

"Everything went fine. What I want to know is how everything went right here?"

Eric stared into his coffee and then looked up at Tom. "It's not what you think, Tom."

"I didn't say I thought anything. You're putting words into my mouth. I think you're a bit touchy."

"It's that woman. She makes me crazy."

"I thought your wife was supposed to do that," Tom said calmly.

"Tom, you know how I feel about Lisa. I love her with all my heart . . ."

"But?"

"There is no but. Teresa is an exciting woman, I admit it, but she holds no attraction for me."

"Then what was she doing, simply getting a bug out of your eye?"

77

"It just happened. I didn't ask for it."

"It didn't look like you were fighting it much, either."

"I think after we take Teresa back, I'll take Lisa and head on home."

"I think that's a good idea, but why don't I just take Teresa to Bryant?"

"But I told Bryant I'd be back."

"Are you sure that's all there is to it?"

"I'm sure." Eric stared into the dying campfire and couldn't believe that he was in love with one woman and attracted to another. "No, that's not all there is to it." He looked at Tom. "I'm attracted to Teresa. I just want to make sure it's nothing more than that."

"And if it is, what do you plan to do? Are you going to tell Lisa that it was nice, but you've found someone else." Tom kicked at the rocks that formed the campfire ring. "Damn you, Eric. First it was Consuelo, now it's Teresa. Have you ever thought that maybe you just can't be content with one woman? Maybe you'll always be tempted by other women." Tom stood up. "If that's the case, I don't want my sister married to you."

"Tom, listen . . ." Eric began, but Tom had already walked out of camp. Maybe he was right; maybe he couldn't be content with one woman. Maybe it would be best to leave Lisa alone so that she could find another man. He threw his coffee cup at the fire ring and stomped away.

Bryant crushed Teresa in his arms, holding him against her. "God, I missed you. I was so afraid I'd never see you again."

"I'm fine, Bryant. Really." Teresa reached up and affectionately touched Bryant's face. "Are *you* all right? I bet you haven't eaten for days."

"Eating was the last thing on my mind."

"Let's go home and get some food into you. You know how you get when you don't eat."

Bryant looked past Teresa to Eric and Tom. "See how this woman spoils me? I don't know what I'd do without her."

"Bryant, how's Lisa? Is she at the mansion?" Eric didn't look at Tom. They hadn't spoken since the night they argued.

Bryant's arms dropped from Teresa. "She left the same day you did, Eric. God, I forgot in all the excitement. I have a letter here from your grandfather." Bryant walked to his desk and opened the drawer. He took out the letter that was sealed with the distinctive red wax and handed it to Eric.

Eric peeled off the wax and read,

"My dear Sandro, I do not like being the bearer of bad news, but you must know what has happened. Lisa was kidnapped by some men who said they ride with a General Vasquez. The last I heard, they were heading for Baja California. I will explain everything to you later, but you must know this—Raya is well and safe here with me. I have had contact with Vasquez on two separate occasions. As you know, I would have been willing to pay him anything, but I'm not sure what he really wants. I *am* sure Lisa is safe, Sandro. He has no reason to harm her, but I believe it is imperative that you return immediately. Your loving grandfather, Don Alfredo."

Eric walked to Tom and handed the letter to him, his face pale. "I have to leave immediately, Bryant. Thank you for everything." He started for the door, but Bryant's voice stopped him.

"Eric, what is it?"

"Lisa's been kidnapped. I have to find her."

"Then you must take Teresa with you."

"What?" Eric asked indignantly.

Bryant walked to Eric. "Listen to me, man. Teresa has family all up and down California. I'm sure she could help you."

Eric looked at Teresa for a moment but shook his head. "No. I'll find my wife on my own."

"She's my sister, Eric. If Teresa can help, why not take her?" Tom looked at Eric, his eyes honest and pleading.

"Bryant, do you mind if Tom and I speak alone for a few minutes?"

"No, certainly." Bryant took Teresa's arm and led her out of the room, closing the door behind Eric and Tom.

"You think I'm in love with her for Christsakes. Why do you want me to bring her?" Eric demanded.

"If she knows the area and has family, then why not bring her? We need help, Eric. Do you know Baja California? Have you even been there?"

"When I was a kid."

"Then we need someone who knows the area."

"I'll be fine on my own."

Tom took Eric by the shoulders. "What the hell's the matter with you? Are you so afraid to be around that woman? Are you so afraid you'll fall in love with her?"

Eric shrugged away from Tom and shoved him backward. "Don't ever accuse me of not loving my wife again, Tom."

"I didn't accuse you of not loving Lisa. It's your feelings for Teresa that scare me."

Eric turned around, pacing back and forth nervously. He walked to the wall and leaned against it, finally bunching his hand up in a fist and punching the wall as hard as he could. "Damn!" he yelled, shaking his hand gingerly.

"Well, did you manage to break it?"

"Leave me alone."

"Now you sound as if you're ten years old. Eric, I'm not your enemy, I'm your friend. I want to help you."

Eric held his hand against his stomach. "I love Lisa, Tom, I swear I do. If anything ever happened to her, I don't know what I'd do."

"But you have feelings for Teresa, too."

"I don't know how I feel about Teresa. I don't even know her."

"Then maybe it's better that she come along with us. What better way to find out how you feel about someone than to be with them day in and day out?"

Eric's eyes seared into Tom's. "And what if it turns out that I do have feelings for her?"

"Then it's up to you to find out who's more important to you, Lisa or Teresa."

"If I were you, I'd strangle me."

"Why should I? I'm the man who was living with your mother when you came back, remember? I just want to ask one thing of you, Eric. Whatever you decide, don't hurt my sister. She's been hurt enough."

"I would never do that, Tom."

"All right then. You better tell Teresa she's coming along. I'm sure it'll make her day." Tom opened the door and motioned for Bryant and Teresa to return to the room. "We've decided that we should take Teresa along. We need somebody who knows the territory."

Teresa went over to Eric. "What happened to your hand?"

"Nothing," Eric responded coldly, then turned to Bryant. "I want to thank you for everything."

81

"No, it's I who should thank you and Tom. I wouldn't have Teresa back if you two hadn't rescued her."

"You're coming along with us, aren't you?"

"Unfortunately, I can't. I can't leave the business alone that long or I'll be robbed blind. I know Teresa will be in good hands with you two . . . So, when will you be leaving?"

"I'd like to leave today."

"I'll make sure you have everything you need. In fact, I'll check on it myself before I take Teresa back to the house."

"I'll come with you," Tom said pointedly, looking over at Eric, who stood next to Teresa. "Teresa, I want you to think about helping your parents. We won't be able to do anything while we're gone, but when we get back, I'd like to take you to their rancho with me. If you don't care, think about your children. That could all be their land someday."

Teresa smiled and took Tom's hand. "All right, Tom. Someday, I'll go out to Rancho de Teresa with you. Satisfied?"

"Very." He followed Bryant out the door.

Eric looked at Teresa. "Look, I can use your help, that's all."

"I know that. I know you love your wife, Eric. This isn't easy for me, either."

"Isn't it? You seemed to be enjoying yourself the other night."

"I was just glad to be alive the other night, and being with you . . ." Teresa folded her hands together in front of her like a schoolgirl. "Look, Eric, I don't want to cause any trouble for either of us. I meant it when I said I don't want to hurt Bryant. That man has been my savior. I want to help you find your wife. It's the least I can do after what you did for me."

82

"Tom was there, too."

"I know. If I help find your wife, I'll be finding his sister. I'd like to repay you both."

Eric looked at Teresa. He couldn't read what was going on behind her dark, oval eyes. "I hope you mean it."

"I do. Neither one of us needs complications in our lives."

Eric nodded in relief. "Do you know Mexico very well?"

"I used to spend every summer there as a girl."

"Where, in Mexico City? I doubt very much if that's where they'll take Lisa even if they leave Alta California."

"No, as a matter of fact, my grandfather's brother had a rancho in Hermosillo, but I've been to many places all through Mexico. But if you don't trust me, find someone else. I'm sure there are others who know it better than I."

Eric knew Teresa was issuing a challenge. Did he have the guts to take her along and still resist her? He didn't know. The thought scared him. "All right, but it won't be easy. We'll be riding all day, every day. Do you understand? We won't stop just because you get tired."

"You seem to think I'm a pampered rich girl, Eric. You forget I spent quite a few years making my living on my back, then wound up begging in the streets. I know what hardship is. I'm not afraid." She started for the door, but Eric reached out and stopped her.

"I'm sorry. I didn't mean to insult you."

"It doesn't matter. You're hurting now; you can't do anything to help your wife. I understand that."

"You understand too much."

"Perhaps." Gently, she took his hand from her arm. "I want to help you. Maybe it's for the wrong reasons;

83

maybe it's because I'm beginning to care for you. But I won't force myself on you, and I certainly won't come between you and Lisa. If I've learned one thing in my life, it's that when a man wants you for yourself, he'll let you know."

"Is that what you want, Teresa? Do you want me to want you?"

"Maybe."

Eric shook his head. "This is crazy. You and I don't even know each other. I'm a married man with a little girl and you're involved with a good man."

"Things like that don't keep people from being attracted to each other, Eric. Don't you know that?"

"Yes, but I also know that there has to be something more than a physical attraction to keep two people interested in each other. I'm going to go help Bryant and Tom saddle the horses. I'll see you later."

Teresa watched Eric as he walked out. God, but he was handsome. He was tall and lean, with dark hair, and the bluest eyes she had ever seen. It was easy for her to say that she didn't want to come between Eric and his wife, but she wasn't really sure she felt that way. This man was everything she had dreamed of. As good as Bryant had been to her, she had never felt truly fulfilled when she was with him. She knew for certain that with Eric it would be a different story.

She took a deep breath and left the room. This would be a real adventure. Either she would find her heart and be truly happy, or she would lose it, and realize that there was no such thing as true love.

Chapter 4

The man sat on his horse, looking down on the ranch in the valley. He'd been a bandit for as long as he could remember. He was nine years old the first time he'd stolen a horse. His mother had just given birth to his little sister and she was very ill. He had needed a horse to ride for the doctor. He stole the horse from a rich man, but by the time he rode to the village and got the doctor, his mother had died. The man who owned the horse wanted to have him thrown in jail, but his father had pleaded with the man to be lenient and, instead, he made him work all day, every day, for two years. His father agreed that the punishment was just, thinking that he had to learn about honor. But there came a time when he could no longer take it, when he saw the injustice of working for a rich man and going home to the hut he shared with his father and five brothers and sisters. It made no sense to him. As much as his father preached to him about religion and honor, he could see no honor in their poverty, or in the way his mother had died.

When he was eleven, he went into the rich man's house and up to his bedroom. He stole as much jewelry as he could get his hands on, two *pistolas,* some food from the kitchen, and the same horse he had taken two years before. Then he rode away. He missed his father and his brothers and sisters, but he knew the only way to help them was to get away from their poor village. But he was just a boy and he knew of no way to make money except to steal it. He went to Alta California and wandered around on his own for a long time until he fell in with a group of *bandidos*. Because he was still so young and innocent-looking, they used him to get into rich people's places and then they robbed them. He never felt bad about robbing from the rich; he knew that they could afford the loss. But he refused to ever take anything from a poor person. In fact, many of the men who rode with him took to calling him Joaquin, after the *bandido,* Joaquin Murrietta, also known as El Famoso. It was said that Joaquin Murrietta stole from the rich and gave to the poor, and this boy did much the same thing.

Now, as he sat up in the hills looking over the Rancho del Mar, he had mixed emotions. Here was a rich *patrón,* a landowner, but he also knew him as Don Alfredo, a man who had once shown him unconditional kindness. He saw the houses that dotted the land, the houses that Don Alfredo had given to the people who worked for him, and again he remembered the kindness this man had once shown him.

During his wanderings he had become ill and had stopped for help. Don Alfredo did not ask his name, he did not ask him what he did, he simply took him in and gave him food and shelter until he was well enough to ride again. He had never forgotten that. It would be good to see the old man again.

He slowly edged his horse down the rocky trail and into the green valley below. He breathed deeply as he rode. This was a beautiful place where a man could live and die peacefully, a place where a man could be proud of who he was. As he edged closer to the rancho, he could see some men riding toward him. He stopped, knowing that they were there to protect Don Alfredo and the people who lived on the rancho.

"Can we help you, señor?"

"Yes, I have come to see Don Alfredo. Tell him it is Cruz."

The man in front eyed Cruz and then nodded his head. "Follow me." Cruz followed the man, aware that the others stayed close to him. When they reached the yard in front of the rancho, the man dismounted. "Wait here, señor. I will tell Don Alfredo that you are here."

Cruz nodded, looking around him. There were trees everywhere, and the sweet smell of orange blossoms filled the air. He remembered how much his mother had liked the smell of orange blossoms. There was a fountain inside the courtyard, and flowers in clay pots were everywhere. He used to sit there when he was recovering from his illness. It was one of his favorite places. He turned when he heard laughter. He saw a woman chasing a small child. The woman was tall and slim with long, flowing hair. The little girl giggled uncontrollably as the woman chased after her. She ran toward the corral.

"Raya, stop!"

He could see the child heading for the lowest rung of the corral; she could easily fit through it. It would be a fun game. Her mother could never fit through. He looked into the corral, where a huge steer stood, looking at the child. Cruz heard the woman scream and saw her start to climb the fence. He pulled his horse to the left and kicked its sides. He rode in one wide circle and headed toward the corral. His horse barely cleared the top rung, its hooves scraping the wood. The steer stared at him, lowering his mammoth head and long, sharp horns. He ignored the animal and rode to the little girl, who was still oblivious to the danger. He leaned over the side of his horse and pulled her up by her clothes, plopping her in front of him. He rode to the side of the corral where her mother stood and he handed the child to the woman.

"Be careful, señor!" the woman yelled.

The steer charged him. He turned his horse and maneuvered away from the huge animal. By this time, men had come running, trying to get the steer's attention. It was too late. The steer charged him again. He looked around the corral. There wasn't enough room inside to get a running start. He would have to stay away from the animal until they could get the gate open.

The steer lowered his large head, pawed the ground, and started for him. He pulled his horse toward the right and galloped to the other side of the corral. The steer stopped and turned, tossing its head in anger. He came at him again. Cruz waited until the animal had committed and then he pulled his horse sharply to the left. The steer almost crashed into the side of the corral.

"Over here, señor. Quickly."

Cruz looked up at the sound of the woman's voice. The men had opened the corral gate. "Ha!" he said to his horse, pressing his heels into the animal's stomach. He raced for the narrow opening and rode through. The men quickly closed the gate behind him, just as the steer butted his head against it. He snorted in anger, his eyes large and bulging. He crashed against the gate one more time. Cruz smiled. It reminded him of when he was a boy and he used to pretend with the young bulls on the rich man's property that he was a matador. He had always gotten away.

"Please, señor, get down."

Cruz looked at the woman who stood on the ground next to him. She was stunningly beautiful, with long, reddish-brown hair and startling green eyes. Her smile was one of relief, as she held her child. He dismounted.

"Are you all right?" she asked.

"I am fine, thank you, señora." He bowed his head in deference.

She stepped forward and put her hand on his. "I don't know how to thank you. You saved my daughter's life."

He reached out and touched the dark curls on the little girl's head. She took his finger and gripped it, smiling. "No thanks are needed, señora. I am glad your niña is all right."

"If I weren't so glad to have her safe, I'd give her a spanking to make her remember what she did."

"It was only a child's game to her. She meant no harm."

The woman held out her hand. "My name is Lisa Anderson. I live here with my husband and his grandfather. You are welcome to stay here as long as you like."

"Thank you, but there is no need for that. I just wanted to pay my respects to Don Alfredo as I passed through."

"No, please, you must stay the night at least. I can't let you leave without a good meal. Besides," she handed her daughter over to him, "you can't leave this little girl yet. You just saved her life. She must get a chance to know you."

Cruz smiled at the delightful child in his arms and the beautiful woman who stood before him. As far as he was concerned, there was no need to hurry off. "Perhaps I will stay the night, but tomorrow I must be going."

"Good. We will arrange something special for dinner. Come, let's go inside and get you something to drink."

As they walked to the hacienda, Don Alfredo came toward them. "What is all this I hear? Did my little Raya get herself into trouble?" Don Alfredo looked at the little girl, and then at the man holding her. His eyes narrowed.

"Hello, Don Alfredo. It is good to see you again."

"Cruz? It is you then? I thought my eyes were playing tricks on me."

"No, it's me, *patrón*."

"And you are responsible for saving this little girl's life?"

"I simply—"

"Yes, Don Alfredo," Lisa interrupted. "He bravely rode into the corral with the steer and scooped Raya up into his arms."

"Well, then, it seems I owe you again."

Cruz handed Raya back to Lisa. "You owe me nothing, Don Alfredo. It is I who owe you."

Don Alfredo stepped forward, taking Cruz's hand in his. "You have saved the life of my great-granddaughter, something that is worth more than any amount of money I have. But I will find a way to repay you."

Cruz lowered his eyes to the ground. This talk made him feel guilty. "Don Alfredo, please, let's not talk about it anymore. If you want to repay me, I would like nothing more than a glass of water."

"I see you have not changed, eh, Cruz? You are still much too proud for your own good." Don Alfredo put his arm around the man. "Come, you will have more than a glass of water."

Don Alfredo led the way inside. "Lisa, would you

mind leading our guest to his room while I talk to Jaime about some food for Cruz?"

"Don Alfredo . . ."

Lisa handed Raya to Don Alfredo and put her arm through Cruz's. "Please don't argue with the *patrón,* Cruz, you will never win." Lisa led Cruz upstairs to the guest room, then, walked to the stand that held the water pitcher and basin. "I'll be back in a minute. I'll get you some water so you can wash up."

Cruz started to protest but saw that it wouldn't do him any good. He looked around the room and a feeling of peacefulness came over him. This was the room he had stayed in over five years ago, the room where he had come back to life.

"Here we go." Lisa came back into the room, pouring some water into the basin. "Soap and a towel are on the stand. And here is a clean shirt."

"Thank you, señora."

"Please, call me Lisa."

"Where do you come from, Lisa?" Cruz asked as he took off his hat and gloves and put them on the chair by the window.

"I am from back East, but I feel as though I've been here all of my life."

"And you are married to Don Alfredo's grandson?"

"Yes." Lisa started for the door. "I'll leave you to wash up now. Cruz?" Lisa walked back to him and took his hand, squeezing it tightly. "Thank you again. I don't know what I would have done if something had happened to my daughter."

Cruz looked into Lisa's clear green eyes and he smiled. He brought her hand to his mouth and he kissed it lightly. "It was my pleasure. Now please don't thank me again."

Lisa smiled. "I'll see you in a little while."

Cruz watched her as she walked out and he shook

his head. He didn't need this; he didn't need any of this right now. He unbuttoned his shirt and put it on top of his hat and gloves, then went to the washbasin and splashed water on his face. He couldn't let himself become attached to Don Alfredo again; it would serve no purpose. And what about the woman? She was married to Don Alfredo's grandson. He washed his face and hands and upper body and then put on the clean shirt Lisa had given him. He couldn't afford to let himself become attached to either of these people. He was far different from them. They would never understand the kind of life he had led, and he would never expect them to.

He walked to the window and looked out. All he wanted was to rest for a while and then go home. He was tired of a life on the run. He was tired of lying and stealing. He just wanted to settle down in a place like this. He needed to know what it felt like to belong somewhere. He needed to start living life, instead of running away from it.

Cruz listened in stunned silence to Lisa's story. It was obvious in the way she spoke of her husband that she was very much in love with him. He had been with the Comanches since he was sixteen years old and had eventually become a chief. Lisa was taken captive by another Comanche while traveling west on a wagon train. The man mistreated her and Eric rescued her from him and eventually he took her for his wife. She was willing to stay in the tribe with him, but he knew the life would be too hard on her. She had already lost a child and almost died. To protect her, he paid a scout to take her west to her brother. They met up again when Eric left the tribe and went back home to his grandfather, where he found Lisa again.

92

"So, you married and had your beautiful little daughter and your life has been wonderful?"

Lisa thought about the argument she and Eric had had before she left San Francisco. It seemed things seldom went smoothly for them. "It wasn't quite that easy. We had a terrible time trying to get along. Things weren't quite as simple as they had been in the Comanche camp. I even left here for a while. I wanted to make sure that Eric loved me for myself. When I discovered I was going to have his child, I wasn't sure if he was staying with me because of that or because he loved me. I wanted to give us both time. I ran away."

"But he found you."

"Yes," Lisa said softly. "He even delivered Raya."

"He must be quite a man. I was hoping to finally meet your grandson, Don Alfredo."

"Unfortunately, he won't be here for a while. He's away seeing to business matters."

"I'm sorry I'll miss him."

"Why can't you stay a while, Cruz?" Lisa asked impulsively.

"Yes, please stay, my friend," Don Alfredo added. "We have much to catch up on."

"I can't stay, for I have business to attend to. I'm riding south, near San Diego. Have you ever been there?"

"No, but friends tell me that it is beautiful. Like a paradise."

"It is very beautiful. I have some land and a small rancho there. It's not much, but in time I think it will be a fine place."

"Is that where you want to settle, Cruz? What about your family in Mexico? I know how much they mean to you."

Cruz had forgotten that he'd told Don Alfredo

93

about his family. "They want to stay in Mexico. I do for them what I can. I send them money, and I have helped some of my brothers and sisters. But they want to stay there. I like it here in California. I never want to go back to Mexico."

"Well, then, let me see what I can do for you. I have a cousin who has a land grant in San Diego. Perhaps—"

"No, Don Alfredo, I don't want your help. You have already done too much. I have some money saved and I plan to enlarge the rancho. I already have some horses and cattle. I will do just fine."

"I'm sure you will." Don Alfredo stood up. "You two will have to excuse me. It is time for my nap." He reached down and took Raya from Lisa's lap. "Are you tired, *niña?* Eh, well, I will take you up to bed anyway."

Cruz watched Don Alfredo as he left the room. "He is a good man."

"You like him very much, don't you? How did you meet him?"

Cruz related how Don Alfredo had taken him in without any questions when he had fallen ill while wandering about the country, how he had fed him and cared for him until he regained his health. "I stayed here for almost six months. It was very difficult to leave, but I knew I couldn't take advantage of Don Alfredo. I was aware of how much he missed his grandson and that I was like a replacement for him. But I knew that I couldn't be a family to him; not the kind he would be proud of."

"No. I can see how fond he is of you."

"He is a kind old man, that's all."

"You don't give Don Alfredo enough credit. He is a shrewd judge of character. If he thinks you're good, then it must be so."

94

Cruz got up. He walked to the window that overlooked the courtyard.

"I'm sorry. I made you feel uncomfortable. I have a bad habit of rambling when I talk."

"It's not you, Lisa, it's me. I don't belong here. I'm not like Don Alfredo or you."

"I don't belong here, either, Cruz, but Don Alfredo has made me feel as if I do. When I felt terrible about myself, he treated me as if I were a special person. He saw the good in me, just as he sees it in you." Lisa walked up behind Cruz. "Please don't leave yet, Cruz. It would break Don Alfredo's heart."

Cruz looked at Lisa. He smiled slightly. "I bet you always get your way, don't you?"

Lisa shrugged. "My brother says I'm as stubborn as a mule and as tough as a wounded bear. So you'd best not argue with me!"

"Well, then, I guess I'll be staying for a time."

"Good. I'm going to check on Raya. I'll talk to you later."

Cruz watched Lisa as she walked out of the room. She was a beautiful woman, but more than that, she was kind and good-hearted, the type of woman a man could learn to love very easily. He turned back to the window. Things definitely weren't going as planned. His compadres would come looking for him soon. They had wanted to kidnap Don Alfredo, but he had talked them out of it. He said he would go to Don Alfredo and find out what he could about his land. He didn't want anything to happen to the old man.

He rubbed his hands together. This was not to his liking. Robbing and stealing had always been easy for him, but not killing. Even when he had killed a man in self-defense, it had been a difficult thing to do. He would never be able to kill a defenseless old man like Don Alfredo. And he knew that's what they wanted.

95

He walked over to Don Alfredo's chair and sat down, resting his head against the high back of the chair. Don Alfredo had been kind to him on two occasions. He would never suspect that he was here to kill him. The old man didn't deserve this. The men that he rode with were a small army, an army of Mexican nationalists who didn't want to see California become a part of the United States. They thought if they killed certain wealthy and influential landowners and took title to their land, they would be able to hold on to the land and keep it from the hands of the white people who were quickly establishing a foothold in California. Cruz wasn't sure if he agreed with them.

California was a paradise—there was no arguing this. It had everything a man could want: mountains, deserts, valleys, an ocean, and the most fertile land in the world. There was nothing anyone could do to keep people from coming here. And California was already a state; there was nothing anyone could do about that. Killing men like Don Alfredo would do nothing but bring the soldiers down on them. It would only cause more bloodshed.

Cruz took a deep breath and shut his eyes. He was so tired. He thought of his mother. If only she had lived, perhaps his life would have been different. But perhaps not. Perhaps he had been destined to be bad from the beginning and nothing could have changed that.

"Are you all right, Cruz?"

Cruz opened his eyes. Lisa was standing in front of him, her hair pulled back from her face, revealing her sparkling green eyes. She was dressed in tight buckskin pants and a man's shirt and held a hat in her hand. *"Perdoname,"* he replied in Spanish.

"I asked you if you were all right. You were mumbling to yourself."

"I'm much more tired than I thought . . . You are going for a ride?"

"Yes. I always take a ride when Raya is napping. Would you like to join me?"

"No, I don't think so."

"Of course. You must be tired."

Cruz stood up, his lean frame towering over Lisa. "No, I just don't think your husband would approve of you riding with a stranger."

Lisa laughed. "You're hardly a stranger. You're our daughter's guardian angel."

Cruz clenched his jaw. He hated this deception. "Please, Lisa, I didn't do anything any other man wouldn't have done. Don't give me so much credit."

"You saved my daughter's life. As far as I am concerned, I'd trust you with my life."

Cruz looked at the lovely smile that lit up Lisa's face. He didn't want to be the person responsible for wiping it away.

"You're quiet again. Is something bothering you?"

"No. I was just wondering what it's like to have a family like this."

"What do you mean?"

"My mother died when I was nine years old, and I left home a couple of years later. I've been on my own ever since. I've never really known much family. I've been home to see my brothers and sisters a few times, but they all have their own lives."

"I can't imagine a man like you not having a family—a wife and children."

"What makes you say that?"

"You must know what an attractive man you are." Lisa smiled. "I'm sure you've had your share of romances. Don't you have a special woman?"

Cruz was genuinely stunned. No woman had ever

97

spoken to him in such an honest manner. Oh, he'd had numerous whores tell him they loved him and wanted him, but he knew it was only for the amount of money he could give them. He had never before had a woman tell him he was attractive. His dark eyes met Lisa's. "Are you always so bold with your compliments?"

Lisa's cheeks turned pink but she didn't avert her eyes. "I don't think of myself as bold but rather honest. I'm sorry if I insulted you. I seem to be doing a great deal of that today."

Cruz reached out and touched Lisa's arm. "No, please, you didn't insult me. The opposite, in fact." He smiled suddenly. "If you're sure your husband wouldn't mind, I think I'll take that ride with you."

"He wouldn't mind."

Lisa led Cruz outside where her magnificent palomino was already waiting for her. "Luis, would you mind getting the señor's horse. We'll be going for a ride."

"Sí, señora."

Cruz walked to the horse and ran his hand over the muscular neck and silky mane. "What a magnificent animal. A present from your husband?"

Lisa smiled. "In a way."

Cruz was puzzled. "I don't understand."

"No one could break him. My husband and I made a wager that I could break him by a certain time and ride him in a race."

"And did you?"

"I did, but I lost the race."

"And what happened?"

"I was supposed to lose Vida, my horse, and become my husband's mistress." She shrugged her shoulders, handing Vida some sugar from her pocket. "Instead, he married me."

"And you were able to keep the horse," Cruz said playfully.

"Yes." Lisa laughed. "Here's Luis with your horse."

They both mounted their horses and rode west, toward the ocean. Lisa pointed out several of her favorite places. She pulled up when they neared the cliffs overlooking the beach and the ocean beyond.

"It's wonderful, isn't it? I never thought anything could be so beautiful."

Cruz looked at the woman next to him. "I didn't, either."

"Why don't we head back toward the valley?" Lisa asked. "There's a wonderful place there I'd like to show you."

Lisa galloped ahead of Cruz, riding quickly, trying to forget the effect this man's eyes had on her. She felt as if he had been looking through her. They rode in silence until they reached the valley by the stream. Oak trees grew in abundance and wildflowers were abloom everywhere. Lisa dismounted and walked over to the stream. She knelt and scooped up some water, sipping it from her hands. She felt Cruz next to her but didn't look at him, instead, leaned back on her hands and gazed up at the sky.

"You're quiet suddenly. Have I offended you?"

Lisa seemed surprised at his question.

"The way you looked at me back there. I thought perhaps you saw something that made you feel uncomfortable."

Lisa looked into Cruz's dark eyes. "I trust you, Cruz. Is there any reason why I shouldn't?"

"No."

"Well, then. Let's enjoy this beautiful afternoon."

Cruz watched as Lisa threw back her head, and he basked in the sunshine of her face. She was unlike any woman he had ever known. She was naive yet forthright. She was lovely yet . . . He stopped. What was the matter with him? Here he was, sitting in the sunshine on a large rancho, enjoying the day with a beautiful married woman. He was acting as if he was one of the *hacendados.* He stood up and walked to his horse, mounting it quickly and rode away in confusion, not looking back to see if Lisa followed him. Already, he was trying to fit in where he didn't belong.

He rode quickly until he reached the foothills. He slowed when his horse started tiring. He turned him so they could look down on the lush, green valley from where they had just ridden. It was unlike anything he had ever seen. He knew what he was trying to do—he was trying to become one of "them" when in truth he would always be a *bandido,* pure and simple. He was not the kind of man Lisa Anderson would want to be with.

He started slowly down the valley and saw the palomino and its rider waiting patiently for him by the trail that led to the rancho. Lisa was sitting with one leg hooked over the horn of the saddle chewing on a piece of wild grass.

"I apologize to you again, Cruz. I told you before, I have a bad habit of talking too much."

"And I told you, it has nothing to do with you."

"All right then, why are you so angry?"

Cruz pulled up on his horse, his dark eyes even darker. "Don't you ever give up?"

"Not often."

He smiled then, unable to resist Lisa's infectious personality. "I can see why your husband is so much in love with you."

"How do you know that he is?"

"He'd be a very stupid man if he didn't love a woman like you." He walked his horse past Lisa.

"You haven't told me why you aren't married,

Cruz. A man like you—"

Cruz pulled up on his horse. He was angry now. "What about a man like me, Lisa? You think I'm good and honorable just because I helped your little girl? You and Don Alfredo know nothing about me. I could be your worst enemy. I could be a murderer for all you know."

"No," Lisa said simply. "Murderers don't have eyes like yours."

Cruz averted his eyes from Lisa's gaze and shook his head in exasperation. This woman had an answer for everything. "What if I wasn't the man you thought I was?"

"I'd say there was probably a reason for it. You have a good heart. I can see it. You genuinely like Don Alfredo and I could see when you were holding Raya that you like children. You're no murderer, Cruz. What are you trying to tell me?"

For a fleeting moment Cruz actually thought he could tell Lisa the whole truth and she would understand, but he quickly decided against that. He had to think of another way to save Don Alfredo's life, for he had already decided that he wouldn't kill him. His grandson was another story. It would be very easy to kill him and take his woman.

"You're quiet again. Do you always think so much?"

"Always. My mother used to call me her *sonador,* her dreamer."

"I bet she was a wonderful person."

"Yes, she was." Cruz began riding again, slowing when he saw the small group of riders ahead. He held up his hand to Lisa. "Stay behind me."

"What is it?" She looked at the riders ahead. "They might be from the del Mar."

"I don't think so. Do you have a rifle?"

"Yes."

"Get it out slowly and place it on your saddle. Just in case." Cruz pulled out his own rifle and laid it across his saddle. He squinted to see the riders better. He could tell from the sombreros that they were Mexican. He pulled up when he was a few hundred yards away from the men. There were four of them, casually sitting on their horses, as if waiting for him. He recognized Arturo immediately. They had never gotten along and Arturo would gladly have found any excuse to kill Cruz.

"Buenas días," Arturo said politely, tipping his hat to Lisa. "Señora."

"Hello," Lisa said softly.

"And you, *amigo,* how are you this fine day?" Arturo asked Cruz.

"Is there something you want, señor?"

"My friends and I were just passing through, and are in need of water. I hope that is not a problem."

"No, you're welcome to the water," Lisa replied.

"Gracias, señora. You are too kind." Arturo looked from Cruz to Lisa. "So, we are on de Vargas land?"

"Yes," Lisa replied.

"And you are Señor and Señora de Vargas?" There was a slight smile at the corner of his mouth when he asked the question.

"No, my husband is away for a time. This is my friend."

"I see."

"We should be getting back, Lisa," Cruz said gruffly. "Why don't you ride on ahead. I'll catch up with you."

"No, I'll wait—"

"Go on ahead," Cruz said firmly; and Lisa rode away.

Cruz waited until she was safely out of range before

102

he spoke. "What are you doing here, Arturo? I told you I'd report back as soon as I was finished."

"It looks to me like you're having a sweet time with the *patróna*." He kissed his fingertips. "She is very beautiful. I can see why you are so distracted."

"I'm not distracted."

"They why is Don Alfredo de Vargas still alive?"

"I've only been here one day. I haven't been able to find anything out."

"The general will not give you much time."

"I'm not sure that it will serve our purposes to kill him."

Arturo sat up for the first time. "You had your orders, Cruz. Why haven't you followed them?"

"I have another idea, a better one."

"I am listening."

"The grandson is away and I am using this time to earn the trust of Don Alfredo and his grandson's wife. If we kill them, there will be no guarantee that we'll get the land. The title is held in San Francisco by the woman's brother. On the other hand, if we were to kidnap the woman and the old man, perhaps we could ask for the land and any money there is in exchange for their safe return. Once I gain their trust, they will do anything for me. If we devised a plan whereby you kidnapped us all and they believed I was not a part of it, I think they would listen to me and wouldn't be any trouble."

Arturo twirled his thin mustache. "It is not a bad plan, Cruz. Sometimes you surprise me. I will tell General Vasquez. How much time will you need?"

"The husband is coming back in two weeks. We should plan the kidnapping for this Sunday, during siesta. No one will expect it."

"What about the men of the rancho?"

"They will all be resting as well. When have you

ever seen men working during siesta?"

"It makes sense. I will tell the general. If you don't hear from us, then we will go along with your plan. But don't cross us, Cruz."

"Why would I do that?"

"You seem very comfortable with the señora. Perhaps you have grown soft."

"Nothing has changed, Arturo. I want this land back as much as you do, perhaps even more."

"All right then. We will be here on Sunday during siesta."

"Remember, Arturo, treat me as you would them, at least until we get them out of here. It will go much easier that way."

"All right. *Adiós, compadre.*"

Cruz watched as Arturo and the other men rode east, toward the hills. Lisa was just a speck in the distance and he rode hard to catch up with her. He wanted to spend all the time he could with her now, because once she found out he was a part of this, things would never be the same between them again.

Chapter 5

Cruz smiled as Raya ran across the courtyard toward him and proceeded to fall, losing the flower she had been so intent upon giving to him. He stood and picked her up from the ground. "Are you all right, *niña,* eh?" He brushed his hand against her cheek. He looked at her tiny little face, and already the sparkling blue eyes of her father shone back. He had heard a lot about the blue-eyed Spaniard with the white father. He had been so angry at his mother for forcing him to stay on this land while his father had sailed at sea and ultimately died that he had taken his father's name, rather than the Spanish name he had been christened by. Where was this man who was so in love with his wife that he risked everything for her? Was tending to his business matters more important than preserving their love?

"I see you're beginning to spoil her, too."

Cruz looked up as Lisa walked up into the courtyard. She was beyond beautiful. She was dressed in a simple white dress, her hair braided and draped over one shoulder, a white gardenia behind her ear. She wore a large silver necklace that contrasted with her dark skin. She held out her hands. "I'll take her now, if you like."

Cruz shook his head and hugged Raya. "No, she's mine for now. She tried very hard to bring me a flower. I'm not going to let her go yet."

Cruz brushed the dark curls from Raya's face and planted a kiss on her cheek. "She's a wonderful child, Lisa You and your husband must be very proud of her."

"Yes, we are. We thought we might never have her. We weren't sure if I could have children."

"I'm sorry."

"No, it's all right. Even if Raya is the only child I'll be able to have, she gives us all the joy we need."

"If you had to choose between your husband and your child, who would you choose?"

Lisa's expression suddenly changed. "That's a strange question. I could never make such a choice. I love them both so much . . ." She shook her head. "I won't ever have to make such a decision, so it doesn't matter. But why are you asking this?"

"I suppose I'm curious as to how much a woman can really love a man."

"I love my husband every bit as much as I love my child, but my child needs me in a way Eric does not." Lisa reached down and handed Raya another flower. "If I had to make a choice, I suppose I would choose my child."

"You remind me of my mother, Lisa," Cruz said without thinking.

"Why is that?"

"She knew that having a sixth child would endanger her life, but she had the baby anyway. She died right after my sister was born."

"I'm so sorry, Cruz."

"She was a sweet woman. She loved her children very much."

"She must have loved your father very much also

106

if she wanted to give him another child."

"I suppose she did. At the time, I blamed my father. I thought it was his fault. But I think you're right; my mother did it because she knew it would give my father great pleasure."

Lisa walked over to Cruz and gently touched his arm. "Maybe you should go back and see your family. It might make you less lonely." She looked up and smiled when she saw Don Alfredo.

"So, here you are. Ah, my *niña bonita,* come to me." Don Alfredo held out his arms as Raya scurried across the courtyard into his arms. "What have we here? A flower for me?" He breathed in deeply. "I think it is the most beautiful flower in the world."

Lisa looked at Cruz, and they both smiled. "He is in love with that child."

"Yes, it's obvious. I know your husband is Don Alfredo's grandson, but what of Don Alfredo's children?"

"He and his wife only had one child, a daughter named Mariz. She lives on the Rancho del Sol, but they have not spoken for some time."

"And what of your husband? Does he speak to his mother?"

"No, my husband left here when he was sixteen years old. When he returned, he tried to get along with his mother but she kept trying to interfere in our relationship. She very nearly destroyed us both. No one here speaks to Mariz."

"It seems sad that she should be alone."

Lisa laughed derisively. "You wouldn't feel sad if you knew Mariz. She is very much like a black widow. That's why my brother Tom left."

"Your brother?"

"Yes, Tom lived on her rancho for quite some time. He is a lawyer and he advised her on many

107

things." Lisa cocked an eyebrow. "They were also lovers."

"I see."

"Mariz is still a very beautiful woman and very dangerous. If you should happen to meet her, Cruz, be careful. She will lure you into her web and then destroy you."

"This doesn't sound like you, Lisa."

"Why? Are you surprised that I can speak so coldly of my own mother-in-law? She thought nothing of having me kidnapped by bandits, Cruz. I was supposed to be murdered by them. I'm not sure Mariz has any feelings except toward her land. She would do anything to protect the del Sol."

"How many acres does she have?"

Lisa shrugged. "I'm not sure. The del Sol is much larger than this place. I think she has at least three thousand acres. Why are you so interested?"

"I just never realized that Don Alfredo had a daughter who lived so close."

Lisa again put her hand on Cruz's arm, but this time she squeezed it. "Cruz, please don't get involved with Mariz. She's not a good person. I don't want to see you get hurt."

Cruz looked at Lisa's green eyes knowing he could never deny anything they asked of her. "Don't worry about me, Lisa, I'll be all right." He took her hand and raised it to his mouth, gently kissing it. He saw the crimson blush spread over her cheeks, but he didn't care. This woman touched him in a way that no other ever had.

"Cruz—"

"Don't say it, Lisa. I know that you love your husband. I know that your feelings for me are simply friendship, but it doesn't mean that I can't admire—"

The voice of Don Alfredo broke in. "What are you two so serious about, eh? Today is a time for relaxation. Why don't I have some wine brought out into the garden and we can enjoy this glorious afternoon?"

Lisa gently pulled away from Cruz and walked over to Don Alfredo. "That sounds wonderful, Don Alfredo. Why don't I help you?"

"No, you stay here with Cruz and enjoy the day. I'll take Raya and meet you in the garden."

Lisa watched Don Alfredo as he carried Raya into the house. She was afraid to turn and face Cruz. She heard his footsteps on the brick path as he walked toward her, and she felt his strong hands on her shoulders as he turned her around.

"I don't want you to be afraid of me, Lisa. I won't hurt you. I respect what you have with your husband. I would never do anything to destroy that. But, my God," his hand went up to her cheek and caressed it gently, "you are the most beautiful woman I've ever seen. If you weren't married, I'd take you away from here and I'd never leave you alone, ever." His dark eyes burned through hers. She started to look away, but he caught her chin and held it. He lowered his mouth to her trembling lips and touched them lightly, wanting to drink in their sweetness, but he was afraid of alienating her even more. He pulled back. "I'll let you and Don Alfredo be alone now. I've interfered too much already."

"No, you haven't interfered. Don Alfredo wants you here. Please, come to the garden with us."

Cruz nodded and followed Lisa through the courtyard and into the garden. He looked behind him, wondering when General Vasquez and his men would arrive.

They walked into a lush green area that was

109

planted with orange, lime, oak, and elm trees. Gardenias and purple and pink bougainvillea flowered everywhere. There was a small swing that hung from the oak tree, and Raya immediately ran to it. Don Alfredo lifted her into the swing and pushed her, reveling in the sound of her childish laughter. Cruz watched Lisa as she sat down on one of the stone benches. She was quiet, and he knew why. He had crossed that line with her and now she wasn't sure if she could trust him.

"So, you are having a little picnic, are you?"

Cruz swung around at the sound of Arturo's voice. "What do you want?"

Arturo, gun drawn, walked forward, followed by a group of men. He motioned for two of his men to grab Cruz and walked toward Lisa, who stood up to face him.

"Who are you?"

"I am Arturo Garcia, señora. We met earlier in the week, do you recall?"

"Yes." Her eyes went to Cruz. "Why are you holding him? What has he done?"

"It's not what he's done, señora, it's who he is. He and his grandfather." Arturo approached Don Alfredo. "Don Alfredo, I regret to inform you that you and your grandson are under arrest."

"Who are you? How dare you come onto my property like this."

"We dare to do anything we please, *patrón*. We will soon be the new government here. We are not happy with the way things are going in California so we are taking things into our own hands."

"What are you talking about?"

"I want you and your grandson to come with me."

"No!" Lisa started toward Arturo, but he shoved her back.

110

"Don't touch her," Cruz said angrily, trying to break away from the men who held him. Cruz struggled, but the men hit him on the head and knocked him out.

"Now, Don Alfredo," Arturo commanded, "will you come peacefully or do we get rough with the woman and the child?"

"No!" Lisa stood up, running to Raya and quickly gathering her up in her arms.

"I will come with you, but please leave everyone else be."

"I cannot do that, *patrón*. You will all have to come with me, I'm afraid."

Don Alfredo stopped. "You aren't using your head, man. If you take the child, she will cause you nothing but problems. Leave her here with her mother."

Arturo thought for a moment. "I will leave the child but not the mother. She comes with us."

"Lisa, find Rocia and make sure that she takes care of Raya."

Lisa started toward the house, but Arturo stopped her. "Two of my men will go with you just to make sure there are no tricks."

"What good will it do for you to have us with you?"

"I am only going to take your grandson and his wife, Don Alfredo. I want you to listen carefully. I will be back in one week by which time I want the title to this land, and I want it signed over to General Vasquez. If you do as I say, no one will be hurt. If you try to do something stupid, you will never see your grandson or his wife again."

Don Alfredo looked over at Cruz lying on the ground. For some reason, they thought he was his grandson. All the better. Cruz was a very resourceful man and hopefully he could find a way for him and Lisa to escape. Otherwise he would have to do as this man said. The land was worth nothing if Lisa would have to die for it. Alejandro would never forgive him if he returned to find that something had happened to his wife.

"Well, Don Alfredo?"

"All right, I will do as you say. Please don't hurt them. They are innocent in this."

"They will be well taken care of as long as you do as I say. Remember, the title to the land, signed over to General Vasquez in one week."

"What do you hope to gain by this?"

"My compadres and I are acquiring land all over the state. We will be wealthy and powerful. We will be the new government in California."

"You are fooling yourself. That will change nothing. As long as people keep coming here wanting land to farm and to build on, the land will either be sold or taken from you. You are a fool if you believe otherwise."

"I don't need to hear an old man's words. Someone will be here in one week for the document, Don Alfredo. Have it ready."

Arturo motioned to the men to pick up Cruz and he headed into the house, dragging Lisa away from her daughter.

"Please, just let me hold her one more time."

"Enough, woman. It is time to go." Arturo pulled Lisa to his horse and made her mount up; he mounted behind her, wrapping one arm tightly around her. Cruz was bound and thrown over another horse that was led by one of the men.

They rode over the land of the Rancho del Mar and up into the foothills, taking a trail that Lisa was unfamiliar with. She kept looking behind her, hoping that someone would follow them, but she saw no one. They traveled far up into the hills until the horses had difficulty climbing. Just when Lisa thought they would have to dismount, the trail evened out and they followed it through a pass. Although it was spring, up here in the mountains it still felt cool. She tried to ignore the tight grip of the man's arm around her but he never loosened it. It reminded her of the time when the Comanches had captured and raped her; she was frightened. She had heard of these men, of these *bandidos,* and she had heard of the things they did to women. She closed her eyes. She had seen firsthand what they did to women when she was kidnapped by Chuka and taken away. She was pregnant with Raya then and the only thing that saved her was that Chuka was double-crossed by Consuelo, Eric's lover, the woman who had paid Chuka to kill her. She remembered the things Chuka's men did to Consuelo, and she remembered the things the Comanches had done to her before Nakon had saved her. Nakon . . . it seemed like a lifetime ago when she knew him, before she found out that he was Alejandro de Vargas and Eric Anderson. A man of many names but still, the man she loved. But this time Eric wouldn't be around to help her; she would have to rely on her wiles. Then she thought of Cruz. She strained to see which horse he was on, but her captor wouldn't let her turn around.

"Don't worry, señora. Your husband will have a little headache when he awakens, but he will be fine."

They traveled for another hour or so until Arturo gave the sign for them to stop. He dismounted and pulled Lisa down. He took her arm and dragged her along behind him, her flimsy white dress and thin sandals no protection from the dirt and rocks. They climbed up a hillside that was covered with rocks and gravel. Lisa slipped several times, and Arturo was forced to stop and pull her along. When they reached the top of the hill, Lisa was surprised to find a camp. It had a few small shacks and a large cooking pit in the middle. Several women sat around, either cooking or sewing. They all stared at her as Arturo brought her into the camp. He took her to a shack on the far side of the camp and pushed her inside, followed closely by Cruz, who stumbled and fell against her. Lisa held on to him, but he sank to the earthen floor. She went to him, running her hand over his forehead.

Cruz opened his eyes and looked up to find his head in Lisa's lap. "Where are we?"

"I don't know, somewhere up in the hills. We went through some kind of pass. I guess this is their camp."

Cruz closed his eyes. Now he remembered. This was Vasquez's camp. He had been here once before. His head throbbed, but he forced himself to sit up. "They didn't hurt you, did they?"

"No, I'm fine. I heard that one man tell Don Alfredo that he had one week."

"One week? What does that mean?"

"He has one week to get the title to the del Mar and give it to him. He said if Don Alfredo didn't have it, he would kill us. He thinks you're my husband."

Cruz knew that Arturo was just playing along to keep Lisa calm. He didn't like the way things were going. He had never wanted to hurt Don Alfredo or Lisa. In fact, the only reason he'd gone to the del Mar at all was so no one else would kill Don Alfredo. He should've warned him. He didn't really believe in Vasquez's cause; had only met the man once before. Now, he was caught right in the middle and he felt responsible for Lisa.

"What are we going to do, Cruz?" Lisa tried to remain calm, but the concern was evident in her voice.

Cruz took her hand. "Just relax, there's nothing we can do now. If we can get some kind of weapon, maybe we can sneak out of here."

"How can we do that, there are men all over the place?"

"Nothing is impossible, Lisa, not where there's a will." Slowly, Cruz got to his feet, grimacing as the pain in his head grew worse. He stooped as he walked around the small, low-walled shack, unable to stand to his full height. The shack consisted of four walls, an earthen floor, no windows, and a flimsy door that was attached by buckskin hinges. It would be easy enough to get out; the hard part would be getting past the guards outside. He walked back to Lisa and sat down, taking her hands in his. "I think you are the way out of here."

"Me? What can I do?" But even as she asked, Lisa knew the answer. She cleared her throat. "You want me to flirt with one of the guards."

"You're going to have to do more than that."

Lisa stared down at the floor. "I don't know if I can—"

"I'm not asking you to let the man rape you, but I think you'll have to encourage him to get friendly so that I can get his gun. Can you do that?"

"I think so." She looked at Cruz. "That man Arturo scares me. I'm afraid of him."

"That's why we can't wait. We have to do it tonight."

"All right, I'll do it. But please don't let him touch

115

me."

"He won't hurt you, Lisa, I promise you." Cruz put his finger to his mouth. "Someone is coming. I'm going to pretend to be knocked out. We may have to do it now."

Lisa nodded and sat on the cold floor next to Cruz. The door opened and Arturo walked in, followed by two men.

"So, señora, your husband is not awake yet?"

"No," Lisa said quietly, resting her hand possessively on Cruz's shoulder.

"You and I have things to talk about, señora. I want you to come with me."

"But—"

"Don't attempt to argue with me, señora. I can force you, surely, you know that."

Lisa's heart throbbed frantically. Why didn't Cruz do something. "What about my husband?"

"He will be fine. He will awaken soon. Please, come with me now."

As Lisa started to stand up, Cruz moaned and opened his eyes. He reached out and took Lisa's hand. "Where are you going?"

"She's going with me, señor. We have some things to talk about."

Cruz sat up very slowly, squinting as he looked at Arturo. "Why don't you want to talk to me?"

"You aren't as pretty as your wife." Arturo laughed raucously and his men joined in.

"She knows nothing of the land grant."

"It doesn't matter, señor. We have other things to talk about."

Cruz looked at the three armed men and he knew he didn't stand a chance. He stood up, carefully watching them as their hands went to their pistols. "I am not the grandson of Don Alfredo de Vargas."

Lisa started to speak, but Cruz squeezed her hand.

Arturo looked at his men and smiled. "Then who are you, the King of Spain?" Arturo laughed again.

"Have you ever heard of a bandit called Joaquin?"

"El Famoso? Everyone has heard of El Famoso."

"Have you heard of another Joaquin, a younger one, one who sometimes robs from the rich and gives to the poor?" Arturo knew him only as Cruz, he did not know him by his other name.

"I have heard of such a man," one of Arturo's men responded.

"Shut up!" Arturo commanded. "What of it? Everyone knows there are many men who try to copy El Famoso."

"Do you know what the younger Joaquin looks like?"

"I have heard he is tall, some say handsome, others say good with a knife."

"And he has a scar on his left arm," Cruz added.

"Yes," one of the men added, "from a knife fight that almost killed him."

"Yes," Cruz said softly. He rolled up the sleeve on his left arm and held it out. "Do you see this, Arturo?"

Arturo stepped forward and looked at the scar that ran from the inside of Cruz's upper arm down to his wrist, then looked at Cruz's face. "This means nothing. I myself have many scars. Do you think I go around telling people that I am Joaquin the Younger?"

"There is one way to tell," one of the men said. "For it is said that this Joaquin is so skilled with a knife that he can kill birds as they fly."

"Perhaps we can come up with something," Arturo said thoughtfully. He took Lisa by the wrist and

117

pulled her out the door. "Bring him!" He walked to a large tree on the edge of camp and made Lisa stand against the trunk. He smiled as he turned to Cruz. "If you are who you say your are, you should be able to pin her to this tree." He made Lisa hold her arm straight out to the side so that the sleeve hung down. "You should have no problem hitting this, no?"

Cruz looked across the camp at Lisa. There was no mistaking the terrified expression on her face. He squinted his eyes. His head was still hurting and he wasn't sure his eyes were that good. He couldn't take a chance. If he came too close to Lisa, he could hurt her or possibly even kill her. "I can't do it," he said firmly.

"I thought not," Arturo said smugly.

"Only a fool would try something like that."

"But I thought you were the best," Arturo said. "If that is true, then this should not be a problem."

"I won't endanger her life."

"Her life is already endangered, Señor Joaquin," Arturo said sarcastically. "If I were you, I would think about that. In the meantime," he took Lisa by the arm, "the señora and I will have that little talk now."

Cruz watched as Arturo dragged her away, then turned to the man, who seemed to believe him. "If you will give me a knife, I will prove that I am Joaquin."

The man regarded him for a moment and slowly took his knife from his waist belt. "I will let you use this, señor, but we all will have our guns pointed at you. Should you try anything, you will be dead before the knife leaves your hand."

Cruz took the knife. "I understand." He looked at the trunk of the tree. "Take the knife and carve a

118

mark in the tree."

The man did as he was told and handed the knife back to Cruz. Cruz stepped backward. He was about one hundred feet from the tree. He took the knife by the blade and held it down by his side. He put his left foot forward and squinted his right eye. Then, almost before anyone could see him, he raised his arm and flipped the knife into the trunk of the tree. They all rushed forward. A hush spread over the group of people. The man who had given Cruz the knife pulled it out of the trunk; it had stuck right in the mark he had made only minutes before.

He turned to Cruz. "I admit that is very good, señor, but many men are as good. Show me something to truly make me believe."

Cruz's mind raced. He thought of Lisa alone with Arturo, and he could hardly concentrate. "What about you? Are you brave enough to stand there with something on your head?"

"I am not loco, señor."

"If I kill you, I will be dead in seconds. If I want to save my woman, I must make sure that my aim is true, *comprende?*"

The man thought for a moment and then shrugged his shoulders. He walked to the tree and began to take off his hat, but Cruz stopped him.

"No, leave on the sombrero. If I put a hole through it, you can wear it and tell everyone that Joaquin the Younger made the hole. You will be famous."

The man nodded. "So be it. But remember, señor, if you do miss and kill me, you and your woman will never leave here alive."

"I understand," Cruz said solemnly. He stepped back and wiped his right hand against his leg. His palms were sweaty and his head throbbed. He put his left foot forward, squinted his right eye, and gripped the blade, all the while concentrating on the point of the hat where he wanted the blade to go. When he was ready, he raised his arm and threw the knife. It landed in the trunk of the tree with a loud thud, its handle shaking slightly. The man against the tree didn't move; his eyes were as large as walnuts. Cruz walked forward and pulled out the knife, and the man stepped away from the tree, smiling as he took off his sombrero. He put his finger through the cut that was right above his forehead.

"You are good, señor, better than anyone I have ever seen." He held out his hand to Cruz. "I believe you are Joaquin the Younger."

"Will you let us go?"

"That I cannot do, señor. I have to answer to General Vasquez, but I will let you get your woman. You two will stay here with us until the general arrives. I am sure he will see things differently when he finds out who you are." He shrugged his shoulders. "It is the best I can do, señor."

"What is your name?"

"José."

Cruz held out his hand. "Thank you, José. I will not forget this." He glanced around the camp. "Where is Arturo?"

"I will show you, señor. You will need the knife, for Arturo is a mean one."

José led Cruz through the rocks and into the trees to a well-hidden shack. "He is in there. Good luck."

Cruz nodded. He put the blade of the knife in his mouth and edged closer to the shack. He brushed through the pine trees that surrounded it and stood by the door, listening for movement but hearing nothing. For a minute he didn't think anyone was inside, but then he heard Lisa's stifled scream. He quickly threw back the door and ran inside, pulling Arturo from her. Arturo was up, gun drawn, but Cruz kicked the gun from his hand. He took the knife from his mouth.

"No guns, Arturo, just knives. I want to prove to you just how good I am."

Arturo smiled and pulled the knife from his belt. He edged his way toward Lisa, but Cruz's voice stopped him.

"Stay away from her or I'll kill you now."

Arturo moved to the side, his knife held out in front of him. "No one is as good with a knife as they say Joaquin is," he stuttered.

"Then why do you look so afraid, Arturo?"

Arturo ran forward, tackling Cruz and throwing him back against the wall of the shack. Cruz grabbed Arturo's knife hand and forced the weapon away from him, then turned under Arturo's arm to suddenly stand behind him.

"You're not very quick, Arturo. You could get yourself killed this way."

Arturo turned around, disconcerted and obviously afraid. He stabbed wildly with the knife, hitting only air. Cruz circled around the shack, letting Arturo tire himself. Arturo came at Cruz again and again, but Cruz adeptly sidestepped him and Arturo clumsily fell against the wall of the shack.

"Are you ready to give up, Arturo?"

"Never!" Arturo stood up, grabbing the knife by the blade and hurling it across the room at Cruz. Cruz didn't move. He watched Arturo and the knife as it came toward him, and he quickly jumped to the side. Arturo's knife stuck in the opposite wall.

"I think you're out of weapons, Arturo," Cruz said menacingly as he walked across the shack to Arturo. He grabbed the man by the shirt and stared into his eyes. "Did you hurt her, Arturo?"

"No, Cruz, I swear I didn't."

"Why is it I don't believe you."

"I didn't hurt her. I was just having a little fun."

"Do you think she was having fun?"

"I don't know—"

"Do you?" Cruz pulled the man's shirt so tightly around his throat that he gasped for air.

"No."

"I want you to apologize to her."

"I am sorry, señora."

"To her face." Cruz turned the man around.

"I am sorry if I hurt you, señora."

"Now what should I do with you, Arturo? Should I gut you like the spineless pig you are?"

"Cruz, please. Don't kill him. It doesn't matter now." Lisa stood behind him, holding her ripped dress in front of her.

Cruz looked away from Arturo to Lisa, and he relaxed his hold. Arturo broke free and ran to his knife. He pulled it from the wood and turned, but before he could do anything, Cruz had thrown his knife, where it landed firmly implanted in Arturo's belly. The man's eyes were large and empty and he dropped to his knees and then completely forward on his face. Cruz didn't have to check to see if he was dead; he had already seen the blood running from the side of his mouth. At Lisa's anguished cry, he grabbed her and pulled her outside into the trees. He held her against him, his hands on the bare skin of her back.

"It seems I now owe you for my life," Lisa said softly, her face against his chest.

Cruz lifted her face up so that he could see her eyes. He wiped the tears that ran down her cheeks. "You owe me nothing, I told you that before."

122

Lisa held her hands against her chest, holding up the front of her dress. She smiled tentatively. "You're a strange man. I almost feel as if . . ."

"What?"

"I almost feel as if you were sent to watch over me, as though you are my protector."

Cruz unbuttoned his shirt and slipped it off, pulling it around Lisa's shoulders. "Since I can't be your husband, then I will gladly be your protector." He ignored Lisa's embarrassment as she slipped her arms into the shirt and tried to cover her bare breasts. He quickly buttoned the shirt. "Are you all right?"

Lisa nodded slightly but walked away from him. She sat down on the ground, pulling her knees up to her chest. "I swore no man would ever hurt me like that again."

Cruz sat down next to her. "Again?"

Lisa dropped her eyes at the memory. "When the Comanches took me captive, they shared me between four of them, every night, until I thought I would die."

Cruz took her hand. "But you didn't."

"Only because Nakon saved me. He took me into his tepee and he cared for me." She looked up at Cruz, her eyes brimming with tears. "He treated me with respect and I loved him with all of my heart."

"I understand."

Lisa nodded. "He made me forget all of those terrible things."

"Did Arturo hurt you, Lisa?" He turned her face toward him. "Tell me the truth."

Lisa shook her head slowly. "He touched me but he didn't violate me. I feel dirty."

Cruz put his arm around Lisa and pulled her to him. She laid her head on his shoulder. "You have done nothing shameful or dirty. He was a pig and deserved to die. You should not torture yourself this way."

"I guess I'm tired, and I'm scared. Will they let us go, Cruz?"

"Not yet. We have to wait until General Vasquez gets here."

Lisa pulled away from Cruz and looked at him. "Is it true what you told those men about yourself? Are you really one of the men they call Joaquin?"

Cruz couldn't lie any longer. "Yes, I am Joaquin the Younger. I am a *bandido,* Lisa, I am not a man to be trusted." He took a deep breath. "In fact, I was sent to the Rancho del Mar to murder Don Alfredo and your husband."

"I don't believe it. You wouldn't do that."

"You're right, I wouldn't kill a man for no reason, especially Don Alfredo."

"How did you get involved with a man like Vasquez?"

"I didn't really, directly, that is. I had been riding with a group of men who were riding with him. They told me of their plans for Don Alfredo and I said I would go to the rancho and speak to him."

"You and Arturo spoke the other day, didn't you?"

"Yes. He wanted to know if I had killed Don Alfredo. I told him I had a better idea. I told him instead of killing anyone, they should kidnap you and Don Alfredo."

"Cruz," Lisa said, her voice full of disappointment.

"It was the only way I could think of to buy time."

"Why didn't you just tell Don Alfredo the truth? My God, Cruz, they could've killed all of us, including Raya."

"I know that now. I did a stupid thing, but I already told you, Lisa, I can't be trusted."

Lisa's eyes searched Cruz's face. "I trust you with my life. You are a good man, you have shown it too many times for it not to be true."

Cruz looked away. "Perhaps I was good once, a long time ago when I was a boy, but I have been a thief for too long now. I am not like you and your husband and Don Alfredo."

Lisa laughed. "Cruz, my husband was a Comanche chief who led raids on other tribes. They constantly stole from each other."

"That is different."

"It's no different. I heard you say you steal from the rich and give to the poor. I don't find that to be such a bad thing."

"I have also kept some of the money. I haven't given it all away."

"Why are you so intent on making me believe you are a bad person?"

"Because I am different from you. You have a good life with a husband and a child. You live on a beautiful rancho. You don't have to steal from people to survive."

"That doesn't make me better, Cruz, that only makes me luckier."

"You do have an answer for everything, don't you?"

"No, I just know that you saved my daughter's life and now you have saved my life. I don't know how to repay you."

Cruz stood up, his mood suddenly changed. "I need to think of a way to get you back to your husband and then I'll be on my way. I've stayed much too long."

"Why do you want to leave?"

"I didn't say I wanted to." He walked back to the shack and pulled Arturo's body outside, removing the knife and wiping it clean of the blood. He put the knife in his belt. "I'll see if we can sleep in here tonight."

"Cruz, wait." Lisa grabbed his arm.

"What?"

"I'm sorry. I mean . . ." She shook her head, sighing deeply. "I don't know what I want to say." She reached up and gently touched his face. "I don't want you to leave. I want you to meet my husband, I think you'd like him."

Cruz put his arm around Lisa and drew her toward him. "I don't want to meet your husband." He lowered his mouth to hers and kissed her deeply. He didn't want to let her go, but he forced himself to back away. "Wait here until I come back. I'll see if I can get us some food."

Lisa watched Cruz as he walked away, his tall, lean form already very familiar to her. She had grown to like him and, more than that, she had grown to count on him. Maybe he was right, maybe it was time he left.

She thought of his involvement in the kidnapping, but couldn't bring herself to be angry with him. She knew that she was lucky he was not like Arturo. Thanks to Cruz, she was still alive, and she trusted him to keep her that way until she got back home safely.

Chapter 6

Lisa was washing clothes in the stream and the cool water felt soothing to her blistered hands. She sat back on her heels, looking around her. These people had picked a perfect hideout—the only way out was down. If she and Cruz did try to escape, the only way they could go was up, and no one in their right mind would attempt that unless they were prepared.

She didn't know how long they had been there, a few weeks she guessed. Cruz had left and returned with the news that General Vasquez was not going to kill Don Alfredo, but he was still going to keep them as prisoners just in case he needed them. Lisa wondered if Eric had returned from San Francisco, and if he had, had he already come looking for her? She wondered about Raya, too, and she wondered if her little girl missed her. She felt tears sting her eyes and she closed them, forcing them to go away. She had to be strong.

"Would you like some help?"

Lisa smiled at the sound of Cruz's voice and looked up at him. He wore tight buckskin pants and a blue shirt. His dark hair was getting long on his neck and his eyes always seemed to be squinting, as though they were trying to figure something out. He had been so kind to her; had been her strength and her sanity. "No, I'm almost finished. These women seem to think I have nothing better to do."

"I can have a talk with José. You shouldn't be doing their work for them."

"It's all right. I did worse things than this in the Comanche camp. And as I'm not an honored guest, I think it would be best if I do as much as I can."

Cruz squatted down and took Lisa's hands. "You're getting blisters. You're not used to such work."

Lisa thought of Eric's similar words in the Comanche camp, and she jerked her hands away. "I'm not a princess, Cruz. I can work as hard as any woman here. And I'll do anything it takes to get out of here alive and back to my little girl."

"And your husband."

Lisa's eyes met Cruz's. "And my husband."

Cruz nodded silently and took some clothes from the bank and began washing them in the stream. Lisa tried to take them from him but he pretended she wasn't there. "I can work as hard as the next woman," he mocked.

"Don't make fun of me."

"I'm not, I'm just trying to help you."

"You've helped me so much already. You saved Raya's life, you saved my life, and because of your influence, you have kept me with you, safe from any harm in this camp."

Cruz brushed the stray hairs from Lisa's face and put his hand in the water, gently wiping the dirt from her chin. "Have you forgotten the reason you're here?"

"How could I forget? If it hadn't been for you, my entire family might be dead."

Cruz shook his head. "Have you been in love with many men, Lisa?"

Though his question came as a surprise, Lisa answered without hesitation. "No."

"I can't believe that."

Lisa shrugged away from Cruz's touch. "Please, don't, it bothers me when you talk like that."

"I'm sorry. It's just that you're so trusting. I fooled you once before. I could do it again."

"You wouldn't do that, I'm sure of it."

"In that case . . ." Cruz picked up more clothes and began to wash them in the stream.

"Stop that!" Lisa said playfully, trying to take the clothes from his hands. "If any of these *bandidos* see you, they'll think you're afraid of me."

"But I am." Cruz looked into Lisa's eyes.

"You are not," Lisa said, slapping the dress she held in her hands against the surface of the water. Water splashed up onto Cruz.

"That wasn't a nice thing to do," he said slowly, putting down the clothing and turning to Lisa. "I think this would be a good time for you to do your own washing." He put his hands on Lisa's shoulders and pushed her into the stream. She fell on her side, her skirt going up around her legs, her long braid hanging limply over her shoulder. She sat up, looking at Cruz with angry eyes. She balled up the wet dress and threw it at him.

Cruz laughed and dodged the flying garment. He bent over and extended his hand. "Here, let me help you out."

Lisa put out her hand. "Until now you've been

129

a gentleman," she said in mock anger.

"You deserved it. Come on, you should get out of there. The water is cold."

"Lisa held on to Cruz's hand and put one foot against the bank. She pretended to stand up, but instead, she pulled with all her might. Cruz lost his balance and fell against her, into the water.

"Now, don't you feel better?" Lisa asked, a smile touching her lips.

"You're a devil." He looked at her. Water droplets ran down her face and her green eyes sparkled. The thin gauze blouse that she wore clung to her breasts and his eyes betrayed his desire. He watched as she lowered her eyes, and her demeanor changed. Her mood was no longer lively. She wasn't a stupid woman. He knew that she liked him but he was also aware that she was afraid to encourage their friendship, afraid that it might go too far. He stood up, his wet clothes clinging to his body. He offered Lisa his hand.

"How do I know I can trust you?" she asked suddenly.

"You can trust me. I would never intentionally hurt you."

Lisa took Cruz's hand and he pulled her up. She looked into his dark eyes and shivered uncontrollably.

"You're cold. Come on, I'll see if we can find something for you to change into."

"Cruz, will we ever get out of here?"

"I've bought us some time, Lisa, but I don't really know what these guys plan for us. I'm going to do everything I can to figure out a way to get us out."

Lisa nodded absently, grabbing her basket of clothes and spreading them on the rocks to dry.

When she was finished, she followed Cruz to the main camp. Women cooked and scurried about while the men sat and talked and gambled. It reminded her of the Comanche camp, where the women did most of the work, the men just sitting about all day long. She had understood after a while why the men were indulged in such a manner—they were the hunters and fighters and quite often they put their lives in danger for the rest of the tribe.

Lisa noticed that Cruz had been easily accepted into this group of thieves. She didn't know if it was because of his name or if he had persuaded them in some other way, but it was easy to see that they had accepted him as one of their own. The only things he wasn't permitted to do was ride a horse alone or carry a weapon.

"They say this man is your husband. Is that truly so?"

Lisa looked at the woman who stood next to her. It was the woman they called Josefa. She was a beautiful young woman who seemed to be extremely proficient with gun and knife. Lisa had already noticed that Josefa didn't do the chores of the other women. "No."

"Yet he protects you like a husband would a wife, why?"

"We are friends."

"Friends do not share the same shack or," Josefa shrugged her shoulders, "come back from the stream wet."

Lisa felt the blood pounding in her veins. It wouldn't be wise to get into a fight with this woman. "Cruz is my friend," she insisted.

"I think you are lying."

Lisa stepped back and stared at the woman, un-

131

able to ignore the insult. "I don't care what you think."

"Oh, but you should, señora." Josefa removed the knife from underneath her skirt and held it up to Lisa's face. "I could carve up your face so that he would never want to look at you again."

Lisa stilled the fear inside her. "You wouldn't do that, Josefa. You're not a coward."

Josefa hesitated. "You are right, I am no coward. You are a defenseless woman. Perhaps that is what he finds attractive about you, eh?" Josefa put the tip of the knife to Lisa's throat. "Are you just a little bit frightened, señora?" Josefa gave a slight gasp as she felt the tip of a knife at her throat.

"Are *you* just a little bit frightened, Josefa?" came a deep voice.

Slowly, Josefa lowered her knife to her side. She looked up at Cruz. "You are always defending this woman, why?"

"We are friends."

"And I think it is more than that. I think you are lovers."

Cruz lowered his knife and grabbed Josefa's arm. "Don't threaten her again, Josefa. I am much better with the knife than you."

"Do you always let this man do your fighting for you?" Josefa challenged Lisa.

Lisa stepped close to Josefa, her eyes looking into the woman's. "If you'd put down your knife, I would be glad to fight you."

Josefa dropped her knife on the ground. "That is easy enough."

"No!" Cruz ordered. I want you to leave her alone, Josefa."

Josefa turned on Cruz. "You cannot give orders

132

here. You are only a prisoner."

"I am only a prisoner until Vasquez arrives. Don't challenge me, Josefa, or you will lose."

Josefa looked from Cruz to Lisa and picked up her knife. "There will be a time when you are not with the señora, and then I will make sure that she understands pain."

Cruz took Lisa's hand and led her through the trees to the shack. "Stay away from her. She's a dangerous one."

"Why did you interfere?" Lisa demanded angrily. "I don't need you to defend me all of the time. I can fight if I have to."

"Do you know how to use a knife?"

"No, but . . ."

"Don't let her fool you, Lisa. She wouldn't have fought you fairly. As soon as she thought she might lose, she would've gone for her knife and killed you."

"I feel like a fool; as if I can't do anything for myself anymore."

"Listen to me," Cruz said firmly, taking her by the shoulders. "We'll get out of here as soon as we can, but until that time, you have to stay away from Josefa and any situation that might get you into trouble." He paused. "Lisa, I'm leaving here tomorrow."

Lisa's face couldn't hide the fear she felt. "What? Are you leaving me here?"

"It's not that. I'm going to talk to Vasquez one more time. I think I have an idea that will be acceptable to him."

"Can't I go with you?"

"They're not going to let you leave here, Lisa. Without you, they have nothing."

Lisa nodded absently, walking over to sit by one

133

of the trees. "You won't be coming back, will you?"

Cruz sat down next to her. "You're not listening to me. I think I have a plan to get us both out of here. Do you really think I'd leave you here after all we've been through together?"

Lisa looked at Cruz's handsome face and her resolve began to fade. She was tired and she was afraid. This man was the only person whom she could trust, and he had not let her down yet. She leaned against him and closed her eyes, unable to still the tears that came. She was glad when Cruz took her into his arms and held her. She felt comforted and safe. "I don't want you to go." The words just came out, and she couldn't believe how feeble they sounded.

Cruz pulled her against him and held her tightly, stroking her hair. She shivered slightly as a breeze blew through the trees. Their clothes were still wet and they were both acutely aware of each other. "It's all right. It will be over soon. I promise."

"What will you do then? Where will you go?"

"I will probably return to Mexico. I have a need to see my family. Then I'll go to my land."

"Why won't you let Don Alfredo help you? With his help you could have anything and you wouldn't have to be a *bandido* anymore."

"I don't want anything from Don Alfredo. He is a good man, but I do not deserve his trust. I am just like the men in this camp. The only difference is, I steal instead of kill."

"That's a big difference, Cruz."

Cruz stood. "I don't want to talk about it anymore. I'll be leaving tomorrow at sunrise and I should be back within a few days. Get up," he ordered Lisa, then placed the butt of his knife in her hand. "I'm going to show you how to use this."

"You aren't even supposed to have a knife."

"José never took it away from me after I killed Arturo. Now, hold it lightly in the palm of your hand, get the feel of the handle. You don't want to hold it too tightly or your arm will tense up. Now, swipe at me with it."

"I can't do that."

"Listen, Lisa, I want you to be able to defend yourself and you may be able to do that with your hands, but Josefa will not be using her hands."

"I don't think I can stab someone." Lisa dropped the knife. "I won't do it. Just go. Don't worry about me."

Roughly, Cruz grabbed Lisa by the shoulders. "You're not listening to me. Josefa is used to killing, and for some reason she's intent on killing you."

"And I know why. It's you. She wants you and she thinks I'm in the way."

"I'm not interested in Josefa. The only thing I'm interested in is making sure you're safe while I'm gone. You're a strong woman; you can take care of yourself if you have to." He bent down and picked up the knife. He took Lisa's hand and placed it in her palm. "Now, do what I tell you to do. Hold it lightly, like I told you, get the feel of it . . . That's good. Now, come at me."

Lisa swiped at Cruz with the knife, feeling awkward and clumsy. "I can't even get near you."

"That's because I'm watching you. I'm ready to move before you are. Don't be so quick to move, be patient. Always watch the other person."

Lisa nodded, watching Cruz intently. He circled

135

around her, making feinting movements toward her, but she continued to watch, keeping the knife held in front of her. Suddenly, Cruz came at her, and Lisa swiped at him with the knife, coming close to his stomach. But before she realized it, he was behind her, his arm around her throat.

"If I had a knife, I could slit your throat and it would be all over."

"I was afraid I'd hurt you."

"Don't worry about me." Cruz loosened his arm from Lisa's neck. "Let's try it again."

Cruz backed away from Lisa and moved around her in a circle. He feinted first to his left, then to his right, then he came at her again. Lisa swiped at him and she turned around, ready to face him. She held the knife in front of her, more confident now. She watched Cruz the entire time, even as he made more feinting movements to try to distract her. When he came at her this time, she swiped at him, ripping his shirt. She dropped the knife and ran to him.

"Cruz, I'm sorry." She tried to examine his side, but he brushed her hands away.

"I'm all right, don't worry." Blood seeped through his shirt.

"I hurt you." She stood in front of him and unbuttoned his shirt. She ripped a piece of cloth from the bottom of her skirt and pressed it against the wound. "I thought you were quick."

"I thought you were inexperienced."

"I learn quickly."

"So I see." He put his hand over the piece of garment. "I'm all right. Now pick up the knife and come here."

Lisa did as he asked and walked to him. She held the knife out to him.

"I want you to keep it. I'll make some kind of a sheath for it. Wear it under your skirt, on your thigh. It'll be hidden but easy to get to."

"Thank you for everything." Lisa reached up and touched Cruz's face. She looked at him for a moment and kissed him softly. "You're a good man, no matter what you say." She walked away.

Cruz watched her as she walked away. He winced at the pain in his side, but that didn't bother him as much as the feelings he had for Lisa. If he was around her much longer, he knew, they would grow too strong. He had to find a way to get her back home.

Cruz had been gone for three days, and Lisa was going crazy. There was no one for her to talk to in camp. The women seemed to make a point of staying away from her. She was sure Josefa had something to do with that. She hadn't seen much of the woman but Lisa still made sure to sleep with the knife by her side at night.

She took walks during the day, but only as far as the guards would let her. Often she looked up the steep, rocky cliffs, wondering if it would be possible for her to scale them and get free, but knowing it was impossible. Even if she got up, she'd have to find a way down.

By the third night, Lisa was convinced Cruz was never coming back. She didn't blame him for getting out; she would have done the same thing if she had the chance. But she missed him. Only he had given her hope. Then she thought about Eric and wondered where he was and if he was looking for her. She felt as if she hadn't seen him in an eternity. She hoped he was taking good care of

137

Raya. As melancholia overtook her, she fought back the tears. She finished her meager dinner of beans and bread, washed out her crude plate, and went to the shack.

It was dark, and very difficult to see the way at night. Cruz always knew the way; he seemed to have eyes that could see in the dark. She felt her way through the trees and saw the outline of the shack. Just as she reached the door, a hand reached out and covered her mouth, dragging her back into the trees. She fought, but her attacker was much stronger. He tied her hands behind her and gagged her, then took her arm and guided her through the thick pine trees. They walked a long time before they started downward. At one point, Lisa slipped and fell, rolling down an embankment away from her captor. She tried to get up and run, but he was there, roughly taking her arm and leading her away. Her eyes couldn't adjust to the dark. She felt disoriented and scared.

They walked for quite a while, the man never saying a word, until finally, she heard the whinny of a horse. He lifted her up onto the animal and carefully guided it through the narrow trail, managing to avoid trees and rocks. They rode for a long time, and Lisa began to tire. She felt her eyes begin to droop and she slept fitfully for a time. They reached their destination when it was still dark. Her captor pulled up and dismounted, pulling her down after him. He led her through some rocks into a small clearing. One person was sitting by a fire that she hadn't been able to see from the trail. Her captor shoved her toward it and she stumbled and fell. When she got up, she saw Josefa standing by the fire.

"So, I told you we would meet again." Josefa

walked toward her and stared at Lisa. "You think you are something special, don't you? You think because you are married to a de Vargas that gives you the right to spit on people like me?" She shoved Lisa backward. "You are nothing because I say you are nothing. No one can help you now, not even your savior. He is far away from here, probably in Mexico by now . . . She paused. "What? You look surprised. He didn't tell you that he was leaving you? Too bad, señora. It seems you were not that special to him after all." Josefa took out her knife and held it in front of Lisa's face. "Is that fear I see in your eyes?"

Lisa stared at the woman in front of her, trying to maintain some composure. She quickly took in the surroundings. As far as she could tell, it was just Josefa and the man who brought her in. Still, her hands were tied and she was helpless. Josefa seemed to like to play games with her knife. What she wanted to see was fear, that was clear, but Lisa was determined not to show any. She stared back at the woman, a cold expression in her eyes.

"You are trying to be brave, but that won't last for long. When I am through with you, you will be squealing like a pig." She shoved Lisa backward and she lost her balance and fell, a muffled sound coming from behind the gag. She looked down at her leg to make sure Josefa couldn't see the knife. It was still covered up.

Josefa knelt next to Lisa, a cruel smile on her face. "I suppose many men have told you you are beautiful." She pressed the tip of the knife into Lisa's cheek until a crimsom spot appeared. "Does that hurt, señora? It is just the beginning."

Lisa looked at Josefa's eyes, and the fear she tried to contain was beginning to overcome her.

139

The woman was mad; she genuinely enjoyed hurting people. There was nothing she could do with her hands tied, but she couldn't just lie here and let this woman cut her up. She jerked her face away from the knife and tried to sit up. Josefa had the knife at her throat before she could move. She closed her eyes. Was it going to end like this?

"Do you have something you want to say to me?" Josefa pulled the gag down.

Lisa took a deep breath and mustered what little courage she had left. "Why don't you give me a chance to fight you? I can't do anything with my hands tied."

"Don't you think I know that? If you are trying to appeal to my sense of honor, señora, it won't work. I have no honor. I do what I please. I answer to no one."

"Not even to God?"

"There is no God!" Josefa spat out angrily, grabbing Lisa's blouse and pulling her forward. "But perhaps you believe in God. If you do, I suggest you start praying to him."

Josefa pressed the knife into the flesh below Lisa's ear, running it across the jawline up to the other side. A thin red line instantly appeared.

Lisa tried to push the pain from her mind. She tried to remember how the Comanches had tolerated the pain. She recalled that when she was first captured, the men from the wagon train were burned at the stake. She didn't know how they had summoned up the courage to be so brave. "Have you ever heard of the Comanches?"

"Indios, sí?"

"Yes. I was taken captive by them once. They knew the best ways to torture people. I don't think anything you could do could be worse than what

140

they did to me," she said bravely, trying to convince herself.

Josefa seemed impressed. She lowered the knife. "You lived with these Comanches?"

"Yes."

"What did you do?"

"I was a slave. I worked for the women all day long. I did their chores for them. If I didn't do something right, I got beaten. I slept on the ground at night, tied up like a dog."

"A woman like you did this?"

"I'm not the kind of woman you think I am."

Josefa shrugged. "But I saw the way you were dressed when they brought you into camp. You look like all of the other *patrónas* I have seen." She pointed to her earrings. "Do you recognize these?"

Lisa remembered that the women had taken her earrings and sandals when she was brought into camp. For some reason, they had left her her wedding ring. "Yes."

"It does not bother you that I wear them?"

"No, they are only things."

"Then it will not bother you if I take your ring?"

Lisa tried not to react. "Why do you want my wedding ring? It means nothing to you."

"It is only a 'thing' to you. You have no need of it." Josefa reached behind Lisa and grabbed her hand, roughly pulling at her ring. Josefa held it up in the firelight. It was a thin gold band with a small diamond in the center. It was delicate and beautiful, but more than that, it represented the love she and Eric shared. She watched as Josefa slipped it on her finger and held up her hand. "Yes, I like it very much. I am surprised that a

141

husband as rich as yours did not give you a ring with more jewels."

Lisa looked away, tired of this bantering. "Are you going to kill me, Josefa?"

"I haven't decided yet. Perhaps yes, perhaps no. But even if I don't kill you, you will never see your husband again."

"Why? What will you gain by keeping me here?"

"That is not my plan. I'll have you taken somewhere, perhaps to Mexico. You could earn a living there in a whorehouse. I'm sure many men would pay for the privilege of using you."

"What about Cruz?"

"What about him? I told you, he is on his way to Mexico."

"Did you and he know each other before? Is that why you don't like me?"

"You fancy yourself too much of a prize, señora."

"I ask again, did you know him, Josefa?"

"We have met before."

"He didn't want you, did he?" Lisa said calmly, finally realizing why Josefa hated her.

Josefa quickly put the knife to Lisa's throat. "Every man who has ever known me has wanted me, do you understand?"

Lisa swallowed hard as the point of the knife pressed into her throat. "Cruz doesn't love me, Josefa. He is only my friend."

"It does not matter now, does it?" She shrugged and quickly drew the knife across Lisa's throat.

Lisa was sure that she was going to die until she realized that Josefa had inflicted only a superficial wound. Still, it was painful and it had scared her. "If you want me to say that I'm afraid, I am."

"That will not change my mind."

"What do you want from me, then? I can't harm you in any way. All I want is to go back to my daughter and husband."

"You have a daughter?"

"Yes. I don't want her to grow up without a mother." Lisa tried to appeal to the woman in Josefa.

"I'm sure a man as rich as your husband will have no trouble finding another wife. Perhaps this time, he will marry with the right blood." She pushed Lisa back and stood up. "I grow tired of this. But we will continue tomorrow. I want you to have tonight to think about it."

Lisa lay on her side, watching as Josefa walked back to the campfire. The man sat next to her, and they spoke in muffled tones. She tried to loosen her hands, but the rope that bound them was too tight. It seemed the more she moved them, the tighter the rope got. She closed her eyes. She was helpless, couldn't do anything to save herself. She would die here, alone, in pain and misery, at the hands of a woman who hated her for no rational reason. This time she let the tears flow freely, thinking it might be the last time she would be able to cry.

Lisa was yanked awake as the man pulled her to her feet. He cut the rope that bound her hands and stood behind her, watching. It had been two days since she'd been brought here, and she felt unsteady.

She rubbed her wrists, trying to get some circulation back into her numb arms. She clenched and unclenched her fists, ready to move if she had the chance. She looked around her. Josefa was nowhere to be seen. She walked toward the campfire, stooping down to warm her hands by the cooling embers. All the while the big man followed her, watching her as he would a prisoner. She wanted to sit but she wouldn't allow herself. She shook her legs, trying to loosen herself up. This might be the only chance she had to save herself. She looked at the man. *"Dónde está Josefa?"* The man stared at her blankly, not answering. She walked slowly around the camp, looking and listening. She couldn't see Josefa anywhere but that didn't mean she wasn't there. Still, she couldn't wait. She stumbled as she walked, falling to the ground. She pulled her knees to her chest, lying on her side. She drew the knife from underneath her skirt. *"Por favor, señor. Ayudame."* Lisa hoped that the man would help her, but he didn't move. She began to cry, screaming in anguish. Finally, the man came to her, stooping down to see if she was really hurt. Lisa didn't stop to think about what she was doing but thrust the knife into the man's belly, moving away as he moaned and fell forward. She reached down and pulled out the knife, also picking up the rifle that was by the fire. She backed up until she reached the rocks and looked behind her. She couldn't see anyone. Slowly, she moved from the camp, looking for the man's horse.

"Very good, señora. I didn't think you had the stomach for killing. Perhaps I underestimated you."

Lisa squinted her eyes and looked around her. "I'm leaving, Josefa."

"How will you get out of here? You don't even know the way in. It will be very easy for me to follow you and kill you. You will be like a

144

trapped animal."

Lisa looked around her. She knew that Josefa was right. She *didn't* know the mountains; it would be easy to get lost. "Then fight me here, Josefa. A fair fight, out in the open, just you and me." Lisa saw a movement from behind one of the rocks and she watched Josefa come out into the open.

"I can fight fair only if my opponent is worthy enough." Lisa stood up, still holding the rifle. "You might as well drop the rifle, señora. It has no shells."

Lisa held the rifle up and aimed at the ground near Josefa. She pressed the trigger, hearing nothing but a click. She dropped the rifle on the ground. "You don't take any chances, do you?"

"That is why I have survived for so long. Now, you want a fair fight, we will have a fair fight. We fight in the open and we each have one knife. That is it."

"Yes."

"You don't have a chance, señora. But I must say, you're much tougher than I thought you would be."

"It isn't over yet, Josefa." Lisa stood her ground, watching as Josefa took out her knife and threw it from hand to hand. Lisa was mesmerized by the knife's movements but forced herself to concentrate on Josefa.

Josefa moved slowly forward, the knife always held in front. "It is much like a dance, is it not?"

Lisa thought it was a strange thing to say but realized that it was a distraction. She watched Josefa as she began to move to the right. She felt her forearm tense up and she loosened her hold on the knife.

145

"I can cut you in many ways, señora, many ways to make you suffer." Josefa's voice was soft, almost caressing.

Lisa forced herself to concentrate. She pushed Josefa's voice from her thoughts and heard only Cruz's voice telling her what to do. She watched as Josefa feinted left, then right, then she came at her, swiping at her left arm and cutting her. Lisa didn't look down. She kept her eyes on Josefa.

"It is only the beginning, señora. It is too bad that your child will have to find another mother."

Lisa watched her, and this time she anticipated Josefa's move and jumped to the side as Josefa leaped forward, her knife meeting with nothing but air. Lisa turned and readied herself again. This time it was her turn. "You're slowing down, Josefa. It was easy to get away from you that time."

Josefa smiled, nodding her head. "You learn this game quickly. But unfortunately, not quickly enough." She moved to the side, feinting left, then right. Then she rushed Lisa, stabbing her in the side. Josefa's knife went in, but Lisa quickly pulled away, plunging her knife forward into Josefa's belly. Josefa groaned and her eyes grew large. She put her hands around the knife and stumbled slightly, then fell to the ground. Lisa put her hand over her wound and walked cautiously to the prone woman, taking the knife from her hand. She rolled her over and pulled the knife from her belly. Lisa's hand began to shake and she felt sick. She knelt next to Josefa.

"I'm sorry," she said softly, hating herself for having killed so easily twice this day, but glad that she was still alive.

"You did well, señora," Josefa said in a whisper, and then her head fell to the side. Lisa tried to stand up, but her legs were wobbly. She looked at her side. Her blouse was red. She lifted it up and looked at the wound. It was much deeper than she had realized. She walked to the campfire to get some water, but her legs gave out and she fell. She tried to get up but she was too weak. Her side throbbed uncontrollably. She thought she had beaten Josefa at her own game, but perhaps she hadn't won at all. Perhaps she, too, was going to lose.

Cruz had little trouble finding someone who knew about Josefa's hideout, for she was in the habit of taking men there. José led him along the trail and through the trees to the high rocks. José motioned him to be quiet and they dismounted. As they approached the camp, all was silent. The horses were still tethered, but no sound came from the camp. Cruz pulled out his pistol and quietly circled the camp, making sure there were no guards outside. When he was sure it was safe, he cautiously approached; As he looked through the rocks, he could see three bodies lying on the ground. He put his gun back in the holster and ran to where Lisa lay. Her side was covered with blood. He looked behind him. Josefa lay on the ground, her eyes open and blank, while a man lay close to her. He went to the campfire and found water. He took the gag from Lisa's neck and wet it, then put the cloth on the wound.

"How is she, señor?"

"I don't know. Are those two dead?"

"Sí, señor. They will not bother you again. What can I do?"

"I'm not going to move her, José." He stared

hard at the other man. "If you could bring us some food and blankets, I would be grateful." Cruz saw José's hesitation. "We won't be going anywhere, José."

José looked at Lisa. "*Sí*, I will do that, señor. And when I come back, I will bury those two."

"Thanks. Is there water around here?"

"You would have to walk quite a ways. I will bring you some."

Cruz nodded. He didn't watch José as he dragged the two bodies from the camp and then rode off. His only concern at the moment was Lisa. He walked to the horse and unsaddled it, taking the blanket from its back. He threw it on the ground and gently placed Lisa on it, then took the bandana from around his neck and wet it, wiping at the caked blood that was on her cheek, throat, and jaw. He lifted the cloth from the wound in her side; it was still oozing red. She would be weak from blood loss; he had to make sure he stilled the bleeding.

He walked outside the rocks and looked around. There were no plants that he was familiar with, and he knew from experience that it could be dangerous to put anything on the wound because it might be poisonous. He slid down a small embankment, where he spotted a bush that he recognized: yerba mansa. He pulled it out of the ground, careful to make sure it still had its roots, and climbed back up the hill. He crushed the roots and put a few leaves in the pan with the little water that was left. When it had boiled for a while, he put the crushed root in the boiled leaves and placed it in the cloth that was on Lisa's wound, making a poultice. He wet his bandana again, laying it across her forehead. He looked at her ashen face. He never should've left her alone with Josefa. She was too inexperienced. He touched the cut on her cheek, angry that he had been so stupid. Inadvertently, his hand went to the cross around his neck. It seemed inappropriate somehow that he had worn the cross for so many years. His mother had given it to him when he was a small boy, and he'd been unable to take it off since. He was convinced that the cross watched over him and kept him from harm. He touched it and lifted it over his head, then slipped it gently over Lisa's head until it was around her neck. "May it bring you luck, *querida*," he said softly. He watched as she lay there, defenseless and weak, and all he could do was wait.

Lisa tried to sit up, but a pain shot through her side. "God," she moaned, lying back down immediately.

"Lisa," Cruz said soothingly. He knelt next to her, his hand on hers. "How do you feel?"

"Terrible." She looked up at the dark sky. "Where am I?"

"You are in Josefa's camp. Do you remember?"

Lisa looked around at the dim outline of the rocks and it all came back to her. "Josefa?"

"She's dead. So is the man who brought you here."

"I can't believe it."

"You killed them both. I don't know how you did it, but you managed to save yourself."

Lisa turned her head away. "I don't feel very proud. I feel sick."

Cruz squeezed her hand. "Killing is not easy, but you had no choice. Would you rather be in

149

Josefa's place now?"

Lisa turned her face back to Cruz. "No." She looked at him in the firelight. "So, here you are again. How did you manage to find me?"

"It wasn't that difficult to get someone to tell me where Josefa took you. In fact, José was more than willing. He had been here before with Josefa and she had cut him with the knife."

"God, it hurts. I used to see Comanche warriors come back to camp with spearheads in their sides and they never uttered a sound. They were always so brave."

"You're not a Comanche," he said. "The bleeding has stopped. I think you'll be all right as long as you stay still for a couple of days."

Lisa felt the strange lump on her wound. "What is it?"

"It's just a mixture that I learned about a long time ago. It usually stops bleeding. Lisa, how did you get the other knife wound?"

"What?" Lisa's voice sounded startled.

Cruz put his finger on an area below Lisa's heart. "Right here, you have a scar from a knife. How did you get it?"

Lisa stared past Cruz into the fire. "I did it to myself." Lisa looked at Cruz. "I was a coward. I want to tell you about it. I had been in the Comanche camp for quite a while. I was living as Nakon's wife and I was carrying his child. He left to lead a raid. We had gotten in a fight because I didn't want him to go. When the other warriors returned without him, they said that he was dead. I waited for over a month but he didn't return. I was afraid to live alone with the Comanches, and I was afraid to have my child and return to the white world. I just didn't want to live." Lisa

150

turned her face away from the fire, ashamed of the tears that rolled down her face, ashamed of the story she was telling Cruz. "I was by the river, near a place where Nakon and I always went. The man who originally took me captive followed me. He said he wanted to help me, but I didn't believe him. I was holding my knife in my hand. When he rushed forward to take the knife from me, I stabbed myself. Nakon finally came back, but I lost the child. After that, he sent me back to my people. I thought I'd lost him forever."

Cruz took his bandana and wiped the tears from Lisa's face. "It doesn't matter now. You are married to him. He loves you."

"Then why does it feel as though I'll never see him again?"

The pain in Lisa's voice cut through Cruz's heart. "Don't give up, Lisa. I'll find a way to get you back to your husband."

"Did you talk to Vasquez? Is he going to let us go?"

"We'll talk about it later, when you feel better."

"I know he won't let us go," she said sadly. "It's me, isn't it? You can probably go anytime you want. He just won't let me go."

"We'll talk about it later, I said." Cruz lifted up Lisa's blouse and removed the poultice. He examined the wound and put the poultice back on it. "Keep this on for tonight. I'll make another one tomorrow."

"Why are you here?" she asked suddenly. "The more I think about it, the more I realize that you could've left anytime you wanted. You're practically one of them. I saw the look on José's face when he found out who you were. You're famous; they look up to you. You're not a captive, are

151

you, Cruz?"

Cruz picked up a rock from the ground and rolled it between his fingers. "I suppose I could leave if I really wanted to, but I won't do that."

"Because of me."

"Yes."

"It's not right. You should go. There's no reason for you to stay here."

"There's all the reason in the world. It's my fault that you're here. If I leave, your life will be in constant danger. Look what happened in the three days I was gone. I won't let that happen to you again."

"You aren't responsible for me, Cruz."

"I won't leave you until you're back home."

Lisa tried to move but cried out in pain. Cruz tried to help her, but she shoved his hand away. "Don't. Just leave me alone." She put her arm over her face to cover the tears. She had never felt so embarrassed in her life. This man knew everything about her, he had seen her in the worst possible condition, and he cared for her as if . . . She was afraid to continue the thought. As she turned her head, she felt something fall against her chin. She reached down and lifted up the cross that Cruz had put around her neck. She knew it was his. She looked up and found him staring at her, and she knew she couldn't hide from him anymore. She knew that he was falling in love with her, and what scared her even more, she was beginning to have strong feelings for him. She wrapped her fingers around the cold metal of the cross and prayed to herself that this would be over soon and she would be back home where she belonged, with her daughter and her husband. The trust she had for Cruz was beginning to turn into something more, and it frightened her. She didn't think she had the strength to fight it anymore.

Chapter 7

Cruz handed Lisa a cup of coffee, then bent down and checked her wound. It was healthy and pink-looking around the edges. It was healing nicely. "It looks good. How are you feeling?"

"Much better. I bet I could even ride if I had to."

Cruz knelt on the ground, resting his hands on his thighs. "What is that supposed to mean?"

"Why can't we just ride out of here?"

"Do you honestly think there's no one watching us? There's a man just below the horses, and they probably have more all around here. They're just not going to let us leave, Lisa."

"You mean *me*." Lisa grimaced as she tried to sit up against the large rock that was behind her. "You said when I was better you'd tell me what Vasquez said. Well, now I'm better."

Cruz ran his hands along his thighs. "You're not going home, Lisa."

"What? But you promised, Cruz. You said—"

"I know what I said, Lisa, but I was bargaining with your life. I did the best I could."

"So, is Vasquez going to kill me?"

"No, but he's going to send you away."

154

"Where?"

"He's going to send you south."

"Why?" Lisa tried to sit up but moved too quickly. Pain shot up her side and she bent forward, her hand over her wound. Cruz was at her side, embracing her. Lisa put her arms around his neck, resting her face in his chest. "Why is he doing this to me? He doesn't even know me."

Cruz ran his hand up and down Lisa's back, trying to calm her. "It has nothing to do with you. You, unfortunately, are caught in the middle."

"Where will he send me?"

"To a ranch near San Diego. It's very beautiful there. You will like it."

"You've seen it?"

"Yes."

"I'm afraid, Cruz. I'm so afraid." She wrapped her arms around his neck.

"It'll be fine. I'll take care of you, I promise."

"What about my little girl? Are you sure she's all right?"

"Yes, she is well. They have no interest in her."

"And Don Alfredo?"

"Well, also. He helped me to bargain."

Lisa pulled back, carefully leaning back against the rock. "I don't understand."

Cruz sat down next to Lisa. "You won't like this, but it doesn't matter. It's over and done with for now. General Vasquez wanted all of the Rancho del Sol and Rancho del Mar in exchange for you."

"Don Alfredo didn't give them to him, did he?"

"No, he got something else instead."

"What?"

"I gave him some land that I have here."

"How much?"

155

"A thousand acres."

"No!"

"I had no choice, Lisa. Then Don Alfredo added to it by two thousand more acres. Vasquez wasn't quite convinced so I offered him some money."

"How much money?"

"Five thousand dollars."

"Where would you get that kind of money?"

Cruz smiled. "Have you already forgotten what I do for a living?"

"Oh. Did he accept it?"

"Not quite. For some reason, you make him nervous. He wants you out of the way."

"You mean 'dead'?"

Cruz nodded. "But I suggested something else. I suggested that as soon as you were well, I take you south to my rancho near San Diego and keep you there."

"For how long?"

"Until I know it's safe."

"That was acceptable to him?"

"Yes. In fact, we'll leave in one week, whether you're well or not. Some of his men will accompany us, just to make sure we don't turn around and go back to Monterey."

"I don't understand. None of this makes sense. Why does he want me out of the way? I'm not a threat to him."

"No, no immediate threat, but if you're out of the way, he can be assured that Don Alfredo will give him the land and not inform the authorities. He has told Don Alfredo that if he keeps his word, you will be safe and will be returned in one year."

"I don't understand why he just didn't take the

del Sol and del Mar. They are much more valuable."

"I persuaded him that that wouldn't be wise, as Don Alfredo is a very influential and powerful man. I told him he might not live to enjoy the land if he took it. He understood that taking my land and the land that Don Alfredo was willing to give him was a much better solution."

"One year," Lisa murmured softly. How much would Raya be grown in one year? Would she even recognize her mother in a year? And what about Eric? Would he wait for her or would he find someone new? She shook her head, not able to believe that this was happening. "It isn't fair."

"I know it isn't fair, but it was all that I and Don Alfredo could do to save your life. It'll go by quickly."

Lisa couldn't contain her smile. "You make it sound as if it's a holiday."

"Well, there are worse places you could be going."

"So, you've saved me again. It seems I owe you my life over and over again."

"How many times do I have to tell you, you owe me nothing." Cruz stood up. "Finish your coffee. I will bring you some stew. We must get some meat on your bones before the week is up. You need to build up your strength before you can travel."

"Cruz, I want to know something and I want to know the truth. I need to know if you still are in on this whole thing?"

Cruz's dark eyes squinted slightly, as if trying to see into Lisa's mind. "I have done many things, Lisa, but I would never take a woman away from her child and husband, especially when she loves

157

them both so much." He strode away angrily.

"Cruz, wait," Lisa implored, but he was across the camp and gone. She laid her head back against the rock, trying to move without activating the pain. So, he was no longer involved with Vasquez. She wondered why the general wanted her out of the way. Why so far south? She wondered if it was Cruz's suggestion. She wondered so much about Cruz. He admitted to being a bandit, he admitted that he was involved with Vasquez in the beginning, yet he was such a kind, gentle man. She didn't know what to think anymore.

"Can I help you, señora? You seem like you are in a great deal of pain." José had come from behind her. He had taken a liking to Cruz and had stayed with him.

"No, thank you, José. I just can't seem to get comfortable."

José walked to his horse and came back carrying his saddle. "Perhaps this will help. Can you lean forward?"

Lisa leaned slightly forward as José propped the saddle between her and the rock. She leaned back against the soft seat of the saddle. It felt heavenly. "José, you are a genius. I don't know how to thank you."

"No thanks. It is good to see you smile."

"Can I ask you something?"

José shrugged his shoulders. *"Sí."*

"Do you know anything about Cruz? Is he really a bandit?"

José found a comfortable rock, one big enough to accommodate his rather large posterior, and he sat down. *"Sí,* he is Joaquin the Younger. I know this for sure."

"How do you know?"

"I have seen the scar."

"What scar?"

"It is said that Joaquin the Younger got in a terrible knife fight with another *bandido,* one named El Diablo. El Joaquin never liked El Diablo because he was a murderer. Well," José leaned forward, looking around him, "they ran into each other once in a cantina in Mexico. El Diablo said some bad things about Joaquin, but Joaquin just walked away. El Diablo didn't like that, so he took out his knife and attacked Joaquin from behind. Joaquin heard a woman scream and he turned away, but El Diablo still got Joaquin in the side." José looked down at Lisa's covered wound. "Very much in the same place as yours. Anyway, it is said that El Joaquin fought bravely, even as the blood poured from his side. El Diablo tried many tricks. He cut Joaquin so badly in his arm, it looked as though it was split open, they say. But Joaquin was able to overcome El Diablo and kill him. People have loved him for it ever since, because El Diablo was an evil man, just like his name, a devil."

"But how do you know it was Cruz? Many men have been in knife fights."

"It is also said that Joaquin the Younger carries a tattoo on his left shoulder." José smiled proudly. "I have seen it."

"What is the tattoo?"

"It is a woman's name."

"What name is it?"

"Soleda. The lonely one."

"Was he in love with this woman?"

"It is said that he loved her more than life itself, but she did not feel the same way about him."

"What happened?"

159

"She ran away with another man. El Diablo."

"That's enough, José." Cruz's voice cut through the camp like a knife.

José quickly got up and walked out of the camp.

Cruz knelt down by the fire and spooned some stew for Lisa onto a clean plate. He looked at her before he handed her the plate. "What did he tell you about me?"

"Not much." She gratefully accepted the plate and spooned the stew into her mouth. "It's very good. Thank you."

"You must be feeling better. You haven't eaten like this since you got hurt."

"You're a good cook."

"I had to learn early, with five brothers and sisters. My mother made me do everything including the cooking. But she always saved something special for me."

"What will you do with me, Cruz?"

Lisa's question caught him by surprise. He didn't know quite what to say.

"I know General Vasquez turned me over to you."

"How do you know that?"

"You must think I'm a very stupid woman. I am of no worth by myself. I can't do anything for Vasquez."

"You are married to the heir of one of the largest land grants in Alta California. Vasquez wants land. He keeps you, Don Alfredo and your husband sign over all of their land to him, then he gives you back."

"But you said he wanted more than the land. That's why you had to bargain with him."

"Land is good, but he wants money and he

160

wants it now. Money will allow him to raise an army and supply it with guns. Now I've told you everything there is to know."

"You haven't told me what you're going to do with me."

"I'm going to take care of you until you go back to your husband."

"Damn it, Cruz, tell me the truth! That first night I got hurt, when you came back, I could tell by the look on your face that there was something you had to tell me but couldn't yet. I can take it now. Tell me the truth."

Cruz stood up, a strange look on his face. "All right, I won't deceive you anymore. The marriage between you and your husband will be dissolved."

"What?" Lisa tried to sit up straighter, but the pain prevented her from doing so. She cried out slightly. Cruz tried to help her, but she pushed him away. "What did you just say?"

"I said that your marriage will be dissolved."

"Why? I don't understand."

Cruz paced back and forth. "Vasquez intends to return you to your husband, but until he does, he wants you under his control. Originally, he wanted you to ride with him. I wouldn't allow that. The only other idea that was acceptable to him was if you were married and living in San Diego with me."

"No," Lisa protested. "I won't do it. You can't make me!"

Cruz stopped pacing and crouched next to Lisa. "You have no choice, do you understand? Either you marry me, or you go with Vasquez and his men. Do I have to tell you what that means?"

Lisa's eyes dropped. She couldn't look at Cruz. He took her chin in his fingers and forced her head up. "If you were to go with Vasquez, it would be worse than it was for you in the Comanche camp because there would be no Nakon to save you."

Lisa jerked her chin away and forced herself not to cry. "And how am I to marry you when I am married to another man?"

"Vasquez will bring a mission priest to his camp. He will dissolve your present marriage and then marry us."

"That can't be legal."

"Vasquez thinks it is, and that's all that matters."

"Was it your idea that I marry you?"

"I told you, I couldn't think of anything else. Vasquez was in no mood for bargaining. I told him that if you were my wife, I could keep my eye on you. I also told him that your husband loves you very much and would pay highly to get you back, whether you were married to me or not. I told him it was the best way to make your husband suffer."

"You bastard. You had no right to do that."

"I had every right. I was fighting for your life."

"And when are we to be married?"

"The day we leave here. We'll ride to Vasquez's camp, the ceremony will be performed, and we'll ride south."

"Maybe I'll die of blood poisoning if I'm lucky," Lisa mumbled loudly enough for Cruz to hear. She closed her eyes and ignored him. She didn't want to talk to him anymore. She was angry with him, yet she wasn't. She knew he had done the only thing he could to save her life. She knew that he could have ridden out of the camp weeks ago, yet he hadn't. He had stayed to be with her. He

162

was a true friend, a friend who would soon be her husband.

She and Eric had faced so much to be together, and now they would be separated again. She didn't know what to do. She felt a gentle hand on her cheek and almost cried. How did he always know what to do? She opened her eyes. His strong, handsome face was close to hers. She could feel his breath on her cheek.

"I promised you that I would take you back to your daughter and husband. I will not break that promise." He looked at her for a moment longer, then pressed his mouth to hers, lingering for only a short, sweet second.

Lisa watched him walk away. She felt an extraordinary pain, only it wasn't a pain in her side. It was a pain in her heart. It felt as if it were being cut in two and she could do nothing about it.

Lisa eased herself into the water, clenching her teeth. Though the water was cold, she hadn't washed in ages and it felt good. Her wound was still healing, so she had to move carefully. She walked to the deepest part of the stream and stooped down so that the water would cover her. She let her head fall back until her long, chestnut-colored hair was completely wet. She had no soap but she ran her fingers through her hair trying to get the dirt out, wetting it again then submerging her body until she touched the sandy bottom of the stream. She felt clean and she felt free.

She ran her hands over her body, wiping the dirt and sweat from it, then stood up and looked at the knife wound in her side. It was still ugly and slightly swollen, but it was healing well. She touched it lightly, then ran her fingers up to the old scar under her breast. Her fingers traced the ugly scar and she was reminded of how desperate she had felt that day. She had been willing to take a knife and stick it into her own body; she had been willing to take her own life. She swore right then, that no matter what happened in the future, no matter how lonely or desperate she felt, she would never hurt herself like that again.

She stayed in the water for a while longer, enjoying the feeling of freedom. She was able to move around in it without it causing her much pain and she scrunched the sandy bottom between her toes, reveling in the sensation. It was good to be alive, even if she couldn't be with her family.

"You look happy," a voice interrupted.

Lisa sat down in the water, quickly turning around. "What do you want?"

"I don't want anything. You wandered off and I wanted to make sure you were safe."

Lisa held her arms in front of her, shielding herself from Cruz's scrutiny. "Don't you have something to do?"

Cruz sat down, leaning back on his arms and stretching his long legs out in front of him. "Not really. My main concern is making sure that you're safe."

Lisa's back was getting tired. The water wasn't deep enough for her to stand in it and the only way she could remain covered up was to squat on the bottom of the stream. She looked at Cruz's bemused expression; she was sure he was enjoying her discomfiture. "Would you please leave so I can get out of here?"

"Why should I leave? All I have to do is close

my eyes. Believe what I say. If I tell you I'm going to close my eyes, I'm going to close my eyes. You can trust me with your life, remember?"

Lisa didn't like Cruz's tone. It didn't sound like he was going to leave. "Can't I be by myself?"

"It's dangerous for a woman to be by herself out here, you know that."

"Yes, I might float downstream," Lisa replied angrily, splashing the water. "Cruz, please turn around. My side is hurting me and I want to get out."

Cruz sat up and turned around. "Come out slowly. You don't want to open up that wound again."

Lisa stood up and walked to the bank, grabbing her clothes. She pulled on her gauze skirt and blouse but they stuck to her wet body. She tried to pull the material away but it didn't help. She carefully sat down next to Cruz, folding her arms in front of her chest. Her long hair hung down her back, away from her face, accentuating her large green eyes.

"Are you done?"

"Yes."

Cruz turned around and propped himself up on his side. He disinterestedly pulled a piece of wild grass and began to chew on it, but his mind and body were going crazy. Lisa looked beautiful. She looked delicate yet strong, and he wanted to take her into his arms and make love to her right there. He kept chewing on the grass. "Do you feel better?"

"Yes." She reached up and wrung her hair out, shaking her head as she did so. She realized that her breasts were outlined by the wet blouse and she quickly dropped her arms.

165

"Why are you so jumpy around me?"

"Maybe it has something to do with the fact that you're a complete stranger and I've been with you for over two months. Or maybe it's that I've just found out you're going to be my husband."

"In name only. As soon as I'm able, I'll take you back home."

"So you say."

"Of course, I could tell Vasquez that you want to stay with him. I'm sure he'd like nothing better than the company of a beautiful young woman for all those long, lonely nights on the trail."

"That's not fair."

"That's the way it is. You wouldn't listen to me before, so now I'll tell you the way it is with Vasquez and men like him. They don't know anything about honor; they aren't like your husband. The only thing Vasquez would want you for is his bed at night. Once he fell asleep, for he is a very old man, the younger men would come for you. You spoke once of how you hated your life in the Comanche camp until your husband saved you. I am not your husband, Lisa, but I *can* save you from this humiliation if you will let me. I won't harm you, nor will I force you to do anything that is against your will. But if you stay here—"

"All right. You don't have to tell me anymore. I see what a hero you are." As soon as the words were out, Lisa regretted them.

Cruz's dark eyes burned, and he got up, shaking off Lisa's grip on his arm. "I have gone to a lot of trouble for you. I could have been to Mexico to visit my family and back to my rancho in San Diego by now. I am wondering why I bothered to help you at all."

"Cruz, wait." Lisa stood up, not caring how she

166

looked. "I'm sorry. I don't want to hurt you. I am grateful for everything you've done for me."

"I have a life also, Lisa. I think you've forgotten that. I have a rancho and people who depend on me. I have been away for a long time. If you decide to come with me, I will extend every hospitality to you, but I don't want you making my life miserable. I don't love you and you don't love me. So, we will just have to put up with each other for a while."

Lisa didn't expect this reaction from Cruz and, for some reason, it hurt her. She turned away, afraid that he would see the hurt in her face. "I understand." She felt as if she didn't fit in anywhere anymore. Tears flooded her eyes and she began to walk along the bank downstream. She was mildly aware of the pain in her side as she walked, but she ignored it. She hadn't expected Cruz to berate her in such a manner, and it had taken her off guard. He would put up with her as though she were an unwelcome guest and nothing more. But what did she expect? She *wasn't* anything more.

As she walked along the bank, she tripped on a rock and stumbled to the ground. She cried out as she felt her wound open. She looked down and saw the blood ooze out. She was surprised at the pain. Her head fell back on the ground and she closed her eyes. Where was her life, she wondered? Where did she belong?

She heard Cruz's voice and she opened her eyes. "I'm sorry."

"Be quiet. I'm going to carry you back to camp."

"No. I want to stay here. Please." She closed her eyes again. Her body relaxed as she felt Cruz minister over her. He pushed up her blouse and poured handfuls of water on the wound, then pressed his bandana against it.

"That was a stupid thing to do. You're a silly woman."

"I know." She felt Cruz's hand on her forehead as he pushed her hair back from her face. He wet his hands again and rubbed her face, cooling her off. "Why are you so nice to me?"

"I don't know," he replied softly. "How does it feel?"

"Better. You should be a doctor."

Cruz laughed. "I don't think so. I make a better bandit than I do a doctor."

Lisa opened her eyes. Cruz's hand was still on her forehead. She took it between her two hands. "Tell me about Soleda."

Cruz's face tensed. He tried to pull his hand away but she gripped it tightly. "No."

"Please. I've told you about my life."

"I owe you nothing. I've paid you back for what I've done."

"I know that." And Lisa knew that he was right. She released his hand and turned her head away. How could she care so much for this man? How was it possible that he could make her cry when she barely even knew him? A tear traced a path across her cheek and she felt his finger gently wipe it away.

"Do not cry. It makes me sad."

"I didn't think anything made you sad."

"Many things make me sad."

"Is Soleda one of them?" Lisa turned back to him. She could tell by the look in his eyes that he was no longer angry.

"Yes."

168

"Was she your lover?"

"She was more than that. She was my wife."

"Did you love her very much?"

"I loved her enough to kill for her," he said angrily, looking away.

"That is a strong love."

"That is a destructive love."

"I'm sorry. I shouldn't have asked."

"But you wanted to know, didn't you?" Cruz was staring angrily into Lisa's eyes. "I was nineteen years old. I had been on my own since I was eleven. I had been a bandido for some time and I was making money. There was a small town near my village in Mexico. I passed through it on my way home. I went into the cantina for a drink and I saw Soleda. She took my very breath away. She was like a fresh breeze blowing through the hot, dusty town. Men hovered around her like flies to an open wound, but she came to me. I was young and had not had much experience with women, and it showed. She took me to a table. I bought a bottle of tequila and we drank until we were both senseless. She took me to her hut and we made love." His eyes burned as he spoke. "It was unlike anything I had ever experienced. I remember that my body ached for her, but she teased me so. She danced for me. She made me sit on her small bed and watch her until I couldn't stand it any longer. I reached for her but still she resisted me. She laid me down on the bed and grabbed a bowl, gently wiping my face with a cool rag. Then she took off my shirt and she began to wipe my chest. Then she made love to me. When I awoke, she was gone."

"She was gone?"

Cruz nodded. "I got up and went back to the

169

cantina, but she wasn't there. So I waited. I waited all night, but she didn't come. As I was leaving the next morning, I saw her on the road walking toward town. She had a way about her. She stood with one hand on her hip, a smile on her lips, and she held her hand out to me. I lifted her up behind me and we rode to a secluded place. I don't think I was a very gentle lover," Cruz said with little embarrassment, "but I wanted her so badly. We were together all day. Finally, it was time for me to go. She asked to go with me. I told her I couldn't take her but that I would come back for her. She got angry and hit me. I remember grabbing her, wanting to shake her, but I wound up making love to her again. I took her with me to meet my family, and it was a mistake. She didn't want to love a poor man. She wanted to find a rich man who would take her away from her sad life. She stayed with my family for less than a week. I woke up one morning to find my gun and horse gone, as well as my mother's silver cross, which hung on the wall next to our family's crucifix. My father was so angry, he asked me to leave. I haven't been back since. It's been five years now. I write to my sister and I send her money. She gives it to my father and tells him that I am doing well. I am hoping that I can get him to come visit me in San Diego. He would like it there."

"What happened to Soleda?" Lisa asked.

"Ah, Soleda found a man who had more money than I. He, too, was a *bandido* but he was a murderer as well. We met up in a cantina months later. She was wearing my mother's cross. She was dancing with this man. I walked over to them, pushed him away, and ripped the cross from her neck."

Lisa's fingers went up to the cross hanging on the silver chain around her neck. "This is your mother's, isn't it?"

"Yes." Lisa started to lift it from around her neck but Cruz stopped her. "No, I want you to wear it. It will protect you."

"But it was your mother's, Cruz. She would want you to wear it."

"No, she would want it to protect whoever needed it."

Lisa ran her fingers over the polished silver of the cross and she thought of Cruz's mother. "Was she pretty, your mother?"

Cruz's face lit up. "She was beautiful. She always had a kind word for everybody and enough food for an extra person. When she died, the priest said God had called my mother to heaven because she was truly an angel. I hated him for saying that at the time but now I believe it was true. My mother was an angel. I have never met a more pure soul in my life."

"You're very lucky," Lisa said sadly.

"What of your parents? You told me you came from the East to be with your brother."

"My father killed himself. Later on, my mother married a very rich man. She never really cared about us, she just cared about the money."

"That can't be true."

"It is true. That's why Tom left. He couldn't take it anymore, and that's why I decided to leave. When Tom wrote and told her that I had been captured by Indians, she replied that it would probably be better if I were killed than to come back alive after living with savages. I knew long ago what was really important in her life. I swore if I ever had a child, I would let it know that I loved it beyond all else, no matter what." Lisa thought of Raya and tears filled her eyes. She squeezed her eyes shut and turned her head away.

"It's all right, don't be ashamed. You love your daughter and you miss her very much. I would think you strange if you didn't."

Lisa wiped her face and looked at Cruz. "I don't understand you."

"There is nothing to understand."

"Oh, I think there is much to understand, but, tell me, what happened to Soleda?"

"That night I got in a fight with her lover, El Diablo. He came at me with a knife and I killed him. Soleda didn't even look at him. She followed me out of the cantina, claiming to love me. I couldn't argue with her. I was bleeding to death. She took care of me and nursed me back to health. When I was well, I determined to marry her. I took her to my rancho and she fell in love with it. We went to the mission and we were married by a priest.

"The rancho was still small but it was beautiful. We spent our wedding night making love under the stars. We lived for a time without any troubles. I think she was beginning to fall in love with me. We had been married for six months when she told me that she was carrying our child. She was not happy about it. She said it would ruin her figure. I told her I would love her even more if she had our child." He laughed derisively. "I found her two days later in the arms of one of my vaqueros. I almost killed the man with my bare hands until I realized that Soleda had wanted it to happen. She told me she hated me and our life together, and that she wouldn't bear any child of mine. I locked her in our room. I told her she could leave after she had the child. That was the biggest mistake of my life. I heard a horrible scream that night and ran to the room. She had used a poker to make herself lose the child. She almost died, she lost so much blood. When she recovered, I asked her to leave. I haven't seen her since."

"I am sorry, Cruz. She was a stupid woman."

"I think she was smart. I have nothing to give a woman. You see, Lisa, I am not like your husband. I have no heritage, I have nothing but what I've stolen." He started to get up, but Lisa grabbed his arm.

"Please, don't go yet. I don't want to stay here alone. I'm in pain," she lied. She didn't want him to be alone and she didn't want to be alone. They needed to be together.

Cruz carefully checked Lisa's wound. "The bleeding has stopped. I can carry you back to camp now."

"No, I want to stay here. It's lovely." She took his hand, entwining her fingers with his. "You're my guardian angel, Cruz, and there's nothing you can do about it." She closed her eyes and tried to keep from smiling.

"Don't be foolish." Cruz jerked his hand away.

"It's true. You saved Raya's life the first minute you rode up, and I can't count the number of times you've saved my life since."

"I don't like this kind of talk."

"Why, because I'm telling you good things about yourself? You're not used to that, are you? You're used to your father telling you you're worthless and your wife telling you you can't give her the things she wants. Well, I'm not either one of them, but I think I know you better than they do. You're a good, decent man, who has given up everything for the last two months to help me."

Cruz looked embarrassed. "We should be getting back now."

"Cruz, listen to me. The only way I can think of to repay you is to make the time I'm with you easy. I'll try not to be a problem. When we're at your rancho, I'll help. I can work around the house and I can help the vaqueros. I'm very good on a horse, you know. I promise, you won't be sorry you took me along."

Cruz stood up and left Lisa without a word. He walked into the thicket and stopped, leaning against one of the trees. If she only knew what she was saying. He had longed for a woman like her to say the things she was saying to him right now. He was falling in love with her. Now what was he going to do?

Lisa looked around her as they rode into Vasquez's camp. It was a ramshackle place near the rocks, and the few belongings that the men and women carried with them were the only signs of permanence. The only thing that seemed out of place was a large tent that was set at the edge of camp. She assumed it was Vasquez's. She was frightened but tried not to show it. She knew that this old man held her future in his hands. If he wanted to, he could have her killed this very day.

Cruz stopped and dismounted. He walked back to Lisa and lifted her down. It had only been a week since the stabbing, and she was still very sore. Cruz took her hand and led her past the staring people.

She looked down at herself and smiled. Cruz had given her one of his shirts to wear with the skirt. He had told her to braid her hair tightly off of her face. He didn't want her to look feminine, he'd said, because he didn't trust Vasquez. So Lisa had pulled her hair back severely from her face and braided it tightly, wrapping it until it caught in a knot. She slipped on Cruz's shirt and wore it so that it hung limply over her skirt. It showed little of her figure. She and Cruz were both convinced that she didn't look very pretty.

Cruz stopped and talked to a guard in rapid Spanish. He turned to Lisa. "We'll have to wait a while. Vasquez is with a woman." He led her to a spot where they could sit down.

"How old is he?"

"Sixty-four."

"Sixty-four! Isn't that a little old for—"

"Don't say that around here. The general fancies himself quite a ladies' man. Whatever you do, don't speak unless you're spoken to. Don't smile. Stay behind me."

"You're scaring me." Lisa clutched Cruz's hand a little tighter.

"It'll be all right . . . Why don't you rest. You can use it. You shouldn't even be riding."

"I don't need to rest."

"Don't argue with me." Cruz forced Lisa's head onto his shoulder and he put his arm around her.

She found herself feeling quite comfortable in his arms, in spite of all the noise of the camp. She closed her eyes. She realized suddenly how much this reminded her of the Comanche camp. It was always noisy there, but she had gotten used to it. Before she knew it, she drifted off to sleep . . .

After what seemed an eternity, she felt Cruz

175

shake her and she opened her eyes. A man stood in front of them. She held Cruz's hand as he pulled her up. They walked together to Vasquez's tent. They heard giggling and laughter, and paused but the guard told them to go in.

Vasquez was sitting in an old tub filled with water. A young woman was busily washing him as he laughed uproariously, chomping on a large cigar and wearing nothing but his sombrero. The sight of the old man in the tub was enough to make anyone laugh.

"Ah, Joaquin, you are here. Good." He squinted his eyes and looked at Lisa. "Come forward, girl. I can hardly see you." Lisa looked at Cruz and he nodded. She stepped forward. "What is this, Cruz? I expected more of a de Vargas. No wonder the man has not demanded a ransom."

"General, I explained why de Vargas has not demanded a ransom. He has been gone for quite some time. He is very much in love with his wife, that much I can tell you."

"I hope you have better taste, Joaquin. This woman could not excite a rattlesnake." He looked at Lisa again, shaking his head back and forth. "Are you sure you want to marry her? Maybe it would just be easier to kill her."

"No, General, I will marry her. She minds well and she works hard." Cruz didn't look at Lisa as he spoke.

Vasquez shrugged his shoulders. "It is your decision then. The padre should be here soon. Then you will be married." He looked at Lisa again, a disgusted expression on his face. "Are you sure you can't do anything with her? What if you take her hair down and put her in a dress?"

Cruz shook his head. "It does no good, General. She has no figure; it is better covered up. And her hair looks like tumbleweed when it is down. She is much better this way."

"As you wish." The general laughed and took the girl's hand and rubbed it over his chest. "It is too bad you don't have this one instead, eh?"

"*Sí*, General. But in my own way, I will make de Vargas suffer." He grabbed Lisa and roughly pulled her forward. "For some unknown reason he loves this woman, so I will make sure she is not the same woman when she goes back to him. *Me entiendes?*"

"*Sí, sí,*" Vasquez laughed. He pointed his finger at Cruz. "You are a clever one, Joaquin. De Vargas will die every time he looks at his woman. He will wonder what you have done to her."

"*Sí*, General. We will leave you alone now. I thank you for everything you have done."

"It was my pleasure, Joaquin. Have my men call me when the padre arrives. I will get great joy in watching this marriage ceremony."

"*Sí*," Cruz said, yanking Lisa's arm and pulling her along with him. "Pig," he muttered under his breath.

Lisa wrenched her arm away. "What did you say?"

"I said the old bastard is a pig. If I hadn't made you look like you did, he would've kept you for himself. You're lucky his eyes aren't any better. Did you see the way he kept squinting at you?"

Cruz was breathing heavily and Lisa was afraid to pursue the subject when he was so angry. She lightly touched his shoulder. "What is it? There's something else wrong."

"I don't like this treachery. If there was just another way."

"Cruz, it's all right. Eric will understand when you take me back. And I understand. I would be dead without you."

"I just don't like it. I don't trust him. He's a dangerous old bastard. He's shot more than one man in the back."

"Did you have to say my hair looked like tumbleweed?" Lisa asked out of the blue.

Cruz finally smiled. "I couldn't think of anything else. I wanted him to believe that you're ugly, but I'm not quite sure I convinced him."

"You worry too much. Can we sit down?"

Cruz took Lisa's hand and they walked to the same spot where they had sat before. "You're in pain, aren't you?"

"A little. It keeps throbbing." Lisa laid her head on his shoulder as if it were the most natural thing in the world to do. "Thank you, Cruz. Again."

Cruz ran his hand along Lisa's shoulder and up to her neck. His fingers rubbed her soft skin. He looked at her. Her eyes were closed and she seemed content. She was so beautiful. If only Vasquez knew how wrong he had been about her. If he only knew that Lisa was one of the most stunning women he'd ever seen in his life. But that didn't matter now. What mattered was getting out of this camp alive.

"Señor, wake up."

Cruz opened his eyes. One of Vasquez's guards was kicking his boot. "The priest is here?"

"Sí. The general wants you and the woman to come now."

Cruz nodded. He pulled his arm from around

178

Lisa. "Come on, Lisa, wake up. It's time."

Lisa opened her eyes and rubbed at them. She started to stand but grabbed her side. "I need help."

Cruz put his arms around her and lifted her to her feet. "I want to check that later. It should be healing better." He brushed her cheek and smiled. "You look too pretty after you sleep. I'm afraid Vasquez will notice."

"All Vasquez will notice is that you are stuck with an ugly, shapeless woman."

They followed the guard to the other side of the camp. A padre in a long brown tunic was seated on a rock, drinking liberally from a cup. He looked up when Cruz and Lisa approached.

"This is the bride and groom?"

"Yes," Cruz answered.

"Am I to understand that the bride is already married to someone else? You know this goes against everything the Church preaches?"

Cruz knelt, his eyes level with the priest's. "Father, this is the only way to save this woman's life. If I don't marry her and take her away from here, General Vasquez will have her shot."

The priest looked at Lisa. "Will you marry this man of your own free will? No one is forcing you?"

Lisa looked at Cruz and then at the priest. "Yes, Padre, I want to marry this man of my own free will."

"Very well then." He reached into a leather pouch and pulled out some papers, ink, and a pen. "You need to sign this document first, stating that you no longer wish to be married to your present husband and sign your name. I will fill in the rest."

Lisa looked at the document and her eyes clouded with tears. Her hand shook as she dipped the pen in the small inkwell and signed her name on the paper. She handed it to the priest.

"Good. Now, both of you kneel before me and take each other's hands." He opened the Bible and read a passage from it, then asked, "Do you Cruz, take this woman as your wife? Will you love her and protect her for as long as you both shall live?"

"I will," Cruz replied solemnly.

"Will you, Lisa, take this man as your husband. Will you love and obey him for as long as you both shall live?"

Lisa couldn't answer. She felt her hands shaking. Her wedding to Eric was so clear in her mind. It had been so beautiful and she had loved him so much. How could she marry another man?

"Well, Joaquin, it looks like the homely little thing has a mind of her own. Perhaps she needs to be persuaded." Vasquez stood behind Cruz and Lisa.

"I will," Lisa said quickly, afraid of what Vasquez would do if she didn't marry Cruz.

"The ring? Where is the ring?"

Cruz shoved his hand into his pocket and brought out a slim gold band. He slipped it on Lisa's finger.

"I now pronounce you man and wife. Both of you sign this document, please. What is your last name, señor?" He looked at Cruz.

"Estacan." Cruz signed his name and handed the pen to Lisa.

"Aren't you going to give your new bride a kiss, Joaquin?" Vasquez prodded.

Cruz looked at Vasquez and then at Lisa. He

put his hands on her face and pulled her close to him, pressing his mouth against hers and kissing her softly, their lips barely meeting.

"What do you call that, Joaquin?" Vasquez came up behind Lisa and pulled her to him, planting his mouth directly on hers. She tried to push him away, but he crushed her arms to her sides.

"She is my wife now, General," Cruz said softly but firmly. "I know what to do with her."

Vasquez backed away, holding up his hands. "All right, if you say so, but I think you need a little help. Felipe, bring the bride and groom some wine."

Everyone began drinking wine, another man pulled out his guitar and began to play, and General Vasquez seemed intent on making sure that Cruz and Lisa were together.

"You must dance. This is a good song for dancing, eh?"

Cruz put his arm around Lisa and slowly led her around the area. "Are you all right? All we need is for your wound to break open again."

"I'm just tired." She started laughing suddenly. "These people probably feel so sorry for you. You married an ugly woman who can't even dance."

Cruz smiled and pulled her close to him. He liked the feel of her against him. She had a strong, lovely body, far from the shapeless one that Vasquez imagined.

"More wine, Joaquin?"

"No, thank you, General."

"Well, then, can I dance with your bride?" Before Cruz could answer, Vasquez pulled Lisa into his arms and danced her around the camp. When the song was over, he led her back to Cruz. "I feel sorry for you, man. This one cannot even dance.

How do you expect to make love to a woman who cannot even dance?"

"I'll find a way, General."

"I'm sure you will." He turned to one of his men. "More wine for the newlyweds."

Lisa finished her cup of wine and eagerly received the next proffered one. She sipped at it. "This is good wine."

"Shouldn't you slow down?"

"Why? It's my wedding night, isn't it? How many women are lucky enough to have two wedding nights?"

"Lisa, don't . . ."

"Don't what? Don't talk about the fact that I'm married to another man?" She put her fingers to her lips. "Shh, I won't tell anyone if you won't."

Cruz tried to take the cup from Lisa but she resisted. "I think you're drunk."

Lisa danced around in a circle. "I want to be drunk. I want to let my hair down, take this old shirt off, and dance until I fall down."

Cruz grabbed Lisa in his arms. "Don't be stupid. We're almost free of Vasquez."

"I think it is time for you two to retire to my tent." Vasquez himself walked up behind them. "My men will accompany you there."

"We couldn't take your tent, General."

"But a couple must have privacy on their wedding night. You do plan to have a wedding night, don't you, Joaquin?"

"Of course."

Vasquez looked at Lisa. "It appears that your wife is more eager than you. Perhaps you need some help."

"No, thank you, General."

"I insist." Vasquez motioned to his men, and

Lisa and Cruz were taken to Vasquez's tent. Vasquez walked inside and sat down on a wooden box. He gestured to the woman who followed him in to attend to Lisa. "Fix her up. Make her desirable." The woman led Lisa to a dark part of the tent, while Cruz remained with Vasquez and his men.

"What are you doing, General?"

"I am simply helping a man and his bride get to know each other a little better. I was young once. Some people are shy on their wedding nights."

"I'm not shy, I just don't like making love to a woman while six men are standing around."

Vasquez looked over the sight of his pistol at Cruz. "I don't see that you have much choice, *amigo,* eh?" Vasquez nodded his head to one of his men, who brought a bucket of water. "Take off your shirt and wash up for your bride. It's the least you can do."

Cruz unbuttoned his shirt and walked to the bucket, all the while looking for a way out. There were six men in the tent, including Vasquez, and all of them carried pistols. Cruz quickly washed and walked over to Vasquez.

"General, you aren't going to stay in here, are you?"

"It's my tent, isn't it, Joaquin?"

"But, General—" Cruz stopped when he saw Lisa walk out of the shadows. He hair was full and loose and covered her shoulders and back. She was dressed only in a thin white slip that left nothing to the imagination. His mother's silver cross rested on her chest, glimmering in the light from the lanterns. He had never seen anyone so lovely in his life.

"Well, Joaquin, it seems there was a butterfly

183

inside the caterpillar after all."

"Yes," Cruz murmured softly. He couldn't take his eyes away from Lisa. He saw the ring on her finger as she tried to cover herself with her hands, and it occurred to him for the first time that she really was his wife. He held his hands out to her and she came to him, hiding in the shelter of his arms. "Can you leave us alone now, General?"

Vasquez shrugged. "Perhaps after I'm sure you two are well on your way. But for now, don't mind me. Just listen to the soft music that Miguel is playing. Feel your lovely wife in your arms and imagine how it will be with her later."

"Cruz . . ." Lisa said softly, looking up at him in the dim light, but she didn't know what else to say. The feel of his arms around her was thrilling; his dark eyes as they looked into hers ignited a fire in her that she thought only Eric could light. Her hands went up to his face as if they had a life of their own to lightly touch his nose and jaw and trace his sensual mouth. Their bodies moved against each other in time to the languid music, and Lisa pressed herself more closely to him.

"Do you mind, General?" Cruz requested without looking at the general. His eyes never left Lisa's face. He noticed how small and delicate her nose was, how sparkling and green her eyes, how straight and even her teeth, how soft her mouth.

"Have a good evening, Joaquin," Vasquez said as he and his men left.

Cruz wrapped his arms more tightly around Lisa. He had never felt such desire for a woman in his life, not even for Soleda. He kissed Lisa, moving his mouth against hers, softly biting her lower lip.

Lisa responded in kind, embracing Cruz as he

184

kissed her. She knew in her mind that this was wrong, but her body told her it was right. Cruz had been so good to her, and now she was his wife. She wanted him. She wanted him to make love to her more than anything in the world. But he pulled away.

"Would you be able to live with yourself if you did this?" Cruz asked, stepping back from Lisa.

Lisa lowered her eyes. She knew the answer to that already, and she knew that Eric could never forgive her if she made love to another man. "I'm sorry. I don't know what's wrong with me." She put her arms over her chest in a protective pose.

"Don't be sorry. Vasquez pushed us together. It was only natural that we—" Cruz stopped as the flap of the tent flew open and Vasquez entered with a flourish, carrying two cups of wine.

"Here you go. I thought you both might get a bit shy."

"I don't want any more wine," Cruz replied harshly.

Lisa touched his arm, afraid that Vasquez might do something to harm Cruz. "Thank you, General." She took the two cups and handed one to Cruz.

"Now, what is the problem?"

"There is no problem. My wife and I want to be alone, that's all."

Vasquez walked around the couple, brandishing his pistol as he did so. "Ah, but that is the problem, is it not? I leave you two alone and you don't seem to be able to do anything."

"Look, Vasquez—"

The old general stepped forward, followed by three of his men. His pistol was in Cruz's face. "No, *you* look, Joaquin. I cannot let you take this

185

woman out of my camp unless I know that she is truly yours. *Me entiendes?*"

"What does it matter? She'll be far away from here. She won't be able to hurt you."

"She can identify me."

"So can I."

"But you wouldn't do that because you are one of us." He pointed his pistol at Lisa, using the barrel to push some strands of hair back from her shoulder. "She is not one of us. The only way I can be sure is if I know she is your woman."

"What do you want me to do, General?"

"I think it is clear what I want you to do, Joaquin. A woman will always be dutiful to a man after he has made her his. That is what I want you to do now."

Cruz wiped the sweat from his brow. "We were in the process—"

"No, you were not. I am not the stupid man that you think me, Joaquin. Either you make her your woman or I will kill her tonight."

Cruz glanced from Vasquez to Lisa. She looked so fragile and sweet. The thought of anything happening to her sent a pain through his heart. "All right, but please leave us alone."

"The last time I left you alone, you were not able to be a husband to her."

"I cannot do what you ask if you and your men are in here."

"All right. I will stand outside the tent and I will make sure that you do as I say. If you do not . . ." Vasquez moved the barrel of the gun from Lisa's shoulder up to her cheek and walked out of the tent.

Cruz turned and watched. He could see the general's shadow outside the tent. He was going to stand out there and listen. "God, I don't believe this. I am being forced to make love to a woman while another man listens." He walked across the tent, rummaging through the supplies.

"What are you doing?"

"Looking for a weapon," he whispered.

Lisa went to Cruz, holding his arm. "Cruz, please, promise me you won't do anything. Vasquez will kill you and then he'll kill me. You can't do anything. He has too many men. Even if you killed him, his men would kill *you*."

"I don't like being forced to do anything," he said angrily, throwing a pan across the tent.

"I understand, Cruz, for I was forced to do many things I didn't want to do when I was with the Comanches, but I did them in order to survive. Life is much too precious to be proud. We must do as he asks. This isn't what I want, either. I want to be home with my daughter and my husband. I want to be in my husband's arms, in his bed, making love to him, not to you." She turned away, crossing her arms in front of her and lowering her head. "But I learned a long time ago, Cruz, that I want to live. I won't give up just because some filthy old man delights in watching other people couple. I have seen worse and I have felt worse and I am still alive. I'll do what I must to get back to my daughter and husband."

Cruz walked up behind Lisa, his breath hot on her bare shoulders. "So, it will be torture for you to make love to me? You didn't seem so tortured a while ago."

"I had had too much wine a while ago."

Cruz handed Lisa one of the cups of wine while he held the other. "I think it's time for you to have some more if we're going to get this out of

187

the way. If we don't do it soon, Vasquez will be back in here." Cruz downed his cup and went to the tent flap, finding Vasquez, as he expected, just outside. "Can we have some more wine, General?"

"More wine for the newlyweds!" Vasquez yelled. One of the men ran across the camp and came back with a bottle and handed it to Cruz. Cruz started to go back into the tent, but Vasquez put his hand on his arm. "Have a drink with me, Joaquin."

Cruz nodded. "Your toast, General."

"To your health," Vasquez said in a low voice, clinking his cup against the wine bottle. Cruz missed neither the threat nor the ominous tone in Vasquez's voice. He drank from the bottle and went back inside the tent.

"May I have some more, please." Lisa held out her cup. Lisa had downed it almost as Cruz had finished pouring it. "Another please."

"You'll get sick."

"It doesn't matter, does it? Either I'll get sick or I'll be dead."

Cruz poured Lisa another cup and he himself drank liberally from the bottle. They said nothing to each other. Sad guitar music filled the silent air as someone began to play a haunting tune. Cruz drank again.

Lisa walked over to Cruz for another cup of wine but she stumbled. "Oops," she said, a smile on her face. "I never could drink. I drank mescal once in the Comanche camp and it made me crazy. I went for a ride in the middle of the night and my husband had to come find me. He wasn't very happy with me." She began to laugh, and took the bottle from Cruz, sipping generously from it. A trickle of wine ran out of the corner of her mouth and Cruz wiped it away.

He drank again from the bottle and tilted his head back. "The first time I drank wine I was ten years old. My friend and I stole some from the church. We drank some and we got so sick that when we went to confession, the priest began to laugh."

"Do you want me, Cruz?" Lisa asked suddenly.

Cruz lowered the bottle and looked at her, startled by her frankness.

"Do you think I'm bold?"

"No, I . . ."

"You don't think I'm a very nice woman," she said lightly, twirling the skirt of her slip around. "After all, I've had many men in the Comanche camp, and I am a married woman. That makes me less desirable, doesn't it?"

"I have never wanted a woman more than you," Cruz said honestly, his voice husky with desire.

Lisa stopped and stared at him. "I was afraid you didn't find me desirable at all." Her eyes sought his. "Many men have had me, but I have really only been with one man."

Cruz walked to her and smiled. "You do get crazy when you drink, don't you? Can't you look at me and see how much I want you?"

"I'm scared, Cruz. I'm so scared." Lisa buried her face in Cruz's chest. "If we do this thing, I will have betrayed my husband and our marriage. If I don't do this thing, I will be killed tonight."

Cruz lifted her chin, looking into her incredible green eyes. "I will do it. It will be my shame, not yours." He pulled her to him and kissed her deeply, pressing his body against hers. The warmth of her breath mixed with the taste of the wine made him crazy with desire. He pushed down the thin straps of the slip. His hands ran down the smooth skin of her shoulders. His hands held hers, squeezing them tightly. "I do desire you, *querida,*" he said softly, pushing the slip the rest of the way down her body. "I am just afraid that once I have you, I will never be able to let you go." He picked her up and carried her to a blanket that was spread out on the floor. He took off his boots, and then he undressed and lay down beside her. He looked at her in the dim light, admiring her beauty. All other women paled in comparison.

He wrapped his arms around her, feeling her naked body against his. He was frightened also. The one time he had ever been in love, the woman had not only stolen his heart, but she had very nearly gotten him killed. He ran his fingers through Lisa's soft hair. This situation was worse. He was holding a married woman in his arms, a woman who was married to a man who had lived with the Comanches.

"Cruz, you are frightened, too, aren't you?"

Cruz propped himself up on an elbow so he could look at Lisa. "I would be a stupid man if I were not afraid. Your husband will be coming for you, we both know that. I'm worried about what will happen to both of us, but I don't want to give you up."

Lisa's hand went to his face. "It seems I'm always getting you into trouble."

Cruz took her hand and kissed the palm of it. "My time with you has been good. But I can't help but worry about your husband. He'll want to kill me, you know, and I don't blame him. I have stolen you away from him."

"You had no choice."

"It doesn't matter. You were his." He rubbed the back of his hand on her cheek. "Soon you will be mine. Don't forget, I am a thief."

"A thief of hearts. You've stolen my heart." She sat up, trying to cover herself. She couldn't believe she had said those words. Did she feel nothing for Eric anymore? Had their love meant nothing? "How is it possible to feel as I do about you and still love my husband?"

"You have been away from him for a long time now. Your mind is helping you to survive in the best way it knows how. You have come to depend on me because I've helped you. You don't love me, Lisa, I know that. You miss your husband and I've taken his place for a while. I know that if he walked in here right now, you would go away with him and not look back."

"That's not true," she said sadly. "You're right— I do love my husband. He is a good man, but we have had our troubles. We have fought too much over silly things. We are both too stubborn. We haven't really had a chance to get to know each other, in any way but our attraction for each other. I'm not really sure we have anything in common."

"You have a beautiful daughter."

"Yes, there is Raya, and we both adore her. But I could feel something happening. Our feelings were so strong, so overpowering, that it was frightening. He needed to get away, and I needed to be without him for a time. I think we were both afraid we had rushed into something we weren't quite ready for. And you frighten me as much as he does. Yet I trust you with my life."

Cruz pulled her head to his. He kissed her mouth. "You are an incredible woman."

191

"Please don't compare me to her," Lisa murmured.

"I would never do that." He pulled her face to his chest.

"I am worried about you, *amigo,*" Vasquez's voice came through the tent. "You two have been talking for much too long. If something does not happen soon, I will have to show you what to do."

"Oh, God," Lisa murmured into Cruz's chest.

"It's all right. He won't hurt you. I won't let him." Cruz kissed her deeply, until he felt her respond, then he gently pushed her down on the blanket. This was not what he had in mind for the first time he made love to her, but he had no choice. If he didn't get on with it, Vasquez would kill him and then kill Lisa.

He pushed her legs apart, running his hands up and down her long legs. He looked at her in the dim light, watching as her head moved from side to side. His hands cupped her breasts and small sounds of pleasure came from her. He wanted to explore her, to prolong her joy and his, but as he looked back at the shadows that stood behind the tent flap he knew time was his enemy this night. He put his hands on either side of her body, covering her mouth with his and thrust himself into her, hearing her moan slightly. He knew he had hurt her, but he didn't stop. He held her head between his hands, forcing his mouth on hers, just as he was forcing himself inside of her again and again. He was ready to stop, but he felt her hips move against his and he became more excited, plunging himself into her with an abandon he had never before felt. He moved his mouth from hers and buried it in her neck. He heard her soft

192

moans of pleasure in his ear and they drove him crazy. He forgot about Vasquez. He forgot about her husband. He forgot about everything but the two of them.

"Cruz!" She said his name with such intensity that he was afraid he'd hurt her. He lifted up and looked at her face and knew that her passion was ready to explode. He put his hands under her hips and pulled her to him. They moved against each other until they exploded in a tumult of emotion. He felt Lisa's arms around his neck and he held her until she finally relaxed. When it was over, he rolled to the side. He lay behind her, one arm held protectively over her, covering her with part of the blanket. He ran his hand along her arm and then kissed it.

"Thank you," he said- simply, for he had never in his life been so fulfilled or excited. He felt Lisa turn on her side and he held her tightly. She said nothing but he felt her body as it trembled, and he heard the stifled cries she tried to hide. All he could do was hold her. Their moment of completeness was gone, perhaps forever, for she now fully realized what they had done. Gently, he kissed her shoulder. He could protect her from many things but not from her own conscience. That, right now, was her worst enemy.

Chapter 8

Eric paced impatiently across his grandfather's study.

"Would you sit down?" Tom tried to calm his brother-in-law. "They'll be down after siesta."

"I can't wait. I haven't seen my daughter in months, and God knows where my wife is."

Eric walked to the table that held the crystal decanters. He started to pour himself a drink but stopped. It would be too easy to drink himself into oblivion and it wouldn't help. He strode into the kitchen.

"Rocia, can you get me two cups of coffee please. And something to eat for all of us."

"Sí, patrón."

"Rocia, the man who stayed here, what was he like?"

"Señor Cruz?" Rocia's eyes became glazed. "He was very handsome and very much the gentleman. He was very good to the patrón. He helped him very much."

"Had you ever seen him before?"

Rocia thought a moment. "No, but I did not start to work in the kitchen until a year ago. Your

194

grandfather says that Cruz came here many years ago, when you were gone."

Eric gratefully accepted the two cups of coffee. "We'll be in my grandfather's study."

"Sí, patrón."

Eric walked back to the study and handed Tom his coffee. "Rocia tells me that this Cruz is very handsome and was very helpful to my grandfather."

"Sounds too good to be true."

"That's what I was thinking." Eric sipped at his coffee, still pacing the floor. "I don't understand why we haven't heard anything from the kidnappers. If they want money, why don't they let us know?"

"Eric . . ." Tom stopped as Teresa entered the room.

She had just taken a bath and changed into fresh riding clothes. Her light hair was pulled back at the neck and she looked lovely in her simple clothes. "I'm sorry, I didn't meant to interrupt."

"You didn't," Eric said sharply. "Are you hungry?"

"I will get something later. This is a beautiful home. I can see why you love it here."

"I don't give a damn about this place right now, Teresa, I care about my wife!" Eric yelled.

"Take it easy, Eric. It's not her fault."

Eric slammed his coffee cup down on a table. "I'm sorry . . ." he said, then suddenly turned around. His grandfather was standing at the entryway to the living room, holding Raya in his arms. Don Alfredo had aged, it seemed, and he appeared to be thinner. Raya had grown. Her dark curls fell about her shoulders and, even from

195

across the room, Eric could see the deep blue of her eyes. He greeted his daughter and grandfather with joy, crossing the room in three great strides, and put his arms around the two.

"Are you all right, Sandro?"

"Yes, I'm fine, Grandfather," Eric answered.

"And you, Tom? I trust you are well."

Tom stood up and walked to Don Alfredo, shaking his hand. "I am well, Don Alfredo. Thank you."

Eric stared at his daughter. She chewed on a tiny finger while scrutinizing him. *She wasn't afraid.* "Hello, Raya. Do you remember me?"

Raya continued to stare, as if trying to recall in her memory who this strange man was.

"Raya, el es tu papá," Don Alfredo said in Spanish.

Raya studied Eric for a moment longer, then in a tiny voice said, "Papa."

Eric was so excited he tore Raya from his grandfather's arms and held her to him. "Hello, *mija,* my little one. How have you been? You've gotten so big."

"Papa," Raya said again.

They all laughed. Eric reveled in the feel of his daughter. "You are a beautiful little thing," he said in wonder, pushing the dark curls from Raya's face.

"Can I hold my niece?" Tom asked, holding out his arms. Raya went to him immediately and they all laughed. "I can't believe how much she looks like you, Eric. She has little of Lisa in her."

"That is not true," Don Alfredo demurred. "If you are around her for anytime at all, you will see that she has her mother's spirit."

"Eric, she's beautiful," Teresa said, walking up behind the group.

"Oh, Teresa, I'm sorry. This is my grandfather, Don Alfredo de Vargas. Grandfather, Teresa Torres, of the Torres family up north."

Don Alfredo took Teresa's hand. "My pleasure, señorita. I have met your family, a long time ago. I'm sure they don't remember me."

"How could anyone forget you, Don Alfredo?"

Don Alfredo laughed. "You are gracious, thank you."

"Grandfather, tell me about Lisa," Eric said seriously, walking across the room. He handed Raya a wooden toy that was on a table and she happily sat on the floor playing with it. "Teresa is going to help us find her. She spent her summers in Baja California. She knows it well."

"Very well. Over two months ago some men came into the garden. They took Lisa and another man who was staying here. They said a General Vasquez would let us know what he wanted."

"Who was the man staying here, Grandfather?"

"His name is Cruz Estacan. I had met him years ago when he was just a boy. He was very ill and I took him in. He came to see me to thank me again for my kindness. It was just coincidence that he was here."

"You think it was coincidence that a man you haven't seen in years comes here, and then a week later, he and Lisa are kidnapped?"

"Surely you aren't suggesting that Cruz is involved with General Vasquez. Impossible!"

"Why impossible, grandfather?" Eric squatted, rolling the toy train back and forth for Raya.

"This man saved your daughter's life, Sandro,

197

and your wife's as well."

Eric stood up. "What do you mean?"

"The first day he came here, Raya had gotten into the main corral. He jumped the fence and saved her from the steer."

Eric rumpled Raya's dark curls. "For that I thank him, but what about Lisa?"

Don Alfredo seemed acutely uncomfortable. "You aren't going to like this, Sandro, but I will tell you. The first time I heard from Vasquez he said he knew that Cruz was not my grandson so he was going to kill Lisa unless I signed over the del Mar and the del Sol. Of course, I was willing to do that, but I knew your mother wouldn't go along with it. Besides, I wanted to know that Lisa was safe. I asked for proof. He sent me a note written by her, saying that she was well. The next time I met with Vasquez, he wanted money. I told him I would give him all the money he wanted as long as Lisa was returned to me."

"And?"

"I heard nothing for over two weeks. The next time we met, Cruz was there."

"And you don't think he's a part of it? You are so blind sometimes, Grandfather!"

"Let me finish, Sandro. Cruz came up with a compromise. Vasquez wanted to get rid of Lisa, wanted to kill her because of her ties to us. Cruz suggested that she cut her ties and I agreed."

Eric's eyes grew cold. "What are you talking about?"

"He suggested to Vasquez that Lisa end her marriage to you and marry him. In return, Vasquez would let Cruz take Lisa south so that she would be far out of the way. Vasquez also got

198

money and land from me, and land from Cruz."

"That's impossible. Our marriage can't be dissolved unless I agree to it. We have to go through the Church."

Don Alfredo got up and walked to his desk, pulling out two pieces of paper. He handed them to Eric. "One is for the dissolution of marriage, the other is the documentation of marriage between Cruz and Lisa." Don Alfredo put his hand on Eric's arm. "I'm sorry, Sandro. It was the only thing I could think of to save Lisa's life. I did not know what to do."

Eric's hands shook as he looked at Lisa's signature on both pieces of paper. He threw them on the floor and walked to Raya, picking her up in his arms. "That's all right. We don't need her, do we?"

"Eric, you can't be serious?" Tom asked.

"Of course I'm serious. Take a look at the papers, Tom. She signed them. If she had wanted to get back here, I'm sure she could have found a way."

Tom bent over and picked up the papers. "These mean nothing. She could have had a gun to her head for all we know."

Eric shook his head. "My wife is now married to another man. I guess it's what I deserve for making such a fool of myself over her."

"Stop it!" Teresa said, walking to Eric and taking Raya from his arms. She handed her to Tom. "Will you gentlemen excuse us while we have a talk?"

"Sure," Tom said, following Don Alfredo out of the room.

"You are a conceited fool," Teresa said slowly,

measuring the words. "You have no idea what your wife has been through. All you can think about is your male pride."

Eric poured himself a glass of whiskey and glared at Teresa. "Stay out of it."

"No, I won't stay out of it. You asked for my help. I won't stand here and let you talk about your wife like that just because your pride is injured."

"It has nothing to do with pride. She could've found a way back to me if she had wanted to."

"Do you honestly believe that, Eric? Could she have found a way out of the Comanche camp when she was a captive there?"

Eric put down the glass and walked to a chair. He sat down, his elbows resting on his knees. "I can't believe I've lost her again so soon. We had so little time together."

Teresa walked to him, putting her hand on his head. "That's really what it is, isn't it? You're afraid you've lost her for good?"

"She's with another man, Teresa. I know what that means."

"Why do you assume the worst?"

"Because my wife is a beautiful woman, and this man is legally married to her. She's his wife now. He can do anything he wants to her."

Teresa kneeled next to Eric, resting her hand on his knee. "You mean he can make love to her anytime he wants to, don't you?"

"I guess," Eric responded without looking at her.

"Eric, look at me. Please." Eric raised his head. With his unruly dark hair and blue eyes, he looked more like a wounded boy than a man. "Do you think that Bryant loves me?"

200

"He's crazy about you. He'd do anything for you."

"That's right. He doesn't think about all the men in my past. He only thinks about the present and how much I care for him."

"It's different with you two, you aren't married."

"I don't think it's different. Bryant saved me from a horrible life and gave me a new one. I owe him everything. He loves me for who I am and holds nothing of the past against me."

"What if she loves this man?"

"You don't think very much of your wife, do you?"

"Of course I do, but I also know how feelings can change. God, she's so beautiful. If I were him, I'd take her away and never let any man touch her."

"She's not a china doll, Eric. From everything you've told me, she's a very strong woman. She's also a very loving woman. She's not going to forget you just because she's away from you. It's possible to find solace with another person when you're lonely, but that doesn't make it love. The kind of love you have for your wife is something you find only once in your life."

Eric put his hand on top of Teresa's. "I didn't expect this from you."

"What did you expect? That I would come running into your arms and ask you to run away with me." She shook her head. "I have pride, too, Eric. I also care very deeply for Bryant. I want to help you, but I don't want to take advantage of you. If something happens between us, then it happens. But I'm not looking for love. I like my life the way it is."

"I envy you. Your life is much less complicated than mine." He stared out at the garden, remembering Lisa as she walked through it holding Raya in her arms. "When you love someone, it makes you weak."

"It also makes you strong. You must draw on that. But now we must be practical and think of finding Lisa. You're the tracker. We find out what we can from your grandfather, find out if Cruz ever told him of any family homes in Mexico, then we start looking. Your wife will be easy for people to remember—she is different from most of the women here."

Eric stood up, pulling Teresa up next to him. He kissed her on the cheek. "I thank you for helping me see a little more clearly. If I weren't married—"

"You aren't," Teresa said softly, "but I won't take advantage of that fact."

Eric ignored what Teresa had just said. "I'll go talk to my grandfather. I'd like to take off tomorrow if possible. Is that all right with you?"

"That's fine. Will that give you enough time with your daughter?"

"It'll have to be enough time. I need to bring her mother back to her."

Eric walked up the steps of the veranda. He hadn't been to the Rancho del Sol for almost two years, since he'd found out his mother had been involved with Consuelo in trying to harm Lisa. But he knew how Lisa felt about it. She had wanted him to talk to his mother. He didn't know if a reconciliation was possible, but he was going

202

to try, not just for Lisa but for Raya and his grandfather. His grandfather had had such a void in his life without Mariz. It was time he had some joy in his life.

He knocked on the door and waited, shuffling his feet as if he were a small boy. He looked around and recalled the many evenings he had sat on the veranda with his parents while his father told stories of the sea, or his mother told him about life in Spain. There had been a time when he loved his mother.

The door opened. *"Ay, Madre de Dios,"* Marta, the servantwoman, said, and crossed herself. She had known Eric all of his life and had never approved of his feud with his mother. She hugged him with her chubby arms and then pulled him inside. "You are hungry? I have just made some fresh bread."

"No, thank you, Marta. Is Mariz here?"

"Your mother? She is in the sitting room reading. Tell me of your daughter. Rocia says she is *muy bonita.*"

"She is. And she's full of life, she's a gift to us all."

"Ah, she sounds much like you were, Sandro. You were so full of life that you broke every cup in the china cabinet. But it did not matter. We all loved you so much, especially your mother."

A frown clouded Eric's face. "I think I'll go in now.

Eric gave the old woman a kiss on the cheek. "Thank you, Marta. You're a good person."

Marta waved him away, muttering to herself in Spanish as she walked back to the kitchen.

Eric walked slowly to the sitting room. He

203

passed his father's study and opened the door. He loved this room. It was full of his father—wooden paneling, ship models, maps, and a huge globe that stood on the floor by the desk. He closed the door quietly and walked down the hallway to the sitting room, the room he had most hated as a boy because he had had to sit so still. His mother had been so intent on him learning the proper manners, never mind that he wanted to be outside riding a horse and playing with his dog. He knocked on the door.

He opened the door and walked in. His mother didn't look up. She was still a beautiful woman, with dark hair and dark almond eyes. She was small and delicate, with the personality of a bobcat. Now that he looked at her, he wasn't sure he could ever get along with her again.

"Hello, Mother."

Mariz put her book on her lap but didn't look up. "Come in, Alejandro. I was just about to have tea."

Eric walked into the room, amazed at his mother's calm demeanor. They hadn't spoken in almost two years, yet she acted as if nothing were wrong. Sometimes he wished he had her strength. "No, thank you. I've come to talk." He stood in front of her.

"What do you wish to talk about?" Mariz poured tea into a delicate cup and dropped a sugar cube in.

"Mother, will you please look at me."

Mariz looked up, setting the spoon down on the saucer. "What do you want? Money? No, let me guess. You want the del Sol back. Suddenly, the del Mar has become too small for you and your

204

wife."

Eric clenched his jaw. As always, his mother was impossible to talk to, but he had to think about his grandfather and his daughter. "I don't want anything from you, Mother. Not even the del Sol." It hurt Eric to say that, especially since the Rancho del Sol was legally his. His grandfather had built it for his mother and Eric's father, but the title belonged to Eric.

"What is it you want then?" She held the cup to her mouth and sipped at the steaming liquid.

"I want you to come to the del Mar with me. I want you to meet my daughter." For the first time, Eric saw a chink in his mother's armor. Her hand began to shake.

"Your daughter?"

"Yes, her name is Raya and she's a year old." He smiled. "You'd like her, Mother."

"Raya is a beautiful name," she said almost nonchalantly.

"She has dark hair and blue eyes, and she's full of the devil."

"Much like you were, eh?" she said with a slight smile.

"Yes, Marta already reminded me of all the china I broke when I was small."

"Lucky for us your father was the captain of a sailing ship. He had access to more china."

"Would you like to see her, Mother?"

Mariz put the cup down and folded her hands in her lap. "Why have you come to me after all this time, Alejandro? You must need me for something."

"I need you to get to know my daughter. She needs her family now.

205

"Why now?"

"Lisa is gone." He looked at her face, knowing that the news would probably please his mother.

"She left?"

"No, she was kidnapped by a General Vasquez. He's taken her south. I'm going to search for her."

Mariz stood up. Tentatively, she reached for her son's hands. "I'm sorry, Alejandro. I never meant your wife any harm."

"Perhaps we can talk about that some other time, but now I'd just like you to come to the del Mar. Grandfather needs you, as well."

"My father, he is ailing?"

"He is older, Mother, and his health is not as good as it used to be. Raya keeps him young, but I think having you there would make all the difference in the world. I don't want him taking care of Raya by himself while I'm gone."

"He has plenty of help—"

"Mother, please. He needs you, my daughter needs you, and I need you. Will you come?"

Mariz removed her hands from Eric's and picked up the skirts of her heavy dress to move to the couch. "What will happen when your wife returns? She won't want me there."

"She's the one who talked me into coming here." Mariz looked genuinely shocked. "She has wanted me to come to you since Raya was born, but I wouldn't do it. She's convinced you had nothing to do with trying to have her killed. She thinks it was all Consuelo's idea."

"But you don't."

"I'm not sure what I think. You tried to ruin our marriage, of that I'm sure, but I don't think you wanted Lisa dead."

206

"Well, if it's any consolation, I didn't have anything to do with it. I didn't want you two together, but I would never have done anything to harm her."

"I'm glad to hear it."

"Is she all right? Have you heard any news?"

"Just that some of Vasquez's men are taking her south."

"I want to help in any way I can."

"No, that's not necessary."

"Yes, I want to help. I can give you money. Perhaps you can buy off this Vasquez. I have heard of him. He thinks he can take over the government of California. He's loco."

"I love her, Mother, and I have to find her. Do you understand that?"

"Yes, I think I do. There was a time when I loved your father very much."

"I remember. I remember a time when you used to laugh all the time."

"It seems like a lifetime ago." Mariz was quiet. "Yes, I will come to the del Mar. I would like very much to get to know my granddaughter, and I want to get to know my father again."

"It will make him very happy, Mother. Thank you."

Mariz smiled slightly, not quite comfortable with the gesture. "Would you like to help me upstairs so I can pack? I'm sure I'll need a few things."

Eric held out his arm for Mariz and she took it. It was the first time since he was sixteen years old and his father had been killed at sea, that he could remember actually talking to his mother. It was a good feeling. Maybe there was a chance for them after all.

207

Cruz looked back at Vasquez's men. They kept an ever-watchful eye on him and Lisa. He would have to wait until he got home to get away from them. He still didn't trust Vasquez, still had the feeling that once he gave Vasquez's men the money, they would kill him and Lisa.

He looked over at Lisa riding next to him. She was silent, just as she had been since they left the hills. He understood; she regretted that they had made love. But he did not. Being with her had been an incredible experience. She was a beautiful, giving woman, and he wanted to make her happy. He wanted to see her smile again. She looked over at him then, and he could see the sadness in her green eyes. How could he make her happy when all she really wanted was to be back home with her family?

He motioned for the men to stop. He dismounted and removed his pack and supplies from his horse. Although it was early to make camp, he knew the men wouldn't protest. He felt that Lisa needed a rest. He went to help her down, but she slid down the side of the horse and untied her pack, following Cruz.

They made camp along a small stream. Lisa silently laid out her pack, planning to cook a dinner, of beans and biscuits, the only foodstuff they carried with them.

"I'm going to go see if I can get us something fresh for dinner," Cruz said as he left the camp. He was determined to be successful on his mission. He was sick and tired of beans.

Lisa gathered pieces of scrub and kindling and

lit them with matches. She added larger pieces of wood until they caught fire. She walked around the area, gathering rocks to put around the fire. Then she found a large, flat rock and laid it in the middle of the fire. She set their largest pot on it and put in that morning's beans to reheat.

As she absently stirred the pot, she tried not to think of Cruz, but she couldn't get him out of her mind. She remembered so vividly what it had been like when he made love to her. She closed her eyes, and she could almost feel his hands on her. She was frightened and ashamed. How, she wondered, could she feel that way about another man?

"Lisa."

Lisa opened her eyes and sat up straight at the sound of Cruz's voice. He was standing behind her, holding two rabbits. She couldn't contain her excitement. "How did you catch them? I didn't hear any shots."

"My knife. It's a lot quieter." He walked toward the trees and knelt there, quickly skinning and gutting the animals. He brought them back to the fire. "Why don't you go find three very strong sticks while I give one of these to the men. As long as they're guarding us, I'm going to try to make them happy."

Lisa nodded and got up to walk around the trees, kicking at branches until she found just the three sticks she wanted. She brought them back and Cruz nodded. He quickly carved a "V" at both ends of two of them, then stuck the other stick through the rabbit. He stuck one stick into the ground on one side of the fire, and the other on the other side, making sure they were anchored by nearby rocks. Then he laid the stick with the rabbit on it across the two V's. Lisa couldn't resist a smile.

"I can't wait. I know I shouldn't complain, but I'm so tired of beans and biscuits."

"I'm sick of them, too. This rabbit will be just what we need."

"Cruz . . ." Lisa tried to speak but nothing would come out. She couldn't even look at him.

"Come on," Cruz said, holding out his hand. "I have a surprise for you."

"A surprise?" She stood up and took his hand, following him into the trees.

Cruz led Lisa back into the trees by the stream. They walked upstream for a while until Cruz stopped and pointed with pride. "There, what do you think?"

Lisa looked at the small pool of clear water. It had been created by a beaver's dam but it looked perfect for her. "It's wonderful. Do you think I could take a swim?"

"I should go in and make sure they aren't any beavers. They can be very dangerous if they think you're trying to invade their territory."

"Can't we just tell them we're going for a swim?"

"All right, come on. We'll go in together. Our clothes could use a good washing anyway."

Cruz took off his boots. He led the way into the cool water, slowly finding his footing, but Lisa was more restless. She stood behind Cruz and pushed him in, laughing as he stood up, completely soaked. "That wasn't a nice thing to do."

"I'm sorry," she replied with a laugh.

Cruz came toward her, but Lisa quickly lunged away. He caught the edge of her skirt and held on to it. She tried to pull away but he pulled her backward and she fell into the water next to him. "I'm sorry," he said sarcastically, looking at the surprised look on her face.

Lisa laughed and sat down in the shallow pond, splashing the water onto her face. She ran her hands along her shirt and skirt, trying to get out the trail dust, then she leaned back and rinsed out her hair. When she came back up, Cruz was gone. She stood up in the pond, looking through the trees. "Cruz, please, where are you?" She looked at the wet footprints on the bank and realized that he had gone back to camp. She floated in the water for a while, trying to clear her mind, trying not to think of Eric or Cruz or her darling Raya, but her mind was flooded with thoughts of each of them. How could she go on without them?

"Are you finished yet?" Cruz stood on the bank, naked except for the saddle blanket wrapped around his waist. His dark hair was slicked back from his face and it made his features look even more angular. Lisa wondered if he had Indian blood in him.

"No, I could stay in here all night."

"I don't think that would be a good idea. The sun is quickly going down and it's getting cold. We have to try to get our clothes dried before morning."

"All right." Lisa stood up and walked to the bank. "You go back and I'll follow you."

"No, I'm not leaving you out here alone with Vasquez's men around. I don't trust them. I'll hold the blanket up and you get your clothes off."

Lisa nodded. She stood behind the blanket Cruz held, taking off her wet boots, the boots that he had traded for with one of Vasquez's women. She poured the water out of them and threw them down, then quickly unbuttoned Cruz's borrowed shirt and untied the sash she wore around it. She slipped out of the skirt and stood only in the thin slip. "Why don't I keep this on?" she asked, grabbing for the blanket.

"No, everything off. I don't need you getting sick on me. I have to get you home."

Lisa looked around suspiciously. "You really don't trust them," she observed, then pulled the wet slip up over her head and dropped it on the other clothes. When she reached for the blanket, Cruz held it away for one brief moment, looking at her with passionate eyes, then he wrapped it around her and held her in his arms. "You're like a sickness, do you know that?"

"Cruz, don't."

"It's true." He crushed her to him. "You're like a sickness that won't go away. It grows worse every day. What am I going to do without you, Lisa?"

She couldn't resist the gentle tone of Cruz's voice and looked at him. "I was thinking the same thing about you," she said honestly. Cruz held her against him and she buried her face in his chest, loving the feel of him against her.

"Come on, we don't have time for this now." Cruz gathered up their clothes and led Lisa back to camp in an uncomfortable silence. Neither one of them could say what they really felt.

Cruz hiked up the blanket and squatted down, turning the rabbit to the other side. "It smells good, don't you think?"

"Anything but beans smells good." Lisa bent

212

down and touched Cruz's left shoulder. The word "Soleda" was written in dark ink. A small rose was entangled in the name. Lisa ran her fingers over the name. Cruz flinched and stood up. "You still love her, don't you?"

Cruz looked at Lisa and gently brushed her cheek with his hand, then he looked past her to some unknown place. "I was wrong when I said you were a sickness, you are nothing so destructive. You are good and sweet. Soleda was more like a sickness. She got in my blood, she was like a sore that wouldn't go away no matter what I did. Even after she left me, I couldn't forget her. There was something dangerously exciting about her. I knew that she could have taken a knife out while we slept and stabbed me to death, but that didn't keep me from her. I had to have her no matter what."

"I'm sorry. I can't imagine any woman using you like that." Lisa turned away as soon as she spoke the words.

"What's the matter?" Cruz's hands were on her shoulders.

"I just accused Soleda of using you, but what have I been doing? *I* have been using you until I get back to my family. I'm no better. In fact, I'm probably worse. At least you knew what Soleda was like."

"Don't do this. You're nothing like her. She was a devil; she had no good in her." He touched his mouth to her shoulder. "You are the best thing that ever happened to me."

Lisa turned around, touching Cruz's face. "Cruz, don't. Nothing can come of this. I have to go back to my family. They need me."

"I know that. I'm not asking you to stay. When the time is up, I'll take you back to your family. But don't ask the impossible of me, Lisa. Don't ask me not to love you."

Lisa closed her eyes. It was the first time the word "love" was mentioned. It scared her more than anything. She felt as if her world was coming apart. Everything she and Eric had worked so hard to build together was crumbling. She hadn't seen him or Raya in over two months and nothing seemed real except Cruz. He was the one on whom she depended every day, and he was the one to whom she was becoming too attached. "My daughter probably doesn't even remember me," she said sadly, tears streaming down her face. "What if she's ill? What if something has happened to her? I feel so helpless."

"There's nothing we can do now. If we try to get away from Vasquez's men, they have orders to shoot us. That won't do your daughter much good, will it? Try to be patient. The time will go quickly. When we get to my rancho, you can write your family a letter. That will make you feel better."

"Yes, and once Eric knows where I am, he'll come for me right away."

"Yes," Cruz said, turning away from Lisa and squatting down by the fire.

Lisa wanted to touch him, she wanted to say something comforting to him, but there was nothing she could say. She pulled her blanket more tightly around her and sat down, stirring the beans. "I forgot the biscuits."

"It doesn't matter."

"But you'll be hungry. I can mix them up

214

quickly."

"I said it doesn't matter. Why don't you spread the clothes out so they can dry."

Lisa did as he said and laid the clothes out on the rocks nearest to the fire. Her mind was a blur.

"Be careful, señora, you wouldn't want your blanket to fall."

Lisa looked up. It was one of Vasquez's men. Lisa held the blanket tightly against her. "What do you want?"

"We were lonely. We thought perhaps—"

Cruz stood up. "What were you thinking, Perez?" Cruz stood. He was defenseless. He had no weapon and he was dressed only in a blanket. "Vasquez said you and your men were to make your own camp and leave us alone."

"I know what Vasquez said, but he isn't here, is he?" Perez picked at his front teeth with a sliver of wood.

"What do you want?"

"Well, señor, I was thinking we could make some kind of arrangement. We all know you were forced to marry this woman. It's not as if you really love her or anything. My men and I are very lonely out here on the trail and we thought—"

Cruz was on Perez in seconds, his hands at his throat. "Finish what you were saying. I didn't quite hear you." Cruz took Perez's gun from his holster and cocked it. He put it to his head. "Now, tell me again what you wanted."

Perez rubbed his throat, gasping for air. "I meant nothing, señor. I only thought—"

Cruz pressed the barrel of the gun against Perez's cheek. "Don't think, Perez, that's not what Vasquez pays you for. You were paid to accompany us to San Diego unharmed. If anything happens to us, you know what Vasquez will do to you, don't you?"

"*Sí*, *señor*."

"Well, then, let me tell you what I'll do if you touch this woman. I'll stake you to the ground and I'll slit your eyelids. Then I'll put hot coals in your eyes. You'll never be able to see again."

"I'm sorry, señor, I meant no harm. I did not think this woman was anything to you."

"This woman is everything to me. She is my wife, *mi esposa. Me entiendes?*"

"*Sí*, *señor*."

"Now go back to your men and leave us alone. And remember, General Vasquez is counting on us getting to San Diego safely. If we do not, and he doesn't get his money, you and your men will be the ones to suffer."

"*Sí*, *señor*." Perez hurried from the camp.

Cruz handed Lisa the gun. "Hold on to this. I don't trust him." He looked around him. "We're getting out of here as soon as we can. It's not safe to stay here anymore."

"Are we still going south?"

"We have to. It would be too dangerous to go back the way we came. There's no telling where Vasquez and his men will be."

"What about the money? Won't Vasquez come to get it from you?"

"Vasquez doesn't know where I live. He thinks I live in San Diego. I live farther north in a little valley."

"But he can ask around."

"He *can,* but he won't find anything out. I am well protected." He bent down and tore off a piece

216

of the rabbit. "It's done. Let's eat."

"Cruz?"

He looked questioningly at Lisa, his dark eyes serious.

"Would you really have put hot coals in his eyes?"

Cruz smiled and cocked an eyebrow. "No, but it scared him, didn't it?" He gave a rabbit leg to Lisa. "Eat, you need it. I want you ready and rested if we need to leave."

Lisa accepted the leg and began to eat. The thought of Vasquez and his men following them scared her, but she trusted Cruz to do what was right.

Lisa felt a hand over her mouth. She struggled until she saw Cruz hovered above her, completely dressed. "Get your clothes on now," he whispered. He handed her the pile of damp clothes and Lisa quickly slipped them on. Cruz took their packs and they silently walked out of the camp to their two horses. He gave her the reins of their two horses. "Lead them downstream. I'll be there in a minute. I'm going to cut their horses loose."

"Cruz, don't." Lisa grabbed Cruz's arm. "They'll have a guard watching."

"Do as I tell you, Lisa. Go." He gave her a little push.

Lisa took the reins and led the horses downstream until they were well out of sight of the camp. She couldn't hear anything. She wrapped the reins around her hand and held them as the horses chewed at the leaves of the nearby trees. She watched them, knowing that if something was

217

wrong, they would react. There was nothing.

She soon grew impatient. She was ready to tether the horses when she heard a noise. She drew the pistol from her belt and held it in front of her, waiting in the darkness, watching as the horses held up their heads and whinnied.

It was Cruz. She breathed a sigh of relief, grabbing at his arm. "You're all right?"

"Yes. Let's go." He took the horses and led them farther downstream until they were out of the cover of the trees, then they mounted. "We'll have to ride carefully. It's hard to see, and the horses could lose their footing."

They rode slowly, Cruz in the lead, leaning over to check the ground they were riding over. Occasionally he looked up at the sky to find the North Star to make sure they were going south. As sunrise came and the sky turned every color of pink and orange, they rode hard. As midday approached, Cruz found a shelter in some rocks. There was a small lake from which the horses drank, and then they grazed on the pastureland. Cruz and Lisa washed up and drank, then lay by the one lone tree that was near the lake.

"This is beautiful. Do you know where we are?"

"We are near Los Angeles. We are probably on Figueroa property. They own most of the land around here."

"Will it be all right for us to be here?"

Cruz nodded confidently. "It will be all right. Get some rest. I'll keep watch."

Lisa lay on the ground next to Cruz, trying to get comfortable. She sat up. "I can't sleep. I keep thinking of Vasquez and his men riding up."

"They won't be riding up."

Lisa was suddenly alarmed. What had Cruz done? What if he had murdered all of the men in their sleep? Perhaps he wasn't the man she thought he was. "Why?"

He smiled, looking like a boy. "Not only do they not have any horses, they don't have any boots."

"How did you do that?"

"I knocked out the guard and took his rifle, then I took his boots. I tied him to a tree. Then I went to Perez and forced him to take off his boots, and everyone else's. Then I told him to tie all the men together, and I tied Perez himself to the whole crew. I took their weapons and their boots and threw them in the pond, under the beaver dam. I don't think they'll be following us."

Lisa sat up and put her arms around Cruz. "I like you very much, do you know that? You're clever and smart, and very nice."

Cruz looked at Lisa and pushed her down on the ground. "I'm not as nice as you think I am," he said, his mouth touching hers, seeking it out, seeing if she still wanted him. When she responded, Cruz kissed her more deeply, his hands running up and down her body. "Do you want me, Lisa?"

Lisa looked up at Cruz. Her hand went to his face, touching it gently. "Yes," she replied, closing her eyes and pressing her mouth against his. "I want you so much, Cruz. Make love to me." She moved her body against his, wrapping her legs around him.

Cruz looked down at Lisa seeing her green eyes sparkling with desire. "You are a witch. You've cast a spell over me."

219

"I don't want to cast a spell over you, Cruz. I'm not a witch. I'm flesh and blood. I'm just a woman who wants to be loved."

"Ah, Liseta," he said affectionately, "you want to be loved by your husband, but he is not here. So I will do."

"That's not true."

"But it is, my love. It is." Cruz kissed her softly and then pulled away, standing up and taking off his clothes. He walked into the lake and dove under the clear water, swimming across to the other side.

Lisa watched him. God, he was beautiful. More than that, he was a good, kind man. He had taught her much about patience and dignity. Right now she felt so foolish, so cheap, like a whore who threw herself at men for money. She stood up and took her clothes off, quickly walking into the water. She washed and swam for a time, always making sure to steer clear of Cruz. When she felt sufficiently refreshed, she swam back to shore and put on her slip. She sat down on the ground, leaning her head back, feeling the warm sun on her face. She heard Cruz come out of the water and slip on his pants, but she kept her eyes closed.

"Would you please put something else on?"

Lisa opened her eyes and looked at Cruz. He was standing with his pants on, barefoot and barechested. Again, his hair was slicked back from his face and she couldn't believe how handsome he was. She looked down at herself and noticed how the flimsy slip clung to her wet body. Without a word, she grabbed Cruz's shirt and put it on, then slipped her skirt on underneath it. She hooked her belt on over the shirt, stuck the pistol in the belt, and sat back down to pull on her boots but stopped suddenly. "Cruz, look." She pointed to some riders in the distance.

"It's all right. Get your boots on. It's probably Figueroa's men."

"What will they do?"

"Just put your boots on and get the horses."

Cruz was almost finished getting his own clothes and boots on and was standing next to Lisa when the five men rode up.

The lead man tipped his sombrero. "Do you know you are on Figueroa land, señor?"

"Yes, I know. How is Miguel?"

The man squinted his eyes and looked at Cruz again. "You know the *patrón?*"

"Yes, I know the *patrón* very well. If you will tell him that Cruz Estacan is here, I think he will be glad to see me."

"Señor!" the man said with obvious admiration. "Certainly we have heard of you. The *patrón* often talks of the man who saved his life. If you and the lady will follow us, we will take you back to the hacienda."

Cruz looked at Lisa and motioned for her to mount. They followed the riders for a few miles until they reached a beautiful hacienda. It was large, much larger than the Rancho del Sol or del Mar, and there were orange trees all around it. The smell of orange blossoms permeated the air as they rode by. When they reached the hacienda, the lead rider led Cruz and Liza through the courtyard to the main house. He went inside, talking to a woman as he went by. They walked down a long hallway. The man stopped and knocked at a door.

When a voice responded, he said, "It is Ramon, *patrón*. I bring a friend of yours."

"A friend?" the voice from inside said. "By all means, come in."

Ramon opened the door and Cruz and Lisa walked inside. The man who sat behind the desk stood up, a wide smile covering his face when he saw Cruz. "Cruz, *mi compadre!*" He came from behind the desk to embrace his friend. "Where have you been for the last two years? I have wondered about you. I have heard stories that you were dead or in Mexico."

"Both untrue, Miguel."

Miguel Figueroa laughed. He looked at Lisa. "And who is this?"

Cruz took Lisa's arm. "This is my wife, Lisa. Lisa, this is Miguel Figueroa, a great man and good friend."

Miguel walked to Lisa. He was a short and compact man, with a thin mustache that looked totally inappropriate on his round, young face. He bowed with a flourish, took Lisa's hand, and kissed it. "It is a great honor to meet the woman who has finally captured Cruz's heart."

"Thank you, señor."

"Señor?" Miguel looked at Cruz. "Do I look like a señor? That is my father. I am Miguel and I will be very insulted if you do not call me by my name."

"All right, Miguel."

Miguel surveyed Cruz and Lisa. "Well, it looks as if you two could use a change of clothing and a hot bath, no? I'll order a bath for you two and I'll have you taken to your room. You will stay here for a while, of course."

222

"Of course," Cruz said with a smile.

Miguel rang a bell on his desk and, within seconds, a servant appeared. "Ah, Manuela, would you please take the señora to the guest room upstairs. Also, find her some appropriate clothes." He looked at Lisa. "It might be difficult to fit you, señora. You are much taller than our women."

"It's all right, Miguel. Just something clean will do fine." She looked at Cruz. "Are you coming?"

"I'll be there in a while. You enjoy your bath. I'll visit with Miguel." He kissed her on the cheek and watched her as she walked out.

"Cruz, you devil, you never told me you were in love. Is this what you have been up to for the last two years?"

Cruz turned around and walked over to one of the chairs by Miguel's desk. He sat down, propping his feet on Miguel's desk. "No, Lisa was an unexpected surprise."

"You are very much in love with her. It is written all over your face."

Cruz crossed one booted foot over the other and folded his hands behind his head. "It's a strange situation, Miguel. I suppose I'll have to tell you about it, but not now. Now, I'd like to have a glass of wine and talk of old times."

"That we can do." Miguel walked to a small table near his desk and poured two glasses of wine, handing one to Cruz. *"Salud y amor,"* Miguel said, drinking half of the glass in one gulp.

"Salud," Cruz said, sipping at the rich wine. "How is it down here? Have you heard much of me?"

"No, nothing since you left. El Joaquin is very

223

active and he doesn't mind taking the credit for everything he does and more. I don't know if he's this far south, but there have been many robberies. I don't even think the authorities are even looking for Joaquin the Younger."

"Good," Cruz said, drinking the wine. "I'm going back home, Miguel. I want to take Lisa to my rancho. It's been a long time since I've been there."

"I do not think you will have a problem. My men have checked for you. Things are going well. Your man, Jesus, he is doing well for you. He is also very loyal."

"Good."

"So, where have you been these last two years, *amigo?*"

"Around. I've been traveling, Miguel. I was on a ship that went to South America. I spent some time in Argentina."

"Argentina? I hear the women are beautiful there. Is that true?"

"Is that all you ever think about, Miguel?"

"Of course it's all I ever think about. So, what else did you do?"

"I went back to Mexico. I wanted to help my family out."

"And how did your father take that?"

"He didn't. He wouldn't allow me to come into his home. He made me leave, but I expected that. I knew how he felt about me."

"What about your brothers and sisters? Did you see any of them?"

"Yes, all of them. It was good, especially with my youngest sister, Caterina. She's beautiful. She looks just like my mother, and she has my mother's heart."

"I'm happy for you, Cruz. I know how much your family means to you. It's too bad your father can't see that you've made something of yourself. You're just not the thief he thinks you to be."

"It doesn't matter anymore, Miguel. He'll think what he wants to think anyway. At least I got to help my brothers and sisters. All of them needed money. It felt good to be able to help them. I'd like to bring Caterina up here. If I don't, I'm afraid my father will marry her off to some poor farmer."

"There are worse things, my friend."

"I don't want her to die young like my mother did, Miguel. I want her to have a chance."

"It is up to you, Cruz. You must decide. Anyway, don't you want to hear about me?"

"Of course, I'm sorry."

"Well, it seems that I, too, am in love."

Cruz took his feet off the desk and planted them on the floor. "I don't believe it. Is this Miguel Figueroa I'm talking to? The man who swore he'd never get married except to have children?"

"Well, I never thought I'd meet this woman. She has changed my life, Cruz. She wants to be a part of everything around here. Wait until you see her. She is incredible. I still can't believe she wants me."

"She'd be crazy not to, Miguel. You own most of Baja California."

"Are you saying she doesn't care for me? You hurt my pride, amigo."

"I'm just telling you to be careful. So, where is this incredible woman?"

"She's out riding right now. You can meet her

at dinner tonight. Why don't you join your lovely wife, have a bath and some wine, then take a nice long siesta. I will send Manuela to get you when it's time for dinner."

Cruz stood up. "All right. Are you sure we won't be putting you out, Miguel?"

"Don't be ridiculous. I wouldn't have it any other way. Your room is upstairs at the end of the hall." He held up his wineglass and winked. "Enjoy your siesta, amigo."

Cruz shook his head and left the room. He climbed the stairs and walked to the end of the hallway, silently opening the door. Lisa was in a small tub, her back to him. Cruz walked behind her until he was standing directly behind the tub. He put his hand on her head and pushed her under the water. She splashed the water with her hands and came up in a fury.

"Cruz!" Her green eyes blazed.

"I couldn't help it," he said lazily, unbuttoning his shirt. For the first time since he and Lisa had been together, he felt completely relaxed. Maybe it was being at Miguel's home. He felt comfortable here. Maybe it was that Lisa had shown him earlier that she wanted him. He took off his boots and pants.

"What're you doing?" Lisa turned around in the tub, staring at Cruz.

"I need a bath, too. I didn't think you'd mind." He walked to the other side of the tub and stepped inside, pushing his legs up against Lisa's.

"Cruz, you can't fit in here! I'll get out." Lisa started to stand up but Cruz pulled her back.

"No, I don't think so." He reached to the knot of hair on top of her head and pulled out the pins, running his fingers through the cascade of long hair that fell around her shoulders. He wrapped his long legs around her body and pulled her to him.

"Cruz, we can't."

Cruz stared into Lisa's eyes. "Now, this is the way to take a bath, don't you think?" He pulled her head to his and kissed her deeply. "Liseta," he said softly, his lips brushing against hers. "You are so beautiful. Do you know that?"

"Cruz," Lisa murmured, her mouth close to his. She wrapped her arms around his neck and he pulled her onto his lap. She could feel his passion rising, and it excited her. Never had she felt this with a man, not even with Eric. "Cruz, Cruz," she whispered his name over and over, kissing his face and neck.

"Liseta," Cruz said, covering Lisa's mouth with his own. He moved against her, encircling her in his arms.

Lisa felt herself sliding, giving in to this man. It would be so easy to love him. It would be too easy. "Cruz, I can't," she made herself say.

Cruz stopped at the sound of her voice. "Why? You want this as much as I do."

"It doesn't matter what I want, Cruz. This isn't right. I love Eric."

"I know you do. I'm sorry." He stood and wrapped a towel around himself.

Lisa reached out and touched his hand. "My feelings for you frighten me, Cruz."

He looked at her and pulled her up, wrapping his arms around her. He understood what she felt because he felt the same way. He had never loved like this before. When the time came, would he be able to let Lisa go back to the man who loved her and the daughter who needed her? All he knew is that he would revel in the feel of her in his arms right now, this very minute. All they had was the present. They could not count on the future.

Chapter 9

Eric, Tom, and Teresa had been riding for over two weeks when they found Vasquez's men, barefoot and weaponless, walking along the trail. They attempted to run away but they didn't get very far.

"You, what is your name?" Eric pointed to the man in front.

"Perez."

"Would you like to live out this day, Perez?"

"*Sí, señor.*"

"Then I would like some information. Do you understand?"

"*Sí, señor.*"

"Good. Have you seen two people, a man and a woman? The man is tall, Mexican, goes by the name of Cruz, the woman is also tall, slim, green eyes and reddish-brown hair. Very beautiful."

Perez looked to the other men. "We have not seen these people, señor."

Eric leaned forward on his horse. "Perez, I don't have much time. I need to find these people quickly. If you've seen them, it will help us greatly. I have a feeling you have. If you don't tell me the truth and tell me quickly, I will have to resort to

229

other means." Eric took out his knife, running it across the leather strap that hung from his saddle.

"Señor, I—"

"I don't want excuses, Perez. I just want the truth."

Perez swallowed hard. *"Sí, señor,* I have seen these people. We were traveling with them."

"You were traveling with them?" Eric looked at Tom. "What happened to them?"

"They ran away."

"They ran away?" Eric looked at their bare feet. "It looks like they did more than that."

"We woke up one night and Cruz, the man, had tied most of us together and taken our boots and our weapons. He made me tie everyone together and then he tied me up as well. It took us most of one day to get free."

"I think I like this man," Eric said with a smile. "Now, Perez, where were you supposed to take them?"

"To a rancho in San Diego."

"Do you know the name of the rancho?"

"No, señor. That is the truth. It belongs to Cruz and I never heard him say the name of it."

"Why were you taking them there?"

"We were to make sure the woman got out of the Alta California. Cruz said he would take her to Baja California and give General Vasquez money if he let her live."

"Were you really planning to take them there, Perez?"

Again, Perez looked at the other men. "We had orders from the general to shoot them after we got the money."

Eric shook his head. "I think this Cruz was too kind to you. He should've slit your throats and left you to rot," he said angrily. "Listen to me, Perez. I want you to tell your General Vasquez something for me. My name is Alejandro de Vargas. Tell the general that if he or any of his men ever come onto my land again, I will personally skin them alive. Do you understand?"

"Sí, señor."

"And be sure to tell the general that we have plenty of men posted all over our property. If we see any strangers, we'll shoot first. Now get the hell out of here."

Tom looked at his two companions and shrugged his shoulder. "I'm sorry to say it but I'm grateful to this Cruz. It seems like he's saved Lisa's life twice now."

Eric got down on his knees and checked the hoofprints of the horses. He ran his fingers around the dirt, then walked around, checking other prints to see if they matched. "They're definitely heading south. We shouldn't have too much trouble tracking them."

"Let's get going then. I'd like to get at least four hours sleep today," Tom said sarcastically.

Eric mounted up. "Look, if it's too hard on you two, you can head back anytime you want. I want to find my wife."

"Is that the only reason you're riding so hard?" Teresa asked.

Eric ignored her and rode on ahead, but he understood her question. He wanted to find his wife and make sure she was all right, but he also wanted to find out about Cruz. He was afraid that

Lisa might have fallen in love with the man, and he wasn't quite sure what he would do if that had happened. He felt he had driven a wedge between them before he left and he just hoped it wasn't too late to get through to her.

Lisa brushed out her hair and pulled up one side with a silver comb that Manuela had brought her. She wore a colorful gauze outfit with a full skirt and loose blouse and a sash at the waist. She slipped on a simple pair of sandals and looked at herself in the mirror. For the first time in months she felt clean and pretty.

Cruz walked up behind her and pulled her blouse off her shoulders. "This is how you're supposed to wear this, you know." He kissed each shoulder then looked at her reflection in the mirror. His mother's delicate silver cross lay on her chest as if it had always been there. "My mother would be proud that you're wearing her cross and her wedding ring."

Lisa looked down. "I don't think she'd be too proud under the circumstances," she said.

"We are married, Lisa. You act as if you are an adulteress."

"I am an adulteress. I'm married to another man." She pulled away from Cruz, but he pulled her back. "No, you're married to me. You're not doing anything wrong." He hugged her fiercely. "When we're together, it can't be wrong."

Lisa couldn't resist the boyish tone of Cruz's voice. "You make me feel so good, Cruz. You have a gift for that."

232

"And you have a gift for making me feel happy." He took her hand. "So, shall we go downstairs and join Miguel. I'd like to meet this lady of his."

Lisa took Cruz's hand and they went looking for Miguel. He was not downstairs yet, but Manuela took them into the parlor and served them wine and fruit.

"How did you get to know Miguel?" Lisa asked.

"It was an accident. I was up in the hills hunting. I'd been on the trail and I was practically starving. I heard a scream and I ran to see what was happening. A bear had Miguel on some rocks. Miguel had dropped his rifle and the bear was climbing the rocks to get him."

"But along came our hero," Miguel said, entering the room, resplendent in a green brocade suit and white ruffled shirt. "He had a small-gauge rifle, certainly not one that could kill a bear as large as that one, so he climbed a tree behind us. He carried some rocks with him and threw them at the gruesome animal. Of course the bear followed Cruz. He started clawing at the tree, shaking it back and forth. I was sure the animal was going to have him for lunch. But Cruz took careful aim and shot into the bear's eye, instead of into his head. That made the beast crazy. He couldn't see. He clawed at his face, but Cruz shot again, hitting him in the head. The poor animal stumbled away, eventually falling before he got into the woods. I'd never seen anything like it. The man was a marvel."

"As usual, Miguel, you exaggerate. Anyone could've shot it in the eye. It's just a matter of

233

having a steady hand."

"While the tree you're in is moving back and forth?" Miguel waved his hand. "As far as I am concerned, you were a hero."

"Miguel brought me home, fed me, and we have been friends ever since. That was over eight years ago."

"My father loved Cruz. I think he thought of him as the son he wished he'd had."

"Don't say that, Miguel. Your father loved you very much and you know it."

"Yes, I do know it, but I also know that I'm not like you. There are things about you that I admire, *amigo,* and I am glad that my father loved you as he did. You have never had a father love you like that."

Cruz nodded silently. He was holding Lisa's hand without realizing it. He smiled at her and brought her hand to his lips.

"I'm not disturbing you two am I?" Miguel asked.

"No, of course not," Lisa said self-consciously, taking her hand away from Cruz's. "Thank you for the bath and the clothes. I can't remember when I've enjoyed a bath more."

"Good. It pleases me to make people happy." Miguel looked past Cruz and Lisa and smiled broadly. "Ah, you are here, my dear. Come in."

A beautiful dark-eyed, dark-haired woman walked into the room, dressed in a red satin gown. Jewels sparkled from her ears and neck. She was small and delicate. As she walked into the room, she went to Miguel, not even looking at Cruz or Lisa.

234

"Hello, my darling," she said in a sensual voice, kissing Miguel on both cheeks. "Have you been waiting long?"

"No, I've been entertaining our guests."

The woman turned and looked at Cruz and Lisa and the smile on her face vanished immediately. She stared at Cruz as if she were looking at a ghost.

"Cruz, Lisa, I want to introduce —"

Cruz stood up. "Hello, Soleda," he said in a calm voice.

"Hello, Cruz," Soleda said, walking slowly forward, her hips swaying suggestively. "You look wonderful." She stood on tiptoes and kissed him on both cheeks.

Cruz pulled away. "Soleda, this is my wife, Lisa."

Soleda looked at Lisa and her eyes traveled to the cross around her neck. "Your wife?" Soleda asked. "But how is that possible?"

"Not now, Soleda," Cruz said, trying to control his temper.

Miguel had walked to the group of people. "I didn't know you knew each other, Cruz. Why didn't you tell me?"

"You never told me her name."

Miguel put his arm possessively around Soleda's shoulders. "Well, isn't she everything I said?"

Cruz's eyes traveled up and down the length of Soleda's body. "Yes, she is."

"So, tell me how you two know each other."

Cruz started to speak but Soleda interrupted him. "Cruz and I grew up in the same town."

"Did you know each other very well?"

235

"Not very," Soleda replied, her eyes making love to Cruz even as she spoke. "Tell me about your 'wife', Cruz," Soleda said.

Cruz took Lisa's hand. "Lisa, this is Soleda. You remember, I told you about her."

Lisa looked at Soleda, her green eyes defiantly taking on Soleda's bold challenge. "Yes, I remember, Cruz." She wrapped her fingers around the silver cross. "You said she was like a sister."

Soleda's black eyes burned into Lisa, her anger barely controlled. "Is that all you told your wife about us, Cruz?"

Miguel looked from Soleda to Cruz. "What's going on here? Is there something you haven't told me?"

Lisa stepped forward and put her arm through Miguel's. "Miguel, I'd love to see the garden. Would you mind? It would give Cruz and Soleda a chance to catch up on old times." She flashed Cruz a smile as she and Miguel left the room.

Soleda put her hands on her hips, walking around Cruz as if appraising him. "I think you have grown more handsome, *querido*," she said seductively.

"Don't call me that."

"Why not? Does it remind you of the times we made love, eh?" She stood in front of him, running her fingers up and down his white shirt. "I have never stopped thinking of you, *querido*." She pulled him closer to her and she pressed her mouth against his, her tongue probing his mouth.

Cruz took her arms and pushed her away. "Stay away from me, Soleda. I have a new life now."

"How can you have a new life, Cruz? You are

still married to me, remember?"

Cruz looked at her, his heart skipping a beat. He couldn't let Soleda know that she had gotten to him. "We didn't have a marriage, Soleda. It was a mistake."

"Ah, but it's a mistake that hasn't been corrected. I am still your wife, so that makes that other woman your whore."

Cruz took Soleda's shoulders in his hands, crushing them in his grasp. "Don't ever call her that. That name belongs only to you, Soleda. I suggest you don't say anything or your chances with Miguel will be ruined. You don't want that to happen, do you?"

Soleda pulled away, rubbing her shoulders. A smile slowly spread over her face. "I think I like you better now, *querido*. You are more of a man. You're not the whimpering little boy I used to know." She walked to the table and poured herself some wine, drinking greedily from the glass. "Tell me, *querido*, how is it with her? Does she please you as much as I did? Does she make you cry the way I did when you begged me never to leave you?"

Cruz forced himself to remain calm. "I was a weak-willed boy then. I'm a man now."

"You did not answer me, *querido*. How is it with the gringa?"

Cruz stepped forward, his expression one of menace. "It's none of your business, Soleda, but I'll tell you just so you'll know. My wife pleases me more than I thought any woman could. When I am with her, I feel as if I could die in her arms and be happy. No woman has ever pleased me as much as she. I love her, Soleda. She is everything to me." Cruz heard the crash of glass against the door as he left the room. It wasn't until he was outside that he realized he was shaking all over. She still had that effect on him. It scared him, but something else scared him more. He had said he loved Lisa. He had never admitted it before, and now he realized just how true it was. He loved her. He shook his head. Perhaps his father had been right about him—he had never been good for anything except stealing. Maybe it would be best if he just ran away and left Lisa here. Miguel would find a way to get her home.

"Cruz? Are you all right?" When he saw Lisa walking toward him, all of his convictions melted away. He wanted this woman more than he had ever wanted anything in his life. He embraced her, kissing her cheek. "Are you sure you're all right?"

Cruz nodded. "She makes me crazy, but not in the way you think. She's evil, and I'm worried about Miguel. I think I should tell him about her."

"He won't believe you, Cruz. He's so in love with her that he'll think you're jealous."

"But I have to try. I can't let her do to him what she did to me."

Lisa cupped her hands around his neck and looked into his eyes. "You are so very good." She kissed him deeply, moving her mouth against his.

"I love you," he said softly.

Lisa watched Cruz as he walked away to find Miguel. She was worried about him. She could already see the effect Soleda was having on him. She was afraid of what he'd be like if they stayed much longer. Then she thought about what he'd just said—that he loved her. She closed her eyes. She didn't know what to think or feel anymore. When she thought of Eric she couldn't remember his face; it was as if he had been eliminated from her mind, only to be replaced by Cruz. But she remembered things about Eric, things he had said, the way he held her, the way he made love to her, the way he laughed and his blue eyes crinkled at the corners. He was so much a part of her she could never live without him. But would he want her back after she had been with Cruz? Could she go on as if nothing had happened between her and Cruz? She knew she couldn't. He, too, was a part of her now.

"So, you think you are Cruz's wife?" Lisa turned. Soleda walked toward her, her fingers caressing the jewels around her neck. "You're fooling yourself, you know. He can never forget me. I am in his blood."

"What do you want, Soleda? You're going to marry Miguel. Why don't you leave Cruz alone?"

Soleda grabbed Lisa's arm in a tight grasp. "Cruz was mine first. Never forget that."

Lisa twisted out of the woman's grasp and stepped forward, forcing Soleda to stumble backward. "Cruz is mine now. Never forget that."

"You *puta!*" Soleda screamed.

Lisa ignored her and walked past her up the stairs to their room, hers and Cruz's. She opened the doors to the balcony and walked out, looking at the vast land that Miguel owned. It was beautiful here, different from Monterey. It was drier, not quite as green, but beautiful just the same. The surrounding mountains were the only boundaries

239

that she could see. There were endless miles of pasture, ponds, cattle, horses, and sheep. She thought suddenly of Don Alfredo and how proud he was of his land and she couldn't keep the tears back. She had forced herself not to think of her family; it was much easier that way. But what would they think of her now? She knew the answer to that. Perhaps it would be better if she never went back because she knew that Eric could never accept what she had done. She wasn't sure she herself could.

"Miguel, I need to talk to you." Cruz grabbed Miguel's arm as he started into the house.

"Let me find Soleda first. We can talk later."

"No. This can't wait."

Miguel stopped at the sound of Cruz's voice. He walked back outside. "What is it?"

"Let's go for a walk. What I have to say isn't easy." They walked through the garden and into the orchard. The orange blossoms were overpowering. "Soleda was my lover, Miguel."

"I thought as much," Miguel said calmly. "I knew there was something more between you two. I could tell by the way she looked at you."

"There's something more." Cruz stopped. "She was my wife."

Miguel nodded his head. "I see. How did the marriage end?"

"She left me. She ran away with another man."

"Cruz, you don't expect me to believe this."

"Miguel, listen to me. I wouldn't lie to you. I'm only telling you this so you'll be forewarned."

240

"What do you want me to do, ask her if she's going to leave me? Cruz, you know as well as I do that I am not like you. I'm not handsome. All I have is money and power. If a woman likes me for those things, then that is all right. Soleda has been honest with me. She has told me she doesn't love me."

"She could rob you blind and then leave you. She did that to me."

Miguel reached up and pinched an orange blossom off a tree and held it to his nose, breathing in. "It doesn't matter. She does things to me that . . ."

"I know, Miguel. She made me crazy with desire. I killed a man over her."

Cruz recounted the story of how, after he had married Soleda and taken her to his family's home, he woke up one morning to find everything of worth stolen from the house. "I went looking for her and found her in a cantina with a man, a killer by the name of El Diablo."

"El Diablo? I have heard of him. He was a bad one."

"She was with him, and when I saw them together it made me crazy. She was wearing my mother's cross that she had taken from the house and I tore it from her neck. El Diablo came at me. We fought. I killed him in self-defense." He lifted up his shirt to show Miguel the scar.

"I'm sorry for your pain, my friend, but it still changes nothing. I love Soleda. I want to marry her."

"You can't, she's still married to me," Cruz said with obvious pain in his voice. "We never dissolved

241

the marriage. We were married by a priest. We would have to go through the Church to get it dissolved."

"But what of Lisa? She is not your wife?"

"We were married by a priest, but that doesn't change anything. Soleda is still my wife."

"Then we will dissolve the marriage. You do want to do that, don't you, Cruz?"

"Of course I do. I love Lisa. I want her for my wife. I don't want to hurt her."

"Then we shall send for a priest and do what we must. Do not worry, my friend. It will turn out fine."

"Miguel, have your heard anything I've said?"

"Have *you* heard anything *I've* said? I know the kind of woman that Soleda is and it doesn't matter. I still want her. She makes me feel more like a man than any other woman I've known. I would do anything for her. Can you understand that?"

Cruz thought of Lisa and their lovemaking that afternoon and he nodded. "Yes, Miguel, I understand. I won't stand in your way. I want you to be happy."

"Good, good. Then there is nothing to worry about. As soon as the priest gets here, the marriage will be dissolved and Soleda and I will be married. Now come, let's go into dinner. The women will be waiting for us."

Cruz found Lisa sitting in a chair on the balcony, her legs curled up beneath her, her head resting against the chair back. He walked up behind her and bent down, kissing her bare shoulder.

242

She opened her eyes and looked up at him, a smile on her face.

"How did it go with Miguel?"

Cruz walked over to the railing and leaned against it, facing Lisa. "He's determined to marry Soleda no matter what. I told him that she and I were still married, but it didn't seem to matter to him. He wants to bring a priest here to dissolve my marriage with her and then marry her himself."

"So you and I aren't really married!" She put her feet on the floor. "I've been nothing more than your . . ." She stood up and walked to the railing next to Cruz. "I've been nothing more than your whore, Cruz. Soleda said it, and she was right." She put her hand over her face. "My God."

"Lisa, don't. We were married by a priest. Our marriage is legal."

"No it isn't, not if you're still married to Soleda. The one thing that helped to keep me going, that helped me not to hate myself, was knowing that I was really your wife. At least, I thought, I wasn't doing anything a wife shouldn't do with her husband. My God. What have I become?" She started for the room but Cruz stopped her.

"Don't you see that you're doing exactly what she wants you to do. She wants you to doubt yourself. That makes you weak. The weaker you are, the more vulnerable you are to her."

"It doesn't matter. It doesn't change anything."

"Listen to me!" Cruz's voice was loud. "You are my wife. We were married by a priest. My marriage to Soleda was an unholy alliance. She was the devil. She cut my heart out and crushed it into

243

little pieces." He looked deep into her eyes. "You put it back together again."

Lisa wrapped her arms around him. "Oh, Cruz, I don't know what to do. Either way, you and I will be hurt. It would have been so easy if we had never met."

"If I must lose you, it will be worth it, Liseta," he said softly, kissing her forehead. "You have given me so much."

"And you have taught me so much. I never thought it was possible to love two men as I love you and Eric. I didn't know my heart was big enough."

"Your heart is big enough to love anyone you wish, Liseta."

Lisa began to cry, her shoulders shaking uncontrollably. Cruz held her in his arms, stroking her hair. The only time she had felt such pain was when she thought Eric was dead. But somehow this seemed worse. Eric and Cruz were alive and she had to decide which one was more important. Yet she knew there was no decision to make, not as long as she had a daughter.

"Come, wipe your face. We must go downstairs."

"I don't want to go down there. I don't want to see her."

"We must. I don't want her to think we're afraid of her. Besides, Miguel would be insulted if we didn't go down for dinner."

Lisa nodded, wiping the tears from her face. She went to the washbowl and poured some water into it, splashing it on her face. She looked at herself in the small mirror and saw her face was

244

flushed, her eyes red and swollen. "I look terrible."

"You look wonderful, as always." Cruz took her in his arms and kissed her. "Don't be sad, *querida*. We will be strong enough to face whatever happens."

Lisa looked into Cruz's dark eyes. It was as if he was willing her to be strong. She nodded and took his hand, and they walked downstairs to the dining room, hearing Soleda's laugh before they ever entered the room.

"Ah, you have finally joined us. Good." Miguel stood up and motioned Lisa to sit beside him, Cruz to sit by Soleda. Cruz ignored Miguel and sat next to Lisa, across from Soleda.

"So, Cruz, are you still a bandit?" Soleda asked, taking a large drink of wine.

"Soleda, please," Miguel implored.

"It's all right, Miguel. No, I don't do that anymore."

"Why, doesn't your wife like it?"

"It was my decision. I thought it was time to stop living off of other people." He looked at her, his dark eyes fiercely angry.

"Tell us something about yourself, Lisa," Miguel pleaded.

Lisa looked at Cruz in desperation. They hadn't discussed her life. If Soleda knew she was married to Alejandro de Vargas and had a child, there was no telling what she would do. "I—"

"Lisa grew up in the East, in Boston. She was coming to California to visit her brother when the wagon train she was on was attacked by Comanches. She was a captive of theirs for almost a

245

year."

"Is that right?" Miguel leaned forward. "I have heard they are fierce people. Is it so?"

"They are fierce people when they want to be but they were good to me."

"Did someone take you for their wife?" Soleda asked, still drinking wine.

"Yes, someone took me for his wife."

"What was he like? Did he torture you?"

"No, he treated me well. He was a good, kind man." Lisa had to look away as she spoke of Eric.

"You speak of this man almost as if you love him. You didn't love a savage, did you?"

"He cared for me and he saved my life."

"How did you finally escape?" Miguel asked, fascinated by her story.

"I didn't escape, Miguel, he let me go. He hired a scout to take me to California."

"He must have cared for you greatly, my dear."

"I think she's lying."

"Soleda, that is enough!" Miguel said angrily. "I won't have you insulting our guests."

Soleda shrugged her shoulders indifferently and poured herself some more wine.

"So, how was it that you two met? Don't tell me you were his captive, too?"

Lisa looked at Cruz, a smile appearing at the corner of her mouth. "I was visiting my brother. He was staying on a rancho in Monterey. While I was there, Cruz stopped by to see the owner. They had met years before. We got to know each other—"

Cruz took Lisa's hand, kissing it gently. "And we fell in love."

"That's very romantic. I shall have to give you both a wedding gift."

"That's not necessary, Miguel."

"But I want to. I will have to think on it. Perhaps we will have a fiesta, too."

"We'll be leaving soon."

"Not before the week is up. You must stay. Besides, we have the *matanza*. You must help with it."

"Yes, and your wife and I can get to know each other better," Soleda said.

"I think you've had enough wine, Soleda."

"I can never have enough wine, Miguel." She reached over and stroked his arm. "You know what wine does to me."

Miguel looked acutely embarrassed. "Soleda, I will have you taken to your room if you don't stop this."

Soleda sat up and looked across at Cruz. "Yes, why don't you have Cruz take me to my room? I'm sure we could find lots of things to discuss."

"Enough!" Miguel said angrily, pounding the table with his fist. "I won't sit here and have you insult my guests at my table." Miguel started to get up and leave but Cruz stopped him.

"Don't leave, Miguel. I will take Soleda to her room. I can handle her."

Miguel looked at Cruz and then smiled. "All right, *amigo*. I trust you."

Cruz walked to the other side of the table and yanked Soleda to her feet, unceremoniously draping her over his shoulder. "Where is her room?"

"Next to mine, upstairs."

"Come on, Soleda," Cruz said, as Soleda kicked

247

and screamed.

"It does not bother you to see them together?" Miguel asked Lisa, still staring at the empty space where Soleda had sat.

"No, it doesn't bother me. I trust Cruz."

"I, too, trust Cruz. It is Soleda I worry about."

"Then why do you keep her here, Miguel?"

"I can't find it in my heart to send her away. She torments me, yet it is a torment that I seem to desire. I cannot seem to live without her."

"Miguel . . ." Lisa said gently, looking toward to the stairs where Soleda's screams could be heard.

Cruz held on to Soleda as he climbed the stairs, gripping her arms but suffering the wrath of her kicks on his back. When he reached her room, he walked in and threw her onto the bed where she landed with a thump. He stood over her, his hands on his hips. "I can stay here all night if I have to, Soleda."

Soleda lay on her side, hiking up her dress to her thighs. "That would be nice, *querido*. It would be like old times."

"No, it wouldn't. I don't want you anymore, Soleda, but I do want Miguel to be happy. If you make him happy, then I won't say anything. But if you keep embarrassing him like you did tonight, I'll make sure that you stay locked in this room until you learn to keep your mouth shut." Cruz knew he had gotten to Soleda. He recalled that the one thing she couldn't stand was being in confined places.

She sat up. "You wouldn't do that."

"Try me."

"Miguel wouldn't let you."

"Miguel would like for me to take over. He doesn't know how to handle you."

"And you do?" Soleda laughed. "You are fooling yourself if you believe that, *querido*."

"I'm not the foolish boy I once was, Soleda. I think you should take a better look."

Soleda swung her legs over the side of the bed and stood up, walking over to Cruz. "I know all about you, *querido*. You would have done anything for me. Anything."

Cruz felt Soleda's body against his, and for a fleeting moment, he was reminded of that small town where he had first seen her and the effect she had had on him. He would have done anything just to have her, it was true. It made him sick to think he had been so weak. He shoved her backward onto the bed. "You either stay in here quietly or I'll tie you to the bed, lock the door, and you'll stay here all night in the dark. Will you do as I ask?"

Soleda angrily kicked at the air. "I will do it if you will do something for me."

"What?"

"This." She stood up and pulled his head toward hers. She moved her mouth against his, her tongue running over his lips. "I know you can't forget me, *querido*. No woman can do to you what I can do." She put her hand between his legs and moved it back and forth.

Angrily, Cruz grabbed her hand. "I warned you, Soleda." He dragged her across the room to her cupboard, opening it up and looking through the drawers until he found some scarves. He took two out and dragged her back to the bed. He tied her

249

hands together and pushed her down on the bed.

"Cruz, I didn't mean it. I'm sorry."

"It's too late. I'm going to enjoy this." He tied her hands to the bedpost and, as she was yelling for Miguel, he tied the other scarf around her mouth. Muted sounds came from behind the scarf. Soleda struggled but could do nothing against the restraints. "If you're good, maybe I'll come up later and turn on a lamp. Good night, Soleda." Cruz walked out the door, slamming it. After he got outside, he closed his eyes and rested his head against the door. He was sweating. Soleda frightened him. She clearly still had a strong effect on him. He walked downstairs, trying to push the feel of her body from his mind.

"These are the same horses," Eric said, running his fingers along the outside of the hoof prints.

"But it looks as if they've gone back that way," Teresa said.

"Do you know whose land this is, Eric?" Tom asked, getting out a land map.

"I think it belongs to the Figueroas, but I'm not sure."

"Do you know them?"

"I met them when I was a boy, but I don't really know them."

"Well, all you Spaniards are related anyway. Just tell them who you are and that you need their help."

"I doubt if they're even there. They probably stopped for food and a change of horses."

"Now why would a rich man give someone like

Cruz food and horses?"

"Instead of sitting out here in the sun pondering it, why don't we go find out for ourselves?" Teresa said.

"You sound like you're getting impatient, Teresa."

"I'm getting tired of listening to you two talk back and forth. And I wouldn't mind a nice thick steak."

Eric and Tom laughed. "This Figueroa won't be able to resist you."

"No, he won't, especially since he's a cousin of mine," Teresa laughed, riding off in the direction of the tracks.

Eric and Tom looked at each other and rode off after Teresa.

"What did you say?" Tom asked.

"I said Miguel Figueroa is a cousin of mine. I haven't seen him in years, of course, but I was always a favorite of his. I'm sure he'll help us if he can."

"And you couldn't have told us that while we were trying to decide what to do?"

"You and Tom were so busy discussing things without me, I just thought I'd let you go on for a while."

"So, tell me about your cousin. What's he like?"

"As I said, I haven't seen him in years, but he was always very sweet. If your wife and Cruz are anywhere around here, he's probably taken them in."

"You're full of surprises, woman!"

They had ridden about halfway to the rancho when they were greeted by riders, inquiring as to

251

their destination.

"I am Señorita Teresa Torres, cousin of Miguel Figueroa. I would like to see him."

"Sí, señorita. And these men? They are with you?"

"Yes, they are my bodyguards."

"Follow us, please."

"Bodyguards?" Eric looked over at Teresa with disdain.

Teresa shrugged her shoulders and continued to ride. They followed the men into the area by the corrals and dismounted.

"If you will follow me, señorita, I will take you to the patrón."

Teresa looked at Eric and Tom, a playful expression on her face. When they reached the door, she turned to the men. "Perhaps it would be best if you waited out here. I can probably find out much more alone."

"All right," Eric agreed impatiently, "but don't take too long."

Teresa was led into the very same study that Cruz and Lisa had been taken to. The man knocked on the open door but before he had a chance to say anything, Miguel was up and out of his chair and across the room. He smothered Teresa with hugs and kisses.

"Mi prima," he said with sincerity. "Where have you been all these years? I have missed you."

"And I you, Miguel. I was sorry to hear about Tío Enrique. I know you and he were close."

"Yes, but it was for the best. I did not like seeing him suffer. So, what of your parents? Are they well?"

252

Teresa walked away, trying to evade the subject. "I haven't seen them in years, Miguel. But I hear from friends that they are well."

"Teresa," Miguel said quietly, "are you still married to that man your father made you marry?"

"No. I left him years ago. He was a hateful person. I don't think I'll ever forgive my father for what he did."

"He thought he was doing the right thing. You know the Spanish tradition our parents followed. He felt that if he arranged a marriage for you, your future would be secure."

"Not only was it not secure, it was hell."

"I'm sorry, Teresa." Miguel put his arm around his cousin. "But you look well enough now. You have a man?"

"Yes, a wonderful man in San Francisco. We live in a big mansion in the city with lots of servants, and I go to the theater and opera whenever they're in town." She looked at Miguel and laughed.

"You haven't changed, Teresa. You are still the same girl I used to know . . . So, what are you doing here? There must be a reason why you've come all this way after so many years?"

"I'm traveling with two men. We're looking for someone."

"Oh, I see."

Teresa smacked Miguel on the shoulder. "Don't use that tone with me. They are both friends. I am helping them because I know this part of California better than they."

"And who are they looking for?"

"A man and a woman."

Miguel walked back to his desk, lowering his eyes. "A man and a woman?"

"Yes, have you had any travelers lately?"

"We always have travelers on our land, Teresa. It covers so much area."

"Don't play games with me, Miguel. This is very important."

"What do they look like?"

"The man is tall, Mexican, goes by the name of Cruz. The woman is fairly tall, reddish brown hair, green eyes, her name is Lisa."

"Why are you looking for these people?"

"It's a long story, Miguel."

"If you want me to help you, perhaps you should be honest with me."

Teresa sighed. "One of the men I am traveling with is Lisa's husband. His name is Alejandro de Vargas, from Monterey. They have a daughter."

"Did she leave this husband and daughter to run away with this other man?"

"No, she was kidnapped by a General Vasquez. It seems Cruz was able to deal for her life. He said he'd take her south and pay the general some money if he let her live."

"I see."

"You know something, don't you, Miguel?"

"I need to know more."

"Damn you!" Teresa pounded the desk. "I have her husband and brother waiting outside. They're worried sick about her. If you know something about them, I want you to tell me."

Miguel dropped into his chair. "They were here, but Teresa, the woman did not look like someone who was kidnapped. She looked like a woman very much in love. They were here for over a week. They were always holding hands or kissing, and they stayed in the same room. I tell you, they are in love."

"God." Teresa turned around and sat on the edge of the desk. "What do I tell Eric?"

"Who?"

"Alejandro. I don't understand it. She was very much in love with her husband."

"If you knew Cruz, it would be easy for you to understand. He saved my life once, a long time ago. He has been a friend ever since. He is a good man, Teresa. I don't want to see him get hurt."

"And what am I supposed to tell her husband and brother? And what about her daughter?"

"I don't know." Miguel drummed his fingers on the desk. "I did notice one peculiar thing. She seemed very dependent on Cruz, almost like a child. She seemed afraid to be without him."

"Maybe it's just as simple as she's come to depend on him for her life. I can understand that." She thought of Bryant.

"How can you understand that, *prima?* You have always been so strong."

"You don't know, Miguel. There was a time when I could barely make it on my own. I'll tell you about it sometime. Right now, I have to figure out what I'm going to tell my friends."

"Tell them the truth."

"I don't know if I can, Miguel. It will break Eric's heart. He is so in love with her."

"I can understand why. She is a lovely woman. She is the kind of woman a man would kill for."

"Don't say that. I don't want to see anyone get hurt."

"Don't worry, Cruz isn't the killing type."

"If he's in love with Lisa, then he might do anything to keep her. Please help me, Miguel."

"All right, I will tell you where Cruz is going. But you must promise me that there will be no bloodshed. Cruz is like a brother to me."

"I don't think Eric is the kind of man who would kill to get his woman back. He has too much pride. I think he would want her to come willingly."

"Then I feel sorry for him. His woman has had her heart stolen by a master thief."

"You sound as if you admire him."

"I do. He's a good man. He did not have the kind of start in life that you and I had, Teresa. He had nothing, and he has managed to do well for himself."

Teresa leaned across the desk. "He's a thief, Miguel. How can you say that?"

"He only stole from people who could afford to lose it. If you go back to the village where he grew up, you will find that he has done much for the people there. Besides, I don't consider us much better. We were born into families that owned great portions of land, we had beautiful homes, servants to wait on us, the best food, the best clothes, how can we judge someone like Cruz?"

"We can't," Teresa said decisively. "If I bring my friends in, will you tell them the truth even if it hurts?"

Miguel rang a bell on his desk and sent a servant to get Eric and Tom. "So, tell me about this man of yours. Do you plan to marry him?" He looked at her hand. "I see you have a diamond on your hand large enough for a blind man to see."

"He's a good man, Miguel. He loves me for me, and he has forgiven me all my mistakes. I hope we will be married someday."

"I am happy for you, Cousin. I, too, plan to marry."

"Miguel! Is she here? Can I meet her?"

"Yes, she is here. She is on a ride now but you will meet her later. I expect that you will all stay here the night so that you can get some good food and rest."

"I think that's a fine idea." Teresa turned around when she heard Eric and Tom walk into the room. She went to them and brought them to Miguel's desk. "Miguel Figueroa, my beloved cousin, Alejandro de Vargas and Tom Jordan."

The three men shook hands. "Our families met once a long time ago, I believe," Miguel said.

"Yes, I think you came to my grandfather's rancho. We were young and not so caught up in life then," Eric said.

"Yes." Miguel looked at Tom. "You look like your sister. She is a lovely woman, very kind. I was happy to meet her."

"So they did stay here?"

"They were here for over a week." Miguel sat in his chair, clasping his hands together in front of him. "It was not my choice to tell you both these things, but my cousin has forced me to be honest. Teresa tells me that Lisa was kidnapped. Well, the woman I saw here was not forced to be with Cruz.

If anything, she seemed very much in love with him."

Eric sat down, putting his hands on the desk. "You're sure? You're sure it wasn't just an act?"

"I'm sorry Alejandro, but I know Cruz. He would never force a woman to do anything she didn't want to do."

"Did Lisa seem unhappy?" Tom asked.

Miguel thought for a moment. "No, she did not. She seemed very happy, very carefree."

Eric pounded his fist on the desk. "That can't be."

Tom reached over and grabbed Eric's arm. "Take it easy. We don't know all the circumstances."

"Alejandro, I am not telling you these things to upset you. My cousin tells me that the truth is the best thing, so I am telling you the truth. If you do not believe me, ask any of the servants in the house. Cruz and your wife appeared to be very much in love."

"Did she say anything about our daughter?" Eric asked in desperation.

"No, she said nothing of you or your daughter."

Eric looked at Tom. "Is it possible she could have lost her memory? Maybe she suffered a head injury."

"That could be," Tom agreed.

"Eric . . ." Teresa said gently. "You will not know the truth until you find your wife and talk to her."

"She's not really my wife, is she?" Eric said angrily.

"Anger will not do you any good. I told you before, you know nothing of your wife's circum-

258

stances. Do not judge her unless you know the facts."

"I think my cousin is right," Miguel added. "Cruz is my friend and I know he would do nothing to destroy anyone's marriage purposefully. Perhaps your wife just came to depend on him when there was no one else."

"Maybe Cruz planned it that way."

"Please, señor, we don't know what happened."

"Eric. You're tired. Why don't you go get some rest. You'll be able to think more clearly."

Tom stood up. "I think that's a good idea. I know I could use a siesta if you don't mind, Miguel."

"Not at all. I will have you shown to your rooms."

Tom started to leave the study but paused at the door. "Are you coming, Eric?"

"I'll be there in a while."

Teresa nodded slightly to Tom to leave the room and she sat in the chair next to Eric. "Will you please do as I ask? You'll only drive yourself crazy if you persist in guessing."

"I'll go in a minute. I have to ask Miguel one more question."

"Sí, anything."

"Did they share the same room?"

Miguel looked at Teresa and then back at Eric. He nodded. "Yes, they shared the same room. I am sorry."

Eric nodded, staring at some far-off place. "Thank you for your honesty, Miguel."

"I probably would have lied if Teresa here hadn't forced me to tell the truth."

Eric smiled slightly. "I guess I'll go get some rest." He stood up and walked to the door, colliding with Soleda. "I'm sorry, señora. I didn't see you."

Soleda looked Eric up and down. "It's quite all right, señor. And what might your name be?"

"Alejandro de Vargas, but my friends call me Eric."

"That is a strange nickname."

"My father was white."

"That is why you have such incredible blue eyes."

"Soleda, this is my cousin, Teresa. She and her friends will be spending the night with us."

"Good, we can use the company. It's been boring around here since Cruz and that woman left."

"That's enough, Soleda."

"No, I'd like to hear more about that woman," Eric said.

Soleda sashayed into the room, swaying her hips to and fro. "I could never see why Cruz was interested in her. She was very pale-looking. She hung on him all the time."

"Do you think she was in love with him?"

Soleda narrowed her eyes. "Why are you so interested in this woman?"

"Because she's my wife," Eric said angrily.

Soleda looked from Eric to Miguel and burst out laughing. "Oh, this is funny." She walked to the table and poured herself some wine. "She is married to you and to Cruz, Cruz is married to me and to her, and I plan to be married to Miguel." She took a big drink of the wine. "I think the Church would frown on all of us, don't you?"

260

"Soleda, I don't think you should be drinking wine in the afternoon."

"I don't care what you think, Miguel," Soleda said derisively.

"I don't think Señor de Vargas is interested in what you have to say."

"I'm very interested in what she has to say, Miguel. So Cruz is married to you?"

"Yes. We were married, five or six years ago, I don't remember exactly."

"So that means that Lisa can't be married to Cruz," Eric said thoughtfully. He looked at Miguel. "Did you know that she was married to Cruz or did you plan to marry her anyway, just like your friend did with my wife?"

"Eric, don't," Teresa warned.

"Actually, Cruz is the one who warned me that he and Soleda were still married. He didn't think it mattered when Vasquez had your wife. Vasquez knew nothing of the marriage, so to him it was legal. He suggested that we bring a priest and dissolve their marriage so I could marry Soleda."

"And that would conveniently make his marriage to my wife legal, as well."

"Please do not insult my friend, señor. I understand that this must be hard for you, but I refuse to listen to such things."

"No, I don't think you do understand how hard this is for me, 'señor'. I was gone for two months and when I came home, I found that my wife had been kidnapped and almost murdered. Then I found out that she had been taken away. Now I find out she's in love with one of her captors." He looked at Soleda. "How would you feel if that

261

happened to her?"

"I would probably feel the same as you."

Eric took a deep breath. "So, was the marriage dissolved? Are you two free to marry?"

"No, I would not give my consent," Soleda said playfully, sipping at the wine.

"Why not?" Teresa asked coldly.

"I did not consent to it because I didn't like her."

"Soleda," Miguel said in a pleading tone.

"Miguel, do you want me to lie? Do you want me to tell them that I liked seeing that woman with my husband? Well, I did not."

"Don't you want to marry Miguel?" Teresa asked.

"Of course I want to marry Miguel."

"So why won't you consent to a dissolution of the marriage?"

"I already told you!" she said angrily. "I hate that woman, and I want her and Cruz to suffer."

Teresa looked at Eric. "Miguel, maybe it's best that we leave right now."

"No, I won't hear of it." Miguel came out from around the desk and embraced Teresa. "Please stay. I need you here."

"All right, we'll stay until tomorrow." She kissed him on the cheek. "We'll be down after siesta." She flashed Soleda a derisive look and took Eric's arm.

Once outside the room, Teresa stopped and said firmly to Eric, "The marriage isn't legal."

"What are you talking about?"

"If Cruz is still married to that woman, he can't be married to Lisa. The marriage is not legal."

"If she's not married to me and she's not married to him . . ." His eyes looked serious. "If they're sleeping together . . ." He shook his head.

"Don't, you don't know that to be true."

"Teresa, if they're sharing the same room, they are probably sleeping together. He would be crazy not to want Lisa. It makes my gut ache. I feel as if she's been disloyal to me."

"Do you love her, Eric?"

"You know I love her."

"Then you will wait for her to explain her actions. Have you never done anything you've been ashamed of?"

Eric thought back to the times he had slept with Consuelo when he was with Lisa. He had made all the excuses in the world but he had still done it. He hadn't been forced into it like Lisa had been. Teresa was right. He was judging Lisa before even hearing what she had to say. He bent down and kissed Teresa on the cheek. "You're a very special woman. Bryant is a very lucky man."

"Thank you. I just know what it's like to be judged only on appearances. Bryant took the time to get to know me. I will always love him for that."

"What do you think of Soleda?"

"I think she's a witch, and she definitely hates your wife. I think she'll do anything to hurt her. I'd be careful of her if I were you, Eric."

"She can tell me about Cruz."

"Do you really think she'll tell you the truth? I think she hates him, too."

"Why would she hate him?"

"Because he was probably smart enough to leave

263

her."

"But your cousin is going to marry her."

Teresa shook her head, taking Eric's arm and leading him up the stairs. "Poor Miguel, he has never had the looks of other men, so he has allowed his pants to think for him when it comes to women."

Eric laughed. "What about men? Is he any better judge of character?"

"If he says Cruz is a good person, I believe him. Miguel is not usually taken in so easily, except by women. Do you think your wife would allow herself to be led around by a liar and a cheat?" She shook her head. "From what you have told me of Lisa, I don't think so."

"I see I'm not going to win with you. You're going to defend Lisa no matter what."

"I don't know your wife but I like her. I like what you have told me about her. She is a survivor. She's not weak, not like I was. I tried to find the easy way out and I almost wound up dead."

Eric thought back to the time in the Comanche camp when Lisa had tried to kill herself. It had been a horrible time for her, but somehow, she had managed to survive.

"You'll like her when you meet her."

"I know I will." Teresa put her hand on Eric's arm. "What is it? There is something else bothering you."

"What if she doesn't want to come home with me? What if she has fallen in love with this man? I don't know if I can face that."

"Then you must make her want to come home, Eric. You must make her see that life without you

264

would be nothing. If she is with this man willingly right now, it must be for a reason. It is up to you to make her see all of the things she saw in you in the beginning. You must make her fall in love with you again." Teresa hugged Eric. "Rest well, my friend."

Eric nodded absently as he stood in front of his door. He should never have fought with Lisa before he left. It had probably just given her the excuse she needed to fall in love with another man. He felt as if someone had just gutted him. He felt empty inside. He just wanted to find Lisa and know that she was well. And he wanted to know that she still loved him.

Teresa and Miguel spent the time before dinner catching up on the past years. Eric and Tom sat in silence, enjoying the easy affection that was between the cousins. The atmosphere was light and jovial until Soleda entered the room, then everyone grew silent.

"What's the matter, are the two cousins running out of things to talk about? I'm sure you could think of plenty of things to tell us about your privileged upbringing. Better yet, why don't I tell you about Cruz and me?"

"Soleda, no one wants to hear about you and Cruz."

Soleda walked over to where Eric and Tom sat on the couch, and she managed to squeeze between them, draping an arm around Eric's shoulders. "I'm sure Eric would be interested in hearing about Cruz, wouldn't you?"

Eric glanced at Teresa and shook his head. "No, not really. I'd rather hear about Teresa and Miguel."

Soleda ran her fingers up and down Eric's neck. "Well, you're no fun at all." She turned to Tom. "So, do you want to hear about your sister who is living in sin with my husband?"

Tom stood up. "If you don't mind, Miguel, I think I'll take a walk before dinner."

"Don't let me chase you off. What's the matter with you people?"

"Soleda, please," Miguel pleaded weakly.

Teresa put her arm through Miguel's. "Miguel, why don't you take the men for a walk while I have a little talk with Soleda." Teresa smiled and kissed Miguel on the cheek. "Please."

"All right. Why don't I show you men my new prize stallion? I paid an incredible sum for him."

Teresa closed the doors behind the men, then she walked to the couch where Soleda was sitting. "Stand up."

"What? Are you giving me orders?"

Teresa reached down and yanked Soleda to her feet, splashing the glass of wine all over her, then took the glass from Soleda's hand and threw it against the wall. Soleda tried to twist away from Teresa's grasp, but Teresa held on tightly.

"I'm not like Lisa," she said angrily.

"What is that supposed to mean?"

"That means that I've been where you've been, Soleda. Nothing you do or say can shock me. I know you, Soleda, I know you as well as I know myself. You'll sleep with any man to get what you want. Nothing matters to you except money, clothes, wine, and a good man. And if the man isn't good enough in bed, you'll find another, like you've probably already done behind Miguel's back."

Soleda's eyes darted back and forth. "Who are you?"

"Don't you recognize me, Soleda? I'm you."

Soleda tried to wriggle away from Teresa's hold but she couldn't. "Let go of me. You're crazy."

"You listen to me, woman. Until we leave tomorrow morning, I want you to treat my cousin with respect. If you don't, I'll tell him you're nothing more than a cheap whore who can be bought for a bottle of wine and a night in bed."

"He won't care. Miguel loves me."

"That may be true, but Miguel also has pride. If I tell him that you've already slept around with half of the men on the rancho, how long do you think he'll keep you here? And that's not all. I don't want you saying anything else about Lisa while we're here, do you understand?"

"Why? Why should she matter to you?"

Teresa smiled, pressing her fingernails into Soleda's bare arm. "She is everything you and I could never be, that's why she matters to me."

"She is sleeping with a married man. I call that — "

Before Soleda could get the rest of her sentence out, Teresa slapped Soleda hard across the face, knocking her a few steps backward. "Don't say it, Soleda. If you're going to use the word, I think you should think about yourself."

Soleda rubbed her cheek, tears filling her eyes. "You are a hateful bitch!"

267

"Just so you know who you're dealing with. Like I said, I'm not Lisa. I'm not good like she is. I've been in the gutter, just like you, Soleda. I'll do anything it takes to defend the people I care about."

"But you don't even know this woman. I don't understand."

"You *wouldn't* understand." Teresa stepped closer to Soleda. "Tell me, why did Cruz leave you, Soleda?"

"He didn't leave me, I left him."

"Why?"

"Because he was nothing but a poor thief. I wanted more for myself."

"It seems he has done well for himself. I'll bet you're sorry you left him."

Soleda put her hand down and faced Teresa. "You don't scare me. You want the truth, I'll tell you the truth. I plan to marry your cousin and become a very wealthy woman. But only after I make Cruz and that woman suffer. I want her to live in sin for as long as it takes. I want her to know what it's like to be treated like a . . ." She stopped, the hand mark still fresh on her cheek.

"Like a whore, Soleda? Why is it so hard for you to say it? You're a whore."

"I'm not a whore. I'm a respectable woman now."

"And what if I were to tell my cousin different?"

"You wouldn't do that. You wouldn't hurt him like that."

"I would rather hurt him now than see him hurt later."

Soleda shrugged her shoulders and walked to the table, pouring herself another glass of wine. "Tell him, I don't care. He is obsessed with me. He will never be free of me," she took a big drink of the wine, "just as Cruz will never be free of me."

"You think too highly of yourself, Soleda. There are other women in the world who can make love to a man and make him happy as well. You will soon find that out."

"There is no other woman who would have the stomach to sleep with Miguel and he knows it."

Teresa was across the room in seconds. She took Soleda by the shoulders and slammed her up against the wall, hitting her head against it. "Don't you ever say such a thing again or I swear I will take great pleasure in wringing your worthless neck. Do you understand?"

"Yes, yes," Soleda cried.

"Are you two through in there?" Miguel's voice came from outside the doors.

"Don't forget what I said," Teresa hissed as she slid one of her hands around Soleda's throat for a moment, then dropped them and walked to the doors and opened them, a smile on her face.

Miguel looked anxiously from Teresa to Soleda. "Is everything all right?"

"Everything is fine, isn't it, Soleda?" Teresa's eyes burnt into Soleda's.

"Yes, Miguel, everything is fine."

"Well, I think dinner is ready. Shall we go in?"

Teresa stood between Miguel and Tom, holding the arm of each man. "Would you two mind escorting me in to dinner?" She glanced back at Soleda, secure in the knowledge that she would

269

keep her mouth shut.

"Aren't you going to escort me in to dinner?"

Eric waited for Soleda and held his arm out to her but she shrugged it away in midair.

"I've been waiting to get you alone, señor. I must tell you something, I must tell you that I walked in on Cruz and your wife."

Eric dropped his arm. "I don't want to hear."

"I think you'll want to hear this. They were in the bathtub together and they weren't taking a bath."

"God, you are cruel."

"I'm not being cruel, señor, I am telling you the truth. Your wife was with Cruz and she was making as much noise as . . . well, you can imagine. It was the middle of the day, too. I was shocked. Anyway, I thought you should know. Cruz and your wife have been together in the most intimate of ways." Soleda walked out, a smile on her face.

Eric stood motionless. He tried to forget what Soleda had just told him, but a vivid picture of Lisa with another man filled his head. His heart beat frantically and his throat felt dry. He actually thought he might be sick. He walked to the window and looked out. Maybe it wasn't worth looking for Lisa. Maybe she was already lost to him.

Teresa walked up behind him. "What did she say to you? Eric, you can't believe anything that woman tells you."

"She saw them making love in a bathtub in the middle of the day." He shook his head, a sardonic smile on his face. "And I thought I knew her."

"Maybe you never did."

Eric looked at Teresa, his eyes questioning.

270

"What is that supposed to mean?"

"Did either one of you ever take the time to get to know each other? You told me that you saved her when she was in the Comanche camp so it was natural for her to love you. Then, after she thought you were dead, she found you again in California, but you still had problems. There was another woman and you told me yourself that you both fought over little things. Maybe you never really knew her, Eric. Maybe you had an idea of what you wanted her to be. When she ran away to have your daughter on her own, maybe she was trying to find out then if you two had a future together. But you brought her back home."

"What is all of this supposed to mean, Teresa?"

"You have made her out to be a perfect woman. But she isn't perfect, she does have faults. She's human, Eric."

"I know that, for Christsakes."

"Do you? Can you forgive her for being with another man? Can you accept that you haven't been the only man in her life?"

"I haven't been the only man in her life."

"Those other men were not her choice, and you know it. Perhaps this man *was* her choice. Can you live with that?"

"I don't know."

"Do you still love her enough to fight for her?"

Eric's blue eyes were clearly sad. "I don't know, Teresa."

"At least you're honest. If you decide she is what you want, then you must be prepared to forget about your pride. Can you do that, Don Alejandro?"

Eric smiled. "I did it once before when I sent her away from the Comanche camp, but I felt as if my heart had been torn from me."

"Still you knew it was the right thing to do. Don't let your pride get in the way, Eric."

"Why is this so important to you, Teresa? You act as if it's you who is so involved."

"Maybe I wish it were. I admire Lisa. She has qualities I wish I possessed. I think she knows in her heart she belongs with you."

"I hope you're right."

"You've decided then?"

Eric nodded. "Yes, we'll leave tomorrow. But you'll have to help me keep my temper in check. When I see Lisa with this man, there's no telling what I'll do."

"I'll be there to help you. I want to see you happy."

"Thank you. You've been a good friend. Who would've thought that could possibly happen?"

"Certainly not I. I hated you the moment I met you . . . but not really. You just made me see myself when I really hadn't looked for a long time. Thank you."

Eric put his arm around her. "Come on. Let's get something to eat. Suddenly I'm starving."

Teresa took Eric's arm, hoping that he would be happy. For the first time in her life, she had found a man friend. It was a good feeling.

Chapter 10

When Lisa first saw the valley she was astounded by its pastoral beauty. They had stopped on a rise overlooking the valley and as far as she could see in all directions were endless miles of green pastureland, looming mountains to the east and the Pacific Ocean to the west. Oak and willow trees grew along the banks of the river, and wild sumac and lilac dotted the hills. Cattle grazed lazily alongside horses. It was a stunning scene.

"Cruz, it's so lovely and peaceful here."

"Yes, I knew I wanted this for my home the moment I saw it."

"How did you manage to acquire the land?"

"Do you mean, did I steal it?" Cruz smiled. "No, I didn't steal it. I bought it. It was part of a land grant, but the owner was willing to sell me some land." He noted Lisa's quizzical look. "No, I didn't hold a knife to his throat. That's not how it happened at all. Actually, when I was a boy and I first came through here, I did some work on the rancho. The *patrón* took a liking to me. I helped him do various things. I was the one who found him one day when he went out riding and didn't

273

come back. He'd fallen from his horse and broken a leg. He claims I saved his life. All I did was help him."

"You have a habit of saving people's lives, don't you?"

"I didn't actually save his life, but he acted as if I'd done something special for him. So, in return, he sold me five hundred acres of his land for practically nothing. He wanted to give it to me, but I wouldn't accept that. I worked on the rancho for the next year to pay for it. Then I left because I missed my family. When I went back home, I met Soleda. My life wasn't the same for quite a while. Then I brought her here. It was the biggest mistake I've ever made. I let her see a part of me that I never wanted anyone to see." He looked across at Lisa. "Except you. She came to this place and for a time, it was never the same for me."

"But you still love it, don't you?"

"Yes, I've never seen anyplace like it." He looked around at the surrounding hills. "I want my children to grow up here."

Lisa looked away, unable to meet Cruz's eyes. She already had a child, a child who she missed desperately. She wondered if she'd ever see her again. It occurred to her then that it was possible she could be carrying Cruz's child, and she became terrified. What would she do if she had two different children by two different men? How could she ever choose between them?

"Lisa . . . ?"

"I'm sorry. I was thinking about Raya."

He reached over and squeezed her hand. "I told

274

you I'd take you back to her and I meant it. I'd never keep you from your daughter."

Lisa looked back down at the valley and it suddenly occurred to her that Eric would love this place, too. She hadn't thought about him in a long time. She hadn't wondered what his thoughts were or what he was doing and she knew why. It was her way of going on. She wasn't sure she could deal with what would happen to Eric when he found out about her and Cruz.

"Don't, Lisa," Cruz said gently. "You're making yourself feel guilty again. Don't do that. You haven't done anything wrong."

"But I have, Cruz. I have. I have made love to you and we're not even married. I don't even know if I'm married to Eric. Sometimes I feel as if my mind will explode if I keep thinking."

"Then don't think. Come on. Let's go to the rancho. Once you get there, you'll relax."

Lisa nodded and followed Cruz, unable to resist his calm voice. They cantered along as Cruz explained to her about the land grants of the area. Most of the land was owned by wealthy families who had been given large land grants by either the Spanish or the Mexican governments. Some owned hundreds of thousands of acres, men with names such as Osuna, Carillo, Figueroa, and Lopez. Mexican vaqueros worked the horses, cattle, and sheep, riding from morning until sunset to make sure a *patrón*'s animals were well within his boundaries. Local Indians and Mexicans did most of the manual labor.

They rode for most of the day along the river until they reached a vineyard. They rode past it and up the steep rise of the hill. On the top of the hill, Lisa saw a small whitewashed adobe house. Corrals for animals were around the yard and orchards of orange and lime trees were everywhere. They rode past a small garden that was being tended by workers. Cruz talked animatedly with the workers, who stood up, smiling and waving, obviously pleased to see him.

"Cruz, this is beautiful."

"It's not the Rancho del Sol, Lisa. It's very simple. I only have a kitchen, a living room, and two bedrooms." He pointed to the top portion of the house. "But, as you see, I'm planning a second story with more bedrooms and a study. There will be balconies all around so there will be a view from every room. Someday, it will be a good house."

"It's already a good house."

"When I'm not here, I let some of my workers live in the house. I trust them and they trust me. I'm lucky."

"Maybe it's because you're one of them."

They rode up to a corral and dismounted. Cruz tethered their horses to one of the railings. They were instantly greeted by an older man with gray hair and a mustache.

"Hello, Cruz. It is good to have you back. Do you see the house? I think we will be finished with the second story by winter."

Cruz patted the man on the back. "You've done well, Jesus. Everything looks good. How is Elena?"

"She is well. She is fat and happy and she talks as much as she ever did."

Cruz laughed. He took Lisa's hand and led her forward. "Jesus, this is my wife, Lisa."

Jesus looked from Cruz to Lisa but said nothing. Obviously, he knew about Soleda. "I am very pleased to meet you, señora. I think you will like it here."

"I'm sure I will." Lisa shook Jesus's hand.

"Can I get you and the señora something to drink? Elena will want to feed you. She'll tell you you look too skinny."

Cruz smiled. "We'll come inside in a minute. I want to show Lisa around." Cruz led Lisa around the house to a well. Flowers were planted all around it and a stone bench was built next to it, under the shade of a willow tree. "This is my favorite place. You can see the valley, the mountains, and the ocean from here."

Lisa couldn't resist the tone in Cruz's voice or the look on his face. He looked like a small boy, finally discovering something that was his very own. She took his hand. "I can see why you love it so. I think it's the most beautiful place I've ever seen." She leaned her head against his shoulder.

"Could you be happy here, Lisa?"

Lisa swallowed hard and kept looking out over the valley, afraid to meet Cruz's eyes. "I think you know the answer to that, Cruz."

"No, I don't," he said, grabbing her shoulders and forcing her to look at him. "I love you, you know that. I just want to know that you care for me in some small way. I know that we can't be together, Lisa. I'm not asking you to stay here. I understand what your husband and daughter mean to you. I just want to hear you say the words."

Lisa's mouth trembled as she looked up at Cruz's handsome face. His dark eyes looked so sad. "Yes, I could be very happy here. If I didn't already have a family, I could stay here with you forever." Tears filled her eyes. "I don't want to hurt you."

"You haven't hurt me." He kissed her softly. "You have always been honest with me; I love you even more for that. You have also made me realize that I can be loved. I never knew that with Soleda."

"Soleda was a stupid woman. How could any woman willingly leave you?" Her green eyes overflowed with love.

"Perhaps I should make you a captive so you can never leave. I'll make you fall in love with me."

"You don't have to make me fall in love with you, Cruz," Lisa said, turning away from him. "I just don't think I could live with myself if I left my family without looking back."

"And I probably wouldn't love you as I do if you did that." He kissed her on her nose. "It's time to be happy and relax. I'll take you in to meet Elena." He appraised Lisa. "She'll take great delight in trying to fatten you up."

Lisa looked around the rancho as they walked. It was built in the typical U-shape, with a courtyard in the middle. Clay pots with flowers filled the courtyard, and birds and chickens chirped and squawked everywhere. "Have you given a name to your rancho?"

Cruz shook his head. "There was no inspiration until now. Maybe I'll call it the Rancho del Amor,"

278

he said with a twinkle in his eye, then walked to the kitchen and peered in. The door was wide open and Elena was singing a Spanish love song at the top of her voice while kneading bread. Cruz continued to lean against the doorjamb, staring, until Elena looked up, jumping in surprise. *"Madre de Dios!* Cruz Estacan, you have frightened me out of half of my life."* She wiped her flour-covered hands on her apron and held out her arms. "Come over here and let me see you." Cruz walked into the kitchen like an obedient child and Elena hugged him. He kissed her on the cheek. "You're much too skinny," she said, shaking her head and making a clucking noise. "We need to fatten you up."

Cruz glanced at Lisa, and she laughed.

"And who is this you bring into my kitchen without an introduction?"

Cruz took Lisa to Elena. "Elena, this is my wife, Lisa. Lisa, this is Elena. I couldn't run this place without her."

"Su esposa?" Elena's eyes widened and then she crossed herself. "You have gotten rid of that evil witch? Good." She practically smothered Lisa in her arms. "Not only are you skinny but you're much too pale."

"That's because she's white, Elena," Cruz said laughingly.

"I know that. Do you think I'm blind. No, she looks as if she could use a good bath, a good meal, and some rest. What have you been doing to this poor girl?"

Cruz rolled his eyes. "We've been on the trail for a long time, Elena."

"Well, you'll be home for a while, I hope. This is your home."

"I plan to stay here from now on."

"Good. Here . . ." Elena ripped large hunks of fresh break from a loaf and smothered them with butter, handing them to Cruz and Lisa. "Eat these and then I will make you both a real meal. Why don't you take your skinny little wife and let her clean up, Cruz."

"Of course, Elena," Cruz replied, shaking his head. "Do you see what I mean, Lisa? She treats me as if I'm ten years old," Cruz said when they were outside.

"It's good for you. You need someone to care for you. Besides, she enjoys it. It's obvious that she really cares for you."

"She and Jesus are like family to me. Come on, I'll show you the house." They walked from the kitchen along a tiled pathway that led to every room in the house from the outside. He opened the doors to the first room, the living room. It was an incredible room. One side was made up entirely of a large window, which Cruz had ordered from Boston. It faced the valley and the mountains beyond, and gave the effect of the room being larger than it was. There was an open beam ceiling, wooden, pegged floors, and heavy wood and leather furniture with lots of cushions. The walls had framed pencil sketches hung on them.

Lisa walked to the sketches. They were all of local people. She recognized Jesus and Elena, but there were also sketches of vaqueros, Indians, the mission, the valley, and the mountains. There was also a sketch of Soleda, her eyes large, her mouth full, her hair hanging in waves around her shoulders. "These are wonderful, Cruz." She looked at him. "Did you do them?"

"Yes," he admitted, looking down at the floor.

"Why didn't you tell me?"

"What was I going to tell you? I can sketch? Many people can do that."

"But these are very good. People in the East pay money for sketches like these."

"What people?"

"Magazines. People back there want to know what it's like out here."

"These aren't for sale. These are mine."

Lisa pointed to Soleda's picture. "This one is especially good. She is very beautiful."

Cruz looked at it a moment then took it down. "It doesn't belong there anymore."

"Cruz, don't. She was a part of your life."

"She was a bad part of my life, a part I don't want to remember."

Lisa took the picture out of Cruz's hand and hung it back up. "It belongs there. It's beautiful. You did that when she was very important to you. Besides, there'll be an empty space if you take it down."

"No there won't. I'm going to do a sketch of you."

"No," Lisa said seriously. "I don't belong up there."

"Yes, you do, more so than Soleda."

"No, please. I don't want to sit for you."

"You don't have to sit. I'll do it from memory."

"Can you do Raya?" Lisa asked suddenly.

281

"I think so." Cruz walked to a desk and took out a pad and some rough pieces of charcoal. He sat down and began to sketch.

Lisa didn't want to bother him, so she kept herself busy by walking around the room. It would be wonderful to have a sketch of Raya that she could look at everyday. She stood by the huge window and she looked out over the valley. She could see the river below. It was so peaceful here. She envied the woman who would become Cruz's wife. She would be a very lucky woman. Hearing him get up, she didn't move but continued to stare out the window. Cruz held the sketch in front of her. It was Raya. Her head was turned slightly and her hair was blown, and she was laughing as only a child can laugh. He didn't shade in her eyes, so they appeared light, just as they were in real life. It was an unbelievable likeness of her daughter.

"This is so good, Cruz." She took the sketch from him and held it to her chest as if by doing so, it would make Raya closer to her. She turned and looked at him. "Is there anything you can't do?"

"I can't make you fall in love with me."

Lisa lowered her eyes. She didn't know what to say to him. "It seems I can never say the right thing."

Cruz tilted her chin up. "You don't have to say anything." He kissed her. "You look tired. I want you to get some rest. I'll wake you when it's time for dinner."

Lisa nodded her aquiescence and followed Cruz down the hall to a large room, simple but very pleasing to the eye. It had a huge mahogany bed in the middle that was covered by a multicolored bedspread. There were colorful rugs on the floor, a washstand with a bowl and pitcher on top, a cupboard for clothes, and a small desk against the wall. There were no drapes on the windows, just as there were none in the living room. "It's your room."

"Yes. It overlooks the valley, and you can see the ocean. Lie down and get some rest. I have some things I have to check on. Don't worry about me."

Lisa looked at the sketch one more time. "Thank you for this. It's beautiful. Now I can look at her everyday."

"We'll put it in a frame later."

Lisa put the sketch on the washstand and sat down on the bed. "I do feel tired. This isn't like me."

"We've had a long trip. I'll see you later."

"Cruz," Lisa said softly, her voice shaking.

He came to her, sitting down on the bed and taking Lisa in his arms. "It's all right. You'll be all right no matter what happens, and so will I."

"How do I know that?"

"You must believe it. We've been lucky enough to have each other for a short time. We can't be selfish, can we?"

"No," she said, and lay back on the bed.

Cruz pulled the bedspread over her legs and he kissed her on the cheek. "Sleep well, *querida*."

He walked out of the room and shut the door, leaning against it, his eyes closed. How could he ever live without her now that he had known her? He wasn't sure that he could. He walked down the hall and out a door that led to the courtyard. He looked around. God, how he loved it here. He remembered how Soleda had been disappointed when he had brought her here. She had been hoping that he would live in a grand hacienda. Lisa had seen the beauty of it immediately.

He walked to the front of the rancho and down by the main corral. Jesus was directing one of the vaqueros on the best way to break a horse. Cruz stood on the bottom of the corral and looked inside. As soon as Jesus let go of the horse, the vaquero and the horse flew around the corral, the horse bucking wildly and eventually throwing the boy off.

Jesus walked to Cruz. "This boy will be good. Every time he falls off, he gets back on."

"How have we done with calves?"

"Twenty new calves born. All healthy."

"And what about our mares?"

"Three healthy colts. One died."

"The sheep?"

"The sheep I still keep down on that back pasture, away from the cattle. I don't like them to mix."

"You don't like those sheep very much, do you, Jesus?"

"I hate them. They're filthy animals."

"But we have to have them for the wool, unless you can find another place to find it."

Jesus lifted his hand. "Don't tell me about that. I've heard it before."

"Have you seen the *patrón* lately?"

"No, but I hear he is ailing. I think you should pay him a visit soon."

284

"Yes, I think I'll go over there tomorrow. I need to talk to him."

"What's wrong, Cruz? I've known you for a long time. Something is troubling you."

"It's nothing, Jesus."

"Is it your wife? She seems so different from Soleda."

"She *is* different from Soleda. She is everything that Soleda was not." He looked at the next vaquero who got up to ride. "I swore to myself that I would never let myself love this much again."

"You cannot control your heart, boy. It is good that this woman has taught you how to love again."

"It isn't good, Jesus. She already has a husband and a child."

Jesus took his handkerchief out of his back pocket and wiped his forehead. He looked out at the corral, and shouted to the vaquero, "Try him again, Renaldo. He's tiring." He turned to Cruz, his old brown face creased and tired. "Why do you do this to yourself, boy? Can you not find yourself a woman who will make you happy?"

"She does make me happy, Jesus. I never thought I could love anyone as much as I love her. I didn't mean to fall in love with her. The only reason she's with me is because I had to get her out of Monterey. She was going to be killed. I had no choice."

"You always have a choice, boy, but I don't understand. How could a married woman be in love with you? It's unholy."

"Don't, Jesus. I don't want you or anyone else saying things like that about her."

285

Jesus took Cruz's arm and led him away from the corral. "I'm sorry, my boy. I don't mean to hurt you. I want to see you happy. I wish this was the woman you could have."

"So do I."

"Then why not fight for her? Perhaps she would stay with you."

"I couldn't do that. She loves her daughter and she'd never leave her."

"And her husband?"

Cruz was silent. "She loves him, too, I believe."

"I am sorry for you then. Your heart will be broken again."

"Don't be sorry for me, Jesus. What she has given me . . ."

"Never mind. I can already see what she has given you. I will say no more about it. Come. I will show you the newborn calves. They should lift your spirits."

Cruz nodded. "Jesus, if something should happen to me, I want you to make sure Lisa gets back to her husband and child."

"Cruz—"

"Promise me!"

"I promise you. If something should ever happen to you, I will do as you ask. Do not worry."

Eric, Teresa, and Tom stood at the front of the rancho, waiting for Cruz. Jesus had gone into the house and told them to wait, obviously none too happy at their appearance.

"What are we going to do now that we're here?" Teresa said.

"We're going to get Lisa and take her home. It's time she came to her senses," Tom replied impatiently.

"No," Eric said emphatically. "I don't want you saying anything to her, Tom. This has to be her choice. I don't want you to force her to do anything she doesn't want to do."

"But you're her husband."

"No, I'm not her husband anymore. I can't force her to do anything, and I won't."

"But you have Raya."

"I won't use Raya to hurt her."

"What the hell's gotten into you?"

Eric glanced at Teresa then at Tom. "Common sense, maybe. Listen, Tom, you know your sister. If I push her, she'll just run away. I have to let her decide on her own what she wants to do. There's no other way."

Teresa put her arm through Eric's. "I'm proud of you. You sound like a different man."

"I *am* different." He looked up when he heard the footsteps on the wooden floor inside the house. When the door opened, he stared at Cruz, unable to take his eyes off the man who had made his wife fall in love with him. He was every bit as tall as Eric himself, with black hair and dark eyes, but his face was almost boyish in appearance. He had a certain quality to his looks that Eric couldn't quite put his finger on.

"Eric?" Cruz said, his eyes meeting Eric's.

"Yes. You're Cruz."

"Yes."

"This is Teresa Torres and Tom Jordan, Lisa's brother."

287

"Why don't you all come inside. It's cool in here." They followed Cruz into the large room. "Lisa is outside in the vineyard, picking grapes."

"Lisa is picking grapes?" Tom asked in astonishment.

"Yes, she enjoys working outside." He glanced at Eric for a moment then turned to Tom and Teresa. "Would you two like something to eat? I'll take you into the kitchen."

"No, just show us where it is," Teresa said, looking at Eric anxiously.

Cruz pointed the way to the kitchen. When they were gone, he turned to Eric. "You'll be wanting to talk to Lisa."

"Yes."

Cruz walked to the large window and looked out at his favorite view. "I don't know what to say to you. If I were you, I'd want to slit my throat." He turned to look at Eric, his eyes honest and sincere. "I never set out to fall in love with your wife. It just happened. I always intended to take her back to you and your daughter when I thought she'd be safe from Vasquez."

"I believe you," Eric replied. There was something about the man's eyes that were so trustworthy. "Cruz, I want you to know that I won't force Lisa to come back with me. It has to be her decision. If she decides to stay here, I'll abide by that."

"And what about Raya? You know she can't live without Raya."

"I won't use Raya to punish her. I'm sure we can work something out."

Cruz shook his head. "You aren't what I expected."

"Neither are you. I was fully prepared to hate your guts."

"So, I guess we just wait. Unless you can think of something else to do."

"No, as I said, I won't force my hand. For whatever reasons, she wants to be with you right now. Maybe I need to find out why."

Cruz turned back to the window and pointed. "She's down there."

"And Cruz, thank you for saving her life. No matter what happens, I am grateful to you for that."

Cruz nodded. He stared out the window until he saw Eric making his way down the hill. His throat was dry. He wanted to take Lisa and run away, but he stood watching, feeling totally helpless. He turned away and walked to his desk, picking up his sketchpad. He flipped it to a certain page and stared at the sketch of Lisa. He picked up the pad and held it to his chest, much the same way Lisa had done with Raya's picture. Soon, this might be all he had left of Lisa.

Lisa stood up, wiping her hand across her forehead. Sweat dripped down her face, and her thick braid stuck to the back of her neck. In the few short weeks she had been here, her arms had grown brown from working in the sun. She closed her eyes, feeling slightly dizzy. The sun was getting to her.

"Get inside," Elena said, taking her scarf and wiping Lisa's face. "You look tired. You shouldn't be out here anyway. I've never seen such a thing, a *patrón*'s wife working in the fields."

"I like it, Elena. It makes me feel good."

"Well, you don't look good right now. Go up to the house and get some food and rest. Don't argue with me."

"I won't," Lisa replied thankfully. As she walked out of the vineyard, she stared down at her blue-stained fingertips. Picking grapes was difficult work, but she liked it. She felt as though she were contributing something. As she started up the hill, she felt as if the ground underneath her was beginning to shake. She stopped and reached out for support, but there was nothing to lean on. She untied the scarf from around her neck and held it over her face, wiping the sweat from it. She took a deep breath. When she took the scarf away and looked up, Eric was standing in front of her.

"Hello, Lisa."

Lisa couldn't speak. She saw him standing before her, and it was as if he were a stranger, a handsome stranger. She looked at him—tall and brown from the sun, dressed in buckskins, blue shirt, and bandana. He held his hat in his hands as if he were a young boy coming to court her. His dark hair had grown long and hung well over his collar. But it was his eyes, those sky-blue eyes that had always mesmerized her, that appeared to look inside her.

Eric took a tentative step forward, cocking his head to one side. "Are you all right? You don't look well."

Lisa started to say something, but before she could, her legs gave way and she started to fall.

Eric caught her before she hit the ground. He held her in his arms, wiping her face with her scarf. "Lisa? Will you please say something."

Lisa opened her eyes and looked at Eric. His face looked so kind and concerned. She hadn't expected this from him; she didn't deserve this from him. "I'm all right. I just felt a little dizzy."

"Have you been sick lately?"

"Just in the mornings. I don't seem to be able to eat much. And I'm so tired all the time."

"Lisa," Eric said her name so intently she sat up. He shook his head. "You don't even realize you're carrying his child, do you?"

"What? No, no I . . ." She paused as the import of all her symptoms hit her. Attempting to stand up, she stumbled instead and Eric pulled her back to the ground.

"Sit down. You need to rest some more."

"No, I need to get back to the house." She looked frantically around her.

Eric took her chin between his fingers. "Look at me, Lisa. You are carrying his child, aren't you?"

Lisa stared into the endless blue of Eric's eyes, and tears filled her own eyes. "It is possible."

"Then you have to tell him."

She looked at him in shock. "No, I can't tell him. If he finds out, he'll never let me go." She covered her face with her hands. "My God, Eric, what have I done?"

Eric put his arms around her. "It's all right. It will work out."

"How can it?" she screamed. "Either way, I am going to lose a child." She tilted her head back and closed her eyes. Her breathing became labored.

"Lisa, look at me."

She didn't respond.

"Lisa." Eric took Lisa's face in his hands. "Please, Lisa, look at me."

She finally opened her eyes. They were glazed and filled with tears. "You can't tell him, Eric. Promise me you won't tell him."

"All right, I won't."

She went limp and fell against Eric. He picked her up in his arms and carried her up the hill to the house. When he walked into the living room, Cruz was gone. He walked down the hall to the first room he saw and put Lisa on the bed. He went to the washstand, wet a cloth, and put it on her face. He wiped her face and neck until she opened her eyes. She smiled slightly. "You're still here."

"I'm not going to leave."

"You should. You deserve someone better than me."

Eric gently put the cloth on Lisa's mouth. "Don't. I don't want to hear you say anything. I just want you to rest. I'm going to the kitchen to get you some water."

Lisa grabbed his hand and held it tightly. "Don't go yet, Eric. Please."

He continued to wipe her face and neck with the cloth, finally laying it across her forehead. He was surprised that he wasn't angry she was carrying Cruz's child. Perhaps it was because he had already accepted the inevitable, or perhaps it was because he knew it wasn't her fault. So much had happened to her in so short a time, and he hadn't been the most patient man. She had begged him not to go on the trip to San Francisco because she felt something might happen. She had been right.

In spite of the fact that she had spent so much time in the sun, her face had a terrible pallor and her eyes weren't the clear green they always were. He was afraid something was very wrong.

She opened her eyes. "Is Raya well?"

"Raya is wonderful," he smiled. "She misses you but she is well taken care of by Grandfather. I even talked my mother into staying at the del Mar until I get back."

Lisa smiled and took Eric's hand. "I'm so glad you did that. It will mean so much to Don Alfredo, and I know Mariz will love Raya."

"You should've seen her the first time she saw Raya. She tried so hard to pretend that she didn't matter, but as soon as Raya went to her, her heart melted. She wouldn't leave her alone."

"I am so glad for all of you." She closed her eyes again and grabbed her stomach. "I think I'm going to be sick." She turned on her side.

Eric reached for the washbowl on the stand and held it next to Lisa's mouth. "Use this."

"I'm sorry," she mumbled, pulling her knees to her stomach. "You should have had a stronger woman, someone who would've made you happy." She grabbed the bowl and vomited into it. When she was through, Eric put the bowl on the floor. He grabbed the cloth and wiped her mouth. "Lisa, you need help. There's something wrong."

"No, please, I just want you to stay with me."

"What if there's something wrong with the baby, Lisa? You need someone who can help you."

She looked at him, her green eyes suddenly clear. "You can help me. You delivered Raya. You saved her life and mine. I trust you."

Eric shook his head. "I have someone here who might be able to help you. You'll like her."

"I don't want any woman in here. I just want you."

"What about Cruz?" Eric couldn't keep from asking the question. "He'll want to know what's wrong with you."

"You can't tell him. You promised."

"He's not a stupid man, Lisa. He'll figure it out."

"No he won't. We'll just tell him I've had too much sun. Oh, God." She reached over the side of the bed for the bowl and Eric lifted it up to her. Again, she vomited into it until there seemed to be nothing left. She lay on her side, limp and weak. Eric stood up. He ignored her pleas as he left the room and walked down the hall, looking for the kitchen. He looked at Teresa. "I need your help."

Teresa immediately stood up, followed by Tom. "What's wrong?"

"Lisa's just had too much sun and she's a little sick. I think it would be best if you stayed out here. Why don't you keep Cruz out of the way if he comes in."

Eric poured some water from the pitcher on the table and led Teresa to the bedroom and closed the door. Teresa sat on the bed next to Lisa. Eric handed her the damp cloth.

"Here, rinse this out again." She put her hand on Lisa's forehead. "She's burning up." She took the cloth from Eric and wiped Lisa's face and neck, finally placing the wet cloth on the back of Lisa's neck. "God, she's so thin. She doesn't look well."

"I know." He walked over to the other side of the bed and sat down, picking up Lisa's hand in his. "If anything happened to her, I don't know what I'd do."

"Nothing will happen to her, but something is not right." She stared at Lisa, noting how thin she was except for the small bulge in her belly the roundness of her breasts. "She's going to have his child, isn't she?"

"How did you know?"

"God, look at her. She's thin as a bone except for her stomach and breasts. No wonder she's so sick. Poor thing." Teresa shook her head, taking the cloth and wiping Lisa's face.

"You can't tell anyone, Teresa, not even Tom, and especially not Cruz."

"Why not?"

"She doesn't want him to know."

"I wonder why."

"I don't know. But I promised her."

"All right. I won't say anything, but she won't be able to hide it for long. I wonder what he'll do when he finds out."

"I don't know, but I'm more worried about her right now. She's usually so strong. I'm afraid she'll do something to hurt herself."

"Stop it. She's not a little weakling. She's a grown woman who happens to be very strong. A lot has happened to her that wasn't of her own doing. She has to sort some things out for herself." Teresa shook her head. "I don't envy her. I don't know if I could decide between two men and the child that belongs to each."

Eric stood up. "I don't think she has a choice. Raya is older and has me, her grandmother, and great-grandfather. This child will only have Cruz and Lisa. She can't take this child away from him, and she certainly can't leave the child here."

"And you think she'll leave Raya with you?"

"I don't know what she'll do, Teresa."

"Well, we can't worry about that now. We just have to make sure she gets well."

"Eric?" Lisa said, opening her eyes and looking at Teresa. "Where's Eric?" she asked anxiously.

"He's right here. Don't worry."

Teresa stood up and Eric took her place. "How're you feeling?"

"I feel terrible."

"I don't think you should work in the sun anymore. It's not good for you in your condition."

Lisa looked from Eric to Teresa. "Don't say anything," she whispered.

"Teresa already knows, Lisa. She guessed the minute she saw you."

Lisa looked over at Teresa. "Please don't say anything to anyone."

"I wouldn't do that. I'm only here to help you. And now I'm going to go into the kitchen and mix something for you. It will make your stomach feel better."

Lisa watched Teresa as she left the room. "She's very nice. Pretty, too."

"She's been a good friend."

"I'm glad. You deserve that, at least."

"Lisa, don't. We can talk later when you're feel-

296

ing better."

Lisa turned her head away. "I don't know if I want to get better."

"Stop it," Eric said angrily. "It's not like you to feel sorry for yourself. You'll do what you think is right, no matter what it is. I can't help you with that decision, nor can Cruz. That you have to do all on your own. But you *can* do it, Lisa. I trust you."

"I'm sorry, I don't know what's wrong with me."

"I do. You're going to have a baby. I remember what it did to you the last two times." He smiled. "It made you a little crazy sometimes."

Lisa couldn't contain a smile. "I was afraid I'd never see you again."

"No matter what had happened, you should have known that I would search for you no matter what. I could never let you go that easily." He leaned down and kissed her on the forehead.

"Will you stay with me until I fall asleep? It feels right having you here."

Eric took her hand, entwining her fingers with his. "I'll stay."

"I'm being selfish, aren't I?"

"No, I think you're trying to decide what you want. I can understand that."

"I didn't expect this from you, Eric."

"You probably expected me to come riding in here and take you away on my horse against your will. A year ago I probably would have done that, but not now. I know that would've made it easier for you, but you're the one who has to decide. Now, that's enough talk. Close your eyes and rest. I'll stay here with you until you fall asleep."

"Thank you," she said softly, her body quickly relaxing. "Your eyes are still as blue as the sky on a cloudless day," she murmured sleepily.

Eric smiled. At least she was thinking of him. That was a good sign, but what about Cruz? No matter how he tried, he couldn't hate the man. He couldn't even dislike him. He had saved Lisa's life and treated her well. Even if he had made love to her, that was something that he couldn't blame the man for. There was a knock on the door and Eric turned. Cruz walked into the room. The look of concern on his face was immediate.

"What happened?"

"I think she had too much sun."

Cruz looked at the bowl on the floor. "She was sick?"

"Yes, and she had cramps. Teresa is mixing something for her that will make her feel better."

"I'm glad you were there."

"I'm beginning to think I should go, Cruz. If I'm here, it's only going to make it harder on her."

"No, don't go. She needs to be with you. She needs to see for herself which one of us she wants."

Eric looked at Cruz and nodded his head. "All right, but it won't be easy."

"I know that. If I were a stronger man, I'd tell you to go away and I'd keep her to myself." He looked at Lisa. "But I can't do that. I know how she feels about you and Raya."

Eric stood up and walked to Cruz, standing face-to-face with him. "I think you're a very strong man, Cruz. I admire you. I'm not sure I could do the same thing if I were in your place."

298

"You already have," Cruz said honestly. He looked at Lisa one more time. "You stay with her. I'm going to go away for a few days."

"Cruz, you don't have to leave because of us."

"I'm not leaving because of you. I have someone I have to see, the man who sold me this land. He's very ill I understand. I should be back in two or three days. It will give you and Lisa time to catch up. Think of this as your home, please."

Eric started to thank Cruz, but he had already left the room. He shook his head in wonder. He had never met anyone like this man in his life. He was almost selfless, and he now understood why Lisa felt the way she did about him. Cruz was a good man. It would be hard to compete with that.

Teresa came back into the room, carrying a cup. "When she wakes up, see if you can get her to drink this."

"What is it?"

"It's a bunch of things thrown together. A servant of ours always used to make it for me when I was a little girl and I was sick. It always made me feel better."

"Cruz is a good man, Teresa. I can't hate him no matter how hard I try."

"Good. Hatred won't serve any purpose. Do you want anything? I'm going to keep Tom company."

"No. You can send him in here if you want. It might do him good to see her, even if she is sick."

"All right." Teresa walked out of the room and down the hall, right into Cruz. "I'm sorry, I didn't see you."

"It's all right."

"I'm sorry we've come here unannounced."

"Why don't we walk outside to the courtyard." Cruz opened the door to the courtyard and followed Teresa outside. They sat on a stone bench. "You're a friend of Eric's?"

"Yes, I met him through my . . ." She stopped. She wasn't quite sure how to describe Bryant. "I actually met him through Lisa's brother, Tom."

"And exactly why are you here?" Cruz's eyes burned into Teresa's.

"I'm here to help Eric."

"Why should a grown man need help from a little lady like you?"

"I'm his friend, Cruz. I didn't know what he was going to find here. I wanted to be here for him just in case."

Cruz reached down and picked a flower from one of the clay pots. He handed it to Teresa. "You're in love with him, aren't you?"

"No, I'm not in love with him. That's ridiculous! I'm going to marry another man. But he's probably the only male friend I've ever had in my life. And for that, I love him."

Cruz nodded. "We're a strange group, aren't we?"

Teresa laughed. "Very strange. What's even stranger is that a man like you would ever be in love with a woman like Soleda."

"How do you know about Soleda?"

"We stayed at Miguel's right after you left. Miguel is my cousin."

"Miguel has been a good friend. I'm sorry that he is with Soleda."

"So am I. She's a witch."

"I see you got to know her."

Teresa smiled. "As a matter of fact, we got to know each other quite well."

"What did you do?"

"I had a little talk with her about Miguel."

"Did she listen to you?"

"She didn't have much choice."

Cruz laughed. "I like you, Teresa. You may be just the match for Soleda."

"I know Soleda as well as I know myself. I was like her once, Cruz." Teresa twirled the flower in her fingers, looking down at it. "I know what she'll do and how she'll act because I was once that desperate."

"It's hard to believe you were ever like Soleda."

"There was a time when I was worse. I would have sold my soul. I couldn't live with something my family had forced me to do, so I punished them by punishing myself. I did that for five years. I'm lucky to be alive."

Cruz covered her hand with his. "I'm glad you are."

"I wonder why you're so easy to talk to?"

"Maybe we just feel comfortable with each other."

Teresa shook her head. "No, it's more than that. Eric feels it and I feel it. And look at Lisa; I think she's fallen in love with you."

Cruz shook his head adamantly. "No, she thinks she's in love with me because I've helped her. There's a difference."

"You don't think a woman can love two men at one time?"

"I don't know."

"Well, I think Lisa loves both you and Eric, and

I think she's going to go through hell trying to decide who she loves more."

"You don't even know her but you seem to like her. Why?"

"As I told Eric, she represents all the things I would like to be in my life. She's a good person with a good heart. In fact, I think it's her heart that gets her into trouble."

"Yes, if she were more like Soleda, she would have no trouble. She would take the rich one."

Teresa laughed again. "She's going to come here, you know."

"She told you that?"

"No, but I know she will. She can't stand the thought of you and Lisa being here alone. She wants to hurt both of you."

"God, I was so young and so stupid. I thought she was so in love with me."

"Don't be so hard on yourself, Cruz. She's a beautiful woman. I can see how she could blind a man."

Cruz bent down and picked some more flowers from the pots and handed them to Teresa. "You are quite a lady."

"I don't think you'd say that if you knew about my past."

"I don't care about your past. All I see is the way you are now — a good and loyal friend and an honest person."

Teresa smiled slightly, bending forward and picking a flower. She handed it to Cruz. "Then please accept this from me, because I think you are one of the nicest men I've ever met. And I know about *your* background."

302

Cruz laughed and stood up. "I must go. I have a friend to visit."

"You're not going because of us, are you?"

"No. My friend is ill, and he is very old. I want to see him before it is too late. Please, this is your home while I'm gone. Don't let Elena boss you around too much. She thinks she's the only person in the world who can cook."

"That's fine with me . . . Cruz?" Teresa stood up. "Miguel spoke very highly of you, and I couldn't figure out why. I just thought you were a bandit. Now I know differently. No matter what happens, I want you to know that I wish you the best."

Cruz bowed slightly. *"Muchas gracias, señorita."*

"Por nada," Teresa answered as she watched him walk away. She didn't envy Lisa her decision. Cruz was everything a woman could desire in a man, and more. She looked at the flowers in her hand and smiled. It was too beautiful a day to feel sad.

Lisa opened her eyes. The sun was shining through the window that faced the mountains. That meant that it was morning. She tried to sit up, but her head ached.

"How are you feeling?"

Lisa looked over and saw Teresa arranging some flowers on a small table on the other side of the bed. "How long have you been here?"

"Since the middle of the night. I sent Eric off to get some sleep."

"You didn't have to stay here."

"He would have worried if you were by yourself.

303

Besides, I didn't mind." Teresa finished arranging the flowers. "Aren't these lovely? I couldn't resist them. I brought this table in here to set them on. Elena will probably have a fit."

Lisa smiled. "So, you've met Elena. Did she tell you how skinny you are?"

"At least ten times."

"And she forced you to eat so much you thought you'd be sick?"

"Yes. She loved feeding Eric and Tom. They couldn't get enough."

"How is Tom?"

"He's fine. He came in to see you, but you were asleep. Don't worry, we didn't say anything to him."

"How did you know, Teresa?"

"I carried a child before. I remember what it was like. I know the signs."

"You must think I'm a horrible person."

"Lisa, listen to me." Teresa took Lisa's hand. "I would be the last person to judge you. I lived on the streets of San Francisco as a prostitute for many years. That's how I supported myself, and that's how I punished myself. I would never judge you."

"Poor Eric. What he must have gone through."

"You have to stop worrying about Eric and Cruz and start worrying about yourself. You need to get strong so that you can make the right decision. They will survive no matter what happens. You need to think about yourself and the baby."

"I don't think I can leave him knowing I'm going to have his child."

"And what about Raya? Can you leave her?"

Lisa closed her eyes. "Sometimes I think it would've been better if I'd never come west. None of this would have happened. So many lives wouldn't be so complicated."

"But that's not the way it is, is it? Listen to me. I have a man who loves me and wants to marry me. I told him all about my past and he still fell in love with me. When he found me, I lived in fear that I would see men I'd been with when I was a prostitute, but he made me face the fact that yes, it might happen. I found that I was strong enough to handle it. The first time, it was horrible. I thought I would die. But then I began to feel pride in myself and I wasn't embarrassed anymore. You have to face the fact that you were married to Eric, you loved him, and you had a child by him. Then you met Cruz, you fell in love with him, and now you're carrying his child. Hiding won't do you any good, Lisa. Trust me. I almost killed myself trying to hide from the truth."

"I can see why Eric likes you so much." She sat up. "Why are you doing this, Teresa? You don't even know me."

"But I want to know you. I feel as if I know you. I have heard such good things about you from your brother and from Eric, I think you are the kind of person I could be friends with."

"That's not all, is it? You wanted to see what I was like. You wanted to see the kind of woman Eric was married to and why she would leave him for another man."

Teresa nodded her head. "You're smart and you're right. At first, that's the reason I wanted to

305

come along. But the more I heard about you, the more I began to like you. I respected any woman who could go through what you had and still survive."

"I'm not sure I am surviving very well. I feel as if I'm losing my mind."

"But you won't. You will make the right decision, you'll see. You are strong enough to do that, Lisa."

"How do I choose between a man and a child?" She shook her head.

"I don't think it's the men you're truly worried about, is it?"

Lisa quickly wiped the tears from her eyes. "I don't know if I can give up Raya, and I don't know if I can give up this child and just walk away. I think a part of me would die."

"If you have to make the decision, you will. And you will live through it."

"You sound so sure of yourself."

"I had to give a child up once. I wasn't competent to take care of her. I don't even know where she is, except that she went to a good family. I think about her all the time."

"I'm sorry, Teresa."

"I'm not. I know she's better off without me. If she had stayed with me, I might have killed her. I could barely take care of myself at the time, let alone a child."

"You're a strong woman."

"I am getting stronger all the time, but I was weak for far too long." She patted Lisa's hand and stood up. "I'm going to get you something light to eat. You must try to keep some food down."

"You don't have to do this."

"I told you before, I want to. Let me help you, Lisa."

"All right. And thank you . . . Teresa, could you send Cruz in when you have a chance? I need to talk to him."

"He's gone, Lisa. He said he was going to visit a sick friend for a few days."

The disappointment on Lisa's face was obvious.

"Eric would like to see you but he doesn't want to push."

"Yes, I'd like to see him," she said. "Wait, am I a mess? Can you brush my hair for me?"

Teresa walked to the dresser and handed Lisa a brush. "You can brush your own hair. You look beautiful enough as it is."

Lisa pulled the bedspread around her and straightened out her simple white nightgown. She pulled her hair over one shoulder and was brushing it when Eric walked in.

"Hello."

"Hello," she said softly, suddenly feeling embarrassed.

Eric walked to the bed. "You look much better. At least you have color in your cheeks."

"It must've been that horrible drink Teresa gave me last night. That would put color into anyone's cheeks." She continued to brush her hair.

"I don't understand how you can look so beautiful after you've just been so sick."

Lisa put the brush in her lap. "Why are you being so nice, Eric? Why don't you hate me for what I did?"

Eric sat down on the bed. "I don't have a right

to hate you, Lisa. I don't know what happened between you and Cruz. Besides, I remember how I acted with Consuelo before we were married. I was surprised you even married me."

"I didn't have a choice, as I recall," she said in a loving voice. "Sometimes I feel as though this is someone else's life, Eric. You and Cruz . . . you're both wonderful men. I don't deserve either one of you. I'm just a simple girl from Boston."

"You're about as simple as the Chinese alphabet. You forget, Lisa, I know you."

Lisa relaxed, a smile on her face. "Yes, I think you know me better than anyone in this world."

"I thought I did," he said gently, reaching out and touching her cheek. "What did I do, Lisa? What did I do to drive you into the arms of another man?"

"You didn't do anything, Eric. It just happened. He was there, and I came to depend on him. There were days I wasn't sure if I'd get home alive. I know that's no excuse, but that's what happened. Please . . ." She took his hand. "You didn't do anything wrong."

"We did rush things after Raya was born, though, didn't we?"

Lisa nodded in agreement. "I think we tried too hard to recapture what we had in the Comanche camp. Nothing could ever be like it was there."

"Is that what it was like with Cruz?"

Lisa's eyes met Eric's. His question was honest, not angry. She couldn't lie to him. "I guess it reminded me of that time. He was kind to me, and good, just like you were. He didn't take advantage of me. He didn't hurt me. He was good

308

to me, Eric."

"I know that." Eric stood up and looked out the window. He was trying to be patient, but he wasn't sure just how much he could take.

"I'm sorry. I'm not saying this to hurt you."

"It's all right. I've been thinking anyway that considering the circumstances, I probably should go on home. It would make things easier for you."

"No," Lisa pleaded.

Eric turned and looked at Lisa. "I love you, but I'm not sure I can stay here and watch you with another man. I know I can't watch you have another man's child. I'm not that strong."

LIsa bit her lower lip, tired of how emotionally weak she had become. "I don't blame you. You deserve better than this. If you want to you, then you should go."

Eric nodded slightly. "Well then, I think we'll rest up for a couple of more days and then head on out. That would be best."

"Will I see Raya?"

"We'll work something out, I promise. I won't let her forget you. Ever."

Lisa turned away, not wanting Eric to see her cry again. The thought of not seeing her beautiful little girl with the dark curls and the blue eyes was almost unbearable. "Maybe you should go now. I'm feeling a little tired." Her voice quivered with emotion.

Eric walked to her and sat on the bed, pulling her into his arms. "Don't cry, Lisa. It will be all right."

"How can it be all right when I'll never see my daughter or you again? I don't know if I can live

309

without either one of you." The words were out before she realized it.

Eric held her tighter, a slight smile on his lips. "Don't worry. We'll talk later. I won't leave until you're well."

"You promise?"

Eric looked at her incredible green eyes and gently kissed the tears that ran down her cheeks. "I promise." He put his arms around her again, just enjoying the feel of her. He wouldn't hurry things, he would just take his time. Perhaps he and Lisa could get to know each other again. And if he was lucky, maybe she would fall in love with him again.

Chapter 11

Eric looked around when the door opened. Teresa was standing by the door, her hands on her hips, a disgusted expression on her face. "What's the matter? Been in a fight with Elena again?"

"We have company," she said angrily.

Lisa pulled away from Eric. "Who?"

"Soleda." Teresa almost spit the name out.

"Soleda is here?" Lisa asked in alarm. "Cruz can't take her, she riles him so."

"Don't worry, Cruz is gone for a few days. As long as we don't let Soleda know where he is, he'll be all right."

Lisa nodded. "Good, then she can take it out on me. She hates me."

Eric looked at Teresa. "Don't worry, I think she might hate Teresa a little more than she hates you right now."

"Why?"

Teresa shrugged her shoulders innocently. "I had to set her straight on a few things, that's all."

"Why the hell did she come here?" Eric asked.

"Why do you think? She wants to make Cruz miserable. I hope when he gets back, he doesn't

311

allow her to stay."

"She's legally his wife," Lisa said. "She can stay if she wants to."

"But what about Miguel?" Eric asked, confused.

"Eric, you don't understand women at all. She wants to punish Cruz and Lisa first. When she's done that and made sure they're unhappy, she'll marry Miguel. She'd never settle for Cruz. He doesn't have the money or power that Miguel does."

"How do you know so much about her, Teresa?"

Teresa glanced at Lisa and winked. "You know my background, Eric. I know all about women like Soleda."

"Where's she going to stay?"

"I think we should make her stay in the barn," Lisa said.

"Better yet, with the pigs," Teresa added.

"Teresa, why don't you and I go out and talk to her. Maybe between us we can find out what she's doing here."

"I already told you why, Eric, and I want you and Lisa to be careful of her. She's dangerous."

"What about you?" Lisa asked.

"I'm not afraid of Soleda," Teresa replied. "As a matter of fact, I'm rather looking forward to seeing her again."

"Where is she?"

"She's in the kitchen trying to get past Elena. Elena was threatening to hit her with a pan if she didn't leave."

"Maybe we should have Elena handle her," Eric said. "That would solve all of our problems."

The three of them laughed. Lisa looked at

Teresa and Eric. They looked good together, comfortable, as if they belonged together. "What's the matter, Lisa?" Teresa asked in a concerned tone, hurrying toward the bed.

"Nothing. I was just thinking it's time I got out of bed. The last thing I want is for Soleda to find out I'm sick."

"No!" Eric said adamantly. "I don't want you getting out of bed."

Lisa smiled warmly. "Thank you for your concern, Eric, but I'm not a child. I'll feel better if I get up and move around. I'm tired of feeling sorry for myself. Maybe Soleda is just the medicine I need." She pulled back the covers and put her feet on the floor.

"What the hell are you talking about? That woman is a she-devil."

"Never mind, Eric. I know exactly what Lisa is talking about. You go on out and I'll help Lisa get dressed. You go entertain our guest."

Eric left the room, mumbling the entire way.

Lisa smiled as she watched him. "I think we're making him crazy."

"I know we are. Come on, stand up." Lisa stood, leaning against Teresa. "How do you feel?"

"A little weak. I didn't feel this way with my other two babies."

"This one might be taking a lot out of you. Besides, these haven't been the best of circumstances. Let's get that nightgown off you." She helped Lisa pull the nightgown off and she handed her a wet cloth and some soap. While Lisa washed up at the basin, Teresa laid out Lisa's blouse and skirt, freshly washed. She also had a pair of buck-

313

skin slippers.

"You washed my clothes for me?"

"I didn't think you'd want to get back into dirty clothes. I think it's time we saw about getting you some new clothes. I'm quite handy with a needle, you know."

Lisa slipped on her blouse and tucked it into her skirt, around which she tied a colored sash. She sat down on the bed and pulled on the slippers. "I guess you didn't like my boots."

"I'm sure they were good for traveling but not for around here. Here . . ." Teresa handed Lisa a pair of earrings, large circles crafted of silver.

"They're beautiful. I can't take them."

"They're too large for me. A taller woman needs to wear them. Besides, they'll go nicely with the cross you're wearing."

Lisa reached up and touched the silver cross Cruz had given her. "This isn't mine. It belonged to Cruz's mother. He gave it to me when he thought I was hurt. He thought it would help me."

"Obviously it did. Come on, Lisa. You're doing fine. How about your hair? Can I do something with it?"

"If you like."

"Sit down on the bed." Teresa went to the nightstand and picked up a comb. She grabbed the brush from the bed and sat down behind Lisa and brushed her long, thick hair. She very quickly pulled it into a thick braid, tying a piece of rawhide thong around it. "Turn around." She appraised Lisa, then brushed a few strands of hair down from her forehead and the sides of her head to surround her face. "There. You look perfect."

Lisa stood up and looked at herself in the mirror. She had to admit she hadn't looked this good in a long time. "Are you fixing me up for Eric or are you trying to make me look good just to make Soleda jealous?"

Teresa shrugged her shoulders. "A little of both. Come on, I think it's time to confront the witch. Let's let her know who she's really up against."

Lisa and Teresa left the room. They could hear the angry voices before they reached the kitchen. When Elena saw Lisa, she hurried to her, immediately solicitous.

"Cómo está, señora?"

"I'm fine, Elena. How about you?"

"I was fine until this, this 'woman' came into my kitchen."

"Ha! This is not your kitchen, you fat old lady! I am still married to Cruz. This is my kitchen."

"You wouldn't know what to do in a kitchen if your life depended on it, you—"

"That's enough, Elena." Lisa stepped forward. "What do you want, Soleda?"

"Oh, so the lady speaks, eh? Where is your devoted husband? Is he already tiring of you and looking for someone new?"

Teresa started to edge toward Soleda, but Lisa held out her arm. "Cruz doesn't want you here, Soleda, and you know that. In fact, he doesn't want you at all. That kills you, doesn't it? You just can't stand the fact that he doesn't want you anymore."

Soleda spit on the floor in front of Lisa. "You *Cabrona!* I'll make you pay for what you said to

315

me."

Lisa stepped closer to Soleda, her eyes narrowing. "Do you actually think you scare me, Soleda? You are nothing. In fact, I find you pathetic. You come chasing after a man who obviously doesn't want you anymore, only because you can't stand the fact that he's forgotten you. And he *has* forgotten you, Soleda. In fact," Lisa tilted her head to one side, "Cruz told me that you made love like a two-cent whore. You disgust him."

Soleda's hand was out like a shot, hitting Lisa square on the face. Teresa and Elena were quick to come to Lisa's defense, but Lisa didn't need any help. She slapped Soleda, knocking her backward. "If you decide to stay here, we'll all make it hell for you. None of us want you here, and you know it."

"I'll kill you for this. I swear I will." Soleda's hand went up to her red cheek.

"Get out. I'm sure there's a vaquero or two who will take you in."

Soleda glared at all of the women and then turned, quickly running out of the kitchen. Lisa grabbed the edge of the table and held on, feeling as if she was going to faint.

"Sit down, señora. I will get you something to drink."

Teresa pulled out a chair for Lisa and she sat down next to her. "When you decide to get better, you don't fool around, do you?"

Lisa smiled. "I won't let her intimidate me. She's a horrible woman. Why does she stay here when she's not wanted?"

"Because she knows she'll drive all of us crazy.

316

As hard as it'll be, we have to try to ignore her."

"I know, but . . ." Lisa stopped when she saw her brother walk into the room. His brown hair had gotten shaggier and he looked tired, but when he smiled, he looked just like the old Tom. She stood up and went to him. "Oh, Tom," she said softly, holding on to him as she did when she was a child. "I've missed you."

"You have been busy, haven't you, Sis?"

"I'm sorry if I worried you. I didn't mean to."

"I know that. When are you coming home? We all miss you, especially that darling little girl of yours."

"You got to see her?"

"She's wonderful, Sis. She reminds me so much of you when you were little. She's going to be a handful."

"So, what about you? Any new women in your life?"

"No, haven't had time for women, just work."

"You're going to grow old before you know it, Tom. You need to take some time for yourself."

"I already have a mother, Lisa."

"Do you have any fun at all?"

"Yes, once in a while I get out. As a matter of fact, I go to Bryant's place quite often. He runs a large tavern down by the waterfront in San Francisco. Tom says he comes there to do business but I think he comes to see this certain woman with red hair who waits for him every week."

"What're you talking about?" A red flush crept over Tom's cheeks.

"Why, Tom Jordan, are you blushing?"

"I've never blushed in my life."

317

"Then why are your cheeks red?"

"Stop this, dammit! There's no redhead. I just help Bryant out with his business." He took Lisa's hand. "Do you feel up to a little walk?"

"Yes, I think some fresh air would do me good."

They walked out into the courtyard and around to the back of the house. They sat on the stone bench by the well. A cool ocean breeze blew, and the leaves of the nearby willow rustled listlessly.

"How are you?"

"I'm all right."

"God, I was worried about you."

Lisa squeezed Tom's hand. "I'm all right."

"Cruz took good care of you, I guess."

"Yes, he did, Tom."

"How could you marry him, Sis? I don't understand."

"I had no choice, Tom. I wasn't thrilled about giving up my family and leaving Monterey."

"But you've stayed with him. Why?"

Lisa looked down at the valley, watching the cattle lazily walk from one place to another. "He's been good to me. He saved my life."

"Do you owe him your life?"

"I don't know. I haven't decided that yet." She looked at the mountains in the distance and breathed in the fresh air. Somehow, this place gave her strength. "I don't expect you to understand."

Tom put his arm around Lisa. "I expect you have a good reason for what you're doing. Who am I to question you? I won't bring it up again. Just know you can always depend on me."

Lisa kissed Tom on the cheek. "How did I get a

318

brother like you?"

"Just lucky, I guess."

Lisa laughed. "So, why aren't you trying to go after Teresa? She's a wonderful woman, and beautiful, too."

"She's also very much attached to a man I work for. Besides," he shrugged his shoulders, "she's crazy about Eric."

Lisa looked at him. "She is?"

"Sure. The only reason she came was to be with him. Then I think things changed."

"What do you mean?"

"She seemed genuinely interested in helping Eric find you. The more Eric and I talked about you, I could see her begin to take an interest in you. She likes you."

"I like *her*. She's a nice woman."

"It doesn't bother you that she's interested in Eric?"

"I am the last person who should say anything about that, aren't I?" She rested her head on her brother's shoulder. "It's beautiful here, isn't it?"

"Yes, it is. But I like Monterey better."

Lisa punched Tom in the arm. "Stop it. You're not going to influence me with your little comments."

"I wasn't trying to influence you," he said, rubbing his arm.

"You were, too. I know you, Tom. We grew up together, remember?"

"And what a handsome man to grow up with," Soleda said, walking up behind them. She paused in front of the bench and looked at brother and sister. "I must say, there is a family resemblance.

Only I think you are better looking," she said to Tom, touching his cheek.

Tom jerked away. "Why don't we go someplace else, Sis?"

"I need to talk to you before I go, please." Soleda looked at Lisa.

"Why?"

"It is very personal."

Lisa looked at Tom. "It's all right, go on ahead. I'll catch up with you later."

"Are you sure?" He eyed Soleda suspiciously.

"Yes, I'm sure. Go on."

"Why don't we walk down by the vineyards. I've always liked it there."

Lisa started to object but decided against it. She couldn't let Soleda know there was anything wrong with her. She stood up, suddenly felt very dizzy.

"What's the matter? You don't look too good."

"I'm fine. Let's go."

As they began the long descent down the hill, Soleda stopped and looked at Lisa. "I know you are carrying his child."

"I don't know what you are talking about."

"Why do you try to lie? We both know it's true."

"I think you've been out in the sun too long, Soleda. You don't know what you're saying."

"It is clear you haven't learned that Elena has a big mouth. She warned me not to upset you because you were going to have a baby."

Lisa was dumbfounded. How could Elena know? The only people who knew were Teresa and Eric, and neither one of them would tell. Soleda was trying to trick her. "I'm not going to have a baby, Soleda."

"That's good, because I couldn't stand it if any other woman had his child."

"He doesn't belong to you anymore. When are you going to understand that?"

"He will always belong to me."

"What about Miguel?"

"What about him? I will marry him and he will give me everything I need, except what I can get from Cruz." She stepped closer. "He is a good lover, isn't he, gringa?" Lisa felt herself blush and turned to walk away. "We have nothing else to say to each other."

Soleda grabbed her arm. "But we do. I want to say that I hate you. I hate you more than I have ever hated anyone in my life."

"You're sick."

"If it's true that you are not carrying Cruz's child, then it will be no problem for you if you have a little fall." She shoved Lisa and watched her as she tumbled down the hill nonstop until she reached the bottom. She lay sprawled on the ground, not moving. Soleda smiled and hurried past the house and down to the corral. She mounted her horse, which was already packed with her saddlebags, and quickly rode off to the north. Someone was waiting for her, and she didn't want to be late.

Eric strolled out to the well, which afforded a spectacular view. He looked out at the mountains and then down at the shining river that meandered below. He squinted his eyes for a minute, then walked farther down the hill. "Jesus," he said to himself, and hurried sideways down the hill until he reached Lisa. She was lying on her stomach, unconscious, her arms and legs sprawled out. Gently, he turned her over. Her face was bruised and cut, but worse, there was blood all over the front of her skirt. Blood was dripping down her legs. He screamed as loud as he could, but most of the workers had already gone in for the day. He lifted her in his arms and carried her up the hill, just as he had done two days before. He hurried through the courtyard and into the house. He laid her on the bed and called in panic for Teresa or Elena.

Elena screamed as soon as she came into the room. *"Madre de Dios."*

"What happened, Eric?"

"She must've fallen. I found her down by the vineyards. She's bleeding badly. I think it's the baby."

Teresa looked up at Elena. "Elena, I want you to bring lots of water in here and plenty of clean cloth. We need to stop the bleeding."

Elena ran out without another word.

Eric washed her face, and Lisa immediately came to. She opened her eyes. "What happened?"

"You must've fallen. I found you down by the vineyards."

"No, I . . ." She tucked her legs up to her chest and wrapped her arms around them, rolling to her side. "It's happening again, Eric."

Eric turned to Teresa. "This is what happened with our first child. She almost died then." His hand went to her face. "It's all right, Lisa. I'm

322

here. I won't leave you."

Lisa moaned as the blood dripped down her legs. As soon as Elena got back, Teresa put pads of cloth between Lisa's legs.

"Elena," Eric pleaded. "Can you help her?"

"There is nothing I can do, señor. I think she is beyond our help right now. When she finds the baby is gone, then she will need us."

Eric looked at Teresa in desperation. "I don't know if she can take this."

"She can take it. She's a very strong woman. You be with her now. If you need me, just call."

Eric took one of Lisa's hands in his and squeezed it tightly. "It's all right, Lisa. I'm here."

"Eric . . ." she said in a daze.

Eric looked down at the blood on the bed. It looked as though she were bleeding to death. He wondered when it would stop. He removed the bloody cloth and put a fresh one on the bed, wiping Lisa's legs. He had never seen her look so frail.

"Eric?"

Eric moved closer to Lisa, holding her hands.

"Tell Raya I love her. I do love her."

"I know you do, Lisa. But you can tell her yourself when you're well."

"No." She shook her head weakly from side to side. "This is my punishment."

"Lisa, that's not true. You're not being punished for anything."

"Yes, I am." She closed her eyes. Her face looked very pale and her lips were dry. "I'm sorry. I never meant to hurt you."

"Don't worry about me. I just want you to get

well."

"You should be with someone like Teresa. She would make you happy." She screamed suddenly, pulling her legs to her chest and rolling to her side again.

Eric was frantic. Lisa continued to bleed and there was nothing he could do to stop it. He sat on the bed and forced himself to be quiet, to think. He remembered a mixture that the women in the Comanche camp had often used when others had bled or had cramps. He got up and ran to the kitchen. "Elena, I need you to make something for me. Listen carefully. Do you know of any kinds of roots or bark that can be boiled and then drunk? I don't know all of the plants around here."

"*Sí, señor,* some of the Indian women use these things. I know of them. There is also something called jimson weed. It can be very dangerous if you don't know how to use it, but if you boil it the right way, you can get a drink. We call it *toloache.* It can make a person fall into a deep sleep."

"Just do whatever you can to help Lisa."

"I'll help you, Elena," Teresa said.

"Thank you both." Eric ran back to Lisa. She was still lying on her side. The cloths he had put beneath her were now blood-soaked. He took them away and replaced them with clean ones. He pulled her skirt through her legs to keep the cloth pads in place and covered her with the blanket. She was breathing heavily, but at least she was resting for the moment. He thought about Cruz suddenly, and he realized that he should send

324

someone for him. He needed to be here. As the room darkened, he lay down on the bed next to Lisa, putting his warm body next to hers, his arm over her side. He kissed the back of her head. He didn't want her to suffer like this.

"Eric?" she asked suddenly. "You won't leave, will you?"

"No, I'll be here. And Lisa, I'm going to send someone to get Cruz. He should be here."

"No!" she exclaimed, wincing with pain when she tried to move. "It would kill him if he knew he had a child and lost it. I couldn't do that to him. I don't want him to see me like this."

"Lisa, the man deserves to know about his child."

"Eric, please don't do this."

"He's strong, Lisa. He should be here, not me. It's his child."

"But I want you here. You've always been here when I've needed you." She tucked his arm around her side and buried his hand in her belly. "Every time I've lost a child, you've been here."

"Lisa," Eric said softly, burying his face in her hair. "I am sorry. I didn't want you to lose this child."

"I know that. That's what makes you so good. I'm just sorry you didn't meet Teresa before you met me."

"Don't."

"It's true. She's better and she's stronger. She's a good woman, Eric, and she cares for you. It's obvious she cares for you."

"It doesn't matter what I want?" He wrapped his arm more tightly around Lisa, pressing his body closer.

"I'm not the same person I used to be."

"Neither am I. Hopefully, we've both done a bit of growing up."

"But I've been with another man, Eric. How can you possibly accept that?"

"I've already accepted it."

Lisa started to speak, but she gasped, squeezing Eric's hand tightly. "Something's happening, Eric."

Eric sat up, but Lisa was already curled up into a ball on her side. Again, blood gushed forth, but this time something else came with it. He saw that she had lost the baby. He took the bloodied cloths and placed them on the floor next to the others, and again covered Lisa with the bedspread. She was relatively quiet again, but breathing heavily.

Teresa and Elena burst into the room. Teresa handed Eric a warm cup. "It may not be exactly like the Comanches, but we did the best we could."

"Thanks."

"I will take these," Elena said sadly, bending over to pick up the bloody cloths. She laid a clean pile of sheets and nightclothes on the floor next to the bed.

"Lisa, I want you to sit up a little." Eric put his arm behind her. "Come on, Lisa. I want you to drink this."

Lisa turned on her back and looked up at Eric. She tried to sit up, the pain evident on her face. He placed the cup to her lips while she sipped at it and then pushed it away. "I don't want any more."

"You have to drink it. It will help with the

cramps."

Lisa didn't object. She emptied the cup and then lay back down. Teresa walked over to turn up the lamp, but Lisa protested. "No, please don't turn it up."

Teresa looked at Eric and he nodded. "All right, Lisa. I'm going to clean up the bed a little and then I'll leave you alone." Teresa quickly cleaned up the blooded bed and stripped Lisa of her skirt. She washed her and helped her into a clean nightgown, then rolled clean sheets under her and covered her with the bedspread.

"Thank you, Teresa. You've been a godsend," Eric said.

"I'm glad I was here." She touched his shoulder. "Do you want anything? Coffee?"

"No, thank you."

"All right, I'll leave you alone then."

"Eric?"

Eric looked at Teresa.

"What about Cruz? Should someone let him know?"

"She doesn't want him to know. She said it would kill him."

"That's her decision to make."

"Yes, but—"

"Don't argue with her, Eric. She has to do what she thinks is right."

Eric nodded.

"I'll be in to check on you later."

Eric lay down next to Lisa in the dark. Her body felt thin and frail. He was frightened. It reminded him of the time in the Comanche camp when he had come back and had found her almost dead, their child lost. It sent a chill through him.

Lisa's voice came out of the darkness. "Do you think God is punishing me?" She sounded weak and tremulous.

"God is not punishing you, Lisa. This is just something that happened. It was an accident."

"It wasn't an accident."

"What do you mean it wasn't an accident?"

"Soleda pushed me down the hill."

"Soleda?"

"Yes, she wanted to talk to me. We started walking down to the vineyards and we began to argue, then she pushed me. I don't remember anything after that."

"That bitch."

"Is she still here?"

"I haven't seen her. I've been here with you."

"You found me, didn't you?"

"Yes."

"I could've bled to death if you hadn't found me. Thank you."

"Just get well."

"Soleda will pay for this," Lisa said, a hard edge to her voice.

"Lisa, don't think about her now."

"I can't stop thinking about her. She ruined Cruz's life once before, and now she's ruined it again."

Eric closed his eyes. "You can have more children, Lisa. I'm sure Cruz will want lots of children."

Lisa turned slightly, her shoulder against Eric's chest. "Do you want me to stay with Cruz?"

"I thought it was what you wanted."

"I'm afraid to lose either one of you."

"You can't have us both, Lisa. It doesn't work that way."

"I know that."

"I think you want to stay here. For whatever reason, you've become closer to Cruz. I won't fight him for you. As soon as you're well and Cruz returns, I'm leaving."

"Oh," Lisa said softly, tears rolling down her cheeks. His arm around her in the darkness gave her a feeling of security she hadn't had in a long time. It was as though this was how it was supposed to be. "Does this have anything to do with Teresa?"

"It doesn't have anything to do with Teresa. It has to do with you and me. We knew this was coming before you met Cruz. There was something wrong between us. I don't know what it was, but we both knew it before we went to San Francisco. Maybe we were forcing it, maybe we should've taken more time to get to know each other. Maybe I should've realized that you needed to be courted like a lady instead of being taken to bed like a whore. I'm sorry for that."

"Don't be sorry for anything. You were always good to me." She cried out suddenly, grabbing her stomach.

"What is it?"

"Cramps again. Don't go. Just hold me, please."

Eric lay on his side, his arms around Lisa, holding her as she fought the waves of pain. He didn't want to turn up the lamp. He was afraid to see that she was still bleeding. "It's all right. I won't

329

leave you."

"God, Eric, I love you," she said gently, sadly. "I do love you."

"I love you too. Now, try to get well."

"What does it matter? If I get well, I'll lose you."

"Yes, but you'll have Cruz. That's what you want, isn't it?"

"I don't know. I don't know."

The door opened, and light from the lamps in the hallway partially illuminated the room. Teresa entered, holding two cups. She set them down on the table and turned up the lamp slightly. "I want you to drink this, Eric, and here's some more of that stuff for Lisa. See if you can get her to drink some more . . . My, God, Eric, she's bled quite a bit more. We've got to do something to stop the bleeding."

Eric disentangled himself from Lisa and sat up. He could see the dark stain through the bedspread. He reached over and grabbed the cup of coffee and began to drink it. "There must be something we can do. Aren't there any women around her who know anything about this?"

"Elena and I asked, but most of them just said to let her bleed. They said there was nothing they could do. Did they do anything else in the Comanche camp?"

"Like I said, they made the women drink this tea. I don't know what it did to the insides, but it helped to stop the bleeding." He thought back to the time when he had returned to the band to find them gone, all except for Lisa and Raytahnee, her friend, and the old woman, Matay, who was a

330

healer. He had asked her what he could do. She told him: "We have done all we can for her. Perhaps what she needs now is you. If you talk to her and stay with her, perhaps she will hear you. You may be the only cure for her now." Eric stood up, slamming his coffee cup down on the table. "Tell Elena to take some blankets and pillows upstairs."

"But the upstairs isn't quite finished, Eric. There isn't any roof."

"I know. Please, Teresa, just do as I say. I'm going to take Lisa up there."

Teresa nodded her head. Eric uncovered Lisa and took the soiled nightgown off and washed her again. He changed her nightgown, then wrapped her in one of the blankets from the bed, and lifted her into his arms. He carried her outside to the ladder that led upstairs. Jesus was already carrying blankets and pillows up the ladder, while Elena was directing him from below.

"Are you sure you want to do this, señor?"

"Yes, Elena, I'm sure. Is there more of that mixture that you and Teresa made up?"

"Yes, there is plenty."

"Good, I want her to keep drinking it until she falls asleep."

As soon as Jesus came back down the ladder he looked at Eric. "Everything is up there, señor. I am sorry about the señora. I hope that she is well soon."

"Thank you, Jesus." Eric held Lisa in his arms and carefully climbed the ladder to the second story. He gently laid her down on the blanket, covering her with another, and put a pillow under

331

her head.

"Here is some coffee for you, and some of that horrible brew for Lisa," Teresa whispered from the top of the ladder.

Eric leaned over to retrieve the two cups. Before Teresa could leave, he grabbed her hand and squeezed it. "Thank you. I don't know why you're doing this for both of us, but thank you."

"You both deserve it, that's why. I'll see you in the morning."

Eric picked up the cups and sat down next to Lisa. He sipped at his coffee, staring off into the black distance. The stars twinkled brightly, and the only sound that broke the still night was the yipping of coyotes, hungry and anxious to find a quarry. When the cup was empty, he placed his arm around Lisa's back and lifted her to a sitting position, holding the other cup to her mouth. "Come on, Lisa, I want you to wake up. Come on."

Lisa moved in her sleep but didn't wake up.

"Come on, Lisa." Eric gently slapped her cheeks until she shook her head.

"No," she said angrily. "I want to sleep."

"You can sleep after you drink this. Come on." He held the cup to her lips and sipped lightly, coughing as the vile-tasting mixture hit her throat. She turned her head away like a petulant child. "No more."

"Yes. I want you to finish it all. As soon as you finish this cup, I'll let you sleep."

Lisa thought about it for a moment, and then turned her head back, sipping at the mixture, coughing each time she took a drink. Within a few minutes, she was finished and lying on her side covered by a blanket. Eric was leaning over her, kissing her cheek and stroking her hair. "I love you so much, Lisa. You'll be all right. You're a strong woman. You have to get well." He laid his head against hers and closed his eyes. He had never felt so much a part of a person as he did at that moment. He could accept losing her to Cruz, but losing her to death he could never accept.

Lisa covered her eyes with her arm. The sun was shining directly into her face and for a moment she thought she was outside. Looking around and propping herself up onto her elbows, she realized that she was on the second story of the rancho. She saw the muscular arm draped over her, and knew that Eric was with her. She looked over at him and smiled. His hair was tousled and his long dark lashes rested against his face as though waiting to burst open at any moment. He looked just like a boy, only he was a man, a man with an enormous heart. She leaned over and kissed him on the cheek. He stirred slightly but didn't awaken.

She sat up and pushed the blanket down from her legs. There was blood on her nightgown and on the blankets, but not a large amount. It looked as though the bleeding had stopped. She rested on her hands and leaned her head back, looking up through the open beams to the clear blue sky. Just what was she going to do with her life now? There wasn't a baby to tie her to Cruz anymore. Her decision would have to be based solely on which man she wanted to spend the rest of her life with.

She looked over at Eric again and her heart skipped a beat. He had been so much to her. She remembered the first time she had seen him in the Comanche camp. He had looked so tall and handsome and he had commended her on her courage. He had then taken her into his tepee. He had saved her from the Apaches and from Kowano, the man who had raped her and wanted her for his woman. He had saved her from Chuka, who had kidnapped her and planned to kill her, and he had helped deliver their daughter when no one else could. But more than all of those things, he was here with her now, helping her and taking care of her. He wasn't pressuring her to come home with him; he wasn't forcing her. He wanted nothing but to help her. It was a side to him she had never seen before.

She lay back down beside him, pulling the blanket back up over them. She pulled his arm tighter around her, reveling in the feel of it around her body. Cruz loved her in a different way, a special way, abut Eric's love was more complete. She couldn't just forget all that he had been to her.

She felt him move against her, and she turned. His lashes moved and his lids opened to reveal eyes that were almost more glorious than the sky. She smiled when she saw them.

"What're you smiling at? Is my hair sticking up?"

"No, you just look like a little boy right now, that's all."

"I'm glad that makes you smile." He touched her cheek. "How do you feel?"

334

"I think the bleeding has stopped. I feel better. But what was that awful stuff you made me drink last night?"

"Don't you remember what Matay made you drink in the Comanche camp? It was something like that."

"No wonder it was so awful."

"It helped, though, didn't it?"

"That's not all that helped. Thank you for staying with me. I know I wasn't being fair to you."

"I told you we'd talk later when you felt better, and I meant it."

"All right. But why did you bring me up here?"

"I thought it might remind you of the Comanche camp, of being in the open air under the stars." He shrugged his shoulders. "It was the closest I could get to an Indian camp."

"It must've worked. Thank you." She put her arms around his neck and kissed him on the cheek. "I could always depend on you, couldn't I?"

"It was meant to be, didn't you know that?" His blue eyes were serious.

"You're not laughing."

"I'm very serious. Matay told me once that you and I were destined to intertwine for the rest of our lives. I believed her."

Lisa looked down. "I'm beginning to as well."

"You have a little color in your cheeks. That's a good sign."

"I'm starving."

"That's a *very* good sign."

"Elena will make me so much food I'll probably get sick again."

335

"Do you feel like going down now?"

"In a minute. I'd like to say something first." She stared at her hands for a minute before looking up at Eric. "You are the first man I ever loved. You showed me what love was."

Eric sat up, pushing the blanket down, an impatient look on his face. "I don't think I want to hear this."

"Eric, please listen." Lisa took his arm. "At first, our love was based on our attraction to each other and then it grew into something different after we had Raya, but we really never got to know each other. I've seen a different side to you since you've been here. You've been nothing but kind and giving, and I've been nothing but weak and complaining. I'm sorry for that. You deserve better."

"What are you trying to say, Lisa?"

"I'm not very good at this," she stammered.

"Just say it."

"What I'm trying to say," she said in a soft voice, tears filling her eyes, "is that I love you. I have always loved you, but I had forgotten how much until I was with you again. But I have to be honest with you, I think I love Cruz, too. He's a good man, Eric. He's one of the best men I've ever known. But I'm not the woman for him."

"Are you sure about that, Lisa? Are you really sure?"

"Yes, I'm sure. Even when I was with him, I couldn't stop thinking about you. You haunted my thoughts, but I didn't know what it would be like when we were together again. Maybe that's why I liked being with him. I felt no pressure from him."

She took a deep breath. "Now the question is, do you still want me?"

Eric put his hand behind Lisa's neck and brought her head next to his. "How can you even ask a question like that? I thought I'd almost lost you yesterday. I was willing to give you over to Cruz myself rather than let anything happen to you, that's how much I love you. Does that answer your question?"

"I don't know what to say. There's so much we have to discuss."

"We don't have to talk about anything right now. You still have to get better. The first thing we should do is get you down and let Elena fatten you up."

Lisa laughed. "I'm sure she'll enjoy that." She started to get up, but Eric pushed her back down.

"Just wait until I stand up. I'll help you down."

"I'm fine. I can get down a ladder by myself."

"No. Don't argue with me." Eric stood up and slowly pulled Lisa to her feet. She wobbled slightly and leaned against him. "You're weaker than you thought, aren't you?"

"I'll be all right. I'd just like to clean up and get something to eat."

"We can arrange that." Eric walked over to the ladder and went down a few rungs. "Come over here to me. Slowly."

Lisa held her blooded nightgown against her, embarrassed at how she must look. She gripped Eric's hand and stepped onto the top rung of the ladder. Slowly, Eric led Lisa down it, picking her up before she reached the bottom. He walked around the house and through the courtyard,

337

opening the door that led inside. He took Lisa to Cruz's bedroom. Another spread was on the bed, and a fresh nightgown lay on the clean linens. Eric put Lisa down on the bed.

"Why don't you wash up and change your nightgown. You can take a bath when you're a little stronger."

Eric walked over and bent down, kissing Lisa lightly. I'll be back later. "I'm going to go clean up."

"Thank you for everything."

"Lisa?" A voice came suddenly from the door, where Cruz stood, an anxious look on his face. He looked at her and at her bloodied nightgown and he ran across the room. He knelt in front of the bed, wrapping his arms around her, burying his face in her chest. "God, I thought you were dead."

Lisa ran her fingers through his hair. "I'm all right, Cruz."

"But the blood. I saw all of the blood that Elena was trying to wash out of the sheets. She said you were hurt. What happened?"

"I'll tell you later."

Cruz pulled Lisa to him. "I don't know what I would've done if something had happened to you."

Lisa's hands went around Cruz's shoulders, but her eyes met Eric's. There was nothing either of them could say. Eric looked at her a moment longer and then left the room. Lisa's eyes followed him until he left, then she lowered her head to Cruz's. "It's all right, Cruz. Don't worry about me."

Cruz looked at her. "How can I not worry

338

about you? You have become everything to me. I didn't want it to happen, but it did. I realized it in the last few days. I love you, Lisa, and I want you to stay with me. I want you to have my children, and I want you to grow old with me."

Lisa bit her bottom lip to keep from crying. How could she leave this man? How was it possible to hurt him without also hurting a part of herself in the process? "Did you see your friend, the *patrón?*"

"Yes. We had a good visit. He convinced me to come back here and fight for you. He said I would be a stupid man to let you go without a fight."

"Cruz, please—"

"I'm sorry, I don't mean to pressure you. I just want you to know how I feel. If you decide to go with Eric, I'll understand and I'll be all right."

Lisa felt suddenly tired. "Cruz, do you mind if I clean up? Then I'd like to rest for a while."

"All right. I'll be here if you need me."

"I know." She smiled and watched him as he left the room. She lay back on the bed and covered herself with the bedspread. She closed her eyes and recalled the time when Eric had taken her into his tepee as his woman but had not forced himself on her. That was what had made her fall in love with him the first time and that was why she was falling in love with him all over again. But how could she ever leave Cruz?

She blocked all thoughts from her mind and tried to relax. She thought of Raya's smiling face and within minutes she was asleep, her mind a blessed blank.

Eric slammed his cup down on the table. "We're leaving tomorrow morning."

Teresa looked at Tom. "Why so soon?"

"Because I'm ready to go. Do I have to give you a reason?" he snapped.

"Eric, don't be like that with Teresa. She was up most of the night checking on you two."

Eric lowered his head and reached out for Teresa's hand. "I'm sorry. I'm tired. I don't know what I'm saying."

"Then why don't you get some sleep?"

"I don't need sleep!" He stood up and paced around the kitchen. "I should've just let it be. It would've been easier if I'd not come after her."

Teresa stood up and walked over to Eric. "Are you upset because Cruz is back? Is that what this is all about?"

"Why should I be upset? This is his home and Lisa is his wife."

Tom raised his eyebrows and stood up. "Look, I'm going to go check on Lisa. Get some rest, Eric."

Eric shoved his hands into his pockets and shrugged his shoulders. "I knew it was too good to be true."

"What are you talking about?"

"Lisa told me she loves me."

"Well, of course she loves you. Anyone can see that."

"But you should've seen the way she looked at Cruz when he came running into the room. He was upset and she hugged him to her like a woman comforting her man." He shook his head. "I can't take it anymore, Teresa. I've got to get out of here."

"Cruz was just worried about her, that's all. Lisa's reaction was a natural one. What is really the matter with you, Eric? There's something else."

"He needs her more than I do. God knows, I love her more than anything in the world, but I can go on. I don't know about Cruz. He's a strong man, but there's something about him . . ." He narrowed his eyes. "It's almost as if Lisa has become his whole world."

"So are you going to give up just because you feel sorry for Cruz?" Teresa stood in front of Eric, her hands on his chest. "Eric, I like Cruz, too. He's a good man, but you can't just give Lisa up and walk away without a fight."

"Why not? Who says I have to fight? I'm tired of fighting. I've been fighting for most of my life."

"Then don't fight. Stay here where she can see you and be reminded of you every day. She won't give you up, Eric."

"How do you know that?"

Teresa tenderly touched Eric's face. Stubble from the previous day had already grown out and he looked tired, but his extraordinary eyes still shined with life. "I know because I'm a woman." She kissed him softly on the lips. "Give up if you want to, but I think you're making a mistake."

"It doesn't matter anymore, Teresa. I need to get home to my daughter. She needs me and she needs a mother." He looked at Teresa and ran the back of his hand up and down her cheek. "It's too bad you're going to marry Bryant. You'd make a good mother."

"Is that all I'd make?"

Eric pulled Teresa into his arms, kissing her passionately, yearning for her to take away his pain. Her slim body moved against his and he felt himself get excited. "What about Bryant?"

"Bryant and I aren't married yet," she mumbled, returning his kiss with such passion that Eric almost stumbled backward.

"Oh, excuse me," Cruz said, standing at the entry to the kitchen.

Eric quickly pulled away from Teresa and turned around. He could only manage to stammer "Sorry" with embarrassment.

Cruz walked over to Eric. "I just wanted to thank you for taking such good care of Lisa. She said you saved her life."

"You don't need to thank me, Cruz."

"What happened to her? Why did she lose so much blood?"

"Why the hell don't you ask her yourself?" Eric yelled, stomping out of the kitchen.

"I'm sorry, Cruz," Teresa said, before she ran out of the room after Eric. She followed him down to the main corral. He was leaning against the corral, watching one of the vaqueros break a horse. She walked up next to him and climbed up a couple of rungs to get at an even level with him. "If you want to go tomorrow, I'll go. And if you really want me to come home with you, I'll do that, too. But don't try to use me as a replacement for Lisa. That will never work. I can never replace her. And don't use me to try to forget her, because you'll never forget her, Eric."

Eric rested his chin on his arm, staring into the corral. "I can't promise you anything, Teresa. I can't even promise you love somewhere down the line. Right now I'm drained, I'm empty. I don't have anything left to give. You'd be better off going back to Bryant."

"I have a lot to give, Eric. Haven't you noticed that yet?"

"Yes, I've noticed. But I'm crazy right now. I don't even know what I'm feeling."

"You're feeling hurt and you're feeling lost."

He stared at her, his clear eyes almost penetrating hers. "Can you live with the fact that I might love another woman the rest of my life?"

"Yes, Eric. I'm not a fragile little thing, I'm strong."

"Right now, you're stronger than I am." Eric turned away from the corral and walked away. "I want to leave tomorrow morning. We'll let Tom decide what he wants to do."

"Eric? Are you going to say good-bye to Lisa?"

"I don't know," he said, walking away toward the valley.

Lisa sat in the courtyard, a blanket on her knees. "Elena, I really don't need this. It's hot out here."

"There's a breeze. We don't need for you to get sick again."

Lisa grabbed Elena's hand. "Thank you for everything. You've been wonderful to me."

"I am just happy that you are well. You make

343

Cruz happy, señora." Elena tucked the blanket around Lisa's legs. "There. I will be out to check on you later."

Lisa closed her eyes, relishing the feel of the warm sun on her face, but opened them shortly at the sound of footsteps. Eric was standing in front of her. He had washed up and shaved, and he'd changed his shirt. His hat was pushed back on his head, and he squinted his eyes. He looked wonderful standing there, almost like one of Cruz's sketches.

"I'm leaving tomorrow."

"No," she stammered. "You can't leave."

"I have to. I don't have any other choice. I can't stay here and watch you with Cruz. We both know he needs you more than I do." He crossed his arms in front of him. "You'll be fine here. Cruz will take good care of you."

"No, you can't just leave me here. What about last night and this morning?"

"Don't you see? None of that matters. As long as you feel the way you do about Cruz, nothing between us will ever change. I'm glad you're getting better." He reached down and picked up the cross she wore around her neck. "Did Cruz give this to you?"

Lisa nodded. "Will Teresa go with you?"

"Of course she'll go with me."

"You know what I mean. Will so go home with you?"

"I don't know, but it's a possibility."

"So, Teresa will be Raya's new mother." She gripped the bench, looking away from Eric. Her eyes filled with tears of sadness and confusion.

344

"You'll see Raya whenever you want."

"And how often will that be? Once or twice a year?" She shook her head. "I think it would just be better if you told her I was dead. It would be easier on all of us."

"If that's what you want."

"Oh, God, Sometimes I hate you," she said angrily, throwing the blanket on the ground and standing up.

Eric went to her, putting his hands on her shoulders. "Be careful. You're still weak."

"I'm not your concern anymore. Just go and leave me alone." Lisa started to walk away, but Eric grabbed her arm.

"I have loved you more than I have ever loved anyone in my life. Don't forget that." He took her face in his hand and pressed his mouth to hers. He savored the feel of her lips, then pulled away. He looked at her and walked out of the courtyard.

Lisa put her fingers up to her mouth and began to cry. She turned around and saw Cruz staring at her from the door of the kitchen. His eyes were hard. She quickly wiped the tears away as he walked toward her.

"Why were you crying?"

"I wasn't crying."

"When were you planning to tell me that you were carrying our child? Or was it just your little secret?"

"How did you find out?"

"Does it matter?"

"Yes, it matters to me."

"I found out from Soleda."

"Soleda! She's here?"

345

"She *was* here. She went to the mission. She said she would be there most of the day."

Lisa felt the rage rise inside of her. "I hate her."

"I'm not here to discuss Soleda. I want to know why you didn't tell me you were carrying my child."

"I just found out a few days ago, Cruz. I needed time to figure things out."

"What were you trying to figure out, which child was more important to you, or was it, which man?"

Lisa couldn't believe how angry Cruz was. "I'm sorry. I didn't mean to hurt you. I would've told you in time."

"When? When you were back in Monterey with Eric and Raya?"

"No, I would never have done that to you. Never."

Cruz grabbed her shoulders and shook her. "Then why the hell didn't you tell me?"

"I was afraid you would force me to stay here, and I couldn't choose between Raya and the baby. I was scared."

Cruz dug his fingers into Lisa's shoulders. "Did you lose the baby on purpose, Lisa?"

Lisa was astonished. "No, I would never do such a thing. Never!"

"Soleda told me she saw you throw yourself down the hill."

Lisa angrily pulled away. "And you believed her? You believe that lying, conniving bitch over me." She clenched her fists at her sides. "All right, Cruz, if you choose to believe Soleda, then you deserve what you get. I won't tell you anything

346

more." Lisa walked toward the house, but Cruz grabbed her arm and pulled her back. "You're not leaving until I get an answer."

"You want an answer, I'll give you an answer. That woman killed our child, our baby. It didn't have a chance, Cruz. I saw its very life bleed out of me yesterday, and part of me went with it. That child was part of you and you are a part of me. You always will be. But I won't be manipulated by anyone, not you and especially not Soleda." She pulled away and walked into the house, going to Cruz's room. She took her saddlebag, packed her belongings, and put on the shirt Cruz had given her. She pulled on her riding boots and quickly braided her hair. She had had enough. She wouldn't take anymore. Walking to the dresser and taking out the revolver that Cruz had given her, she checked to make sure it was loaded, then stuck it in the saddlebag. She stomped out of the room, going out by the front door, hoping to avoid seeing anyone in the kitchen or courtyard area. She saw Teresa coming toward her but continued walking.

"Lisa? Are you all right?"

Lisa stopped and turned around. "I'm better than I've been in a long time, Teresa. Have a good life with Eric."

She practically ran down to the corral and asked Jesus to saddle her horse. When he hesitated, she threw her saddlebag over her shoulder and went into the tackroom.

"I will do it, señora."

"I'll need a bedroll and some water, Jesus."

"Are you going for a long ride, señora?"

"Long enough," Lisa answered.

"Does Cruz know where you're going?"

"No, and he doesn't need to know." She put the halter on the horse while Jesus cinched the saddle. When Jesus was through tying on the bedroll and handing her the water bag, Lisa mounted. She looked down at Jesus. "Thank you, Jesus. Tell Elena that she's a wonderful cook and thank her for everything she did for me. Take good care of Cruz."

"But, señora . . ."

Lisa didn't stop to listen to what Jesus had to say, but just rode away as fast as she could. She felt the pain immediately, but still she rode hard and fast, feeling the animal underneath her, and she felt herself grow stronger the faster she rode. It felt good to be on her own. It felt good to feel free. The only thing that mattered to her right now was Soleda. She was going to find Soleda. And then she was going to kill her.

Chapter 12

Lisa saw the riders coming in the distance. She pulled up, reaching for the pistol in her saddlebag. She could tell there were at least six of them. As they approached, she could see that one of them was a woman, and she knew it was Soleda. She put the pistol on the saddle, and pulled up part of her skirt to cover it. As soon as the riders neared, she saw it indeed was Soleda, and she was with Miguel and some of his men. So, the woman wasn't as brave as she appeared!

"Ah, Lisa, it is wonderful to see you again. You are out for a ride?" Miguel asked innocently.

Lisa's eyes never left Soleda's face. "No, actually, I've come to settle some business with someone."

"Oh, I see. Is Cruz at his rancho? I'd like to speak with him." He smiled like a schoolboy. "Soleda has finally consented to marry me. I'd like to ask Cruz to dissolve his marriage to her."

Lisa shook her head. "Poor Miguel, I feel sorry for you."

"Perdoname," he said in polite Spanish.

"Do you really want to marry this she-devil?"

"What did you call me?" Soleda asked.

"You know what I called you. You know what you are."

"Lisa, please, I don't think you know what you're saying."

"I know exactly what I'm saying, Miguel. If you marry this witch, you'll wish to God you had never been born. She will make your life a living hell."

"Miguel, are you going to let her talk to me like that?"

Miguel looked confused. "Lisa, Soleda told me of your terrible ordeal. Perhaps you need to rest —"

"Did she also tell you how it happened, Miguel?" Lisa edged her horse closer to Soleda's. "You are such a coward."

"I am no coward."

"Then get off your horse and stay here, alone, with me. I want you and me to settle this thing now."

Soleda's eyes met Lisa's and she nodded. "All right. I will stay here."

"What are you doing, Soleda? You can't stay here in the middle of nowhere. You must come to the rancho with me."

"You go on ahead, Miguel. I will be there later. Lisa and I have some things to discuss."

Miguel looked from one woman to the other and shrugged his shoulders, riding off to the east. As soon as the horses were out of sight, both women dismounted. Lisa held the pistol in the folds of her skirt. She stared at Soleda, her eyes cold and hard.

"So, Lisa, what is it you think I've done?"

Lisa reacted before she could even think. Her pistol hand went out and hit Soleda across the face, knocking her to the ground. Soleda cried out, but she quickly pulled a knife out of a sheath on her thigh. "I thought you'd be prepared to fight. But it's more your style to stab someone in the back, isn't it, Soleda? You also like to push pregnant women down hills?"

"You slipped."

"You lying bitch! You pushed me and you know it."

"You didn't deserve to have his child."

"What gives you the right to decide that? Who made you God?"

"I am his wife, that is what gives me the right. You think you've fooled everyone, don't you? You act as if you're such a good, sweet woman, but I know different. You are just like me. You whore around just as I do, only I'll wind up rich and you won't. Cruz will never be rich."

Lisa smiled. "Cruz is already rich in ways you'll never understand."

Soleda looked confused. "Cruz is rich? Does he have money hidden somewhere?" She smiled greedily. "Somewhere at his rancho?"

"You don't understand what I'm talking about, Soleda. I'm not talking about money. I'm talking about the kind of person he is. But I'm sure you never took the time to get to know him."

"I got to know him. I got to know him very well, in fact. I remember the way he liked me to strip for him before we made love, and I remember—"

"I don't want to hear what you remember. I want you to listen to what I have to say." Lisa lifted the pistol and aimed it at Soleda. "I can never forgive you for what you did to me and to Cruz. You took away something precious and good, and now you're going to pay for it." Lisa pulled back the hammer on the revolver. She watched as Soleda lifted her knife, but it didn't frighten her. She squeezed the trigger and the sound exploded in her ears. Soleda screamed and jumped as the bullet hit the ground near her feet. Lisa pulled back the hammer again and took aim. "I won't miss this time, Soleda."

"What do you want from me?"

"You have a knife. Why don't you fight back?"

Soleda lifted her knife hand. "I wish the fall had killed you and the baby."

Lisa squeezed the trigger, hitting Soleda in the hand. Soleda screamed, dropping the knife and grabbing her injured and bloodied hand with her good hand. "My God, are you crazy? Do you see what you have done?" She began to sob.

Lisa stepped closer, surveying the damage. She cocked the revolver again. "You look fine to me, Soleda. At least you're alive. That's more than I can say for my baby." Lisa aimed the pistol, but Soleda fell to her knees crying out.

"Please, do not do this. Please."

Lisa watched as she wailed, bent over on her knees, her shoulders shaking. She didn't expect this from Soleda. She had expected more fight from her. She stood over her, suddenly feeling quite powerful. "Get up," she said in a cold voice.

"I can't. My hand, it's bleeding."

Lisa kicked Soleda in the thigh. "I said get up or I swear I'll shoot you where you are. Like a dog."

Soleda quickly got to her feet, holding her bloodied hand in front of her. "What do you want from me?"

"What do you think I want from you, Soleda?"

"You want me to say I'm sorry? All right, I'm sorry. Now, will you put the gun down?"

"No, that's not good enough. I want the one thing you can't give me."

"What?" Soleda screamed.

"I want my baby." Lisa lifted the gun and cocked it, aiming it at Soleda's head. "You should never have been born, Soleda. You were a mistake." Her hand was steady as she aimed the gun at Soleda. Her finger started to squeeze the trigger. "You're not scared, are you?"

"Don't do this. You're making a mistake. Miguel will make sure you pay for this."

Lisa laughed. "Do you think I care what Miguel thinks? He is a spineless creature who can't tell the difference between a woman and a rattlesnake."

Soleda's eyes widened as she looked straight at Lisa and then past her. "If you are going to kill me, you should do it now. Miguel is coming back with his men."

Lisa didn't turn his head. "I don't think you heard what I said before, Soleda. I'm not afraid of Miguel, and I don't care what happens to me. I don't care if I die killing you, just as long as you die first."

For the first time, Soleda looked truly frightened. She began to sob hysterically. "Please, let me live and I will change. I will go to confession and I will change. I promise."

Lisa laughed. "You're good, Soleda. You're probably the best actress I've ever met." Lisa heard the horses behind her, but she didn't turn. "I guess I should kill you now before someone kills *me*." She held the gun farther out in front of her, both hands on the handle, the first finger of her right hand on the trigger. "Good-bye, Soleda." She squinted as she looked down the barrel of the revolver. She had never felt so calm in her life.

"Lisa, don't." Eric's voice broke the stillness. He walked up to her. "She's not worth it."

"I think she is. Leave me alone and go back home. Take Teresa and go to Raya. I'm sure the three of you will make a lovely family."

"Lisa, listen to me. If you kill Soleda, what will you have accomplished? Will her death make you feel any better?"

"Yes, I'll rest much better at night knowing she's no longer on this earth. Get out of here, Eric!"

"I don't care if you want me here or not, I'm staying." He walked toward Soleda and stood next to her. "Why don't you shoot me, too? You can put me out of my misery."

Lisa's hands began to shake. "Get out of the way, Eric." She pulled the trigger. The bullet hit the ground right next to Soleda's boot. She screamed and hit the ground, covering her head with her hands.

"You missed. You used to be a better shot."

Lisa turned the gun toward Eric, pulling back the hammer. "I wish I could kill you. I wish I'd

354

never seen you."

Eric took a step closer. "Well, you did see me, and I remember the first time I saw *you*. You were filthy and rolling around on the ground fighting that Comanche woman. You were beating her badly. You thought I was going to punish you, but you didn't realize how brave I thought you were."

"That doesn't have anything to do with this."

"But it does. I think you've been brave the last few days. You could've given up, but you didn't. You fought, just like you always have. God, Lisa, don't let filth like her ruin your life."

Lisa couldn't control the shaking of her hands. She heard footsteps behind her but before she could react, Cruz had wrapped his arms around her, while Eric came from the front, grabbing the gun.

"Let go of me." Lisa kicked and screamed.

Cruz loosened his arms and looked at Lisa. "You weren't actually going to kill her, were you?"

"Why, were you worried you might lose her?"

"Lisa, don't. I'm sorry I didn't believe you before. I should've known better."

"Yes, Cruz, you should have, but you didn't. That's the problem."

She pulled away from him and glared at Eric. "You've done your good deed for the day, now you can go home." She walked toward her horse. Eric grabbed her and whipped her around.

"Stop it! I know you've suffered a real shock and that you're probably still trying to get over it, but I won't let you be consumed by hate."

"You don't really have anything to say about it.

You have your own life to lead and I have mine."

"And just what did you plan to do? Murder Soleda and then simply resume your life?"

"I told you to leave me alone." Lisa tried to pull her arm away but Eric held on tightly. "I won't let go of you, not until I know you're all right."

"It's not that simple, Eric. Just go away and leave me alone."

"God, you are so stubborn, woman," Eric said angrily, pulling Lisa after him as he walked away from the others. He walked down a slope and pushed Lisa to the ground and then he sat down next to her. "Now, you listen to me. I'm not leaving here until I find out what's really bothering you. I love you, you know that. The only reason I said I was leaving was because I thought you should stay with Cruz. I don't feel that way anymore. I think he's a good man, but I won't give you up without a fight. I love you. You're my wife and the mother of my child. I won't just walk away."

Lisa pulled a stalk of wild grass and twirled it in her fingers. "That still doesn't change anything. You were ready to walk away from me this morning."

"And you were ready to have another man's child and live with him."

"You didn't know that. I hadn't made up my mind yet."

"If that baby had lived, I know you would've stayed with Cruz. I know you so well, Lisa. You would never have left him if you'd had his child."

"If you know me so well, why is it you didn't think I'd go after Soleda?"

356

"I didn't know she was still around here. It was only after Cruz had spoken to me and Teresa said she'd seen you going to the corral, that I thought something was wrong. Then Miguel rode up and told us that you and Soleda were having a talk."

"I should've killed her when I had the chance. I've never hated anyone so much in all my life."

"Then don't hate her, forget her. There's nothing you can do about it now. The hatred will only eat you up. I know all about hatred."

Lisa looked at Eric for the first time. "I feel as if I've lost my way. I don't know where to go." Her voice wasn't cold anymore, but frightened.

"Let me help you." Eric reached out and put his arm around her neck, pulling her to him. Her head rested against his. "I won't be anything more than your friend right now, if that's what you want. But don't push me away. I know I can help you."

She nodded. "I know you can, too. You always have. You've always found a way to get through the darkness." She closed her eyes. "I feel so tired."

Eric pulled her into his arms and she rested against his chest. "You've been through a lot, Lisa. You need time to get over it. Let me take you back to the rancho so you can rest."

"I don't want to go back. I don't want to see Cruz again."

"Don't blame him. He was crazy with grief. He didn't understand why you didn't tell him about the baby."

"But he believed Soleda and not me."

"He was angry and he was hurt. You should

understand all about that."

"I just don't want to talk to him right now."

"I think you should. Talk to him and make him understand. I won't go anywhere. I'll be waiting right here for you. If you still want to leave, then I'll take you away today. All right?"

Eric stood up and went back to where Cruz was standing, tending to Soleda's wound. He didn't seem the least bit upset. "She wants to talk to you. But let me give you some friendly advice. Take it easy. Remember, she's still recovering from the loss of the baby. You aren't the only one who lost a child here."

Cruz nodded and walked up behind Lisa. She had her knees pulled up to her chest and she was hugging them, her chin resting on them. "How do you feel?"

"You mean after I almost killed someone?"

"No, that's not what I mean. I know you're still weak. Do you feel all right? You look tired."

"That's funny, Cruz, a little while ago you didn't seem too worried about me. The only thing you seemed worried about was what Soleda had to say."

"I was angry. I know that's no excuse, but—"

"You're right, that is no excuse. I didn't want to lose our child. I wanted it, and I had decided to stay here with you and give Raya up. It seemed like the best thing to do."

Cruz sat down next to Lisa. "I didn't know."

"You didn't ask."

"What're you going to do now?"

"I don't know. I just know I don't belong here. Whatever we had together is over. You were good

358

to me and you took care of me, but I'm not sure that's love."

"You're going back with Eric?"

"I don't know what I'm going to do. I just might have Eric take me somewhere where I can be by myself for a time. I need to be away from everyone. Then I want to go home and see Raya."

"I'm sorry for everything I put you through. You didn't deserve any of it."

"You didn't put me through anything, Cruz."

"Yes, I did. I put pressure on you the entire time we were together. I made you try to fall in love with me, I made you need me. I wanted you to be my wife, that's why I came up with that idea of you marrying me. I thought for sure the longer you were away from Eric, the more chance I'd have of making you fall in love with me."

"I did fall in love with you, Cruz. I did." Her eyes were tender when she looked at him.

"But not in the way you love Eric. It's different with him, isn't it? It goes much deeper. I can see it. You trust him in a way you could never trust me. You belong to him more than you realized, Lisa."

"Maybe, but I'm not counting on anything right now. I just want to get healthy and strong and then see my daughter. Whatever happens after that . . ."

She put her hands up in the air in a questioning gesture.

"Why don't you stay here?"

"I don't think that would be a good idea."

"I won't be here. I'm going to Mexico to see my family. It's time I tried to reconcile with my father.

He's getting old and I don't want him to die with a heavy heart. So, stay here for as long as you like. Eric, too."

"No, I couldn't do that. There are too many memories."

"There are good memories here, also, aren't there? And I know you like it here. It would be stupid to leave. Miguel will be taking Soleda north with him as soon as she can travel. You'll be safe. I'll make sure there are always men around the rancho to keep watch."

"Thank you, that's very generous. I'll think about it." She looked out over the peaceful valley and the mountains beyond. "Someday you'll have children running wild all over this land and you'll wonder how you ever thought you loved me."

"I don't think so. I have no interest in marriage anymore. I don't seem to choose my women very wisely."

Lisa glanced at him, her eyes showing the hurt. "I understand why you feel that way about me, but please don't ever compare me to Soleda." She stood up. "I don't think I'll stay here at the rancho. It already has too many memories for me."

Cruz stood up and took Lisa's hands in his. "I'm sorry I said that. You've shown me so much and I'll always be grateful for that. You haven't done anything wrong. You always told me you missed your husband and little girl. I was just hoping you'd fall in love with me." He kissed her on both cheeks. "If you ever need me, you can always depend on me."

Lisa put her arms around Cruz's waist and looked up at him. "You will find someone someday, someone who doesn't have a history like mine. There is a beautiful woman out there somewhere who will give you everything you want. Trust me. I know about these things."

Cruz smiled and kissed her lightly. "I know where she is, it's just that she's leaving."

"A part of you will always be with me. Always."

Cruz nodded. "Well, we should be getting back. Miguel will be going crazy." They walked back to the others. Eric was leaning against his horse, looking as if he might fall asleep. Soleda was complaining endlessly about her hand, but Eric didn't seem to be the least bit interested in listening to her.

"We're ready to go back now," Lisa said to Eric.

"All right, but, Lisa, are you sure you're feeling well?"

"I'm just a little tired, that's all." As she started to mount her horse, she was pulled down by Soleda, who had run up from the back, a knife in her hand. Flailing her arms, she tried to stab Lisa in the back but missed, hitting the saddle. Eric and Cruz dragged her back.

"What is the matter with you? Are you asking to be killed?" Cruz said angrily.

"She deserves to die. Look what she did to my hand."

"You deserve a lot worse for what you did to our child." Cruz looked at her. "Get up on your horse. If you say another word, I swear I'll kill you myself."

Lisa mounted her horse, ignoring Soleda and the men. No one spoke as they rode back to the rancho. All Lisa wanted to do was rest.

361

When they reached the rancho, they were met by an angry Miguel. "What has happened?" He looked in horror at Soleda's hand. He helped her down from her horse and held her against him.

"That woman, she shot me."

Miguel looked at Lisa. "Is this true?"

Lisa ignored Miguel and dismounted.

"Is this true, Cruz?"

"Yes," Cruz answered impatiently, dismounting.

"I demand payment for what this woman did to Soleda."

Cruz went to Miguel, his face angry. "That's enough, Miguel. I tried to tell you about Soleda but you wouldn't listen. Now, I'm going to be brutally honest. Do you know what I found her doing one night while we were married? I came home and found her sleeping with men in my bed for money. She was earning money by sleeping with men whenever I wasn't around."

"I don't believe you."

"I wouldn't lie to you, Miguel."

"You hate me because I have her and you don't."

"I don't care if she's dead, Miguel. She means nothing to me. She is worthless."

Miguel hit Cruz in the face. "I will not allow you to say such things about my intended."

Cruz took Miguel by the shirt collar and walked him backward to the corral until he was slammed up against it. Miguel's men started to draw their guns, but Eric had drawn his first.

"Leave it alone, men. Go mind your own business. Now!" He slid out of the saddle and walked to Soleda. He pulled her away from Miguel and

362

pushed her toward the men. "Take her with you." The men walked away but Eric stayed, walking to Lisa and handing her gun back to her.

"It's time you listened to me, Miguel. I tired to be your friend and warn you about Soleda but you wouldn't listen. Do you want to know the kind of woman she is? She pushed Lisa down a hill a few days ago so that Lisa would lose our child." His hands moved around Miguel's throat. "She did lose the child, Miguel, all because Soleda couldn't stand the thought of another woman having my child."

"No, she wouldn't do that."

"Do you want to know something else? She was the one who would never let go of our marriage all these years. I tried, but she said she would never let me go. So I left and prayed I would never see her again."

Miguel's body went limp against the railings. "I can't believe she would do such evil things."

"Soleda would do anything to get what she wants. Don't marry her, Miguel. If you do, your throat will be slit before you've been married a month and Soleda will wind up a rich young widow." Cruz dropped his hands.

"I am so sorry, my friend. Your child—I don't know what to say."

"I think you owe Lisa an apology."

Miguel nodded his head and walked to the horses. "Lisa, I am so sorry about your child. I apologize for what Soleda did to you. She must not be in her right mind."

"It wasn't your fault, Miguel."

"But I feel so responsible. I must go see her."

Lisa leaned against the fence. Cruz walked to her. "Let me help you to the house. You need to rest."

"I'm all right, Cruz. I'm not helpless."

"I'm sorry, I'm just now finding that out." He glanced at Eric and walked away.

Eric looked at Lisa. "Shall we go up?"

She nodded, and they began walking in the direction of the house.

"You wouldn't like to give me that gun back, would you?"

"I don't think so." Lisa held it down by her side, walking alongside Eric. "Don't worry, I'm not going to harm myself."

"It's not you I'm worried about," Eric said playfully.

Lisa smiled slightly. "Thank you for what you did back there. I'm sure I would've killed Soleda if you hadn't talked me out of it."

"What did I tell you? We're destined to be together?" He flashed a brilliant smile and quickened his pace, leaving her to walk the rest of the way by herself.

Lisa couldn't contain a smile; he was always able to make her smile. She watched his long, confident stride as he reached the courtyard and Teresa rushed out and into his arms. Lisa stopped, not wanting to get close to them. She watched as Teresa put her arms around Eric's neck. It sent a stabbing pain through her heart; she felt as if she couldn't breathe. She had forgotten about Teresa. She had forgotten that Eric was ready to leave with Teresa. She walked the other way, toward the front of the house, and went inside. She went to

Cruz's room and shut the door. She didn't even care where Soleda was. She lay down on the bed with the pistol in her hand. She closed her eyes. She had never felt so tired in her life, or so alone.

Teresa rubbed Miguel's hand. "You'll be fine, Miguel."

"I won't know what to do without her. She is like fire to me."

"And fire can burn, remember?"

"Yes, but she is so beautiful. I will never find another woman like her."

"Stop it, Miguel! You can be so stupid sometimes. This woman is worthless, yet you waste so much time worrying about her. She is bad, just like a rotten apple. She needs to be thrown away."

"What will she do on her own?"

"She'll do what she's always done on her own, she'll survive."

"I can't help but feel sorry for her."

"If you feel sorry for anyone, feel sorry for Cruz and Lisa. They lost a child because of her. Miguel, you are such a good man. Don't let her ruin you. There are so many good women out there, women like Lisa."

"Women like you, Cousin."

Teresa kissed him on the cheek. "What you need to do is come to San Francisco. I have lots of girlfriends, beautiful girlfriends, who would love to meet a rich *patrón*. You need a good woman, Miguel. Someone who can take care of you."

"I feel very stupid, you know. I feel as if I'm not a man."

"Why, because you fell in love with Soleda? Don't feel that way. She's good at what she does. Cruz even fell in love with her once, remember?"

"I worry about him. Not only has he lost his child, but he has lost his woman."

"What do you mean?"

"Lisa was ready to kill Soleda, but Eric talked her out of it. She listened to him. There is something very special between them. I can see it."

"Yes," Teresa mumbled, trying not to lose her composure. She stood up. "Will you be all right?"

"Yes, I'll be fine. Where are you going?"

"I have some things to do. I'll see you later."

Teresa walked down the hall and opened the door to Cruz's room. Lisa was sleeping on the bed and Teresa sat down in the chair in the corner, waiting for her to wake up. She had been a fool to think that Eric might love her; she had known all along how he felt about Lisa. She had befriended Lisa out of the kindness of her heart; yet it still hadn't kept her from falling in love with her husband. Poor Bryant, how he had misjudged her.

Lisa rolled to her side and opened her eyes. She sensed someone was looking at her and, glancing over her shoulder, saw Teresa sitting in the chair staring at her.

"I must know if you plan to go back to Eric," Teresa asked, swallowing the lump in her throat. "It's a simple and direct question."

Lisa sat up, rubbing her hands over her face. "I thought you were in love with another man, Teresa."

"And I thought you were in love with Cruz."

"What do you want from me?"

366

"I don't want to play games, Lisa. I'm not Soleda. I just want the truth."

"The truth is, I don't know. All I know right now is I want to leave this place and go somewhere by myself and after I spend some time alone, I want to see Raya."

"So you are going back to Eric."

"I didn't say that. I said I was going to see Raya."

"But you know he'll be there."

"Of course he'll be there, he's her father. Look, Teresa, I don't really care what you do with Eric. I just want to see my daughter. That's all that matters to me right now."

"But you still love him, don't you?"

"Love isn't everything."

"I would settle for that right now."

"Then take it if that's what you want. I'm not standing in your way."

"But you are, and you know it. As long as you're on your own, Eric will never decide anything."

"I can't live Eric's life for him. He'll do as he pleases no matter what. If you don't realize that by now, Teresa, you don't know him very well." Lisa stood up. "I really don't know what you want from me. Do you want a promise that I'll never see Eric again? I can't give you that promise. He and I have a child together. All I can tell you right now is that I'm not interested in marriage. In fact, I'm sick of men all together." She walked to the door and turned. "If I were you, I'd talk to Eric about how you feel. He'll be honest with you."

Lisa walked down to the corral and stood on

367

the bottom rung, looking over the top. She watched as the men tried to break the wild horses and worked with the ones that were already broken. Jesus walked over to her.

"Can I do something for you, señora?"

"No, thank you, Jesus, I was just watching. Your men are very good."

"Yes, we have some of the best vaqueros around. There are not many horses that they cannot break."

"Cruz has a nice place here. He will do well."

"You are not staying." It was a statement, not a question.

"No, I don't belong here, Jesus. Cruz is a good man. He will find the right woman someday."

"I think Cruz was hoping that woman would be you."

"It can never be me. Cruz and I were thrown together. Under other circumstances, we would never have been together."

"I admire your honesty, señora, but what will you do now? Will you go back north with your husband?"

"I don't think so," she said almost inaudibly then jumped down from the railing. "Thank you, Jesus, for being so kind. I'll see you before I go." Lisa walked toward the back of the house and the well. She stood on the hill, looking down into the vineyards, remembering the day Soleda had pushed her. Had it actually made everything easier for her?

"What're you thinking about?" Eric walked up next to her.

"I was thinking that I've made a mess of my life

and it's time I did something to straighten it out. I'm not exactly sure what, but I have to think long and hard. Once I make my decision, I have to live with it the rest of my life."

"Are you going to include Raya in that decision?"

"I don't know Eric," she replied honestly. "Sometimes I think it would be best if I never went back to her."

"And who would be her mother?"

Her green eyes blazed into his. "I'm sure you can find someone to take my place."

"You're getting hard. I don't like that."

"I really don't care what you like, Eric. It's time I learned to protect myself from people."

"Even from me?"

"Especially from you," she said angrily, walking along the edge of the hill. She stood with her arms crossed in front of her, tapping her foot. "You don't have to follow me around. I'm not going to kill myself. If anything, I might kill someone else."

"I just don't want it to be me."

She looked away from him, to the mountains in the distance. They were beautiful, and peaceful-looking. Maybe if she went to a place like that, she could find what she was looking for.

"Those mountains aren't going to give you the answers you're looking for." Eric interrupted her thoughts.

"Would you just leave me alone?"

"That would be simple wouldn't it? I could just ride away and your decision could be made for you. You could even talk yourself into hating me.

But I won't do that. I won't make it that simple for you. I plan to hang around as long as you do."

"Why? Why won't you just leave me alone?"

Eric took a step toward her and Lisa moved slightly backward, losing her balance. A look of terror came over her face as she realized she might fall, but Eric grabbed her. He wrapped his arms around her, holding her close. "I'll never let you fall again."

Lisa closed her eyes and laid her head against Eric's chest. "Will you take me upstairs? I like it up there."

"I'll take you up there if you promise me you'll rest."

They walked to the ladder that led to the second story of the rancho. Lisa climbed the ladder first and stood up above, looking out over the valley. "It is so beautiful here."

"Yes, I can understand why you might want to stay."

Lisa turned, surprised. "I didn't say I want to stay."

"What do you want then?"

"I don't know." She looked back at the valley. "I just want some peace in my life."

Eric took her hand and led her to the place where they had lain the night before. The blankets were still there. He sat against one of the poles and pulled Lisa against him. "Close your eyes."

"I'm not really that tired. I just want to be someplace where no one can bother me."

"No one will bother you up here." He pulled the leather thong out of Lisa's hair and undid the braid with his fingers. As he ran his hand through her hair, he could see her eyes drooping. He knew she loved to have her head rubbed.

Lisa closed her eyes, snuggling up to Eric's chest. "Just a little while. Then I'll be fine." Her hand automatically fell across his waist.

Eric smiled at the feel of her in his arms. She had been through too much lately, physically and emotionally, and he worried about her. He wanted her someplace where he could keep an eye on her.

He rested his chin on her head and closed his eyes. He wouldn't want to rush her. If it took her months to decide what she wanted to do, he would wait, but he wouldn't leave her alone. He knew now that she didn't love Cruz, at least not in the way she loved him. She had depended on Cruz, but she didn't love him. He would wait as long as it took for her to recover, and then he would do whatever it took to make her fall in love with him again.

Eric jerked awake. It was dark. They had both fallen asleep. He carefully moved away from Lisa, covered her with a blanket, and stood up, stretching. He couldn't believe he'd fallen asleep. He decided to go down and get something to eat and drink. Maybe it would do them good to stay up here alone on the second story. He started down the ladder but stopped when he heard voices. He quietly climbed back up to the top again and knelt, listening.

"The general says to wait out here."

"Why? There's nothing here. Do you see how

easily we got in. I don't understand why he doesn't get what he came for and leave."

"He's looking for the woman, remember? The one with the green eyes."

Eric didn't move a muscle. He just hoped the men didn't think to climb up the ladder in the dark.

"Why does he want the woman? What is she to him?"

"I have heard that she is married to a rich *patrón* and that he will pay much money to get her back."

"Then why did the general let Joaquin take her south? I don't understand." The man took a drink from a bottle and handed it to his friend. "Here."

"*Gracias*. I can use it to keep warm." The man took a drink and handed the bottle back. "Joaquin was to give him money for the woman, but now the general wants her back. She is more valuable to him if he takes her with him." He took the bottle and drank again. "So, once we find the woman, we will be heading back north?"

"*Sí*, if we find her. The general says she should be here, but we can't find her. We will be ordered to stay until we do, knowing the general."

"Ah, this is nonsense. Why not just kill her? Why come all this way for her? Her husband wouldn't know whether she was alive or dead. Once the general had the money, he could leave. I think he's growing old."

"Be careful what you say, my friend. If anyone else hears you say that, you could be dead where you stand."

"But you know what I mean, Justino. He *is* old.

He does not think with his head anymore."

"He never did think with his head. Come, let's go down by the corral and pretend we are keeping watch."

Eric listened to make sure that the men were gone, then went to Lisa, shaking her. "Wake up, Lisa."

Lisa opened her eyes and sat up. "What—" Eric put his hand over her mouth.

"Be quiet and listen. I think General Vasquez and his men are here looking for you. I'm going to go down and take a look. You stay here and keep your gun ready. If anyone comes up here, hit them with the butt of the gun. Shoot only if you have to."

"Why are you going down there? His men will be all over."

"No, I just heard two of them talking. They don't think they have too much to worry about. They're down by the corral."

"What about the vaqueros?"

"I don't know. I'll have to take a look."

"Let me come. I can help."

"No, I want you to stay here. If I have to worry about you, too, God knows what will happen."

"All right . . . but Eric, do you know the vaqueros have a camp down in the valley, by the river. They go there at night to drink and take women, I'm sure."

"So some of them might still be there, some Vasquez hasn't found?"

"Yes."

"You know where it is?"

"Yes, Cruz showed it to me."

373

"All right, you wait here until I get back, and then we'll decide what to do. If Vasquez has too many men, then we may have to try to find more people to help us."

"Please be careful," Lisa said, grabbing Eric and putting her arms around him.

"I will," he replied, kissing Lisa softly. "I don't want to lose you now that I've found you again." Eric quietly climbed down the ladder. When he touched the ground, he looked around, his gun drawn. When he was sure he didn't hear or see anyone, he continued around to the back of the house and stopped by the well. From there he could see into the living room without being seen. Tom, Cruz, and Teresa were all sitting in a line on the couch. Soleda and Miguel moved around freely. Two of Vasquez's men were standing by the door that led to the courtyard. He walked a little way down the hill and around the house until he came to the kitchen side. He climbed up the hill and looked into the small window. He could see Elena, Jesus, and several other men, including Miguel's. They didn't appear to be prisoners.

He crept back to the living-room window and looked inside. Miguel was now there, talking with Vasquez. Soleda was drinking a glass of wine, looking at the three on the couch as if they were dirt. He walked up to the edge of the thin glass and listened, easily able to hear the voices from inside.

"So, Soleda and I and my men are free to go? Are we agreed?" Miguel asked Vasquez.

"Sí, as long as you pay me the money you promised. If you do not, señor, I can promise you that you will be sorry."

"I can't believe you're doing this, Miguel," Teresa spoke up.

"I'm sorry, Cousin, but I have to do what I think is best for me. I want to take Soleda and get out of here. I'm sure you will be fine. You have a rich family."

"You're a pig!" she yelled.

Soleda laughed. "Empty threats, *cabron*." She walked to Teresa and stood in front of her. "I hope Vasquez's men have their way with you." She threw her wine in Teresa's face. Before Soleda could react, Cruz was on his feet. He slapped Soleda so hard she stumbled backward and fell.

One of Vasquez's men ran across the room and hit Cruz across the face with his gun. Cruz fell back on the couch. Teresa looked at him, and then at Miguel.

"I hope you burn in hell for this, Miguel." She looked at Soleda. "But then you will, as long as you're with her."

"Enough!" Vasquez yelled. "I want no more fighting in here or I will shoot you all myself." Vasquez walked over and stood in front of Teresa, then looked back at Miguel. "You did not tell me this woman was your cousin, Miguel. You are willing to sacrifice your own family?"

"I'm not sacrificing her. Her family is rich. All you have to do is ask them for money and they will give you plenty."

"And what if I were to ask you for money for her, would you pay it?"

Miguel looked acutely uncomfortable. "I am not really her family. After all, she is only my cousin."

375

"Only your cousin?" Vasquez yelled. "What is the matter with you, man? A cousin is almost as close to you as a brother or sister. Have you let that *puta* blind you to what really matters?"

Miguel walked across the room. "You of all people are telling me about what really matters, General? What about a wife's relationship to her husband? You didn't seem to honor that too strongly with Señora de Vargas, did you?"

"I think I may have misjudged you, señor." Vasquez nodded to his men and they took Miguel's arms and forced him to sit down. "I think I will have to rethink my situation with you. Any man who would cross his own blood would easily cross an enemy." He looked at Cruz. "Are you all right, Joaquin?"

"Yes."

"Good. We need to talk. Where can we go?"

"Outside, in the back. There's a place there where we can sit down."

Vasquez drew his gun. "Don't try anything, Joaquin. I wouldn't like to have to shoot you."

Eric quickly scrambled back down the hill and lay with his belly to the ground right below the stone bench and the well. It would be easy for him to hear what they were saying but difficult for them to see him. He heard their footsteps and he gripped his gun.

"So, where is the woman?" Vasquez asked, belching loudly after taking a long drink of wine.

"I don't know. I told you she disappeared with her husband. For all I know, she could be back in Monterey by now."

"I doubt that."

"Why do you doubt it, General? You know she never wanted to marry me anyway."

"I doubt it, because my men and I have been around for several days. We have seen no one leaving here who fit their description."

"That doesn't mean they haven't gone. There are lots of places they could've gone to. Maybe they're in Mexico."

"What are you trying to tell me?"

"I'm not trying to tell you anything. I'm just saying that I often spoke of my village in Mexico. Perhaps they've gone there."

"Why is it I feel as though you're trying to trick me, Joaquin, eh?"

Eric crawled to the top of the hill, peeking over the edge. Vasquez had his back to him. Slowly, he got to his knees, standing up behind Vasquez. Cruz saw him but acted as if nothing was wrong.

"I don't know, General. Why would I trick you? I have nothing to gain."

"I think you love the woman and you want her to be free."

"You're right, I do love her, but I don't want her to be free. If anything, I want her to stay here." He looked past the general to Eric, who quickly moved forward, putting his arm around Vasquez's throat to choke off any sound. Cruz grabbed his gun, and together they dragged him down the hill.

Cruz held the gun to Vasquez's throat. "Don't utter a sound, General. I would love nothing better than to blow your head off."

"And if he doesn't, I will," Eric said angrily, yanking Vasquez's belt from his pants and turning

377

him over on his stomach. He pulled his hands behind his back and tied them together with the belt. He took off Vasquez's bandana and stuffed it into his mouth, then took off his own and tied it around his mouth. Then he yanked him onto his back. "I don't much like what you've done to my wife, Vasquez. I think you're a cowardly little man who likes to prey on people who are scared." He looked over at Cruz. "Lisa said you had some vaqueros who have a camp somewhere away from here. Can you get to them?"

"If I can get a horse. I could never get there and back on foot."

"He has men down by the corral. Do you know how many are with him in all?"

Cruz thought for a moment. "I think he said he had twelve men. He only has two in the living room and a few more in the kitchen. The rest have to be out here somewhere."

"I don't think we have any other choice. If we go down by the corral, maybe we could get to some of my men in the bunkhouse."

"Let's just hope Vasquez hasn't killed them."

Cruz checked Vasquez for other weapons, and found a knife in his right boot and a small derringer in his left. "I think we should drag him down farther. I don't want him inching forward."

Eric pulled Vasquez farther down the hill. There would be no way the man could get back up to the top. They crawled up there and looked around. None of Vasquez's men were around the house. They stood up and quietly walked past the well and stood on the side of the house. They could hear men talking in the font.

378

"So what do we do now?"

"How about the kitchen?"

"I've already been there. Vasquez and Miguel's men are in there."

"We don't have any other choice. We have to go for my men on foot, even if it takes us all night and the next day."

"We can't do that."

"We don't have a choice, Eric."

"I can't leave Lisa."

"Where is she?"

"Yes, I'd like very much to know where the *puta* is," Soleda asked confidently.

Both men turned around. Soleda was standing with a rifle in her hands, surrounded by some of Miguel's men.

"So, I've caught you both trying to be heroes. Tell me where she is, Cruz."

"I don't know."

"You liar!" she screamed.

"What's wrong, Soleda? You can't stand it that she's safe, that she may even get away. You really hate her, don't you?"

"Yes, I hate her."

"You hate her because she's everything you're not. I feel sorry for you."

"Don't you ever feel sorry for me," Soleda replied angrily, shoving the butt of the rifle into Cruz's stomach.

Cruz stumbled, but Eric helped him regain his balance. "You're very brave with a weapon in your hand, Soleda. But we all know you're a coward without a weapon. We saw that today. You were scared to death that Lisa was going to kill you,

379

weren't you?"

"Stop it!"

"She should've killed you and saved us all a lot of trouble."

"You'll be sorry for that, de Vargas. When I find your wife, and I *will* find her, I'll make sure that you watch when I cut her up. I don't think you'll enjoy looking at her after I'm through with her."

Cruz started toward Soleda but Eric pulled him back. "Don't, Cruz, she's not worth it."

"I hope you burn in hell, Soleda. I just hope my soul doesn't go along with yours because I was married to you."

"You still are married to me, remember, *querido?*" She moved forward, putting her hand on Cruz's inner thigh. "You used to like this, remember?"

Cruz grabbed Soleda's wrist and snapped it backward. She stuck the barrel of the gun into his stomach. "Why don't you pull the trigger, Soleda?"

Soleda stared at Cruz in the faint light, her gaze wavering under Cruz's angry scrutiny. "Bring them inside," she ordered and the men pushed Cruz and Eric through the door.

"Where is Vasquez?" Miguel asked.

"I don't know," Soleda answered, "but I think they've done something to him. "All the better for us, eh, *querido?*" Soleda kissed Miguel on the cheek.

"So, de Vargas, you have decided to join us. And where is your lovely wife?"

Eric stared at Miguel. He said nothing.

"What about you, Cruz? Do you know where

she is?"

"I should've let that bear kill you, Miguel," Cruz said slowly.

"But you didn't and here we are."

"I want to know where she is," Soleda said angrily.

"It doesn't matter, Soleda. What can one woman do to us?"

"I'm not afraid of her, I just want to find her." She held up her injured hand. "She'll pay for shooting me."

"It's too bad she didn't shoot you in the head and put us all out of our misery," Teresa said sarcastically.

Eric, Cruz, and Tom all laughed.

"Are you going to let them laugh at me like that?"

"What would you like me to do?"

"You should punish them."

"Soleda, I'm not in the habit of punishing men for laughing. Let's go into the kitchen and get something to eat and drink." He turned to two of his men. "Make sure they don't move. Shoot them if they do."

Eric and Cruz sat down next to Tom and Teresa on the couch.

"I don't understand why Vasquez's men aren't putting up a fight," Tom said.

"Because Miguel is paying them much more than Vasquez ever did," Cruz answered. "Vasquez probably promises things, but he never pays up. Miguel always travels with money. I know him. He's probably already paid them something, and promised them more when they reach his rancho."

381

"So what do we do now?" Teresa asked in a lowered voice.

"We wait," Eric said softly.

"For what?" Tom asked.

Eric looked at the two men who stood by the door. "Our only hope is outside. She's smart. She'll find a way to help us."

"My God, you don't expect Lisa to help us all by herself," Tom said in an angry tone.

"Eric's right," Cruz agreed. "She will think of something if she can. If she can't, I just hope she can get herself out of here."

Lisa had seen everything that had gone on below her. She knew that she was the only person who could help her friends. She quietly walked all around the second story of the rancho, making sure that no one was around, and then she began to climb down the ladder. She took each rung softly and slowly until she hit the ground, and then she ran quickly for the hill, hitting it and rolling down. She bumped into something as she rolled, and she realized that it was a body. She stopped and recognized Vasquez. He was muttering something under the bandana. She sat and thought for a moment. If she untied him and forced him to go down to the corral, it was possible that she could steal a horse. But it would be very difficult.

Then she remembered the horses in the pasture down by the vineyard. Cruz seldom brought them in at night. It would be difficult catching one of them without a rope, but it didn't seem impossible.

She slid down the hill on her rear end, coming instantly to her feet when she hit the bottom. She walked around the vineyards and out to the pasture. The only light came from a partial moon and she could see nothing but a few shadows. She kept walking until she heard noises. She stopped, hearing the distinct sound of a horse pulling out clumps of grass and chewing. She walked slowly until she saw the outline of the animal. When she got close, it lifted its head and flared its nostrils, trying to figure out her scent. Lisa moved slowly forward until she was almost next to the animal. She couldn't figure out a way not to scare it away. Then she made a clucking sound with her tongue. The horse nodded its head but didn't move. She moved closer, putting a tentative hand on the animal. He whinnied but stood still. Lisa knew that these animals were used to being handled and they were only left out in the pasture when the main corral was filled with new animals that needed to be broken.

"Hello, boy. It's all right." She stroked his neck, talking gently to him. "Just how am I going to get up on you, huh?" she asked aloud. She rubbed his nose, and he put his mouth in her hand. He was clearly used to being fed. Lisa bent down and pulled out a clump of grass. She handed it to the horse and he greedily chomped on it. "Good boy." She bent down and pulled out some more, waiting patiently while he chomped his second helping. She untied the sash around her waist and made a slip knot on one end. Carefully, she slipped if over the horse's nose. "It's all right," she said in a

383

soothing voice, patting his neck. She gripped the sash and then wrapped her left hand in his mane. She took a deep breath and swung herself partially up onto the horse. Frightened, the horse took off at a gallop, leaving Lisa clutching his mane. She tried desperately to pull herself up onto his back, and by the time he had slowed down, she was sitting astride.

"Good boy. Now we need to go for a ride. Come on." She pulled the sash to the right and the horse responded. They rode at a gallop along the river, slowing to a canter as Lisa tried to figure out the direction of the camp. She knew if she followed the river east, she would eventually find it.

It wasn't long before she heard voices and singing and saw campfires. She rode the horse to the edge of the camp and slid off.

At least twenty men stared at her, not only because she was a beautiful white woman, but because she had just ridden a horse bare-back with no hackamoere. *"Yo necessita ayuda.* I need help."

One man stood up. "What is the matter, señora? Do you remember me? My name is Constantino."

"Yes, Constantino, I need your help. There are men at the rancho who are holding Cruz and the rest of my friends captive. They are very dangerous."

"We do not care about the danger. Who are these people?"

"A bandit named Vasquez and a man and woman who were guests, Miguel Figueroa and Soleda."

Constantino looked back at the men in the

camp and spit on the ground. "Yes, we all know of Soleda. How many men are there?"

"I'm not sure. I think Miguel has five or six, but I'm not sure about Vasquez."

"It is no matter. There are enough of us to take care of things." Constantino turned to his compadres and spoke to them in Spanish. Without hesitation, they rose and began to gather their weapons.

"Thank you, Constantino."

"We are happy to help, señora. Cruz has been good to us. He has helped us all in one way or another." He walked to Lisa. "I think you should stay here."

"No, I want to come with you. I might be able to help."

"And you might get hurt. I could never face Cruz if something happened to you."

"Listen to me, Constantino. I can ride a horse and I can handle a gun. I can take care of myself. I don't want to stay here."

"If that is what you wish, señora. Tell me, are they all inside?"

"No, Vasquez is tied up outside. In fact, he is on the hill behind the house, on the way down to the vineyard. You'll need to get him out of the way. I think Miguel Figueroa bought off Vasquez's men. They don't seem to be with him now."

Constantino thought for a moment. "Perhaps you can help. We can ride up through the vineyard and come in through the back, up the hill. If you distract them somehow, we can get in position all around the house."

"There are also some men down by the corral. I

385

don't know how many."

"We will take care of that. You ride with us, and then when we get there, you go in from the back side."

"I think it would be better if I rode in from the front. They'll take me right away and hopefully, no one will pay attention to the back."

"*Bien*. Do you have a weapon?"

Lisa pointed to the pistol in the belt around her shirt. "Only this."

"That will not work. You cannot hide it. We need something smaller." He looked around and spoke to a few of the men. He took Lisa's gun and handed it to one of the men and, in return, handed Lisa a knife and a smaller revolver. "Put the knife in your boot and the gun here." He pointed to the area between her legs.

"How do I keep a gun there?"

"We will fashion a kind of holster for you. I hope you do not embarrass easily, señora," he said, lifting up her skirt. He took off his holster and held it in his hand, cutting off the bottom quarter of it. He knelt and fastened it around Lisa's upper thigh, cutting off the excess portion of the belt and tightening it to secure it to her leg and then took the gun from her hand, sticking it in the holster. "It will feel very strange, but it's important that you try to walk normally. Try it."

Lisa walked with the cold steel of the pistol against her inner thigh. It felt awkward, but she knew she could do it. "It feels like it's slipping down, Constantino."

"I think we can fix that." He cut off a small piece of thong and put it through the belt buckle.

He pulled it up and tied it to the waist of Lisa's skirt. "I apologize, señora. I don't usually go reaching underneath women's skirts."

Lisa couldn't refrain from smiling.

"Walk and see how that feels."

Lisa walked again. The thong pulled at the waist of her skirt but it held the holster up, and Cruz's long shirt covered anything that showed. "It feels fine."

"Good, take it out until we get there. It will be very difficult for you to ride with that in your holster."

Lisa took out the gun and put it back in her belt. "I'm ready."

"All right, you ride up to the front. Act as if you don't know what has happened. Now, *va-manos, amigos*."

They all mounted up and rode to the rancho. When they reached the pasture below the vineyard, Constantino and his men rode slowly. "It is up to you now, señora. Be careful. We will be in soon."

Lisa thanked Constantino and put the gun in her thigh holster, holding her leg awkwardly so the gun wouldn't rub against the horse. She rode around the vineyard and up the front of Cruz's land to the large corral. As she neared, she could see shadows moving. She pretended not to notice. She dismounted and started to walk up to the house when a man grabbed her.

"So, you have come back, eh, señora?"

"Who are you?" Lisa cried out indignantly.

"We are with General Vasquez."

"We *were* with General Vasquez," the other man corrected him.

"What is happening? I don't understand."

"Perhaps we should keep her with us a while, Felipe, eh? She is a pretty one."

Immediately, Lisa fell limp in the man's arms. "Please, could you take me up to the house. I just lost a baby two days ago and I'm still bleeding." Lisa smiled to herself, knowing that most men didn't like to hear about women's problems.

"Take her up. Miguel will know what to do with her."

The man literally dragged her up to the house and through the front door, pushing her through it. "I have a present for you, Miguel." When he saw that the room was empty, he looked at the two guards. "Tell Miguel to get in here now."

One of the men walked down the hallway while Lisa tried to move toward the couch, but the man gripped her arm. She looked at Eric. "Are you all right?"

"Yes." Her eyes glanced at the bruise on Cruz's face. "And what happened to you?"

"It doesn't matter."

"So, you decided to return to us," Miguel said grandly as he walked back into the room.

"Well, well, well," Soleda said smugly as she walked across the room to Lisa. "I've been waiting for this all day. She stood only inches away from Lisa, their faces close together. "You will be sorry that you ever crossed me, *puta*."

"I think you've got it wrong, Soleda. That word is for you." Lisa stared coldly into Soleda's dark eyes and spit into her face, expecting the full wrath of the woman to rain down on her.

"You *cabron*," she screamed, going at Lisa with

388

her hands up raking her fingernails across her face. Lisa summoned all her strength to push her away.

"You can't hurt me, Soleda. You are nothing, remember?"

Soleda screamed in anger, but before she could go at Lisa again, Miguel grabbed her from behind, holding her kicking and screaming. "That is enough, Soleda. We will deal with her later. Right now we have to figure out what to do with all these people."

"Kill all of them, but leave her and Cruz for me."

"We can't kill them all. People will know we've been here."

"What does it matter? Someone will find Vasquez and blame it on him. I want her, Miguel," Soleda grinned. "You must promise me."

"All right, Soleda."

Soleda smiled. "Good. I can't wait to make her pay."

"Let's finish our meal before we do anything. I'm still hungry."

Soleda looked at Cruz and Lisa and smiled. "The longer they have to wait, the better." She put her arm through Miguel's. "You are such a man, Miguel. Wait until I get you in the bedroom tonight," she said seductively, laughing lightheartedly as they left the room. Lisa walked to the couch and sat between Eric and Cruz. Both men reached up to examine her scratches, but she pulled away.

"I'll be all right. Listen to me," she said quietly, looking at Miguel's men. "I was able to get to your vaqueros, Cruz. They're here. We have to be ready."

"You were right," Cruz said to Eric.

"I know her," Eric said, looking at Lisa's scratched face.

"Are you sure you're all right, Sis?"

"I'm fine, Tom. Listen. I have a knife in my boot. I also have a gun."

"So do I," Eric said quietly, reaching behind her and pulling her into his arms. As he embraced her, he had managed to hand the derringer around Lisa to Cruz.

Cruz took the small weapon and concealed it in the palm of his hand. He lifted a leg up on his other knee and smoothly slid the derringer into his boot.

"I'm glad you're all right, Lisa," Teresa said sincerely. "I just hope we get out of here so you and I can have a real talk with Soleda."

"Thank you, Teresa. I would like nothing better than for you and I to take Soleda out alone."

"I'd hate to be Soleda," Eric said with a smile.

Footsteps pounded down the hall, and Miguel and Soleda emerged. "We have made our decision," Miguel said authoritatively.

"You've never made a decision in your life," Teresa said angrily.

"I have made one now, Cousin. All of you will be shot, with the exception of Cruz and Lisa. For them we have something special in mind."

Cruz looked at Lisa and then at Soleda. "Let her go, Soleda, and I'll do anything you want."

"Anything, *querido?*"

"Yes," Cruz said, trying to control his anger.

"It is too late, *querido,* because when I am done

390

with you and your 'wife,' you will both be dead."
She kissed her fingertips and waved her hand at
Cruz. "Prepare to die, my love, for it will not be
easy."

Lisa felt the cold steal against her thigh. She
looked absently out the windows that faced the
courtyard. When would Constantino be here? They
were quickly running out of time.

Teresa put her arms around Eric. "Well, if I am
to die, I want to die happy." She kissed him passionately, pushing him against Lisa. "I want you,
Eric."

Eric stared at her wide-eyed, but he didn't fight
her. He put his arms around her, kissing her back.
"What're you doing?" he whispered against her
mouth.

She kissed his cheek and neck and hissed into
his ear, "Perhaps we can distract them."

Eric wrapped his arms around Teresa and rolled
on his knees to the floor, not letting go of her.
The knife he had taken from Vasquez was still in
his boot. Teresa wrapped her legs around him,
making moaning sounds.

Lisa looked at Tom and Cruz, then at the men
across the room. They were amused and slightly
distracted. "I don't know where Constantino is,"
she said softly.

"He's just waiting for the right time. He can't
come rushing in here or Miguel could have his
men kill us all."

Eric and Teresa continued to roll around on the
floor, to the amusement of the guards across the
room. Cruz propped one foot on his knee, preparing to take out the derringer. The men were laugh-

391

ing and pushing each other as they came closer to watch the lusty couple.

"You idiots!" Soleda screamed, marching into the room. "Don't you realize that they are doing this to distract you?" Soleda pointed her shotgun at one of the men. "Shall I shoot you first, to make an example of you?"

"No, señorita. We meant no harm."

"You cannot trust any of them, do you understand? If they get away, I will shoot you myself." She looked at Cruz and Lisa. "It is time for you two to come with me."

"Go to hell!" Cruz said angrily.

Soleda smiled and put the barrel of the shotgun to Lisa's head. "It's up to you, *querido*. I would just as soon kill her here."

Cruz stood up, his hands trembling. He ached to put his hands around Soleda's throat and choke the very life out of her. "I can't remember why I was ever attracted to you, Soleda."

"You know why, *querido*. I made you feel like a real man."

"You made me feel like a small boy."

Soleda's face turned red. "That's enough, Cruz, or I swear I'll kill her now." She motioned to one of the men. "Take him to the kitchen and tie him to one of the chairs. She stared at Lisa. "Stand up." She laughed derisively at Eric and Teresa. "Your trick didn't work. I'll deal with you later."

"Don't hurt her, Soleda," Tom said, standing up.

"What's the matter, Brother, are you afraid for your little sister?"

Tom started forward, but Soleda grabbed Lisa, placing the barrel of the shotgun into the small of her back. "I am not playing games. I will shoot her."

Eric stood up, standing close to Lisa. "Don't worry." He touched her face gently.

"I'm not worried. She can't hurt me."

"That's enough. Move." She shoved Lisa forward with the barrel of the gun. "Make sure these people don't move."

"*Si, señorita.*"

Lisa turned and looked at Eric, a slight smile on her face. She wouldn't let Soleda know that she was scared. She forced herself to be brave, even though she knew there was a good chance she could be dead within the next few minutes. She prayed to herself that Constantino and his men would come soon.

Chapter 13

Lisa stared at Cruz, who was sitting across the table from her. They were both tied to chairs, their hands behind them. Soleda was standing beside the table closest to Lisa, hot tongs in her hand. She waved them in front of Lisa's face.

"Do you see these? Do you see how red they are from being in the fire?"

Lisa forced herself to be calm. She remembered the men who had been captured with her on the wagon train, and how they had been burned at the stake. She had watched them suffer, and part of her had suffered with them. She didn't know how they could endure the pain.

"Are you afraid, *cabrona?*" Soleda now held the tongs close to Lisa's cheek. She didn't utter a sound.

"Soleda, don't. She didn't do anything to you."

"How touching, Cruz. Now you are pleading for her life."

"Her life is worth pleading for."

Soleda walked to Cruz, leaning close to him. "Is *my* life worth pleading for, Cruz? Is it?"

Cruz's dark eyes burned into Soleda's. "Your life

394

isn't worth anything, Soleda," he said slowly.

Angrily, Soleda pressed the hot tongs into the flesh of Cruz's neck. The smell of burning flesh wafted throughout the kitchen.

"Soleda, don't!" Lisa screamed. "Torture me, I'm the one you want. Not him."

Soleda lifted the tongs and walked over to Lisa. She put them even closer to Lisa's cheek, but a gunshot made her pull away. "What is it?" She screamed, but no one answered her. She cut Lisa's ties and pulled her to the back wall of the kitchen, looking around her frantically. Lisa tried to pull away, but Soleda hit her on the shoulder with her gun. "Don't try that again."

Miguel came running into the kitchen. "Some of Cruz's men are outside. We have to get out of here."

"Our only chance is to take him with us," Soleda said. "Hand me the rope from the chair." She pulled Lisa's hands behind her and quickly tied them together, then looked at Cruz. "Just remember, if you try to get away or hurt Miguel, I'll shoot her."

Miguel quickly untied Cruz from the chair and retied his hands behind him. "What now?" he asked Soleda.

"We use them to get us out of here. I know of a place—"

The kitchen door burst open and three of Cruz's vaqueros came running in. "Cruz, are you all right?"

"Don't shoot!"

"Tell them to let us out of here."

"Why should I, Soleda? If you're going to kill us anyway, why not just get it over with now?"

Soleda looked worried. "But I know you don't want this one to die. I know you, Cruz."

"I would rather she die here and now than be tortured by you."

"I don't believe you." She waved her gun hand in front of Lisa.

"Do it, Cruz. Have them kill her," Lisa said confidently.

"Shut up!" Soleda screamed. She pressed the barrel of the gun into Lisa's head. "I mean it. I'll shoot her right now."

Cruz walked forward. "If you do it, Soleda, you'll be dead in five seconds. Then I'll make sure to spit on your body."

Soleda looked wild-eyed. "Do something, Miguel."

"What do you want me to do, Soleda?"

"Be a man for once."

"You don't know what you're saying."

"I know exactly what I'm saying. You're nothing but a spineless little man. You don't even know how to make love to a woman. You are nothing compared to Cruz."

Miguel walked forward. "Don't say things like that, Soleda. You're upset."

"I'm upset by you, Miguel. You make me sick." She cocked the pistol and pressed it to Lisa's head. "Say good-bye to your woman, Cruz."

Cruz ran forward, ramming Soleda's shoulder with his head. The gun fired but missed Lisa. Lisa pulled away and Cruz rammed into Soleda again. The pistol fired again but this time it hit Cruz in the chest, knocking him backward. He fell against the table and down to the floor. Lisa ran to him.

"Cruz," she said softly, kneeling against him as

he lay on the floor. With her hands tied behind her, she was unable to help him. One of Cruz's men reached down to set her free from her binds. She quickly went to Cruz, untying his hands, and cradled him in her lap. She looked up at Soleda, who was aiming the gun at her. Lisa felt no fear at that moment. She looked into Soleda's eyes and felt only burning hatred. She heard the gun fire and prepared for the searing burn of the bullet but nothing came. She watched as Soleda slumped against the wall and slid to the floor, her eyes blank. She looked around. Eric was standing by the hallway, his gun raised.

"Soleda," Miguel screamed, running to the woman he loved.

Lisa ignored Miguel and opened Cruz's shirt. His wound was right in the middle of his chest and it was bleeding profusely. "Cruz, can you hear me?"

He opened his eyes. "I can always hear you." He tried to smile.

She ran her hand across his forehead. "Why did you do such a stupid thing?"

"I can't resist being a hero in your eyes."

"Oh, Cruz," she said gently, lowering her head to his.

"How is he?" Eric asked.

"I don't know." She ripped off a piece of her skirt and placed it on the wound.

"I'll get Teresa. She might be able to help."

"Soleda, *querida,*" Miguel moaned in the background.

"Get them out of here," Lisa said angrily to Cruz's men.

"How is he, señora?" Constantino asked, walking in from the hallway.

"I don't know. It's a large wound. I don't know what to do for him."

"I will get Elena and Jesus. Between them, they know many cures."

"Thank you." Lisa kissed Cruz's cheek.

Cruz opened his eyes. "Where is Soleda?"

"She's dead. Eric shot her."

"Tell him I owe him one." He began to cough.

"God, I don't know how to help you."

"You are helping just by being here."

Lisa felt the cross around her neck and started to take it off, but Cruz stopped her. "No. I want you to have it back."

"I don't ever want you to take it off. It belongs to you. It will protect you."

"But maybe it can protect you now." She leaned her head against his. "You have to get well."

Cruz lifted an arm and put it around Lisa's back. "Even if I do die, you and I have forged a bond that can never be broken. Remember that."

Lisa began to cry softly. "I'm so sorry."

"It is I who should apologize. If you hadn't been around me, you would never have had to worry about Soleda."

"I'll stay for as long as you want me to stay."

"And what if I say I want you to stay forever?"

Lisa looked into Cruz's dark eyes and she knew she couldn't hurt him. "Then I would stay forever." She leaned her head against his.

Eric stood by the door to the kitchen, listening to what Lisa was saying. He felt Teresa's hand on his arm, but he couldn't move. Lisa had just told Cruz she would stay with him forever. Teresa tugged at his arm and they walked to Cruz and

Lisa.

"May I see?" Teresa asked Lisa.

Lisa backed away, wiping her face. She glanced at Eric, but her attention quickly turned back to Cruz. "Do you know what to do, Teresa?"

"I think the first thing we have to do is get the bullet out." She looked up at Eric. "We need a steady hand."

Eric shook his head. "Don't look at me. I don't want to dig a bullet out of his chest."

Lisa stood up, grabbing at the front of Eric's shirt. "Eric, please, you delivered our baby, and saved me just a few days ago when I was practically bleeding to death. I know you can do it."

Eric looked at Lisa and clenched his jaw. How could he say no to her. He looked down at Cruz. He couldn't just let him die without at least trying to save him. He was too good a man. "All right, I'll try. But I'll need your help."

"We'll do anything we can to help," Lisa said anxiously.

"All right, take his shirt off and get some alcohol. Force him to drink some even if he doesn't want to, I don't want him to be in pain."

Teresa ran to get a bottle of whiskey while Lisa carefully removed Cruz's shirt. Eric looked around Elena's kitchen for a sharp knife.

"Oh, *Madre de Dios*," Elena yelled as she came in from the courtyard with Jesus. "My poor boy."

"Elena," Eric said, "I need your help. I need a sharp knife. I need to get a bullet out of Cruz's chest."

Elena thought for a moment and looked through a box of kitchen utensils. She took out a long, thin utensil and handed it to Eric. "It's not

399

really a knife. I use it for the prickly pear cactus."

Eric looked at it and nodded his head. "I think it'll do just fine. Can you pump me some water, I want to wash my hands. Then hand some to Lisa." He looked at Lisa. "I want you to clean him up the best you can. I can't see anything with all that blood."

Teresa hurried back into the room with a bottle of whiskey. She uncorked it and took a drink, then knelt next to Cruz. "Hold his head up, Lisa."

"Cruz, open your eyes," Lisa said firmly.

Cruz opened his eyes slightly. "I must be in heaven. I have two beautiful women at my side."

Teresa smiled. "He's still strong. Cruz, we want you to take a drink of this whiskey. It will help with the pain. Do you understand?"

Cruz nodded slightly and accepted the bottle. He sipped but was unable to swallow, spitting it up on his chest. "I'm sorry."

"It's all right. I'm going to lift your head up further, Cruz," Lisa said. "There, now try to see if you can swallow a little." She held the bottle to his lips and Cruz swallowed. "Again," Lisa said anxiously, turning to see what Eric was doing.

He had rolled up his sleeves and washed his hands. Now he carefully scrubbed the utensil Elena had given him. He bent down close to Cruz. "Cruz, the bullet is going to have to come out."

Cruz opened his eyes. There was an awkward smile on his face. "This is your chance to pay me back for stealing your wife away from you, *amigo*."

"If I wanted to pay you back, I would've done it long before now." He nodded to Lisa, who held the bottle to Cruz's lips. "Drink some more. I want you so drunk you don't care what I do to you."

"What are you going to do?"

Eric held up the utensil. "I'm going to try to probe for the pullet and hope that I can get it out. I can't promise you anything, Cruz, but I'll try my damndest to help you."

Cruz's hands went up to Eric's shirt and pulled him down. "If I don't make it, make sure you take care of Lisa. She's a special woman."

"I know that."

"Promise me."

"I promise, Cruz. Just relax."

"Listen to me. I want her to have this place if I die."

Eric looked at Lisa. "Cruz, don't talk of such things."

"Bring me a piece of paper. I want it down on paper."

"I'll get one," Teresa said, hurrying out of the room.

"Cruz, why are you worrying about this now? You should be concerned with getting well."

"I want this to be yours if I die. There is no other person who would love it as much as I do," he said in a soft voice, then closed his eyes.

Lisa bent over him, kissing his cheek. "Don't worry. Everything will be all right."

Eric sat back on his heels, watching Lisa comfort Cruz. They looked good together, they looked right. He needed her now. He loved her so much, he had literally taken a bullet that was meant for her.

"Here it is, Cruz," Teresa said breathlessly, followed by Tom. "Tom is a lawyer. He will take it all

401

down and make it legal."

Tom knelt next to Cruz, holding a pen and paper. "What do you want to say, Cruz?"

"Just that I want everything I own to go to Lisa, and I want the people who are here now to stay after I'm gone."

Tom glanced over at Lisa and nodded, writing it all down. "Okay, all I need is your signature."

"He's in no shape for this, Tom," Lisa berated her brother.

"I want to sign it," Cruz said. "Will you please hold me up for a moment?"

In spite of the intense pain he was in Eric and Tom helped prop Cruz up. He signed the paper and Tom folded it. "I'll make copies of it, one for you, one for Lisa, and I'll keep one on file."

"Thank you," Cruz said almost inaudibly.

Eric looked at Lisa and pointed at the whiskey bottle. "Pour some of the liquor over my hands and over this thing." He held the utensil out. Lisa did as she was told. "Now, give Cruz another drink." Lisa held the bottle to Cruz's lips and he sipped, smiling as he did so.

"Did I ever tell you people that I was a *bandido?* I was very good, too. People trusted me."

Eric looked at Lisa, and they both smiled. "I think he's feeling the liquor," Eric said.

"It's true," Cruz continued. "If I had been tougher, if I had been a killer, I could've been one of the best *bandidos* in all of California." He closed his eyes and began to murmur something unintelligible.

Eric looked at Lisa and Teresa. "Now pour some over the wound. Okay, now I want both of you to hold his shoulders. He'll probably jump when I

402

stick this in him. You've got to try to hold him still."

"I'll help," Tom said, kneeling behind Cruz.

Eric took a deep breath and looked at the wound. It was below the heart, but he didn't know what damage it had done. He had only done this twice in his life, and both times, they were wounds to the arm. He nodded and stuck the point of the instrument into the wound, his hand firm and steady. Cruz moaned but he didn't move. It was as if he knew Eric was trying to help him. Eric probed with the instrument and the wound bled profusely. Lisa quickly wiped the wound with pieces of cloth that Elena had given them. Eric kept probing and shook his head. "I can't feel anything. I'm going to have to use my fingers." He took a deep breath and stuck his index finger into the wound, moving it around, trying to feel the bullet. The blood was pouring out now and Eric was afraid Cruz was going to bleed to death. He stuck his finger in a little further and stopped when he felt the hard lead of the bullet. "I feel it," he said quietly. "But I'm not sure how to get it out. It's in deep."

"Can you cut around the wound? Lisa asked anxiously.

"Possibly. I'll need a knife."

Lisa took the knife from her boot and poured whiskey over it. "Will this do?"

"It should." Eric shook his head. "I don't know if I can save him, Lisa. He could bleed to death before I get the bullet out."

"We don't have much choice, do we?"

Eric looked at Cruz and nodded. He handed Lisa the other instrument as he began to cut with

403

the knife, calmly, as if he had done it a hundred times before. He had watched Matay cut people many times in the Comanche camp. Her hand had always been steady and she had always gone around the wound, sometimes trying to come in from the side to get at the bullet or arrowhead.

When he made an incision laterally to where he thought the bullet was, he again stuck his finger inside the wound. This time, it was easier for him to move his finger and he felt it. Although it was embedded in tissue and not easily movable, Eric managed to free it and guide it out with his fingers. He held the bullet up for a second and then dropped it on the floor. "Elena, I'm going to need something to sew him up with."

"I have a strong needle and good thread. Don't you worry." She rummaged through a basket and quickly handed Eric what he needed. "Jesus and I have made a good poultice for him when you are through, señor. It will help to heal him."

"Good." Eric pinched the skin together and quickly sewed up the incision, leaving the bullet wound open. He cleaned it and placed the poultice on his chest. Eric sat back on his heels, washing his hands in the bowl that Elena had set on the floor next to him.

"Should we try to move him?" Tom asked.

"It would probably be easier now when he's out. If we try in the morning, he'll be in too much pain."

"I can help," Jesus said quickly. "I can call some of the men."

"I think we can all do it. If Tom and I take his shoulders, you and the women can take his feet. Elena, make sure the bed is ready for him." Eric

404

got up and moved to Cruz's shoulders. "You ready, Tom?"

"Yep."

The men lifted Cruz's shoulders, while Lisa, Elena, and Jesus lifted his legs. They maneuvered carefully down the hall and into the large bedroom, laying him gently on the bed.

"I will stay with him," Elena said, touching his face and looking sorrowfully at him.

"No, there will be no need for that. *I* will stay with him. You get some sleep. Thank you."

"But señora, you are still not completely rested yourself."

"I am fine.

"Elena, let's you and I make some coffee," Teresa suggested. "I think we're going to need it."

"I'll help," Tom said, leaving with the two women.

Eric walked up behind Lisa. "I hope he's all right."

"So do I," she said, affectionately running her hand over Cruz's face. "He's a good man. He doesn't deserve this."

Eric started to say something but stopped himself. Now was not the time. He walked to the door of the room and turned to look back at Lisa, her hand on Cruz's face, her concern more evident than she realized. It was obvious that she loved Cruz more than she thought. It was definitely time for him to go.

It had been a week since Cruz had been shot and he had made a rapid recovery. He was already sitting up in bed, impatient to be up and walking around. Lisa seldom left his side, except to eat and clean up. She even slept on the bed with him. Lisa was washing Cruz, ignoring his grumbling, when Teresa and Tom came into the room.

"Lisa, we need to talk to you."

"What is it?" She put down the cloth and stood up. "Has something happened?"

"Eric's gone, Sis. He left early this morning."

"He's gone? How do you know he's gone? Maybe he's just gone for a ride."

"Jesus talked to him, and he left this." Tom handed Lisa a letter.

Lisa took it in her hands. She was afraid to unfold the piece of paper.

"Why don't you go outside? We'll stay with Cruz," Teresa said gently.

Lisa nodded absently, walking down the hallway and out the door to the courtyard. She sat down on one of the benches and opened the letter. "Dearest Lisa," she read, "This is not an easy letter for me to write. I have been watching you for the past week with Cruz, and I realize now that your life is with him. What we had together is in the past. It doesn't exist anymore. You and Cruz get along in a way that you and I never have. You and I are like fire and ice. I don't want to leave you with him, but I know it's the best for all of us. You and I would've found something to fight about anyway. I just want you to know that I do love you; I always have. No woman will ever touch me like you have. Don't worry about Raya. I'll send her down with Tom to visit with you once or twice a year. I'll never let her forget her mother. I love you, green eyes. Thank you for our time together. Eric." Lisa held the letter to her chest and

406

closed her eyes, feeling the tears that streamed down her face. How was it possible to live without Eric? How would she find the strength?

Lisa folded the letter and put it in her lap, quickly wiping the tears from her face.

"Are you sure this is what you want, Sis?" Tom asked as he sat down next to her on the bench, putting his arm across her shoulders. "Is this where you want to spend the rest of your life?"

"Cruz needs me, Tom.

"That's not what I asked you."

"Yes, of course this is what I want. I wouldn't be here if it wasn't."

"You're talking to the wrong person, kid. You forget I know you." He turned her face to his. "I'm sure Cruz would understand. Eric is your husband, and you have a daughter to think of."

"I know that, Tom, but I also know that Eric will take good care of her."

"Your mind's made up then?"

Lisa nodded absently, looking past Tom. "I didn't have much of a choice."

"What're you talking about?"

"I owe Cruz my life over and over again. I can't just leave him, Tom. I can't."

"And what about everything Eric has done for you?"

"I don't know, Tom. I don't know," she broke down, crying in her brother's arms. He held her until she had cried herself out, and then she wiped the tears away. "When you go home, will you tell Eric thank you for everything?"

"Is that all you want me to tell him?"

"I think it's enough."

"What about Raya?"

"I'm going to write her a letter. I'd like you to read it to her when she's old enough to understand."

"Okay. For what it's worth, Sis, I admire your loyalty. I just think it's to the wrong man." He stood up and walked away. Lisa watched him cross the courtyard. She stood up and headed for the house. Teresa was coming outside.

"If you're going to lecture me, too, Teresa, please don't."

"I wasn't going to lecture, Lisa. I was going to tell you I understand your choice."

"You do?"

Teresa took Lisa's hand and led her back to the bench. "I thought I was in love with Eric, but I was in love with a dream. He was handsome and brave and I liked being with him, but the truth is, he isn't the man for me. Bryant is. I realized this past week that I was really beginning to miss him. He has a special way about him and a special way of making me feel happy. I don't think I'd trade that for anything in the world."

"I'm glad for you, Teresa. You deserve happiness."

"So do you."

"I'll be happy here."

"Will you?"

"You said you wouldn't lecture."

"I'm not going to lecture, but I am going to tell you something. Eric loves you more than I've ever seen a man love a woman. I know Cruz loves you, too, and he needs you, but so does Eric. Eric needs you in a way Cruz doesn't, and that's because he's known you in a way Cruz hasn't. He'll suffer every day when he looks at your daughter

408

and realizes that you're not there to share her with him."

"Teresa, don't. I have to do what I think is right."

"I know you do, Lisa, but you also deserve to be happy. Just think about it."

"And what about Cruz? What happens to him if I leave?"

"I think you're giving yourself too much credit and Cruz not enough, Lisa. He's much stronger than you realize, and he's a very attractive man. It won't take him long to find another woman."

Teresa stood up. "I'm going to go look for Tom. We're making plans to leave. We're both anxious to get back home."

"You're leaving?"

"It's time. We all have to resume our lives." She looked at Lisa affectionately and then kissed her on the cheek and left the courtyard. Lisa watched her walk away and felt as if she was losing the last friend she had in the world.

Cruz watched Lisa as she worked in the garden, toiling endlessly in the dirt. If she wasn't working in the garden, she was working the vineyard, or helping with the house, or helping with the horses. She was doing anything to keep busy.

It had been two months since he'd been shot and two months since Eric had left, and nothing had been the same between them since. It was as if a part of her had left with Eric. Although they shared the same bed, they had no intimate relations. It was not that she would have fought him, but he knew that it wasn't what she wanted.

He knew it was time. He walked to her, watching her dig the hole with her small shovel and drop in the seeds. "Lisa, I want to talk to you."

She barely looked up. "Later, Cruz. I want to finish planting these seeds. I think this will make a fine garden, don't you?"

Cruz bent down and took the shovel from her hand, pulling her to her feet. "I want to talk to you now."

Lisa stood up, wiping the dirt and sweat from her face. "Is something wrong?"

"Yes, something is very wrong." He took her hand. "Let's take a walk."

Lisa nodded her agreement and they walked for a while in silence until they reached the river. "Are you happy here, Lisa?" Cruz asked.

"Of course I'm happy here. It's a beautiful place." Lisa avoided Cruz's eyes.

"You want nothing else out of your life?"

"No."

"Well, I do. I want a woman who can love me fully, with all of her being."

Lisa looked at him square in the face. "What are you talking about?"

"You know what I'm talking about, Lisa. You don't want to be here, not really. Your heart is someplace else and that is where you should be."

"No, that's not true."

"Yes, it is true. I've watched you every day for two months and I've seen the life drain out of you. You haven't been the same since Eric left."

"I miss my daughter. That's natural."

"Yes, I believe you do miss your daughter, but I also think you miss Eric—much more than you thought possible."

"Why are you doing this, Cruz? Are you trying to hurt me?"

"No, I'm trying to help you. The only reason you're staying here is because you think you owe it to me. Well, I'm telling you that you don't owe me a thing. You nursed me back to health but, more important, you taught me how to love again. You taught me that all women aren't like Soleda."

"You want me to go?" Lisa asked.

Cruz caressed Lisa's face with his large hand. "I want you to stay, Liseta, but it wouldn't be fair to either one of us if you did. You belong with your family."

"Cruz, you have done so much for me—"

"No more than you have done for me. I will always be your friend, Lisa. Always. And I hope you will always be mine. But you have a husband and daughter waiting for you. I think it's time you got back to them."

Lisa threw her arms around Cruz. "I will never forget you. I envy the woman who finally becomes your wife."

"And I envy Eric. He is a lucky man." He pressed his mouth to hers, tasting the soft sweetness of her lips. "Now, go pack. Jesus is ready to take you to San Diego. A ship leaves tomorrow for Monterey. I want you to be on it."

Lisa reached up and took the cross from her neck. "This doesn't belong to me anymore. It belongs to the woman who becomes your wife." She took the thin band from her finger. "And this, too. I have no right to either of them."

Cruz held the objects in his hand and looked at them. "You have every right to them." He put the cross back on Lisa's neck and the ring on her

411

right finger. "Think of the ring as a gift from a friend, and the cross as your protection. Give it to Raya someday, from me."

"I will. Thank you, Cruz."

Cruz watched Lisa walk back up the hill toward the house, and for the first time his heart wasn't heavy. He had done the right thing. Now, perhaps, he could truly live his life.

Lisa got down from the buggy and walked through the courtyard of the Rancho del Mar. She took a deep breath before she knocked on the door. She was afraid. She didn't know how Eric would react, and she wondered if Raya would even remember her.

The door opened and Rocia stood, open-mouthed. "Señora! I can't believe it's you!" Then before Lisa realized it, she was encircled in Rocia's large arms. "Come. Come inside. I will get you something to eat."

"No, thank you, but something to drink would be fine, Rocia."

"Where is Don Alejandro?"

"He isn't here, señora. But Don Alfredo is in the other room. He will be so happy to see you. And wait until you see your beautiful little girl."

"Thank you, Rocia." Lisa opened the double doors to the sitting room and walked inside. Don Alfredo was sitting by the garden window, reading a book.

"Yes?"

"Is that all the greeting I get after all this time?"

Don Alfredo dropped the book on the floor and

stood up, rushing over to Lisa. He literally crushed her in his arms and kissed her on both cheeks. "I was afraid I wouldn't see you before I die."

"Is there something wrong? Are you ill?" Lisa asked worriedly.

"No, I just didn't know when I would see you again."

"You look wonderful, Don Alfredo. You don't ever seem to age."

"And your compliments have grown more flowery. So, how is it you happen to be here? Sandro told me you had decided to stay with Cruz."

"Cruz told me to leave. He told me I was only staying with him out of loyalty, not out of love. He was right."

"I knew that Cruz was a wise man."

Lisa smiled. "Yes, he is, and he sends you his best regards. He thinks very highly of you, Don Alfredo."

"And I of him."

Lisa sat down in a chair, looking down at her hands. "What you must think of me." She shook her head. "I can hardly believe myself what I have been through in the last two years."

"I think you are a wonderful person, Lisa. I admire your courage and your sense of loyalty."

"I am touched by your kind words," Lisa murmured, then looked around the room. "Where is Raya?"

"She is out with Mariz. They take a walk every day at this time. You should see them, Lisa. They are almost like mother and daughter."

Lisa felt herself stiffen. She wasn't sure if she could stand it if Raya thought of Mariz as her mother. "I'm glad that you and Mariz are getting along again. It's good for the family."

"You haven't asked about Sandro."

"How is he?"

"He's well enough. He works too hard, if you ask me. He's out every day at sunrise and he stays up late into the night. He never seems to sleep. He is now involved in running both the del Sol and the del Mar. He still likes to be involved in the rounding up and breaking of the horses, as well as the branding. I'm surprised you didn't see him in Monterey. He was there with some cattle, selling them to ships for fresh meat."

"Has he talked about me at all, Don Alfredo?"

"He has said only that you made your decision and he would abide by it. He has not spoken of you since he returned."

"Maybe I shouldn't have come back."

"Of course you should have, this is your home. It will take time for the scars to heal, my dear. But he knows that whatever happened, you did what you thought was right."

Lisa nodded. She removed her gloves and hat, setting them on the table next to her. She heard voices in the entryway and stared in wonder as Raya came running into the room, jumping into the lap of her great-grandfather. She didn't look at Lisa.

"Raya, look, someone special is here." Don Alfredo held Raya in his lap. "Come over here, Lisa. Don't be afraid."

Lisa got up and walked over to Don Alfredo's chair, kneeling next to it. "Hello, Raya."

Raya stared at her mother, cocking her head to one side. "Papa," she said suddenly.

414

"Raya, this is your mama. Can you say hello?"

Raya stared at Lisa and adamantly shook her head, crawling down from Don Alfredo's lap and running across the room to Mariz, who was standing in the doorway. She clutched Mariz's skirts. "Mama," she said, hugging Mariz's legs.

Lisa felt as if a knife had been put through her heart, a wound she fully deserved. She didn't blame Raya for not knowing her. She was just a child. She stood up. She wasn't ready to confront Mariz but knew it was necessary. "Hello, Mariz."

"Buenas días, Lisa. You are looking well."

"You also. Thank you for taking such good care of Raya. She looks wonderful."

Mariz smiled and stroked Raya's dark curls. "She is an utter joy." Mariz looked at Don Alfredo. "Papa, would you please take Raya into the kitchen. I think she is probably hungry after our walk."

"Of course," Don Alfredo said good-naturedly, taking Raya by her little hand.

Mariz crossed the room and stood staring at Lisa. "Believe it or not, I'm glad you're back."

"I don't know what to believe, Mariz. You never liked me, I know that, and now my daughter thinks you are her mother. You must love that."

"I have changed, Lisa, ask my father. I know that if it weren't for you, I wouldn't even be here now. Eric came to me before he went south and told me that you wanted him to talk to me. I don't think he ever would've come to me if you hadn't spoken to him."

"I'm glad it's working out for you all. I can see by the look on Don Alfredo's face that he's very happy."

415

"He would be much happier if you stayed. He thinks of you as part of this family."

"Why the change of heart, Mariz?"

Mariz shrugged her shoulders. "I either had to get to know my family again, or die a lonely old lady. I don't want to die alone, Lisa."

"How is Eric? Don Alfredo only told me that he works too hard."

"He's heartbroken, although he won't say it. He misses you very much."

"But will he want me back?" Lisa walked to the garden window and looked out. "I don't blame him if he doesn't."

"That doesn't sound like you. I thought you were more of a fighter."

Lisa turned around, a smile at the edges of her mouth. "That doesn't sound like *you*. You never cared whether I was alive or dead before."

"That was before I got close to my son and my father again. I also got to know Raya, and, through her, I got to know you. She is so much like you, Lisa."

Lisa was taken off guard. She didn't expect this from Mariz. "I feel strange being here. I'm afraid Eric will walk in and ask me to leave."

"He would never do that. You are the mother of his child."

"True, but he might not want me as his wife anymore."

"Then you must make him want you again."

Lisa was embarrassed. She couldn't believe she was having this conversation with her mother-in-law. "I never thought in a million years that you'd want me to stay with Eric. I thought you'd be glad that I was gone."

416

"As soon as I got to know my granddaughter, I knew what I was missing by not getting to know you. Also, my father told me many things about you, and when Eric got back, I saw how miserable he was without you. I decided that there must be some good in you if all of these people loved you so much."

"Thank you," Lisa said simply.

"You can't leave, Lisa. Eric needs you, Raya needs you, and my father needs you. You can't let them all down."

"I never thought I'd have a mother-in-law to talk to. My mother and I haven't been close since I was young, that's why I was so close to Tom. It would be good to have you as my friend."

Mariz put her arms around Lisa. "I apologize for all the pain I caused you last year, but I swear to you, I didn't know that Consuelo was trying to kill you."

"I know that. I never thought you were responsible for that."

"I know I have a lot to make up for, but I'd like you to do something for me."

"What?"

"I want you to stay, at least for a while. You have to give it a chance."

"I'm afraid, Mariz. I'm so afraid Eric won't want me back."

Mariz smiled and took Lisa's hand. "That's why we have to make him want you. You must look wonderful when he comes back."

"No, I don't want to play silly games. Either he'll want me or he won't."

"He'll want you, Lisa, but it won't hurt to make yourself look good."

417

"Mariz, I—"

"Don't argue with me. I know all about these things. Do you have any clothes?"

"I just have what I bought in San Diego."

Mariz thought for a moment. "You have all of your clothes here. We can pick out something for you to wear, then you can bathe and I can fix your hair."

"I don't know, Mariz."

"Don't argue with your mother-in-law. My son may still be in love with you, but it won't hurt to remind him just how beautiful you are. Come on." She took Lisa's hand and led her upstairs to the guest room. Lisa looked around and smiled at the familiar surroundings, then Mariz took Lisa's hand again and they walked to Eric's room. Lisa hesitated before she entered the room she had shared with her husband. Mariz walked to the armoire and opened the doors. "Here you are."

"He didn't move my clothes?"

"No. I think he was hoping you'd come back."

Lisa walked to the armoire. Her white wedding dress hung inside. She ran her hand along it and smiled. "I don't have to decide what to wear. This dress will do just fine."

Mariz looked at the dress. "It's simple, but it will look good on you. Do you have any jewelry?"

"Don Alfredo gave me a necklace and earrings that belonged to your mother." Lisa opened a small drawer in the armoire and pulled out the emerald earrings and necklace. She handed them to Mariz. "They should belong to you."

Mariz's eyes filled with tears. "I remember when my mother wore these. She was so beautiful. I don't think I've ever met anyone like her." She

418

looked at Lisa. "Except maybe you."

Lisa hugged Mariz. "Thank you, Mariz. Thank you so much."

Mariz held up the earrings and necklace. "I will save these for Raya. I have some sapphires that will go wonderfully with her eyes when she is older."

"She doesn't need jewels, Mariz," Lisa said in mock anger.

"They are family heirlooms, not gifts. Get undressed now. I'll order a bath for you."

Lisa went back to the guest room and undressed in silence. She stood in her worn white slip and walked to the window, looking out on the courtyard. She wondered when Eric would return. More than that, she wondered how he would feel when he saw her. One thing she had already decided, she wouldn't stay if he didn't want her. She would move to San Francisco and live with Tom, and she would find some kind of job. She wouldn't force herself on a man who didn't want or love her. If she had to, she would make a life without him. She would learn how to go on.

Eric sat in the tub, leaning his head back against the edge, his long legs propped on the sides. He barely fit in the circular brass tub, but it felt good to be clean after his ride. After he had visited with Raya and his grandfather, he had come up to his room. He had passed his mother in the hall and she had acted very strangely. She told him they had a guest who would be joining them for dinner and that she would be resting until then. He grimaced. He knew his mother and he knew that she was probably already planning to marry him off to some rich landowner's daughter.

He closed his eyes and thought of Lisa. She was never far from his thoughts. He wondered how her life was going with Cruz. As much as he tried, he couldn't hate Cruz. He was a good man, and Eric knew he would treat Lisa well. He wondered if they would have children together, and the thought gave him a knot in his gut.

After his bath, he dried off and got dressed. His mother had asked him to dress a little more formally this evening because of their guest, but all Eric could manage were his tan trousers and a pale-blue shirt. He made a slight attempt at brushing his hair, but it had grown wild and long and he didn't even mind, for it reminded him of the days when he had first met Lisa in the Comanche camp.

He left his room and went to Raya's. He played with her for a while and kissed her good night before Rocia put her to bed. He went downstairs to the library, where his grandfather was reading.

"Cómo estás, abuelo?"

Don Alfredo looked up with a smile, closing the book. *"Bien.* I was just catching up on my reading. Well, you look more refreshed."

"You mean I look dressed for dinner," Eric said sarcastically.

"There's nothing wrong with dressing for dinner once in a while, Sandro. You were raised that way, after all."

"I know, Grandfather. You don't have to remind me."

"Don't forget, we also have a guest for dinner."

"Who is this guest anyway? Is she a friend of Mother's?"

Don Alfredo considered the question. "Yes, you

could say that she is a friend of your mother's."

"Where is Mother?"

"You know how long it takes her to get ready for dinner, Sandro. Pour yourself a glass of wine and sit down. Tell me about Monterey."

Eric complied and sat down in the chair next to his grandfather. "Monterey is growing rapidly. Before we know it, the people from the city will be spreading to the country."

"There is nothing we can do about it, Sandro. We must get used to the idea."

"I hate it, Grandfather. This land was so unspoiled before. I see the people who are here now and it scares me."

"All we can do is make sure that this land stays in the family for Raya and her children."

Eric nodded. "I suppose you're right."

"Have you written to Lisa?"

Eric looked shocked by the question. "No. Why would I do that?"

"You told her you would be in touch with her. You didn't break that promise, did you?"

Eric stared into his wineglass. "She hasn't written to me, Grandfather."

"Why not be the one to take the first step?"

"I don't really want to talk about it," Eric replied impatiently.

"I miss her," Don Alfredo said. "It's not the same around here without her."

Eric turned and glared at his grandfather. "She made her own choice. She could've come with me but she chose to stay with Cruz. She really isn't my concern anymore."

"I see."

"Don't do that. You're trying to make me feel

421

guilty and it won't work. It's over between Lisa and me. I'll send Raya with Tom to visit her, but other than that, I won't have any contact with her."

"I understand."

"You are an insufferable old man!" Eric yelled.

"Yes, so I've been told by many people."

"I'm sorry, Grandfather, it's just that I don't want to talk about Lisa anymore."

"All right, Sandro."

"Where is Mother? I'm hungry."

"Perhaps we should go into the dining room. At least you can have some bread. I'm sure Rocia wouldn't mind bringing you a little."

The men went into the dining room and sat down. Rocia bustled about like a mother hen, serving hot bread to Eric the second he sat down. She filled their glasses full of wine. Before long, Mariz came into the room, resplendent in a black satin gown and diamond jewelry.

Eric stood up and kissed his mother on the cheek. "You look lovely, Mother."

"Thank you, Sandro." She cocked an eyebrow and looked him up and down. "Couldn't you have dressed a little more formally?"

"Don't criticize me, Mother. I'm not in the mood."

"Forgive me, dear." Mariz kissed her father on the cheek and let Eric seat her to the right of Don Alfredo.

"So, where is our mysterious guest?"

"She should be down soon. She was tired from traveling."

"Mother, if you're trying to arrange another marriage for me—"

"Sandro, I would do no such thing."

"You would, too. You've been trying to do it since I was sixteen years old."

Mariz ignored Eric and sipped at the wine. "Oh, his wine tastes particularly refreshing tonight, don't you agree, Father?"

Don Alfredo smiled, his brown eyes twinkling. "Yes, I think it's one of our better years."

"If you two don't mind, I'm about to starve to death. If your guest doesn't come down soon, I'm going to . . ." Eric stopped in midsentence as Lisa walked into the room. She was dressed in her white wedding dress. Her skin was brown from working in the sun, and Mariz had put gardenias in her hair, which fell loose and long around her shoulders. The only jewelry she wore was the silver cross, the silver earrings that Mariz had given to her, and the wedding band, which she still wore on her right hand. She stopped at the edge of the table and met Eric's eyes. She felt a flush creep over her skin, as if she were seeing him for the first time. He looked more handsome to her than she had remembered. She kissed Don Alfredo on the cheek and walked to the chair opposite Mariz, to the left of Don Alfredo and to the right of Eric. Eric got up and stood behind the chair, staring into her eyes.

"Hello, Eric."

"What are you doing here?"

"I wanted to see Raya," Lisa lied.

"Oh," Eric said obviously disappointed. He formally pushed Lisa's chair up to the table and then sat back down.

"Well, I think this calls for a toast," Mariz said, lifting her glass. *"Salud y amor,"* she said, winking

423

at her father, then clinked glasses with everyone.

Lisa held her glass to Don Alfredo's and Mariz's and then held it next to Eric's. *"Salud,"* she said softly.

"Salud," he responded, his blue eyes searing into hers.

Mariz and Don Alfredo dominated the conversation throughout dinner, Lisa and Eric remaining quiet. When dinner was over, Mariz asked her father to play chess.

Eric looked at his mother suspiciously. "When have you ever played chess, Mother? I thought you hated the game."

"I've changed, Sandro. There's a lot you don't know about me now. Come, Father," she said playfully, taking Don Alfredo's arm and leading him from the room.

Eric finished his wine and looked at Lisa. "How long do you plan to stay?"

"I was hoping I could stay for a while."

Eric looked down at the table, fidgeting with a piece of silverware. "How long is that—until you grow tired of me and want to go back to Cruz?"

Lisa set her glass down on the table, trying to control her anger and disappointment. "I don't blame you for feeling that way. There's nothing I can say to you that will make things different. I did what I did because I thought it was the right thing at the time."

"And now?"

"I know I was wrong."

"How do you know, Lisa? What made you change your mind?"

"I was unhappy without you and Raya."

"I'm sure Cruz could give you another child if

424

you worked at it hard enough."

Lisa's eyes filled with tears. She stood up, pushing the chair over as she did so. "It was a mistake to come here. I'd like to visit with Raya for a few days, then I'll go. If that will inconvenience you, then I'll leave tomorrow. Raya can visit me on Tom's rancho."

"That would be fine. But just stay out of my way."

Lisa hurried from the room, covering her mouth to stifle any sound. Eric sat back in his chair and watched Lisa leave the room, humiliation and hurt written all over her face. He didn't feel any better for having hurt her so deeply, and he hadn't accomplished anything. He poured himself another glass of wine. Why did she have to come back? And why, dear God, did she have to look so beautiful?

He got up and walked out the front door to the veranda. He sat on the edge of the railing and leaned his head against the post. Lisa was sitting on the swing. "I didn't know you were out here."

Lisa stood up. "I'll leave. I wouldn't want to get in your way."

Eric grabbed her arm as she walked past. "Why did you really come here, Lisa?"

Lisa stood motionless, trying to get a grip on her emotions. "I missed my daughter."

"Why else?"

"I came because I missed you and I was hoping you missed me."

"Did you honestly think it would be that easy to put the pieces back together again?"

"No, I didn't, and I don't expect anything from you, Eric. All I want to do right now is spend some time with my daughter."

"And then what?"

"I don't know. I haven't thought that far ahead."

"What will you do?"

"I told you, I don't know. I'll probably stay with Tom and hopefully I'll be able to find a job."

"What kind of job?"

"I don't know. I'm not really qualified for anything."

"Maybe Teresa's boyfriend could give you a job in his place," Eric said coldly.

"That was cruel," she said sadly, trying desperately to pull away from Eric. "Let me go."

"You don't want me to let you go. You want me to hold you and make love to you and tell you that I forgive you. Isn't that what you want, Lisa?"

"God, you are so conceited. You think the world revolves around you. I can live without you, Eric, I know I can. Now that I'm with you again, I'm not even sure what we ever had in common."

"We had a lot in common." Eric pulled Lisa to him, dropping the wineglass on the ground and wrapping his other arm around her. "Have you forgotten already?"

"No, I haven't forgotten."

Eric's face was next to Lisa's, his breath hot on her face. "Tell me, Lisa, what was it like when Cruz made love to you?"

"Don't," she said in a pleading tone.

"What's wrong? You're not embarrassed, are you? You weren't too embarrassed to run off with the man and live with him. You almost had his child, damn you!"

426

"I won't apologize for that child!" Lisa replied angrily. "I'll never be sorry I carried that child. It was a life inside me, and that made me feel more complete." She tried to pull away.

"Every night I go to bed and dream about what it was like to make love to you, and every night I picture you and Cruz together. It makes me sick."

Lisa closed her eyes, trying to fend off this vicious attack. "I never meant to hurt you, Eric."

"I was the one who took care of you and nursed you back to health, but you stayed with him."

"You wanted me to stay with Cruz. It helped to fuel your anger."

"I thought you'd go with me. I never thought you'd stay with him."

"He needed me then, Eric, and you know it. We both knew it."

"So, did Cruz get tired of you and throw you out? Is that why you're here?"

"I told you why I'm here."

"And I don't believe you. If you had wanted to see Raya so badly, you would've found a way back to her a long time ago."

Lisa couldn't fight the tears any longer. They streamed down her face. "I'll leave in the morning. It was a mistake to think I could come back here."

"You're not taking Raya to San Francisco with you."

"But you said I could see her anytime I wanted."

"How do I know you won't run off with her? How do I know I can trust you?"

"Eric, please don't do this," she sobbed. "She's my baby."

"You should've thought of that before you ran off with Cruz."

"If you won't let me take Raya and you don't want me to stay here, when can I see her?"

"I guess you can't." Eric finally released his hold on Lisa and stood up. "As far as I'm concerned, you aren't her mother. After you leave here tomorrow, I don't ever want to see you around here again."

"Eric, you can't mean that. You promised—"

"And you promised that you would love me forever, remember?" he said coldly. "I don't believe in promises anymore. I want you out of here in the morning." He strode across the porch and into the house, slamming the door behind him.

Lisa walked to the railing and gripped it for support, trying to control her sobs. Eric was actually gong to take Raya away from her and there was nothing she could do about it. What could she say to a judge? She had lived with another man, but it had all been a mistake? She had almost had another man's child, that they were almost married? She knew she didn't have a chance of keeping her daughter and she had never felt such despair in her life.

She went inside and up the stairs to Raya's room and lay on the floor next to the crib. She reached inside and stroked her daughter's smooth skin and she cried as she had never cried in her life. This might be the last time she would ever see her daughter.

Eric woke up suddenly, his head throbbing. He'd had too much wine. He sat up slowly and walked to the nightstand, pouring himself a glass of water. He drank greedily and poured himself another, then walked to the window and looked out. The moon lit up the courtyard and the mountains in the distance. It created an eerie scene, much like the shadows that were created when the sun went down. He vaguely remembered talking with Lisa. As he recalled, he had been quite cruel. He splashed water on his face from the bowl and walked across the room. He was still dressed in his pants and shirt, having practically passed out on the bed when he came upstairs. He crossed the hallway and entered Raya's room, checking on her, as he always did, to make sure she was sleeping soundly.

The moon shone through the window and partially illuminated the room. As he walked toward the crib he almost stepped on Lisa lying on the hard wooden floor, her hand over the side of Raya's crib. Gently, he took her hand away and lifted her into his arms. She moved slightly but didn't awaken. He carried her to her room and put her on the bed. He looked at her for a moment and couldn't believe anyone could be so lovely. He ran his hand across her cheek. She stirred and turned on her side, mumbling something in her sleep. He bent down and kissed her head. He knew as he watched her sleep that he didn't want to live without this woman, but he wasn't sure that he could forgive or forget what had happened between them. He would just have to wait and hope that they could find a way back to each other.

Chapter 14

Lisa stood on the veranda in her worn traveling suit, her one small bag next to her on the floor. She leaned against the post and looked out at the distant mountains thinking how much she would miss the ranch. The door opened behind her and she turned around. It was Don Alfredo, holding Raya in his arms. He knew that she was leaving early and had brought Raya to her.

"How are you this morning?"

"I'm going to miss it here, Don Alfredo, and I'm going to miss you." Her eyes rested on Raya and she gently touched her cheek. Without hesitating, Don Alfredo handed Raya over to her and the little girl started to squirm in her mother's arms. "Tell me about your horse, Raya," Lisa asked. Raya turned her head toward the main corral and pointed. "Do you want to go see your horse?"

Don Alfredo looked with affection at mother and daughter and laid a comforting hand on Lisa's shoulder. "You are always welcome here. I want you to think of this as your home."

"Thank you, but I don't think Eric agrees."

"This is not Eric's home. If he feels that way, he can go back and live at the del Sol."

"Thank you, Don Alfredo, for everything. You have been so good to me."

"Horsie," Raya said impatiently, pointing to the corral.

"I guess we're going for a walk," Lisa said with a half-smile.

"I'll see you when you get back." Don Alfredo watched Lisa as she walked across the yard to the corral. She was such a lovely woman with so much spirit, he couldn't believe his grandson was being so stubborn.

"What're you doing out here so early, Grandfather?"

Don Alfredo didn't turn. "I'm saying good-bye to your wife. She's leaving soon."

"Where is she?"

"She took Raya to the corral." Don Alfredo turned, leaning against the railing on the veranda. "You are a foolish man, Sandro."

"It's nice to see you this morning, too," Eric replied.

"Don't use that tone with me, young man. I'm still your grandfather and you will show me the respect that is due me."

"Perdoname, abuelo," Eric replied instinctively.

"Lisa is a good woman. You are going to lose her and then what will you do? Your life will be empty without her."

"I would appreciate it if you would let me make my own decisions about my life, Grandfather."

"Just like the time I let you get so angry at your mother that you left here for so many years? I'm

431

not so sure you're capable of making good decisions."

Eric shook his head. "What do you want me to do?"

"I want you to give her a chance. She is the mother of your child, Sandro."

"I know that, Grandfather. I'm just not so sure I can forget that she lived with Cruz and almost had his child."

"Forgive me for bringing this up, but did she not live with you in the Comanche camp and almost bear your child?"

"That was different. We were married."

"You were not married in the eyes of the Church, so she was just living with you. You didn't seem to think she was so bad for doing that. As I recall, you weren't even anxious to marry her after you arrived here."

"You don't forget anything, do you?"

"Sandro, I love you, and I love Lisa. I think you would be making a big mistake if you let her leave today."

"But how do I make myself forget?" He shook his head. "I don't think I can do that."

"How do you know if you don't try? It seems to me, Lisa was able to forget that you were with Consuelo, or is that different?"

Eric threw his grandfather a surly look and walked down the steps and headed toward the corral. Raya was sitting on the top rung, Lisa's arms around her, while they both watched a vaquero working a horse. "She loves horses," Eric observed matter-of-factly.

Lisa didn't look at him. "Can't I spend a few minutes alone with her before I go?"

432

"I just wanted to know what your plans are."

"It's none of your business."

"Papa," Raya said affectionately, smiling at her father.

Eric smiled back and kissed Raya on the cheek, swinging her down from the corral. "Go see Enrique. He'll show you the horsie." They watched as Raya ran off to Enrique. "I know it's none of my business, but I want to help you."

"I don't want your help."

"How do you plan to support yourself?"

"I'll find a way, without your help and without the help of Teresa's boyfriend." She turned her back on him, looking at Raya across the corral with Enrique.

"Everyone says she looks like me because of her dark hair and blue eyes, but I think she looks very much like you. She has that same small nose and pretty smile. Her nose even crinkles up when she gets mad the same way yours does."

"Will you please let me see her, Eric? Please. I don't think I could live without seeing her."

Eric looked at Lisa, putting his foot on the bottom of the corral. "You can see her, but you have to stay here. I don't want you taking her away from the del Mar."

"Really? I thought you wanted me to leave today."

"Well, I don't suppose it would hurt if you stayed around for a few days."

"I'll stay out of your way, I promise. I just want to spend time with Raya."

"Well, today I was going to take her out to the lake."

Lisa seemed disappointed. "All right. I won't

433

interfere with your plans."

"Why don't you come with us? We could pack a lunch and spend the day out there."

"I don't think so."

"Why not? It would be good for Raya to see us both together."

"Why are you doing this? Last night you didn't want to see me again. What changed your mind?"

"I had a little too much wine last night. I said some things that were cruel and I'm sorry for that. I won't keep you from seeing Raya as long as you come here to see her."

"Thank you, Eric. You don't know how much that means to me."

"What about the picnic?"

"I don't know . . ."

"Why don't you go for a ride? It always clears your mind."

Lisa nodded. "I think I will." She walked around to the tackroom, looking for the right saddle. "Can I help you, señora?" came a voice that Lisa recognized immediately. It was Hector. He had worked at the del Sol for many years and he had helped her to train Vida. She smiled and walked up to him, taking his hand in both of hers. "It's so good to see you, Hector. What are you doing here?"

"The *patrón* he asked me to come here and work with the young vaqueros. They need some guidance."

"You look well, Hector."

"And you also, señora. It is good to have you back. So, you are going for a ride?"

"Yes, do you have a good horse for me?"

"I have just the one." He spoke to someone in

Spanish and minutes later the man returned with a spectacular-looking palomino. "Will he do, señora?"

"Vida," Lisa exclaimed affectionately, walking up to the horse. She stroked his strong neck and rubbed his soft nose. "I've missed you, boy."

"He has missed *you,* señora. No one rides him like you do."

"What is he doing here?"

"The *patrón,* he tells me to bring him here, then he says that no one is allowed to ride him. I think he was hoping you would come back, señora."

Lisa smiled. "Could you saddle him for me, Hector?"

"*Sí, señora,* it would be my pleasure."

Lisa took off her hat and traveling jacket and hung them on one of the hooks in the tackroom. She rolled up the sleeves to her blouse and walked back over to Hector. "It's been a long time since I've ridden a horse like him."

"He will be spirited. He`hasn't been ridden since you've been gone. You take care."

"I will, Hector."

When Vida was saddled, Hector led him out into the yard, holding the reins while Lisa mounted. "It is good to have you back, señora. Have a good ride."

"*Gracias,* Hector." Lisa took the reins and cantered out of the yard, past the main corral and Eric. When she reached the open land, she pressed her knees into Vida's side and he galloped at full speed. Lisa let him have his lead. They rode hard and fast until they were both tired out. Lisa slowed him down to a walk, patting his neck. She felt exhilarated. She'd forgotten what it was like to ride a horse like this. But she couldn't grow too comfortable with anything here because soon she'd have to leave and find a place of her own in San Francisco. The thought of it frightened her.

She rode back to the rancho and walked Vida up to the main corral. She noticed that there was a carriage in the yard, but she didn't pay much attention to it. She dismounted and led Vida to his stall, finding him some feed.

"I will take him, señora. How was your ride?"

"It was wonderful, Hector. He's still a wonderful horse."

"He looks happy. I think it was good for him also."

Lisa smiled and patted Hector on the shoulder. She grabbed her hat and jacket and went back to the house. She heard voices coming from the library and stopped to look. Eric was standing with his arms around a woman, and Lisa could tell from the color of her hair that it was Teresa.

"I've missed you," Eric said, nuzzling Teresa's neck.

"I've missed you, too, but I couldn't get away. Bryant has me busy doing everything."

"How long can you stay?"

"I don't know, but that doesn't matter now." She wrapped her arms around Eric's neck and kissed him passionately.

Lisa ran past the room and up the stairs, stifling the tears that stung her eyes. She had no right to be upset by what she had just seen. She and Eric had no future together. Their only tie from now on would be Raya. Just as she reached her room, she heard Mariz's voice call out from her room.

436

"Lisa, is that you? Will you come in here, please?"

Lisa walked down the hall to Mariz's room and opened the door. Mariz was sitting up in bed with a tray of food over her lap. She was dressed in a pink nightgown and her hair was already done up perfectly. Lisa shook her head. "Don't you ever have a hair out of place?"

"Never. It is a trick of mine." She patted the bed. "Come, sit down here." She poured some coffee from the pitcher into another cup. "How do you like it?"

"Cream and sugar, please."

"So, my father had some disturbing news to tell me this morning. My son has asked you to leave. Is this true?"

"Yes." She accepted the coffee from Mariz. "He told me last night that he never wanted to see me again and that he wasn't going to allow me to see Raya again."

"He can't do that."

"He can do whatever he wants, Mariz. You know that the laws do not favor women. Besides, this morning he decided that I could see Raya, but only if I stayed here. I cannot take her away from the del Mar."

"I don't know what is the matter with that boy. He is so stubborn. He was always that way."

"I wonder where he got that from," Lisa remarked with a smile.

Mariz tilted her head. "Do you know who is here?"

"Yes, I saw them together."

"I don't like that woman."

"She's actually a very nice person, Mariz. She

437

helped nurse me when I was ill. She was very good to me." She looked down at her coffee cup. "I'm sure she'll be very good for Eric."

"You don't really believe that, do you? You aren't going to give him up without a fight?"

"I'm too tired to fight anymore. Besides, he's already told me he doesn't think very much of me. He says he doesn't think he can ever forget what I did."

"That son of mine has a very short memory. What about Consuelo?"

"It doesn't matter anymore, Mariz. I appreciate your concern. It means a lot to me, especially knowing that you'll be here to take care of Raya. But Eric and I have no future together."

"What will you do?"

"I don't know. I'll go live with Tom, I suppose, until I can get some sort of job."

"I will help you out. I don't want you working in that horrible city."

"I can't take money from you, Mariz."

"Nonsense. If you don't take it from me, all I'll do is send it to Tom and have him hold it for you. I want to help you."

"It's funny, isn't it? Now that you and I are finally getting along, Eric and I won't be together. I'm truly sorry for that. I'll miss getting to know you better."

"You'll be here quite often, if I have anything to say about it."

Lisa finished her coffee and set the cup on the tray. "Thank you, Mariz. Your friendship means a lot." She stood up and walked to the door, stopping. "What did you do without your husband, Mariz? How did you manage to go on?"

"I had something which you don't have, Lisa. I had hatred. That hatred almost lost me my son and granddaughter and made me a lonely old woman. That won't happen to you. You have too much love inside."

Lisa smiled slightly and shut the door as she went out. She stood absently, her head against the door, her eyes closed. What would she do with the rest of her life?

"What are you thinking about?"

Lisa opened her eyes. Eric had just come up the stairs and was standing directly in front of her. "Nothing. I'm just tired." She started to walk away, but Eric grabbed her arm.

"What about the picnic today?"

"I don't think so."

"Why not?"

"I don't feel up to a picnic."

"But you said you wanted to spend some time with Raya."

"Why don't you take Teresa on the picnic and Raya and I will stay here." Lisa said angrily.

"When did you see Teresa?"

"It doesn't matter." She walked to her room, but Eric followed her inside. "Would you just leave me alone?"

"See, your nose is crinkling up, just like Raya's." He shook his head. "It's amazing."

Lisa tried to change her expression. "Would you please just go. I'm sure you have other things to do."

"I just thought you'd like to spend some time with your daughter."

"I can spend some time with my daughter right here at the ranch." She walked to the window,

439

trying to pretend he didn't exist.

"I won't go away just because you want me to," he said softly.

"Why are you doing this?" she asked angrily. "This morning you wanted me to leave and now you're asking me to go on a picnic with you. Why don't you just take Teresa and have a wonderful day."

"If that's what you want," Eric said casually. "But Raya's coming with me."

"Are you playing games with me again?"

"No, but I promised to take her on a ride to the lake. She loves it there. You wouldn't want me to deny my own daughter, would you?"

"Well, take her. I'll stay here."

"You're being silly. This isn't like you, Lisa. You want to be with Raya and she wants to be with you, so come on the picnic. I promise I'll be civil to you."

"I don't know . . ."

Eric stepped closer. "What's the matter? Will it bother you to see me with Teresa?"

"Why should it bother me? You've made it perfectly clear that we have no future together." She smiled slightly. "I do think it's ironic, however, that you've chosen a woman who made her living at what you accused me of."

"I'm surprised you'd say something like that."

"I'm surprised you'd blame me forever for what happened between me and Cruz." She shrugged her shoulders. "It doesn't matter anymore. I've already made plans to leave at the end of the week. Tom will be in touch with you. I'm hoping you won't change your mind again about letting me visit with Raya. I can make arrangements to visit

440

with her when you aren't here."

"I won't change my mind. You're welcome here anytime."

"That's kind of you." Lisa turned away from him. "Just go on your picnic, Eric, and leave me alone."

Lisa tried to ignore the fact that Eric and Teresa would be together but it was making her crazy. She was angry and hurt and she didn't know what to do. She tapped her foot frantically for a moment and then left her room and went downstairs. She decided to go for a walk. Perhaps that would clear her mind. She went outside into the courtyard and stopped. Teresa was holding Raya in her arms and Raya was giggling. She wrapped her little arms around Teresa's neck.

"You are so beautiful, Raya."

Lisa looked at the woman holding her daughter and she felt sick. She couldn't blame Raya. She hadn't seen her in so long, her daughter didn't even know who she was.

Teresa swung Raya around in the air but stopped when she saw Lisa. "Oh, hello, Lisa. I didn't see you standing there."

Lisa walked up to Teresa and held out her arms to Raya. "Would you like to take a walk, Raya?" She smiled.

Raya buried her head in Teresa's shoulder. "No," she replied in her little voice.

Lisa forced herself to be strong. She couldn't fall apart in front of Teresa. She stroked Raya's hair. "It's all right. Perhaps we can go for a walk later." She walked off toward the corral.

"Lisa, wait a minute," Teresa implored.

Lisa stopped and turned, breathing deeply. "We

441

don't have anything to discuss, Teresa." She shook her head. "It seems you've won. You wanted Eric and now you have him. I can't blame you and I can't hate you. In your shoes, I might've done the same thing." She walked to the corral and watched absently as the men worked with the horses.

"What do you think, señora?" Hector asked Lisa.

Lisa smiled. "They're very good. I admire them."

"Still, I don't think anyone of them could have broken Vida."

"I was lucky."

"No, you are good with the horses. You have patience. A good horseman must have patience in order to break a horse."

Lisa propped her chin on her arms and looked over the railing. "That's about the only thing I have patience for," she said quietly.

"What is the matter, señora?"

"Nothing, Hector."

"Señora, you were gone for a long time. Now you just come back and you and the *patrón* are not getting along. I don't know what happened and forgive me if I am speaking out of turn, but I know you. I have worked with you. You are tough and you are strong. It is not like you to give up so easily."

Lisa looked at Hector, a smile appearing on her face. "How do you know so much about me, Hector?"

"I saw you work with Vida. You never gave up on that horse, not even when the *patrón* did. I have seen you with your daughter and I know the love you have for her. I have also seen the love

442

you have for the *patrón*. It is not something that dies easily."

"What if the *patrón* does not share the same love for me, Hector?"

Hector shrugged, taking his bandana out of his back pocket and wiping his forehead. "You are talking about this other woman?"

"Yes."

"Does she matter so much to you?"

"Hector, I don't know what you know, but the *patrón* is very angry at me. In fact, I don't know if he'll ever forgive me. Teresa is very beautiful. She can help him to forget me."

"Impossible," Hector said confidently.

"What did you say?"

"It is impossible. She cannot ride a horse like you. The *patrón* would never marry a woman who could not ride a horse."

"Hector, *tu eres muy tonto.*"

"I may be silly señora, but I have lived on this earth long enough to know when two people are in love."

"So, what do you propose I do?"

"I do not propose anything, señora. It is up to you."

"But?"

"I just cannot believe a woman like you would give up your husband and child without a fight. It almost seems . . . cowardly."

"Cowardly?" Lisa asked indignantly.

"Are they not the two most important things in your life, señora?"

"Yes, of course they are."

"Then how could you walk away without fighting for them?"

443

Lisa rested her chin on her arm again, sighing deeply. "I'm tired, Hector. I don't know if I'm up to a fight."

"You are always up to a fight, señora. You forget, I have seen you when you are angry."

"And if he doesn't want me?"

"Then you will know you have tried your best, *verdad?*"

"Yes, that is the truth." Lisa stood up and hugged Hector. "Thank you, old friend. Thank you." Lisa walked away but stopped and turned to Hector. "Hector, would you bring Vida around for me again? I think I'll take another ride."

"Sí, señora. With pleasure."

Lisa hurried into the house and up the stairs to Mariz's room. She knocked and then walked in. "Mariz, I need your help."

"What are you so excited about?"

"I've been doing some thinking and I'm not sure I want to give up on my family so easily."

"That is good to hear. What can I do for you?"

"I need a pretty slip."

Mariz looked puzzled. "You need a pretty slip?"

"Yes."

"That is all?"

"That's all for now."

"All right." Mariz walked to her armoire and opened the doors. She pulled out one of the drawers and stood aside. "I'm not sure what you are looking for."

"I'm looking for something that a man can't resist."

"Ah, I understand." Mariz nodded her head, lifting up the neatly folded slips until she came to the one she wanted. "How about this one?"

Lisa held it out in front of her. It was simple but lovely. The thin straps were made of lace and the bodice was hand-stitched lace with tiny satin bows all the way up the front. It was made of silk. "I couldn't possibly wear this under my riding clothes, Mariz."

"Why not?"

"Because I plan to go swimming in it."

Mariz shrugged her shoulders. "All the better. It no longer fits me anyway. It will be shorter on you, but that should not matter."

"Thank you, Mariz." Lisa gave her mother-in-law a hug.

"Do not thank me, just go."

Lisa hurried from the room and went to her room. She quickly slipped off her clothes and put on the silk slip. It fit her a bit too tightly but it felt wonderful against her skin. She looked at herself in the mirror and smiled. She had to admit she looked rather pretty in it. She quickly slipped back into her riding skirt and blouse and pulled on her boots. She brushed out her hair and let it hang loose, then searched for her silver hoop earrings. She hurried down the stairs and out to the courtyard. Eric and Teresa were standing with Raya. She walked up to them. "I've changed my mind. I've decided to go on the picnic with you."

"Good, you can ride with us in the carriage."

"No, I'm going to ride Vida out there." She reached out and touched Raya's cheek. "Do you want to ride the horsie with me, Raya?" At the mention of "horse," Raya went running toward the corral. "I'll see you out there." Lisa sauntered off toward the corral and scooped Raya up into her arms. Hector was already holding Vida's reins. "I need you to do something else for me, Hector."

"Anything, señora."

"It involves some deception."

"I will not mind, especially if it's for a good cause."

Lisa smiled and spoke to the man. Then she mounted Vida and held out her arms for Raya. She sat Raya in front of, her on the saddle, putting her arms on either side of her. *"Adiós, Hector."*

"Hasta luego, señora."

Lisa cantered off in the direction of the lake, not looking back to see if Eric and Teresa were following. It felt wonderful to be riding with her daughter in front of her. Raya seemed perfectly content and not the least bit afraid. They rode at a leisurely pace until they reached the stand of oak trees by the lake and Lisa dismounted, lifting Raya down after her. Raya immediately ran toward the water. "Oh, no you don't," Lisa said playfully, running after Raya and lifting her up and swinging her around just before she reached the water. Raya giggled, and Lisa hugged her. "You are so pretty and I love you so much, *mija,*" Lisa said sincerely, kissing Raya on the cheek. Raya squirmed to get down and Lisa put her on the ground. She chased her around the edge of the lake and through the trees. By the time Eric and Teresa arrived, Lisa was lying on her back on the ground, holding Raya high above her.

Eric helped Teresa down from the carriage and walked over to Lisa and Raya. "Well, you two seem to be having a good time."

"We are, but she wants to go for a swim."

"She always wants to go for a swim."

Lisa sat up, letting Raya go to her father.

"Don't you ever take her in?"

"No. She's too young."

"Don't be ridiculous. If she doesn't get used to it and learn how to swim, what will happen if she's alone out here? It's for her own safety, Eric."

"Lisa, she's only a baby."

"Do you remember how early the Indian children started swimming in the river? You never had to worry about them."

Eric shook his head. "Never mind, I'm not going to argue with you about it." He looked at Teresa and took the blanket from her. He spread it out on the ground and took the basket from the carriage. "I'm sure Rocia packed us some wonderful things."

Lisa looked at Eric and Teresa. "I think I'll take Raya to the water."

Eric watched her walk away. "Stubborn woman," he mumbled to himself, uncorking the wine bottle.

"You can't even admit to yourself how much you love her, can you?"

"Don't you start now, too, Teresa."

"Then why am I here? You brought me here to help you. So why don't you take advantage of the time you have with her? Go talk to her now."

"I don't want to talk to her now."

"Why, because she told you something you didn't want to hear?"

Eric sat down next to Teresa on the blanket. "Can you just stop talking?" He watched Lisa as she chased Raya around the water's edge. It was an unbelievable feeling, watching his wife and daughter together again. It was almost more than he could bear.

"Here she comes," Teresa said disgustedly, "and

447

if you won't do something, I will." She put her arms around Eric's neck and kissed him passionately, pushing him back on the blanket.

Lisa was walking up to the blanket when she saw the two. Part of her was hurt, but the other part was angry. She went to the blanket and sat down, pulling off her boots and stockings. Eric pulled away from Teresa's grasp, obviously embarrassed. "Don't let me disturb you two," Lisa said lightly. She stood up and unbuttoned her blouse, dropping it next to the boots. Then she unclasped her belt and skirt and pushed it off.

"What're you doing?" Eric asked, unable to take his eyes from Lisa's tight-fitting slip.

"Raya and I are going swimming," she said, running down to the water's edge and grabbing Raya. She took off Raya's dress and shoes and stockings and carried her into the water, laughing as Raya playfully splashed the water.

Eric took off after them. "What do you think you're doing? You can't take her in there."

"Of course I can. Look at her, she loves it."

"Lisa, don't be ridiculous. Come out of there."

Lisa ignored Eric and swam farther out, holding Raya in one arm.

"Damned fool woman!"

"You just can't stand it, can you Eric?" Teresa asked, adamant in her confrontation. "You can't stand the fact that you can't live without her."

"I feel another lecture coming on."

"You're right. You've accepted me as a friend and I've known more men in my lifetime than most ten women would know. Bryant knows all that about me and he doesn't care. I don't know why you can't forget what happened to Lisa. It

448

wasn't her fault, it was just circumstance. Don't tell me the same thing couldn't have happened to you. You just put her on a pedestal and you can't let her down."

"That's enough, Teresa!"

"Eric, I—" Teresa turned when she heard the sound of a horse.

"*Patrón,* I have a message for Señorita Torres."

"What is it, Hector?" Teresa asked in alarm.

"I don't know, señorita. There is a letter for you at the rancho. Would you like to ride back in the carriage with me? I can leave the horse for you, *patrón.*"

Teresa looked at Eric, narrowing her eyes. "No, thank you, Hector. I'll follow you in the carriage."

"Teresa, just go in the carriage with Hector. You're trying to interfere."

"I'm doing nothing of the sort." She walked down to the edge of the water and yelled for Lisa. "Why don't you let me take Raya back with me?"

"Why?" Lisa asked, puzzled.

"If you can't figure that out, then you aren't the woman I figured you for."

Lisa smiled and handed Raya to Teresa. "Thank you." She picked up Raya's clothes and gave them to Teresa.

"I'm not against you, Lisa. I think you and Eric belong together. Enjoy your swim."

Lisa waded back out in the water and watched as the carriage pulled away. She swam to the middle of the lake, feeling better than she had in a long time. She looked at Eric lying on his side on the blanket drinking a glass of wine. Now was the time, she knew, to confront her demons. She swam back to shore and stood up, walking slowly out of the water. She felt the slip stick to her body and she knew it left nothing to the imagination. She walked seductively up to the blanket, standing in front of it, shaking out her wet hair. "The water is wonderful. You should go for a swim."

"I'll just watch you."

"Too bad Teresa had to go back to the rancho."

"Yes, too bad," Eric said, staring at Lisa.

"May I have a glass of wine?"

Eric nodded and poured her a glass. "Are you going to sit down or stand there half-naked?"

"Why, does it bother you?"

"Not at all. I just thought you might be getting a little cold."

"Cold? It's lovely outside." She sat down and sipped at the wine. A drop rolled down her chin and Eric reached up and wiped it away with his finger. "Thank you," she said, her eyes connecting with his.

"Do you know how really beautiful you are?"

"Beauty isn't everything, Eric. If you can't forgive me my mistakes, then nothing matters."

"I've never claimed to be a forgiving person, Lisa."

"How were you able to love me in the Comanche camp when you knew that all those braves had had me? Didn't that bother you?"

"No, because I knew it was against your will."

"You don't think I was taken against my will? You know, you never even asked me what happened. You just assumed that I went off with Cruz."

"I didn't assume that. I knew you were kidnapped. I just didn't understand why you had to

450

give into him so easily. Why did you have to marry him?"

"I didn't have a choice, Eric. Vasquez threatened to kill me. Would you prefer that I be dead right now?"

"I didn't say that."

"But it would've been easier for you, wouldn't it? The poor widower. He loved his wife so much but she was brutally murdered." Lisa snapped her fingers. "Then you could've found a new woman to console you in your grief."

"You're crazy. I wouldn't have done that."

"You wouldn't have? You did it before with Consuelo, and what about Teresa? God, Eric, you're such a hypocrite." She slammed the glass of wine down on the blanket, spilling the contents all over. She ran back down to the water.

Eric went after her and grabbed her by the shoulders. "Maybe I am a hypocrite, but I can't stand the idea of you willingly being with another man. It kills me. I want to be the only man you've ever wanted."

"And I want to be the only woman you've ever wanted, but that's not the way it is. This isn't a dream, Eric, it's reality. Too many things have happened to me. I'm a tarnished woman. I'm not the sweet, pure thing you're convinced I am. I never will be. I'm a woman, plain and simple."

Eric cupped her chin in his hand. "You will never be plain and simple, Lisa."

"I can't be what you want me to be, Eric. I can't." She pulled away and waded until she was deep into the water. She swam to the middle of the lake, secretly hoping that Eric would follow her, but he didn't. She had already decided she

451

was going to leave. They had no future together. As much as she hated to admit it, and as much as she loved and wanted Eric, he clearly could never forgive her for being with Cruz.

She swam in long, easy strokes on her back, her eyes looking up at the clear blue sky. She couldn't imagine life without him; she couldn't imagine being a part-time mother to Raya. But there was no other choice.

She was getting tired and decided to swim back to shore. When she looked back she couldn't see Eric or Vida. Had he taken the horse and ridden back to the rancho? It would take her the rest of the day to get back there on foot. When she reached the shore and stood up looking for her clothes, she found they were gone. She stomped her bare foot on the wet ground. "Damn you, Eric Anderson!" she yelled.

She went up to the oak tree. The blanket and basket were still there. If she was going to have to walk, she had to have something to eat first. She opened the basket and took out one of the sandwiches. She shook her head. She couldn't believe he would do this to her. She pushed her dripping hair from her face and lay down on her back. How had everything gone so wrong? All she had ever wanted was to come west and be with her brother.

"Have a nice swim?"

Lisa jumped at the sound of Eric's voice. She sat up, covering herself. Eric was leaning against one of the trees, chewing on a blade of grass. "Where did you come from?"

"I just went for a little walk."

"Where's Vida?"

"He must've run away. Can't seem to find him."

"What about my clothes?"

"I didn't do anything with them."

"How are we going to get home?"

"I guess we'll have to stay here all night."

"We can't do that. We'll freeze to death."

"Then we'll have to find a way to stay warm, won't we?"

"I don't think this is very funny."

Eric sat down next to her. "You're afraid to be alone with me, aren't you?"

"Don't be ridiculous." She finished eating her sandwich, all the while aware that Eric was staring at her. "Would you please stop staring at me. It bothers me."

"Why should it bother you? You're the one who chose to swim in your slip."

Lisa pulled part of the blanket across her. "What did you do with my clothes? I want them back."

"I didn't touch your clothes."

"Would you stop playing with me, Eric. I can't stand it. Last night you acted as if I had a disease and now you're looking at me like you desire me more than anything in the world."

"I do desire you. My desire for you was never the problem."

"But my desire for Cruz was," she said without anger, staring into Eric's clear blue eyes.

"Yes," he answered honestly.

"Then why are you here?"

"I came to have a picnic with my daughter."

"And to be with Teresa."

"Why not? Teresa is a beautiful woman."

"Of course, and it's natural for you to want to

453

be with another woman, but it's sinful for me to even think of another man."

"Just tell me this, were you attracted to Cruz before you were ever kidnapped?"

Lisa looked at Eric and then lowered her eyes. "Yes, I was attracted to him, but it didn't mean I knew I was going to sleep with him."

"But you did."

"I told you why and you won't believe me. There's really nothing else I can say to convince you, Eric. You were right last night. I think I should just go away."

"I had too much to drink last night. I was angry."

"I don't think the drink is the issue. You aren't going to forgive me for what I've done, and I won't spend the rest of my life trying to convince you that I only did what I thought was right at the time." She stood up, tugging at the blanket. "Will you please move?"

"What are you going to do, walk back to the rancho?"

"That's exactly what I'm going to do. Please move."

"I'm comfortable right where I am."

"You are without a doubt the most stubborn, bull-headed man I've ever met in my life." Lisa started off toward the rancho.

"Lisa, I'd be careful if I were you. You won't make it back to the rancho before dark and there's been a wounded mountain lion that's been after some of the cattle."

"A mountain lion?" Lisa asked, trying to remain calm.

"Yes, it's already killed four head of cattle. We

think we might've wounded it, but we're not sure. Even if we did, they're even worse when they're wounded. Nothing will stop them."

"So what am I supposed to do?"

"I don't think you have much choice. You either stay here or you start walking."

"You won't go back with me?"

"Why should I? I figure they'll send someone for us in the morning. Might as well stay here and be comfortable."

"What about the mountain lion? What if it comes here tonight?"

"We'll have a fire, and I have my gun. I think you'll be much safer here with me."

Lisa ignored Eric and headed toward the lake. She walked around it, staring at the water. When she got to the other side, she sat down, rubbing her sore feet. She hadn't walked barefoot in a long time and her feet felt every little pebble and sticker on the ground. She looked across the lake. Eric hadn't moved. How could he be so calm? She didn't want to be out here alone with him because she knew the effect he still had on her. Maybe he was just trying to use that against her to prove that she was a weak woman.

She ran her fingers through her long hair and shook it back from her shoulders. She was so tired of all of this. She lay down on the rough grass and covered her eyes with her arm, letting the sun warm her bare limbs. It felt good. She didn't want to think about anything right now. All she wanted to do was rest.

Her whole body jumped at the screeching sound

of the bird. She opened her eyes and sat up. It was almost night and the bird that flew overhead was an owl. She shivered. She couldn't believe that she had fallen asleep and slept for most of the day. She was so worn out. The last months had taken their toll on her.

A slight breeze blew down from the hills and she wrapped her arms around herself, looking across the lake. She could see a campfire glowing in the night, and it looked wonderful. She stood up and started back around the lake. She walked slowly, not able to see much in the darkness. "Ouch," she said aloud, balancing on one foot while rubbing the other. She started walking again when an eerie, shrill sound stopped her. It echoed down the valley from the hills and made her shiver. "The mountain lion!" she gasped, quickly picking up her pace. She could barely see the outlines of the trees as she walked, but the sound of the wild animal kept her going. She just wanted to get to the fire. Again, the animal's shrill cry filled the night air and Lisa felt a different kind of fear. She began to run as quickly as she could, imagining that every noise she heard was the animal following her. As she ran toward the light of the campfire and the safety she knew would be there, she saw Eric.

"Lisa?" His voice sounded close.

Relief flooded her. "Here," she called, trying to sound brave. "Eric? I can't see you." She squinted into the darkness, but she couldn't see anything.

"I'm right here," he said confidently, striding toward her. He had his hand on her arm and was rapidly pulling her toward the fire. She didn't resist. When they reached the campfire, Eric threw more wood on it. He looked at Lisa shivering in her thin slip and he unbuttoned his shirt and took it off. "Here, put this on."

"Won't you be cold?"

"I'll be fine. Get over here by the fire, with your back to the tree."

"I thought you were just trying to scare me," she said, buttoning up the shirt and looking around in the darkness.

"No, I wasn't. That cat is out there and I can't believe I was so damned stupid."

"What do you mean?"

"I sent Vida packing, with your clothes. I thought it would give us time together. I wasn't thinking."

"When your grandfather sees Vida come home, he'll send someone out after us, won't he?"

"He probably thinks that we're having a romantic interlude."

Lisa leaned against the tree, Eric's large shirt coming midway down her thigh. The sleeves hung below her hands. "What if he comes at us? Will the fire attract him? Are we going to stay awake all night?"

Eric smiled for the first time. He shook his head. "You look like you're about fourteen years old in that shirt, and which question did you want me to answer first?"

"I'm sorry. I guess I'm a little nervous."

"I don't think he'll come for us, but I don't know for sure. Like I said, he's wounded. That changes everything. Wounded animals are unpredictable."

"So I guess we just have to wait."

"Yes, we just have to wait." He walked next to

457

Lisa. "I'm sorry. I didn't mean to put you in any danger. I wasn't thinking."

"It's all right. I trust you to get us out, Eric."

"Are you hungry? We still have some sandwiches left."

The cat's shrill cry resounded throughout the valley. Lisa looked at Eric, her fear evident. "I'm not very hungry."

"I don't think he'll come after us, Lisa. I just want to be prepared, that's all."

"I don't know why this scares me so much. I've certainly been through much worse."

Eric put his arm around her shoulders. He thought of what the Comanche warriors had done to her before he had returned to camp. She had never lost any of her spirit. "Yes, you've definitely been through worse."

"The only time we seem to get along is when one of us is in danger. I wish we could care about each other like that all the time."

Eric stroked Lisa's hair. "Let's sit down. Standing here all night isn't going to do us any good." He slid down the trunk of the tree, his arm around her, until they were both sitting on the ground. "You're sure you're not hungry?"

"No, I'd just like to be back at the rancho."

"I've never known you to shy away from a little excitement."

"This is more than just a little excitement, Eric. This is sheer madness. I don't want to be dinner for that mountain lion."

"You won't be, don't worry." He leaned forward and stirred the fire with a stick. "I don't love Teresa, you know. She's a friend, that's all."

"I believe you. Now, will you believe me when I

458

tell you that I don't love Cruz, I love you. He sent me away because I was miserable. He said he didn't want a woman who didn't love him. I told him I was afraid to come back here, but he told me to fight for you and Raya. He's a good man, Eric."

"I know that. I knew it the moment I met him." He stirred the fire some more, watching as the flames rose higher. "You told me that you did what you thought was right by staying with him." His eyes looked at hers in the firelight. "I practically forced you to stay with him because I thought it was right, too. He needed you more than I did, or so I thought."

Lisa laid her head on Eric's shoulder. "Why can't things be easy for us? Why can't we just love each other and be together?"

"Maybe we had to go through all of this so we'd realize how much we really love each other." He turned her face to his and kissed her. "I don't want to live my life without you, Lisa."

"Are you sure? I don't think I could take it again if you decided you didn't want me anymore."

"I'd be crazy if I didn't want you," he said deeply, pulling her into his arms. He kissed her passionately. "I need you, Lisa."

Lisa closed her eyes and let herself be guided by Eric. She had waited so long for this moment. It seemed like ages since they had been together. She wanted him desperately, and she loved him even more. But a part of her wondered if he would feel the same way afterward. She couldn't stand to lose him again. She wrapped her arms around his neck. "Eric . . ." she said softly, murmuring his name over and over.

He pressed his mouth against hers, devouring her with his desire. He took her shirt off and ran his hands up and down her body, remembering what it was like to touch her, remembering the passion she aroused in him. He opened his eyes and looked at her face. "Look at me," he said in a deep voice. He ran his hand along her cheek. "You are all I want in this world. I love you," he said simply, kissing her passionately. He felt Lisa's hands running up and down his back and he rose to his knees, unbuckling his belt. He stood up and took off his boots, then his trousers. He knelt next to her, untying the upper bows of the slip. He lowered his mouth to her breasts, kissing them, moving his mouth on them. At the sound of her passionate moans, he pushed up her slip, running his hands along her long legs and up to her hips. He knelt above her for a moment, poised like a statue, unable to believe he could feel this way about any woman. He knelt between her legs and his hand moved to her, probing and rubbing, feeling her hips move against his hand. He felt himself harden and he knew it was time. It had been much too long for them already. Slowly, he pushed himself inside her, waiting for her to move against him. When she didn't, he thrust into her again, pulling her hips against his, moving almost frantically. Her hands went around his neck and she wrapped her legs around his waist. He lowered himself so that his mouth was above hers. He watched her face as her passion rose. He had never seen anything so beautiful in his life. As he moved even more rapidly inside her, she began to gasp. Her hands tightened around his neck and her legs clamped around his waist. He felt himself ready to give in to her desire. His mouth covered hers, and when he thrust himself hard and fast inside her, her cry was muffled by his own. They moved against each other so rapidly that they both thought they would burst from the sheer joy of it. As their passion exploded, he gripped her tightly, his arms around her waist, his face buried in her breasts.

Eric rolled to his side, pulling the blanket over both of them. He pulled Lisa into his arms. She lay with her head on his chest, her eyes closed. She didn't say a word. He ran his fingers through her hair. God, he thought, how could anyone make him feel the way she did? He kissed her head.

"Are you all right?" he asked.

"I don't know," she said, her voice soft and low.

"Did I hurt you?"

She lifted her head and looked into his eyes. She touched his cheek. "No, you didn't hurt me, Eric. You made me feel as no other person has ever made me feel. It frightens me."

"It's not supposed to frighten you."

She laid her head back on his chest. "I don't want to lose you again."

"You won't."

Lisa was silent again. "I love the way you love me," she said in a low voice.

Eric smiled to himself. It was such a girlish, innocent thing to say. "I love the way you wrap your legs around me whenever—"

"Don't!" she said. "It's embarrassing. We're not supposed to talk about those things."

Eric laughed. "I think we changed all of that in

the Comanche camp, Lisa. You and I aren't like everyone else."

"Still, it's embarrassing. It makes me feel . . ."

"It shouldn't make you feel anything but good about yourself. You know how to please a man. You shouldn't be ashamed of that."

Lisa looked at him, smiling for the first time. "You're certainly a different man from the one I talked to last night."

"Love seems to do that to me." He kissed her on the nose. "I should get dressed." He stood up and pulled on his pants and boots. "Put the shirt back on. It's cooling off."

The cat's cry suddenly resounded around them. Eric pulled his gun out of his holster. "I want you to get up in the tree," he ordered, pulling Lisa to her feet. "I'll be up in a minute." Eric gave Lisa a foothold and she shinnied up the rough bark of the oak. She sat on a thick branch, leaning against the main part of the trunk. "Can't mountain lions climb trees?" she shouted down nervously to Eric.

"They can, but they have to jump first. I'll shoot it before it gets up there." Eric added more wood to the fire then climbed up the tree after Lisa. He stuck his gun in his belt.

"I heard a horse whinny." Lisa turned her head. "You don't suppose Vida is still out here, do you?"

"He should be back at the rancho."

"But if he's still out here, would the cat attack him?"

"I don't know, Lisa," Eric admitted.

The cat's cry sounded even closer. It was an eerie sound, combined with the frightened whinny of a horse. "Isn't there anything we can do? What if you shoot your gun, won't the noise scare the cat away?"

"I doubt it, Lisa. Besides, these are the only bullets I have. I need to save them."

They sat and waited. From time to time they heard the cat's cry, but there were no other sounds. Lisa put her head on Eric's shoulder and fell fast asleep in spite of her resolve to stay awake.

Hours passed as Lisa slept and Eric kept a fitful watch. When Lisa awoke, Eric climbed down from the tree and stirred up the coals of the fire, adding more wood to it. He bent down, carefully building the fire back up. They didn't see the cat sneak up behind, from the shadows. As Eric stirred the fire and added more wood to it, the cat crept even closer, jumping on Eric's back and knocking him to the ground.

"Eric!" Lisa screamed.

Eric struggled to keep the cat's jaws away from his neck, all the while feeling the daggerlike claws bite into his chest and arms. He tried to reach for his gun but couldn't move his hand.

Lisa knew she couldn't just watch while the huge cat killed Eric. She reached over and broke one of the branches off the limb next to her and slowly climbed down the tree. The cat didn't see her; he was too busy attacking Eric. She walked up behind him, and with both of her hands poised on the branch, she stuck it into the animal's side. A horrific sound emanated from the pained animal and, instantly, it turned on her. But before it could do anything, Eric drew his gun and he fired three times. The cat fell at Lisa's feet, breathing slightly, but unable to move.

Lisa rushed to Eric, crouching next to him. "God, Eric. Are you all right?"

"I've been better," he said, trying to sit up. "Here, take this and make sure he's dead. Shoot him in the head."

Lisa took the gun and walked to the animal. Its eyes stared up at her like an innocent pet. Lisa hated to kill the animal but she knew she had no choice. She aimed at the cat's head and pulled the trigger. This time its breathing stopped. She walked back over to Eric. "You're a mess. You didn't even have your shirt to protect you." She looked at the gashes on his chest, stomach, and arms and winced. Already, he was losing a lot of blood. She went to the picnic basket and took out the bottle of wine. "I'm going to pour this over your wounds."

"Why don't you let me have a drink before you do that?"

Lisa held the bottle to his lips and he sipped generously. He laid his head back on the ground, closing his eyes. "There's not enough alcohol in that stuff to do my wounds much good. Why don't you just let me drink it instead."

"You're bleeding badly. I've got to get you back to the rancho."

"There's no way you can get me back there tonight, Lisa. Just forget about it until morning. Don't worry, I won't bleed to death."

Lisa looked at Eric's wounds and she wasn't sure she agreed with him, the bleeding was so profuse. "Here, go ahead and drink some more." She held the bottle to his lips until he said he'd had enough. She stood up and wandered away from the camp. She wondered if Vida was out there in the darkness. She put her fingers to her mouth and blew hard. A loud whistle filled the night, a whistle that would be familiar to Vida if he was there. She blew two more times, then walked back to camp. Eric's chest and stomach were almost completely covered with blood. She ran down to the lake and soaked her shirt in the water, then ran back to Eric, placing it over his stomach and chest.

"Ow," Eric said softly, not really objecting to Lisa's ministrations.

Lisa pressed the wet shirt onto his stomach. She leaned down and kissed him. "I love you, Eric. I refuse to live my life without you."

"Good," he mumbled, trying to open his eyes but unable to.

Lisa started to go back down to the lake but stopped when she heard a noise. She thought she heard the sound of hoofbeats. She put her fingers to her mouth and whistled again. Vida came galloping into the camp. He stopped when he saw her, shaking his head up and down. Lisa ran to him, patting his strong neck. "Good, boy. You did stay." Vida's breathing was labored. "What's wrong, boy?" She slowly ran her hand along his left side. There was nothing. "It's all right," she said in a soothing voice, walking around to the front of the horse. His right rear hoof was off the ground and she looked closer. There was a wide, deep gash that extended the length of the animal's right flank down to his hind leg. It was bleeding profusely. "Oh, you poor boy. It's all right. It's all right." She patted him on the neck and walked back to Eric, kneeling next to him. "Eric, I'm going to ride back to the rancho and get help. I'll build up the fire and I'll leave the gun with you."

"No, I don't want you riding out here at night by yourself. We can wait until the morning."

"You could bleed to death by morning." She picked up the gun and put it in his right hand. "Hold on to this, Eric."

Eric grabbed Lisa's wrist. "Don't leave. If something happens to you . . ." His voice trailed off as if he wanted to argue but didn't have the strength.

"You're not going to get rid of me that easily this time. I love you." She kissed him on the mouth and stood up, then walked to Vida. "It's up to you to get me home, boy," she said, patting him gently on the nose. She mounted the saddle, careful to avoid touching his right flank as she swung her leg over. She didn't know how strong Vida was or if he would make it to the rancho, but he was her only hope. She pressed her left leg into his stomach. He started off slowly but soon went faster. They rode west to the rancho. Lisa couldn't see anything, but she knew that Vida would find his way. Horses had a sense about where they belonged.

It was painful for her to hear Vida gasping for breath but she had no other choice than to ride him back. When the horse slowed to a walk again, she patted his neck and encouraged him to continue. She didn't know how long they had ridden before she saw the torches in front of the rancho. "Not much farther, boy. Come on." She walked Vida into the yard and dismounted by Hector's bungalow. She banged on the door until he appeared.

"Hector, I need your help. Eric has been attacked by a mountain lion. He's out there by the lake. I need you to go out there with me in the buckboard."

"*Sí, señora.*"

"Can someone tend to Vida? He's badly hurt. He brought me here even though he was in such pain."

"*Sí,* I will have Enrique look at him. He is good with animals. And I will have Rocia prepare some medicine for the *patrón.*"

"Thank you, Hector. I'll be back in a few minutes." Lisa ran to the main house and up the veranda. She pushed open the door and took the stairs two at a time until she was in front of Don Alfredo's room. She entered without knocking. "Don Alfredo, Eric has been badly hurt. Hector and I are bringing him back here."

"Then I must go, too."

"No, you stay here and help Rocia. She will be preparing something for Eric's wounds." She kissed him on the cheek. "Don't worry. We'll get him back here soon."

"Be careful, Lisa."

Lisa ran down the hall to Teresa's room. Teresa opened the door just as Lisa was about to knock. "I need your help."

"What is it? I heard the noise."

"Eric has been attacked by a mountain lion. He's badly hurt. I need you to help Rocia prepare a poultice for him."

"Of course. Are you all right?"

"Yes, but I must go now." She went to Mariz's room and told her what had happened. Lisa wasn't sure what to expect, but Mariz was very calm.

"You go on. We will be ready for you when you return."

Lisa ran down the stairs and into the library, where she grabbed a bottle of whiskey, then raced out the front door. When she got to the bungalow, Hector already had the buckboard and horses ready. There were two men in back. She climbed up. "Thank you, Hector."

"It is no problem señora." He handed her a torch. "Put this next to you. It will help to light our way. And do not worry. Rocia is already in the kitchen preparing poultices for the *patrón* and your horse."

Lisa nodded, sitting anxiously on the edge of her wooden seat. It seemed as if it took forever to get to the lake. When they finally arrived, Lisa saw the fire had died down. She jumped down from the buckboard and ran to Eric, who was still lying in the same position, the gun still in his hand.

Hector quickly appraised the situation and spoke to the two men. They lifted Eric's torso while Hector lifted his legs. Carefully, they walked him to the buckboard and laid him on the blanket. The two men pulled him up. Eric groaned slightly, but he didn't open his eyes. Lisa and Hector climbed back up and Hector drove back to the rancho. Lisa grabbed for the bottle of whiskey.

"What were you planning to do with that, señora?"

"I thought Eric might need it but he doesn't seem to."

"I think it would be wise for *you* to have a drink, señora. It will calm you down."

Lisa uncorked the bottle in her hands and took

468

a drink of the whiskey, coughing as she swallowed it. She handed the bottle to Hector. "Here."

Hector took the bottle and took several drinks from it, handing it back to Lisa. "So, the day did not turn out well for you?"

"Actually, it turned out better than I anticipated. I just want him to be all right, Hector."

"He will be fine, señora. He is young and strong. He will survive this."

Lisa nodded to herself, unable to face the possibility that Eric might die from his wounds. She clenched the whiskey bottle, unable to look back at the man she loved, afraid he would disappear before her eyes.

"We are almost there, señora. See the torches?"

Lisa nodded silently as they drove up the dirt drive to the rancho. Hector pulled the buckboard close to the house and he and the men lifted Eric from the back. Lisa ran up the steps of the veranda and opened the front door, following Hector and his men as they carried Eric upstairs to his room. Teresa and Don Alfredo were already waiting. Lisa sat on the bed next to Eric, carefully taking off the pieces of blood-soaked cloth. Her hands were steady as she wiped the blood away.

"Why don't you let me do that, Lisa?"

"No, thank you, Teresa. He's done this for me too many times. Now it's my turn." She looked up at Don Alfredo, her eyes glassy but her voice strong. "He'll be all right, Don Alfredo."

"Yes, I know he will." He turned to Hector. "Would you tell Rocia that we're here . . . and *muchas gracias,* Hector."

"Por nada, patrón."

Don Alfredo thanked the other men and walked

469

to Lisa, placing his hands on her shoulder. "Are you all right?"

"I'm fine, but I'm worried about Eric's wounds."

"Do not worry, señora," Rocia said, hurrying into the room with a large pot. Hector followed, carrying pieces of clean cloth. "Here, señora," she handed Lisa a wet cloth, "clean the wounds the best you can."

Lisa pressed the wet cloth against the widest gash on Eric's stomach. The white cloth soaked through immediately. She took another cloth from Rocia and pressed it to the other wounds on his chest and arms. Eric didn't move. "They won't stop bleeding, Rocia."

"We will clean them with alcohol while he is still unconscious. Then you will put these poultices on him. He will still bleed for a time, but it should stop. When it does, we will change the poultices." She took a bottle of whiskey and poured part of it over another cloth. She handed it to Lisa.

Lisa grimaced as she thought about the feel of the alcohol against the open wounds, but, thankfully, Eric still didn't move. She quickly wiped each wound and then took the poultices from Rocia. Rocia had prepared wet pieces of cloth soaked with herbs and roots and numerous other ingredients. The Comanches, she remembered, used different plants for different conditions, but she didn't know what Rocia used now. The poultices were warm, and when she finished putting them on Eric's wounds, she covered him with the sheet and blanket. She reached up and touched his face, then leaned forward and kissed him on the cheek.

"Why don't you let him rest, señora. There is nothing more we can do now."

"I'd be glad to stay here with him," Teresa said, putting her arm around Lisa.

Lisa started to object but she saw the sincerity in Teresa's eyes. She knew that Teresa thought of Eric only as a good friend. "Thank you, Teresa. I'd like to go see about Vida. If it weren't for him, I wouldn't have gotten back here tonight."

"I will take you to him, señora," Hector said, guiding Lisa by the arm.

"Lisa," Don Alfredo said gently. "Come back to the library when you are finished. Mariz is making tea. I think you can use it."

Lisa nodded and followed Hector out of the room. They walked in silence to the stables and found Vida leaning against his stall, his rear hind leg up off the ground, his large nostrils flaring as he tried to take in air. Lisa walked to him, stroking him on the neck and rubbing his nose. "Vida," she said softly. "How are you doing, boy?"

Vida's ears pricked up and he tried to turn his head when he heard Lisa's voice.

"He knows you are here, señora. That is good."

Lisa looked at the long gash on Vida's flank and leg. It seemed worse than before. "Will he be all right, Hector?"

"I hope so, señora. He is a fine animal with good spirit. It is amazing that he didn't leave even after that cat attacked him. He must have sensed something."

"Most people would say you're loco, Hector."

Hector shrugged. "Perhaps, but I know he remembered your kindness toward him. He wouldn't leave you just to run home."

"You're going to be all right, Vida. Good boy." Lisa smiled and rubbed the horse's soft nose.

471

"Isn't there anything we can do?"

"The same thing we are doing for the *patrón*. Enrique will treat him with the poultices and then we must wait for him to heal."

Lisa leaned forward once more, resting her head against the horse's. "Thank you, Vida."

Lisa walked back to the house and went to the library, where Don Alfredo awaited her, a tray of hot tea on the table.

Lisa sat down in the chair next to Don Alfredo. "Thank you," she said, taking a cup of tea and gratefully sipping the warm, sweet liquid. She rested her head against the back of the chair. "I've never seen Eric injured before. I can't stand it."

"You can stand it. You are strong."

"He's seen me injured so many tines and has always helped me."

"Just as *you* helped *him* tonight. Drink your tea," he said. They sat in silence before Don Alfredo spoke again. "So, have you both decided what you are going to do?"

"What do you mean?"

"Don't play with me, child. You are both two very stubborn people. You love each other very much but you seem to have trouble being together."

"I know. In fact, earlier today I had decided that I was going to leave the rancho at the end of the week and only visit Raya when Eric wasn't here."

"What changed your mind?"

"Seeing him hurt. I knew I didn't want to live without him. When we're in trouble, we always seem to pull closer together. It's the other times I'm afraid of."

"Then you both must work at making your love strong all of the time. You must be a little more giving and trusting with each other. If you both do that, you will have a good life together."

Lisa put down her teacup and reached for Don Alfredo's hand. "You are such a good man. I'm so glad that I know you. I only wish I had known your wife."

"You would have loved her. She is very much like you." Mariz stood at the door, a sad smile on her face. "My mother was kind and good, Lisa. She was the kind of mother I wish I had been to Eric."

"You are that kind of mother now, Mariz," Lisa said gently.

"I don't know if I can make up for past mistakes, but I will most certainly try. And if I can do that, I don't see why you and Alejandro cannot as well."

Lisa stood up, looking first at Don Alfredo, then at Mariz. "I don't stand much of a chance with you two, do I?"

"I think not," Don Alfredo said.

"Go and be with your husband, Lisa. He needs you."

Lisa kissed Don Alfredo on the cheek and then went to Mariz, taking her hands. "I don't know how to thank you. Since I've been back here, you have made such a difference in my life." She kissed Mariz on the cheek and left the room.

Mariz sat next to her father, pouring herself a cup of tea. "Well, Papa, it seems we have a real family for the first time, eh? Who would've thought that it would have taken this white girl to bring us all together again."

473

"Yes, Mariz, I know how important it was to you for your son to marry a Spaniard."

"It no longer matters, papa. All that matters is that Lisa makes Eric happy and she has brought this family together. I will be eternally grateful to her for that."

Don Alfredo took his daughter's hand. "So will I, *mija,* so will I."

Eric opened his eyes. The sun was shining brightly. He tried to move, but the pain in his chest and stomach stopped him. He lifted the blanket and sheet and saw the poultices covering him. He lifted the one on his chest and looked at the wound underneath. It was open and ugly.

He smiled when he saw that Lisa was sitting in the chair next to his bed, her legs pulled up under her, her head against the back. Her hair was tangled and she was still wearing the same clothes from the picnic, but he thought she was the most beautiful thing he'd ever seen. As he looked at her, it occurred to him that nothing was more important to him than Lisa and Raya. His pride meant nothing to him now. They had both made mistakes but they had learned from them, and they had grown stronger as a result. He sensed that their love had taken a different turn the night he'd been attacked.

He tried to sit up, but he couldn't maneuver himself into a comfortable position. "Damn," he muttered in frustration, trying to get himself situated more comfortably.

Lisa opened her eyes. "Eric? Are you all right?"

Eric smiled. "I'd be a lot better if I could just

sit up."

Lisa got up and went to the bed, sitting next to him. She put her hand on his head. "You don't have a fever anymore and you look much better. Let me check these." She moved the blanket and sheet and looked underneath the poultices. "They have a good color to them. Hopefully, you'll be fully recovered in a few weeks."

"A few weeks? I can't stay in this bed for a few weeks."

"You don't have a choice, *querido*."

Eric narrowed his eyes. "You've never called me that before."

"I know. I'm just glad you're all right."

"So am I." He reached out and took Lisa's hand. "Thank you for getting me home."

"How do you know I was responsible for that?"

"I remember you saying you were going for help. I don't remember anything after that."

"Do you remember anything *before* that?" Lisa asked playfully.

"I remember *everything* before that."

Lisa smiled. "You've been in bed for almost three days."

"Three days?" Eric shook his head. "And all this time I thought I was so tough."

"You *are* tough, that's how you managed to survive *this*. But it'll still be sometime before you can get out of that bed."

"So what am I supposed to do all day?"

"How about if we talk? I want to know about us, Eric, and I'm not afraid to tell you that I love you more than anything in this world and that I want to spend the rest of my life with you. My time with Cruz wasn't planned. He was good and

475

kind to me and I guess I responded in the wrong way. For that, I'm sorry. But I came back to you because I love you. I think we've always both been afraid of our feelings because they were so strong. Well, I'm not afraid anymore. I know that I want you, I need you, and I love you."

"I feel the same way about you. That night when I said all of those things, I didn't mean them. I think I was more angry at myself for being so stupid. I do love you, Lisa, you know I do. I want you so badly I ache."

"I think those are your wounds that are making you ache," Lisa said playfully.

"Don't interrupt me when I'm getting passionate."

"You can't afford to get passionate now. You need to get well first."

"Then can we talk about passion?"

"Yes."

"All right, as soon as I'm well, we're going to have a huge fiesta and we'll dance, just like the night we got married. Then I'll bring you up here, and I'll make love to you all night." Eric grimaced as he moved.

"I'll believe it when I see it."

"I'll be strong before you realize it, then you and I are going to make up for lost time. By the way, we're still married."

"What?!"

"I found the padre who married you and Cruz and dissolved our marriage. He said because Cruz was already married, you didn't really have a marriage to him, which means you and I are still married. I needed to make sure you wanted to stay here for the right reasons, before I told you." He

476

took her hands in his. "Are you happy?"

"Of course I'm happy. It's what I want." She leaned forward and kissed him gently.

"My lips aren't in pain, Lisa," he whispered, pulling her head to his mouth and kissing her passionately. "I do love you, green eyes. I will love you forever."

"Oh, Eric, this is like a dream come true."

"Only this time, we're going to live out our dream, Lisa. Nothing will come between us again."

Lisa laughed and clapped her hands, watching as the men and women did the Mexican hat dance. It was a joyous occasion. She and Eric were celebrating their new life together. She looked up at him and smiled. It had been a month since his accident and he looked wonderful. He was as strong as ever and she couldn't remember when she had ever loved him more.

"Are you having fun?"

"It's wonderful."

"I told you we'd have a big fiesta, didn't I?"

"I'm so happy."

Eric took Lisa into his arms and moved her out onto the dance floor. The musicians immediately started playing a slow tune and Eric held Lisa close to him. "You deserve all of this and more. You are one of the bravest women I've ever known. I love your strength, your courage, and your heart." He smiled. "Your looks aren't bad, either."

Lisa pressed her face against Eric's chest. She hadn't felt this secure in his love since they'd been in the Comanche camp together. "I love you so much."

"Do you want to show me how much?"

"Hey, Sis," Tom interrupted, "how about a dance?" Tom pulled Lisa away from Eric.

The evening continued much the same way, Lisa dancing with every other man, and Eric dancing with every other woman. Finally, Don Alfredo walked to the center of the courtyard and held up his hands. "I would like to propose a toast to my grandson and his lovely bride. I wish them all the love, happiness, and health that two people can have in one lifetime." He held up his glass. "*Salud,*" he said solemnly.

Eric took Lisa's hand and walked to Don Alfredo. He hugged his grandfather, then he took Lisa in his arms. Again, the musicians started playing and Eric gracefully moved Lisa around the courtyard. As they neared the doors to the sitting room, he took his wife's hand and led her inside.

"What are you doing?"

"I'm taking you to bed," Eric said, and he picked Lisa up in his arms, carrying her up the stairs and into their room. He put her on the bed and sat down next to her taking her in his arms. "You are so beautiful."

"You're only saying that."

"No, I'm not." His voice was serious. "No matter what happens in the future, just believe that I love you more than I thought it possible to love anyone. You are everything to me."

Lisa put her arms around Eric's neck and pulled him close. His body forced her backward on the bed. She looked up at him, her eyes filled with desire. "Make love to me, Eric."

Eric kissed her. "I'll make love to you, Lisa." He

478

ran his fingers along her mouth. "And after we make love, you will be a part of me forever." His mouth touched hers softly. "I love you, green eyes. I love you."

PASSIONATE NIGHTS FROM ZEBRA BOOKS

ANGEL'S CARESS   (2675, $4.50)
by Deanna James
Ellie Crain was a young, inexperienced and beautiful Southern belle. Cash Gillard was the battle-weary Yankee corporal who turned her into a woman filled with hungry passion. He planned to love and leave her; she vowed to keep him forever with her *Angel's Caress*.

COMANCHE BRIDE   (2549, $3.95)
by Emma Merritt
Beautiful Dr. Zoe Randolph headed to Mexico to halt a cholera epidemic. She never dreamed her caravan would be attacked by a band of savages. Later, she refused to believe that she could love and desire her captor, the handsome half-breed Matt Chandler. Captor and slave find unending love and tender passion in the rugged Comanche hills.

CAPTIVE ANGEL   (2524, $4.50)
by Deanna James
When handsome Hunter Gillard left the routine existence of his South Carolina plantation for endless adventures on the high seas, beautiful and indulged Caroline Gillard learned to manage her home and business affairs in her husband's sudden absence. Caroline resolved not to crumble and vowed to make Hunter beg to be taken back. He was determined to make her once again his unquestioning and forgiving wife.

SWEET, WILD LOVE   (2834, $3.95)
by Emma Merritt
Chicago lawyer Eleanor Hunt was determined to earn the respect of the Kansas cowboys who openly leered at her as she was working to try a cattle-rustling case. The worst offender was Bradley Smith — even though he worked for Eleanor's father! She was determined not to mistake passion for love; he was determined to break through her icy exterior and possess the passionate woman who lurked beneath her.

Available wherever paperbacks are sold, or order direct from the Publisher. Send cover price plus 50¢ per copy for mailing and handling to Zebra Books, Dept. 2983, 475 Park Avenue South, New York, N.Y. 10016. Residents of New York, New Jersey and Pennsylvania must include sales tax. DO NOT SEND CASH.